DOCTOR WHO™

SHORT TRIPS:
TIME SIGNATURE

A Short-Story Anthology
Edited by Simon Guerrier

BIG FINISH

Published by Big Finish Productions Ltd
PO Box 1127
Maidenhead
SL6 3LW

www.bigfinish.com

Range Editor: Ian Farrington
Managing Editor: Jason Haigh-Ellery
Consultant for BBC Worldwide: Justin Richards

ISBN 978-1-84435-235-7

Cover art by Stuart Manning 2006
Original sleeve design by Clayton Hickman

First published September 2006

An Overture Too Early was first published in *Doctor Who: Short Trips – The Muses* (2003)

With thanks to
Richard Atkinson, Sharon Gosling, Netty Rhodes, Paul Rhodes, Gary Russell and Steve Tribe

Typeset in Quadraat

Printed and bound in Great Britain by Biddles Ltd
King' s Lynn, Norfolk

An Overture Too Early

Simon Guerrier

An Adventure of the Third Doctor, with Sarah Jane Smith

'Let me tell you about the piece I'm working on at the moment,' said Isaac as he poured himself another glass of wine. The reporter and her assistant did not look pleased. Isaac knew full well he had kept them here twenty minutes and only answered three of their questions. But he was wallowing in the attention. He had never realised before just how good it felt to be listened to. And this reporter wasn't bad-looking either, in the stern, modern way fashionable here. The glossy sections of the newspapers some of the orchestra left around reckoned the West was leading the global struggle for women's rights and recognition. The conceit of it made him laugh. Their carefully thought-out costumes – symbolic of utility as good as any man – just made him think of the dourly dressed matriarchs back home. Whatever the generals might think, it was those mothers and maiden aunts who really ran the country, who really had the power.

'Please do,' said the reporter, with an edge Isaac chose not to notice.

'Nothing is worse than getting some morsel of a tune inside your head,' he said. 'You don't know what it is, or where it comes from, this fragment. And you can't shake it. You understand?'

The reporter had the grace to lie and say she did, though her assistant yawned quite explicitly. The man had made no secret of his opinion of the concert either. Not that he'd said anything as such, but his manner suggested he had spent the evening compiling a mental list of all the places he would rather have been. He looked like the worst sort of music lover – classically educated, knowledgeable to a point and compensating for his intellectual shortcomings with brash affectation. He had behaved the whole time during the interview like a bored, petulant child, staring round the room, or inspecting his fingernails, or pulling faces to himself – whatever he could do to show off his disdain. Isaac studiously ignored him back.

'The *frustration* of not knowing the tune, of having just a tantalising fragment, motivates my work. I've been consumed by this one piece for nearly twenty years. I don't have a choice. And I can't honestly say whether I've got nearer to what I think I heard, or warped it into something new and unrecognisable. And my own.'

'There's no risk of you being accused of plagiarism, then,' the reporter said smoothly. 'The ambassador,' she went on, looking over her notes, 'Nikolai Faro. He believes this work you're doing will prove to be your masterpiece.'

Isaac nodded demurely. 'But that's not for me to say, is it?'

'Faro got you over here on the basis of what he saw in the manuscript you gave him, though. And he thinks it's good enough to get you a passport. We've not yet talked about your request for asylum...'

'You *have* done your research.'

'Faro claims that it's dangerous for you back home, that your well-being is compromised by links to revolutionary elements. Is that true?'

'As Dr Faro has said himself, a musician should be able to appeal to all kinds of people, whatever their politics.'

'So, it's just a hazard of your celebrity back home?'

'I'm not sure "hazard" is the word I'd use, Miss Smith.'

'Fine. And what about "celebrity"?'

'What are you trying to say?'

'I've talked to several people from your country over the last few days. Not one of them had heard of you. Why is that?'

'Is that what this is?' he scoffed, genuinely surprised. 'I'm not famous enough?'

The reporter's assistant muttered something about not being talented enough, barely concealing the remark as a cough. Isaac, astonished by such open rudeness, allowed Miss Smith to admonish him herself.

'Doctor!' she said. 'You said you'd behave.'

'This has been a wasted journey, Sarah Jane,' he said, no hint of apology. 'You promised me an alien. I didn't realise you were being so parochial...'

Isaac ignored Sarah's efforts to apologise. He was staring at the man, who now wouldn't meet his eye. Isaac couldn't believe it.

'I know who you are,' he said. 'You're the Doctor.'

Miss Smith looked between them, trying to work it out.

'How?' she said. Isaac couldn't keep the smile off his face.

'Twenty years ago,' he said. 'I used to travel with him in the TARDIS.'

'I can't *believe* you sometimes!'

'I won't change my mind, Sarah Jane. I can't! That's all there is to the matter.'

'He obviously convinced you he is who he said he is, otherwise you wouldn't be like this. Why's it so awful? You two are old friends!'

'He's from my future, Sarah. Don't you see? The travelling companion of a me I haven't become yet. I can't know what's going to happen to me, not in advance. It would do terrible damage to time, to causality. Can't you see that?'

Sarah supposed she could, but wouldn't admit it, not now. She sat in silence as the Doctor got them onto the motorway. He was leaning forward, straining to see through the rain bashing and battering the windscreen. Inwardly Sarah tried to get on top of her anger. Having fought all the way from the doorstep of the concert hall, this was a chance to regroup. To rework her strategy.

'You could still try to help him,' she said later, her tone more reasonable. 'You needn't ask him any questions. You probably owe him that much.' She left a pause, and when he didn't respond she tried something she knew he'd react to. 'He's an exile because of his travels with you.'

'Of course,' was all he said, tight-lipped and staring ahead at the road. It wasn't good enough. Isaac had been so relieved to see the Doctor, to recognise him. He said he'd been back on Earth since the 1950s, since leaving the Doctor. A girl had been involved, he said. Presumably it didn't work out. There was no mention of a wife in his file, in any of the interviews. And even before he had said what he was, she'd been sure he was hiding something. That's what her interview had been driving at.

The Doctor had stormed out, though, and started up the car. He would even have left her behind if she hadn't run out after him right then. That was when she'd lost her temper.

If she hadn't, if she had been more in control of her wits, Sarah would certainly have noticed the two tall top-hatted men in grey on the far side of the road. They waited out on the street until the Doctor had driven off. Sarah would have been intrigued by the way they stood, tall and unmoving like street performers working late. She would have responded on instinct – something about them just wasn't right. At the very least she would have watched them over her shoulder as the Doctor drove away.

And so would have seen one of them saunter up into the concert hall she and the Doctor had just left, where Isaac would now be alone. The other grey man stood outside, looking all around. Sarah would have sized him up in a glance: professional, sleek and deadly.

The Doctor joined Brigadier Lethbridge-Stewart for breakfast first thing next morning. They sat at a small table in the Brigadier's office away from his desk.

The day had started off brightly after the previous night's rain, the view out of the window crisp and green. Nowhere did a fried breakfast quite like UNIT HQ. It was definitely one of the perks of the job, and the Brigadier rarely missed the ritual. While he ate, he would usually read the paper or even catch up on a novel. Anything that wasn't work. He'd made an exception this morning to hear all about the Doctor's latest crisis.

'You certainly know how to treat the hired help, don't you, Doctor?' he mocked cheerily, having been brought up to speed. 'What is it you do to them? Just look at these recent adventures Ms Grant – *Mrs Jones* has had!'

'What?' said the Doctor, entirely thrown. 'Is Jo all right?'

'Is now, I hear,' the Brigadier said, reaching for more toast. 'Dealt with it on her own. Training she got here, I expect. She'll have it all in the letter she's sending, anyway. I sometimes get my gossip in advance because of the wires her husband's lot send in. Still, the locals think it's your crystal's fault and Jo wants shot of it. Should arrive back here any day now.'

'Hmm.'

The Doctor had already lost interest, or didn't want to talk about Jo. He was still funny about her, even after all these months. That reporter had been a tonic, of course. Just what he needed to get him out and about again, stop him moping. This latest thing would be all her doing too. He would bet on it.

'This composer chap,' said the Brigadier, getting back on track. 'You must realise how irregular it would be for UNIT to get involved in immigration...'

'The chances are that Isaac is a UK citizen,' said the Doctor primly. He really had got out of bed on the wrong side. 'Or has been. Or will be.'

'You do know his background, then? Ms Smith said –'

'Never mind what she said, and no, I don't,' he snapped. 'It's his accent that's the obvious giveaway, Brigadier.'

'His accent.'

'He hasn't lost the English pronunciation of some words. A real foreigner, if you'll excuse the term, would have to have been in England, or amongst English speakers, for years to get that. I'd guess Hampshire, but Home Counties definitely. Just an adequately qualified linguist would spot it a mile off.' He grinned, the first time he had smiled all morning. 'You could test him for his innate Englishness.'

'Fine,' said the Brigadier. 'But that might not be enough, and I'm not sure why UNIT should have to carry –'

'UNIT should "carry" him,' the Doctor interrupted, 'because, if he will be a companion of mine – and I've no doubt that he will, or was – he's a UNIT operative by proxy. I owe it to the man because he got caught up in my adventures and, unless my future self decides to be a villain like the Master, I'd guarantee that Isaac helped get the Earth out of trouble. On more than one occasion.'

'Fine,' said the Brigadier, holding up his hands. He'd long known how pointless it was to argue with the Doctor. He could get so hot-headed and grand, and was more often than not right. 'I'll come up with something about wanting him as a special adviser. That's worked before.'

The Doctor remembered to say thank you before he left.

At around the same time, Sarah locked her MG and crossed back over the road to the small flat where Isaac was living. He opened the door looking groggy, pale and unshaven in a tatty old dressing gown. She had got him out of bed. When she had seen him the night before, conducting his music, he had seemed ordinary, anonymous. Then he'd been in black tie. Now he looked even worse. He was in his late fifties, not tall and no longer slim. The hair he had left was greying in a way that just looked untidy. She couldn't picture him younger, full of energy and pluck as he and the Doctor fought Daleks. Those days were long gone.

He didn't seem surprised to see her, but nor was he particularly pleased. Resignedly, he invited her in for tea. Had he been expecting an apology?

she asked, as they went through to the kitchen. Did he even want one? No, he said, he just knew she still had questions.

'You are a journalist, after all,' he said. 'A man from the future's a scoop.'

'It's not so much that,' she said, eager to make friends. 'You mentioned some things last night that I've not been able to shake. I do have a few more questions.'

'I see,' he said warily. She noticed he kept glancing out of the window. He had opened the front door cautiously, now she thought about it. Did he think she'd brought the Doctor along?

'I'm more interested in your own future,' she said gently. She had to convince him she was on his side. Which she was, of course. 'You were trying to tell the Doctor something last night.'

Isaac sat down with the tea. It might just have been the morning sunshine, but she'd not seen the darkness round his eyes last night. He really had changed for the worse.

'The Doctor's right,' he said with a sigh. 'I can't tell you anything about what's going to happen to him. How we met, things we did. Nothing like that.'

'Was that what you tried to tell him? Something about his future?'

'I shouldn't have even tried. I know the rules just as much as you do.'

'Even so –'

But he had clearly made up his mind – and from the weary way he looked it must have taken him all night. She wouldn't affect his resolve by force, she could see.

'There is something you could do for me, though,' he said.

'Anything.'

He watched her for a moment, again making a difficult decision. He obviously concluded that she was worth the risk, and then got down on his knees. With ease he pulled at the skirting board under the kitchen cabinets. A long board of wood-effect plastic came away and Isaac began rooting around in the space behind. He emerged with a large brown envelope, the stiff-backed sort she used herself when sending manuscripts. The bashed corners suggested it had travelled well. Isaac got up – she glanced away as he rearranged his gown – and handed the envelope, this precious secret, to her.

'Go on,' he said with a funny look. The envelope was open; the sealing flap had lost its stick. Sarah gingerly removed the stack of pages inside. There were probably fifty or sixty sheets in all. She could see at once that there were various paper stocks and densities involved, and some pages were a slightly different size. It had taken him twenty years to assemble this, he had said. She looked over the first page, at what he'd written.

'I don't read music,' she said, unsure why she felt so embarrassed, so wanting. Isaac was clearly pained by her confession. It had taken a lot for him to share this with her.

'It's probably for the best,' he said, but his words sounded hollow and lifeless. Sarah carefully returned his work to the envelope, but he didn't take it from her.

'Would you hold on to it for me?' he said. 'Make sure it survives...'

He wouldn't say more. She couldn't get him to say anything, and suddenly he was making excuses about other things he had to be doing, commitments to the orchestra and so on. She knew it was a put-off – if his schedule was so urgent he'd already have been up and dressed when she arrived. But he clearly didn't want her there, and she wasn't going to push him. She would just come back when she was in a stronger position. She'd get someone to look at the music. Maybe she'd talk to Nikolai Faro, the ambassador who had discovered Isaac, for herself. There'd be something, there had to be, something to draw him out.

He was brisk with her at the door, and then took her hand on an impulse and shook it. He really was nervy now, full of jitters and continually looking over her shoulder.

'I'll take care of this,' she told him, hugging the envelope with her free arm. 'And you'll be fine,' she added.

By the time she got back to UNIT, Isaac was already dead.

The Brigadier had taken her to the police station himself, keen to show support. He could have delegated, probably should have, but he had always been a doer, and it got him away from his paperwork. Miss Smith seemed grateful for the thought, though. Indeed she probably appreciated just getting away from the Doctor. He really wasn't good when it came to saying the right things. He could sound so uncaring.

In the car and in reception they had sat in companionable silence, respectful both to Isaac and to one other. When the officers took Sarah into the interview room, she surprised the Brigadier by asking him, simply and without fuss, to wait outside. Of course he did as she asked, but it bothered him. What did she think he'd do? He was there for her, not to take over the investigation. What didn't she want him to hear? If the Doctor did prove to be tied up in anything, it would be him who would have to sort it all out. He was just thankful he hadn't yet made the call to the immigration people. That would just have made this whole sorry business even more involved.

He made himself stop watching the clock. When they eventually released Miss Smith, he was engrossed in a leaflet about keeping children away from fireworks; typical, he thought, you only ever see these things at police stations and hospitals – presumably long after it's too late. Despite her efforts to walk tall, he could see she'd been crying. That was why she hadn't wanted him in there. The silly girl, she didn't want him to see. Actually he liked that.

'He called the ambulance as soon as I left him,' she said as he walked her back to his car. She tried to sound matter-of-fact, like this had been an information recce and hadn't been ghastly for her. 'He must have made up his mind while I was there.'

The Brigadier thought it best to play along with her bravado. She certainly wouldn't like it if he tried to put his arm round her, would take it entirely the wrong way. Best to keep things strictly professional.

'I checked in with the Doctor,' he told her. 'He's still as baffled as the rest of us. He has at least looked at that music you gave him, and he thinks it's important. Says it's like something he's heard before. He tried humming a bit of it to me over the radio, but then he reckons that there are various melodies all going on at once and it needs to be properly staged. I didn't make anything of it, anyway.'

'The police don't doubt it's a suicide.' She shrugged. 'They don't think there's a case any more. Now they've spoken to me there isn't anything to follow up.'

'Tell that to the Doctor,' the Brigadier said. 'It's got his interest now.'

Nikolai Faro was genuinely sorry about Isaac and pleased to talk to anyone who had known him. Welcoming the Doctor and his reporter friend into his sumptuous rooms in the embassy, he made every effort to be genteel and accommodating. The Doctor obviously wanted to know about his friend, the reporter wanted to extend an interview she had conducted with Isaac into a full feature on the poor man, his life as well as his work. Both clearly intended to ask him *why* Isaac had done such a thing, but their questions skirted the issue. Either they were nervous about confronting him openly, or they didn't actually want to find out.

He answered what questions they did ask him as openly as he could. He had known Isaac for only a year or so, but the Doctor's name had come up a few times, and Isaac had spoken of him fondly.

'Isaac, I think, saw you as an older brother, a mentor,' said Faro. He meant it as a comfort, the sort of thing you say at a funeral to the bereaved.

'Yes, well,' said the Doctor, squirming in his chair. For all the flaunting exhibitionist he appeared in those clothes, he didn't seem to like the attention.

'Can you tell me how you and Isaac met?' asked Miss Smith, neatly changing the subject.

'He came to me,' said Faro. 'In an interview I'd given, I said I hoped to introduce the peoples of the United Kingdom to our artistry and culture. We were donating some artefacts to your British Museum for a special exhibition. I said that this was what being an ambassador was all about, championing our little nation, making links.'

'Isaac approached you?' asked Miss Smith.

'Yes. As I said, about a year ago.'

'Did you know who he was? His reputation?'

'No. I'd never heard of him before.'

'But you thought he was good enough to bring him over here?' she asked.

'Yes. He showed me some of his work and it impressed me.'

'And he asked you to get him out of the country?'

'That's why he came to see me, showed me the music, yes. He didn't want to talk about his reasons, but I found out some things about him. I don't know how useful this will be to you, of course.'

'Go on,' she said.

'The case for granting him asylum is... *was* based on some threats he claimed to have received. I found out he'd been high up in *Ul Esdaphro* – that means 'The Rebels' – during the 1950s. Some accounts say he was actually the right-hand man to Ettyn – who brought the government down in '53 if you don't know our history. Isaac's wife – she's been dead for years – may even once have been Ettyn's girlfriend. Accounts of those times are hard to come by and contradict each other, so it's not easy to know exactly what happened, or what anyone's role was in it all. But Isaac did feel there was something hanging over him from those days and desperately sought to escape.'

The Doctor asked a question now. 'May I ask, Dr Faro, what it was about the music that stood out?'

'Just reading it off the page impressed me greatly,' he said. 'It seemed so simple, so elegant if you just followed one part at a time, but combined altogether it was... transcendent.'

'Did it seem familiar to you at all?'

Dr Faro stopped, too shocked to say a word. The Doctor sat back in his seat smugly. Thoughts tumbled over each other in Faro's mind. How could he have been so naive, so blind? *Of course*, that had been what he had connected with in the music. Some part of it chimed within him, like he had heard it played before. Or not quite. It resembled something important and long forgotten, an echo of a tune lying dormant in his head and still not tangible even now, even when he was looking for it.

'I don't know *what* it reminds me of,' he said. 'I would not be able to tell you whose work it was he copied. But, yes. Now you say it, Isaac's music...' He paused again, a new thought lighting up inside him. 'You don't notice it when the thing is played,' he said. 'But if you read the notes off the page...'

'That's it exactly,' beamed the Doctor. He leapt to his feet. 'Thank you, Dr Faro, you've been enormously helpful!'

He hurried out. Miss Smith took her time packing away her notebook and pen, obviously just as surprised by the Doctor's behaviour as Faro had been. She thanked him herself, asking if she could call during the afternoon if she thought of any details to check with him. She also said she'd have a copy of the paper sent to him in the morning, so he could see what she'd said. Faro said he would look forward to that.

When she had gone, he stood at the window, looking out over the busy street below. The Doctor was at the wheel of his remarkable-looking car, fidgeting eagerly while he waited for Miss Smith. Faro watched until Miss

Smith appeared, taking her time as she clambered into the flying saucer. She was teasing him.

As the car spun round on the spot and whizzed off down the road, Faro wondered what they were saying, what conclusions he'd helped them to, what her story would say. If she sent her telephone number along with the paper he would call her back, he thought.

But the paper never came.

'It really doesn't matter now,' said Sarah. She did not share the Doctor's conviction that this could all be sorted out.

The Brigadier had been on the phone much of the morning, trying to reach the Defence, Press and Broadcasting Committee. Since he often advised them personally himself, the fact they were not answering his calls was not a good sign. Sarah and the Doctor had sat in his office, talking quietly and waiting for some progress to be made. It was evident the Brigadier had finally got through to someone, and had no time for the efforts being made to wrong-foot him. The Brigadier had already pulled rank, reminding them of what UNIT stood for, what part it played in the great scheme of things.

'It *does* matter, Sarah,' the Doctor said. 'If your editor's been told the story's covered under a D-notice, it means they're claiming national security is at stake. Someone senior in the military or in the Government is working directly against our investigation. Someone your editor's prepared to believe.'

Sarah shrugged. Whatever the case, it had killed her story. If she had checked with her editor before writing up her piece, it would have saved wasting an afternoon.

The Doctor must have guessed the reason for her forlorn manner. 'We'll get this thing repealed,' he reassured her. 'Your story will get told.'

The Brigadier had evidently been put through to someone who could answer his questions – and who knew what the questions were going to be. He had only just begun asking when whoever it was must have interrupted. The Brigadier listened for a good few minutes, his expression getting steadily graver.

All the while, the Doctor had grown more and more impatient. Eventually he could stand it no longer. 'I hope you're not allowing them to batter you down,' he snapped.

The Brigadier answered him with a look that Sarah had never seen before: angry didn't begin to describe it.

'I actually have the Doctor here,' he said into the receiver. 'If you'd care to repeat that back to him.'

The Doctor wandered round behind the Brigadier's desk. He rolled his head and stretched his arms back like he was preparing for a boxing match, then took the receiver. The Brigadier stepped back out of the way. He looked stunned.

'Now look here,' the Doctor started. Then he too was overruled. Sarah sat forward in her seat. What on earth where they saying to him?

'All right,' said the Doctor rather meekly. 'I understand. Yes, you too.'

He put the phone down, and collapsed back into the Brigadier's seat. Sarah looked from him to the Brigadier, stood behind him by the window. Neither would look at her. They looked like a pair of naughty schoolboys after being ticked off by the headmaster.

'Who was that?' Sarah asked. 'Who requested the D-notice?'

The Brigadier took his time to answer. He nodded forward. 'He did,' he said.

The Doctor looked mournfully up at her. The edge of his mouth creased in a half smile. 'Or rather,' he said, 'I will.'

The Doctor didn't blame the others for losing interest. Sarah was furious at him, despite his best efforts to explain. The D-notice he had, or would, request had ended the investigation as far as she was concerned. And their failure to sort it out had nothing to do with the terrible consequences of overstepping time. It made no difference what his future self was up to, she had said. He – the one of him here and now – had had his chance with Isaac and had blown it. That rankled with the Doctor more than anything because it was true. Wherever his travels took him, however long he took to meet Isaac, he had let him down when he was needed. Nothing he could do now would make amends for that.

Still, he refused to give up on such a tantalising mystery. He couldn't let the loose ends go. Why had Isaac died? What did the music signify? What linked it to the coup Isaac – and maybe himself – had taken part in twenty years before, if anything? Why did he recognise the tune? At three in the morning, the Doctor was still working away in his lab, puzzling over the manuscripts.

He had made copies so he could add his own notes, and these were scattered about the worktop and around him on the floor. He would glance from one page to another, seeking links or a springboard, convinced he would find something, somewhere at the heart of it all, he remembered. It was so frustrating!

'I'll be here a while longer,' he called when someone poked their head into the lab. He looked round to see who it was, wondering if they'd make him some coffee.

He didn't recognise the two men who had entered the laboratory. They were tall and all in grey. Their eyes and skin were grey too. A grey like moonlit clouds, like eerie magic. They wore morning dress, strange and identical apart from their different buttonholes. One had a perfectly white tulip in his lapel, the other a black rose.

'How do you do, gentlemen?' said the Doctor. 'Is there something I can help with?'

Black Rose knelt gracefully, and started gathering up the pages on the floor. White Tulip ignored the Doctor as he came over to the worktop. He took the envelope first, then lithely gathered up the Doctor's copies.

'Excuse me,' said the Doctor, reaching for the man's wrist. The man struck out at him, but the Doctor caught his arm, pivoted down and round and rolled him over his shoulder, bowling him directly into the kneeling Black Rose. The Doctor would have made a quip if they had given him time. But both grey men bounced to their feet like cats and came at him. He feinted to one side as Black Rose flew at him, and brought the man down with a keenly aimed chop. But White Tulip bashed him in the nose with the back of his hand, and Black Rose, down on the floor, grabbed his ankle. The Doctor fell over backwards and that was all it took. He struggled to his feet as quickly as he could but by then they were gone.

'Wait!' the Doctor shouted, giving chase. But there was no sign of them in the corridor outside the lab. And all his copies of Isaac's music were lost with them.

Though she hadn't yet seen for herself, Sarah had heard several reports about the Brigadier's ill temper. The two officers on watch the night before had taken the worst of it, of course. And then Benton got a roasting when he reported that nothing had been found. The search had taken up the whole morning. When the Brigadier strode into the Doctor's laboratory later that day, his expression suggested the Time Lord was next for the chop. That momentarily changed as he tripped over the line of wires in the doorway and landed on his face.

'Do look out for the apparatus, old chap,' said the Doctor from where he crouched in the corner. He hadn't even looked round, didn't see the Brigadier seething as he picked himself up. Sarah, perched up on the tabletop, swinging her legs in the space underneath, bit her lip. Her presence was enough to ensure the old soldier collected himself before starting on the blue murder. She watched him count slowly to ten. He looked around the room, at the coils of wire organised in some lunatic pattern all over the floor.

'I do hope you're doing something constructive, Doctor,' he said gruffly.

'More than you've been doing, I should say,' replied the Doctor, still not looking back at him. He had some thrown-together mechanism in front of him, the sort of thing he dashed off all the time and which rarely worked. He beavered away on it, leaving the Brigadier and Sarah to mug 'What can you do?' faces at each other. Then the Doctor used his sonic screwdriver to finish whatever he was making.

'There, that should do it!' He beamed as he got up. 'You can stay and watch with Miss Smith if you like, Brigadier.'

'What have you been up to, Doctor?' the Brigadier muttered.

'My dear fellow, I've done what your men – sterling as they are – could not. I've found the two intruders.'

The Brigadier folded his arms. 'How on earth –'

'That's just the point, Brigadier,' the Doctor chided. 'They weren't "on Earth" at all.

'Aliens, you mean?' said the Brigadier.

'Quite possibly,' said the Doctor. He began to connect some of the odd bits of mechanism on the worktop beside Sarah.

'The Doctor thinks that his attackers materialised in the lab,' explained Sarah. 'Rather than breaking in.'

'That would explain how they got past security,' said the Brigadier. 'But can you tell for sure?'

The Doctor looked up from his work. He seemed weary, thought Sarah. Some of the soldiers who had known him for years said he looked old and worn-out these days. Maybe he had just got fed up answering their stupid human questions, the hassle of it all.

'There are elementary tests for space-time scarring,' the Doctor said irritably. 'By a process of elimination you can determine whether you're at the end point of a hyperspace tunnel or transmat linkage or what-have-you.'

'And are we?' asked the Brigadier, obviously in no mood for the Doctor's flouncing.

'Yes, Brigadier,' said Sarah. 'The tunnel opened just about where you're standing.'

The Brigadier stepped quickly forward towards the desktop and then looked back at where he had stood.

'I can't see anything there,' he said.

'Well, obviously not, Brigadier,' muttered the Doctor. 'It's closed now.'

'Can you open it?'

'Not as such, no. But I can use the scar it has left behind to lead us back to wherever the tunnel was opened.'

'And that will get you to your two grey men.' The Brigadier nodded. 'Want me to gather some men to help you apprehend them?'

The Doctor considered it. 'I'm hoping that won't be necessary,' he said. 'I just want a quick chat with them.'

The Brigadier laughed. 'This is driving you mad, isn't it? The not knowing?'

The Doctor didn't dignify that and continued with his work. 'Used to hate these things when I was at school,' he said – as much to himself as anyone. 'One of my old tutors used one to catch me stealing sweets from the school pantry. Ah, that should do it.'

The Doctor hurried round to connect this last piece of equipment. Looking at the complex, disordered set-up, Sarah wondered how the Brigadier had learned to cope with his freelance eccentric. But the Brigadier, for all he had criticised, looked on indulgently.

Soon the Doctor was satisfied. He got them both to stand behind the worktop, and told them not to come and help him if he looked like he was stuck. The Brigadier shook him cheerily by the hand when the Doctor tried to say a sombre goodbye. Evidently the old soldier didn't take any of this seriously. Or he was making it easier for the Doctor to do whatever absurdly dangerous thing he was about to. Sarah shook the Doctor's hand as well, but couldn't convince herself he could be in any danger really. Not pressing a switch down on just the other side of the worktop.

The Doctor looked quickly at them both one last time then pressed the lever.

There was a warbling from the machine behind them, the one he'd been working on when the Brigadier came in. The Doctor looked expectantly at the laboratory doors, as if willing the grey men he'd described to come walking back through them. Then, Sarah could see something. It was like heat haze, a smearing of the lines of the doors. The air smelt of something sweet and tangy, alive with energy.

Then the Bri–

[The wormhole is wide open. He can see right down it, the lucent white membranous walls leading to a point of indistinct darkness far away at the end. He takes a step forward, then realises his friends have said nothing. Surely they are impressed. He looks back.

The Brigadier and Sarah stand stock still. Not even involuntary, reflex movements. They are not dead, just frozen in time. Time has stopped. His machine has not done this. So who?

'We did, Doctor,' says a man in a neatly tailored pinstripe suit who now stands at the mouth of the tunnel. He has not emerged from it; he is just suddenly there in front of it. He blocks the Doctor's way. The man raises his bowler hat cheerily.

'You've come to explain all this, then?' he answers angrily.

'I'm afraid not,' says the man in the suit pleasantly. 'The story ends here for now.'

'You're not serious.'

'You will understand. But not now.'

'I don't need to know about Isaac, but that music! I already know it means something. It's right on the tip of my tongue and I just need to know what!'

'You have had just a glimpse of something to come. That is all.'

'Of course it's not!'

'This is not a choice I'm offering you.' The man in the pinstripe suit does not say this last bit so pleasantly. He isn't really pleasant at all.

'It'll drive me mad not knowing,' he replies bitterly. He is bitter because he will do what the man says. He takes a step back from the man, from the tunnel. 'How am I going to get any peace?'

The pinstripe man shrugs. 'There will be times ahead,' he says, 'when you will need something to keep you going.' He looks for a moment like he will say more, explain what that means. He raises his hat and is gone.

The clock on the mantelpiece ticks suddenly loud, too slow and not real as seconds start to pass by once more.]

* * *

–gadier turned to her to say something. A 'pop' from the machine behind them stopped him. They both looked back at the Doctor. The strange haze in the air had faded. Everything was back as it had been.

'It didn't work?' asked the Brigadier sympathetically.

The Doctor didn't say a word. It wasn't just disappointment. If he had looked old before, that was nothing to the way he looked now. Sarah leaned forward and put her hand on his arm.

His friends could see he wanted to be alone and left him. He was grateful for that kindness. Alone in the lab, tired and worn out, he didn't know where to begin.

As he fussed with pulling the apparatus apart and putting it away, a bit of the melody he had tried to sing to the Brigadier over the radio came back to him unbidden. At first he tried to think of something else, anything that would come. But what came was the counter-melody, weaving in and out of and through and around the first tune.

He let the two phrases play inside him as he tidied up. Only as he came to the end of his work did he realise he could not recall the third part. The notes were tantalising, just beyond his grasp.

The Doctor looked round the lab for some paper, eager despite himself to work it all out. If it took him the rest of his days, he would get it.

Some weeks later, RSM Benton looked in on the Doctor's lab. He felt wistful. UNIT headquarters was a very different place these days. The Doctor and Sarah were no longer about and things were quieter all round. They had already sent the cars off to storage, to be properly looked after should the Doctor ever return. The familiar old lab would be stripped out to make room for computers, they said. Benton would have to learn to use them if they did. He didn't like the thought of that. Maybe he'd resign his commission before that day came, go do something else, something hands-on.

A shadow in the corner caught his eye and he went over, squatting down to see what it was. A smart smoking jacket lay long discarded under one of the benches. He picked it up, bashed some of the dust off. It was the one the Doctor had worn when he'd changed, wasn't it? The one he'd died in...

Benton wondered what to do with it. It didn't seem right just to leave it here. Someone might pinch it. Then again, he didn't want to keep such a ghoulish relic for himself. Without really knowing why, maybe just to do something, he checked the jacket pockets. There was nothing in them. It didn't seem right for the Doctor's pockets to be empty.

And then Benton found the paper.

It was a scrap torn from something else, a triangular fragment beginning to yellow. Something had been written on it, though it was only when Benton held it up to the light he could see it wasn't writing. Musical notes were strewn messily across the page.

Benton knew the old Doctor's handwriting from years of supply requests and favours. But this was a cruel parody of that confident, spidery scrawl. Benton took a moment to realise what he was holding: the desperate jottings of a dying man.

For years to come, Benton would return time and again to three questions he could never answer. He couldn't shake them from his head.

How long was the Doctor travelling, dying from whatever that Tibetan lot did to him, before he got back to UNIT HQ?

Did he really not think he'd make it?

And, if the reborn man had discarded this once-so-important page, had he been right?

The Ruins of Time

Philip Purser-Hallard

An Adventure of the First Doctor, with Susan, Barbara Wright and Ian Chesterton

The Twilight City

'What colour would you like to be, Ian?' Susan asked, proffering a handful of the wooden counters.

Ian considered. 'I suppose I'll be silvery-grey. But you'll have to explain to me how all this works.'

'Oh, but it's easy,' the girl said at once. She launched into a tortuous explanation, as Ian gazed in bafflement at the landscaped board.

Barbara smiled to herself. Ian was both too kind and too stubborn to admit to their young friend that this game of hers was beyond him. 'Won't we be arriving quite soon, Susan?' she asked.

'I don't know.' Susan looked over at the Doctor, fussing away at his controls as usual. 'Once the ship's in flight, I don't think even Grandfather can tell. But it's very simple really, Ian. This house is yours – it's the same colour as your counters, you see – and you're trying to get home.'

Now Ian glanced over at the Doctor. 'Isn't that the truth,' he said ruefully. Susan gasped, dismayed at her own tactlessness.

'Have you had the game long?' Barbara asked quickly, wondering which planet – and which century – had produced the ornate box-board, with its wooden dice and counters.

'Oh, yes,' Susan replied. 'This set's been in Grandfather's family for thousands of years.'

'Thousands?' Ian stared at her. 'Surely you mean "hundreds"?'

Susan gave him a mischievous smile. 'Well,' she admitted, 'it's hundreds of thousands really. But I didn't want to shock you.'

A once-grand piazza, unchanging beneath a grey sky. Its fountains dry, its buildings and its paving-stones empty of life.

A walkway, arching gracefully overhead. The sky above, drab twilight, scant of stars.

There was no movement here. No breeze perturbed the scraps of dust and rubbish. No rats scampered from the darkened doorways, and the sky was bereft of birds. Not a sound escaped from the surrounding city.

Where previously had been a vacant flagstone, now stood a squat and foreign presence – an English police box. Its beacon flashed sharp white, tearing apart the glowering dusk.

* * *

The four companions wandered down a broad and empty boulevard. Skeletal trees accused the grizzled sky.

Ian was carrying the box containing Susan's game board and pieces. He'd just been getting to grips with the rules when the ship had landed. Susan was hoping they could set it up again somewhere.

The women were instinctively whispering, but the Doctor insisted on breaking the museum silence. 'Oh, I shouldn't think there's any reason to worry. This city's been deserted for some time, I should say. Besides,' he added sagely, 'there's nobody about.'

Ian was unconvinced.

The Doctor had been mistaken before, to say the least. And, if any locals were still lurking in the desolation, they'd hear him streets away.

'It must have been beautiful once,' Barbara mused, 'when there were people living here. It feels desolate without them. Why do you suppose they left?'

'My dear Miss Wright, every civilisation comes to an end eventually,' the Doctor said. 'I should have thought a history teacher would know that.'

He scraped at the dust beneath their feet with his walking cane, revealing the intricate mosaic that formed the pavement here. In daylight it might have been colourful, but this dim undifferentiated twilight rendered it in shades of dark and paler grey. 'Some day your own city, London, will be deserted just like this one.'

A shriek cut through the silence. Susan stood some way ahead of them, hands to her mouth.

Ian was at her side instantly. 'What's the matter, Susan? What did you see?'

Cross at being startled, her grandfather snapped, 'What is it now, child?'

'A man!' the girl gasped. 'Over at that window. Standing there completely still, just watching us.'

Her shaking finger pointed across the street to a dark aperture near the base of a tapering tower. 'Ian, he's still there!'

He put a hand on her shoulder. 'I'll go and look,' he said. 'I'm sure it's nothing, though. You stay here with the others.'

Susan's horror did not dissipate over the next hour, as the travellers found more of the immobile figures. Once they knew what to look for, the natives were everywhere: standing at windows, slumped on floors, propped awkwardly amidst the dusty furniture. Not sleeping, and apparently not dead; but not alive.

They looked like human beings, more or less... but so had people on so many of the worlds Susan had seen. Horrifying though they were, now she was more used to them they seemed terribly sad as well, like faded photographs.

'So many of them,' said Barbara as they entered a pillared hall where dozens of pathetic figures huddled motionless. 'Doesn't it remind you of Pompeii, Ian?'

'Pompeii? What's she talking about now?' Grandfather muttered. He was agitated, and Susan could easily understand why.

'What do you think happened to them, Doctor?' asked Ian.

'They're frozen, aren't they, Grandfather?' said Susan. 'Not in temperature, I mean. In time.'

'Yes, well. I thought I'd taught you not to jump to such absurd conclusions, child.'

'But haven't you noticed? The light.' She pointed through a shattered skylight at the toneless sky. 'Since we arrived it hasn't changed a bit.'

'There must be... there could be all kinds of reasons for that,' the old man blustered. 'Perhaps this world just moves too slowly around its axis for us to see the change in the light. Or we may be in one of the polar regions. Yes, I dare say that's it. We're simply beyond the region of this planet's day and night.'

'*Ian!*' Now it was Barbara who cried out. From a shadowed corner, one of the stiff figures stepped towards them.

As it moved forward between the pillars, a pale face came into the light. Marred by a scar across one cheek, it remained strangely beautiful.

Calmly, it said, 'I wish that was the case.'

'Thank you so much for your hospitality, Vedirioi,' Barbara said.

Smiling wryly, the alien – the Torcaldian – inclined his head. 'It isn't much to offer you, I know.'

The village of Cantosi, Vedirioi's home, was built in what had once been a city park. Tents and ramshackle sheds were set amongst low ornamental walls and hedges, with row on row of crops planted in what had been flowerbeds. A paved convergence of paths had been cleared of its statues and now-useless sundial to form a rudimentary village square, where the Cantosians sat at wooden trestles with the strangers. In all directions, graceful, lifeless buildings buttressed the skyline.

'We don't see many visitors,' Vedirioi went on. 'Not friendly ones, at least.'

'Oh, don't worry about that, my friend,' the Doctor replied generously. 'Your food may be basic, but it's most adequate. Most adequate, I can assure you!'

Ian frowned – troubled, Barbara supposed, by this scarcely appropriate reaction to the villagers' selfless hospitality. 'You've really been extremely kind, Vedirioi,' he said. 'You've more than made up for the fright you gave us out there in the city.'

'It's the least I can do,' Vedirioi said. 'And I'm sorry for not announcing myself to you sooner. We've been having trouble recently with bandits from the other cities.'

'Bandits?' Susan's eyes were wide.

'I'm afraid so. Our world's resources are scarce. Not everybody chooses to come by them peacefully.'

Barbara traded a glance with Ian. The question had to be asked.

'What happened here, Vedirioi?' she said. 'Was there some terrible disaster?'

The Torcaldian gazed gravely at her. 'No,' he said. 'Not really.'

'What happened, then?' asked Susan eagerly.

Barbara saw Ian wince at her poor manners.

Vedirioi considered the question.

'Nothing,' he said. 'Nothing happened. There was a city, and noise and hurry and change. And then it all gave way to... nothing.'

'What can it have been?' asked Susan. 'Do you know, Grandfather?'

'I don't, my dear,' he said. His eyes were focused on the distant buildings. 'I simply don't have any inkling.'

But he refused to return her questioning gaze.

The Dying World

'I just can't help it,' Barbara said. 'I feel we should be helping them somehow. They've been so kind to us.'

Ian sighed and looked across the square to where Susan was chatting animatedly to Vedirioi. 'What can we do, though? The Doctor doesn't seem to hold out much hope.'

She said, 'But that's just it. I don't think he *wants* to help. It's a scientific puzzle to him. And meanwhile we're using up what little food these people have.'

Ian shook his head. 'Yes, I know. I wish there was something we could do as well.' She followed his gaze. 'At least Susan's made a friend,' he said more cheerfully.

'I'd noticed.' Barbara smiled. 'I think she's developing a bit of a crush actually.'

He turned back to her, shocked. 'You think so? Really? That's a bit... unexpected, isn't it?'

Amused, she said, 'What, because he isn't human? Alydon wasn't either.' And nor was Ganatus, she thought, rebellious suddenly. 'You know, we can't be sure Susan is herself.'

'Well, that's as may be, but –'

'As a matter of fact –' she was teasing him now '– I think Vedirioi's rather a dish myself.'

'Barbara!'

'Well, he is.' She faltered. Why was Ian so appalled by a harmless schoolgirl fancy?

'Hold on a second,' he said, frowning. 'What do you mean, "he"?'

Both turned to stare at the Torcaldian.

* * *

Vedirioi and Susan fed the little horned animals who provided Cantosi with its scarce supplies of milk and wool. 'It happened generations ago,' Susan's friend was saying. 'Before any Torcaldian now alive was born.'

'Even Astebo?' Susan asked. Cantosi's leader was the oldest Torcaldian she'd seen, except among the frozen figures in the city.

'Even Astebo,' Vedirioi confirmed. 'Back then, we had a truly global culture. Our – what's the word? – our *nations* had been at peace for many generations. Our learning grew with every passing decade, and so did our civilisation. That's what my grandparents told me, anyway,' Vedirioi added, 'and with all the fine buildings and works of art around me, I couldn't see any reason to doubt them.'

Torcaldi's cities, Vedirioi said, had been built around places of wisdom and enlightenment – libraries and museums and observatories – in the same way, Susan knew, as those on worlds like Earth grew up around temples and cathedrals. 'This whole city was Cantosi then,' Vedirioi said. 'Now we're all that's left. We scrub around in the ruins and compete for what little time remains to us.'

'Can't the other worlds help you?' she asked.

'As far as I'm aware, you and your friends are Torcaldi's first visitors from elsewhere.' Although the ancient astronomers had observed compelling evidence of intelligence among the stars, Vedirioi explained, it had all been far away from Torcaldi... and, finding on their own world everything they might wish for or need, the Torcaldians had had no desire to establish contact.

'And that,' Vedirioi said now, 'may have been our undoing.'

And, for the moment, refused to elaborate.

When they finally managed to get the alien woman – and surely she *was* a woman – on her own, Ian said, 'Look, Vedirioi, old... old stick, there's something we need to ask you.'

He looked to Barbara for moral support, but it wasn't forthcoming. He soldiered on.

'I know it's not exactly the polite thing to ask, but – well, you are a woman, aren't you? And, er, not a man?'

Vedirioi looked utterly mystified. Ian hoped he hadn't offended her.

Barbara's idea was absurd, of course. Vedirioi might be considered boyish, in a lissom sort of way, but she was clearly female. It was ridiculous to think otherwise. Surely.

He went on rather desperately: 'I'm afraid you all look a bit androgynous to us. I mean, we know Astebo's a man because of his beard, and Gartami's obviously a woman because... well, she's expecting, but the rest of you...'

He petered out.

'Well,' said Vedirioi politely, 'as you can see I don't wear a beard, and I've never been pregnant. So I suppose I'm neither.'

Ian stared at her.

Barbara stepped in. 'When you were introducing everybody, you told us that Freltese was Ecsilo's mother and Hathemia was her –'

'His,' Ian corrected her. Ecsilo and Gartami were a couple, he was fairly sure.

'– *her* father. So Hathemia must be a man, and Freltese's a woman.'

There was an awkward pause.

'Your society must pay more attention to these things than we do,' said Vedirioi. 'Yes, Freltese and Hathemia are Ecsilo's mother and father. But their other child, Jeyi, Freltese fathered and Hathemia gave birth to.'

'They *what?*' Ian was flabbergasted.

'Are your people supposed to specialise in one or the other?' Vedirioi asked. 'That must be very limiting for you.'

'You mean you didn't realise?' Susan said kindly, trying not to giggle. 'They're hermaphrodites, of course, like the flowers and snails you taught us about in biology, Mr Chesterton.'

They were in Cantosi's village guest hut. It was small but the worn furniture had once been surprisingly luxurious. Presumably it came from the abandoned houses in the city.

'You mean you *knew?*' Barbara seemed surprised.

'Oh, yes – it was only from a distance that I thought one of them might be a man. Grandfather and I saw something similar on Yaqexis.' She started telling them about the Yaqex and their peculiar coming-of-age ceremonies, but Ian stopped her quickly.

'That's... very interesting, Susan,' he said. 'I wonder how the Torcaldians came to be this way?'

'Oh, I don't think they were ever any different. The animals are hermaphrodites too. On Yaqexis, all of the organisms were. They'd simply never evolved single sexes.'

'And what's so unusual about that, my boy, hmm?' Susan's grandfather was suddenly at the hut's door. He must have finished talking to old Astebo at last. 'You really must cast aside these preconceptions of yours. Why ever would these people have the same reproductive arrangements as yourselves, hmm? Consider the snails of your own planet –'

'That's just what I was saying, Grandfather.'

He looked mildly crestfallen. 'Oh, were you? Oh.'

'Well,' the Doctor said shortly afterwards, 'it's just as I feared, I'm afraid. There's very little we can do here. It's been a very pleasant visit, but I think it's time that we were getting back to the ship.'

Ian exchanged a look with Barbara. 'You mean you've found out what's going on here, Doctor?'

'Oh, I think so, Chesterton, I think so.' The Doctor adopted his lecturing stance, gripping his lapels, chin jutting high. 'It all fits in with what Astebo's told me. This constant twilight, the fact that the buildings are intact – it's been many years, you know. Some of them should have fallen down by now. It seems as if whatever catastrophe occurred here has drained this world of time, and it's left these people short. There's very little left to go around now. The people we saw frozen in the city had simply run out of time.'

'But can't anything be done for them?' Barbara asked.

'No, I'm afraid not, my dear. Astebo's very clear on that. When somebody's time runs out no one else can give it back to them. They should have used it more wisely.'

Ian protested. 'But that doesn't make any sense. Time isn't a commodity, to be shared around like that!'

The Doctor bristled. 'Isn't it, my boy? And yet you humans talk of spending time and saving it, of sparing time for others or keeping it to yourself. You even have a saying about "time burning a hole in your pocket", isn't that so?'

Ian sighed. 'No, Doctor, that's money.'

'Oh, is it?' Again the Doctor deflated slightly. 'But then you also say that "time is money," don't you, hmm? If you people could buy and sell time itself, then I'm quite sure you would. These people can.'

Ian said slowly, 'So these bandits Vedirioi's so concerned about – they don't just steal food? They steal *time*?'

'So it would seem, Chesterton. So it would seem.'

Above the park, a tower. Its silhouette stark against the colourless sky, a giddying staircase curling up to its summit.

From that rooftop, a comprehensive view spread forth across the city that had once been called Cantosi.

A newcomer to the city was taking advantage of that view. A figure dressed in black, tight-fitting clothes – a belted knife, a slender, cruel gun slung over its back – stared down towards the park, the village, its people and their visitors.

The Raiders from Labeth

'That's right, Vedirioi,' said Susan cheerfully. 'You've thrown a 13, so now your counters move 13 spaces up the mountain. Now it's my turn.'

Susan had insisted on 'just one game' with her friend before they returned to the ship, but Vedirioi was proving a slow learner.

'Susan doesn't seem very bothered that "he" isn't a he,' Barbara whispered to Ian.

He immediately changed the subject. 'I don't see why the Doctor won't let us talk about the TARDIS. What harm can it do? The Torcaldians must realise we came here in some kind of spaceship.'

'Well, I suppose they've never met space travellers before,' she whispered doubtfully. She too had difficulty understanding the reason for the old man's prohibition, but he had been quite insistent.

They both started as a cracking noise resounded through the square, echoing from the park's dead outer reaches.

'Er... Susan?' said Vedirioi. 'The board's just split in half.'

'Oh, yes, it's supposed to do that. Grandfather?'

The Doctor was dozing in a nearby chair. 'Hmm? What is it? Are you still dallying about with that foolish game?'

'What is it we shout when the board splits open?'

'Oh, I don't remember, child. You know I can't be bothered with that sort of thing.'

Susan pouted. 'You used to play this all the time at home.'

'Yes, well. It's really time that we were going.'

Susan screamed again and again as the bandits attacked. Torcaldians in dark clothing, wielding long-bladed knives and strangely elegant guns, charged through Cantosi, scattering its people everywhere.

'Run,' Astebo insisted. 'Both of you. This isn't your fight.'

Grandfather barely hesitated before grasping Susan's wrist and pulling her away. They stumbled past the guest hut, trampling the crop beds in their haste, aiming for the open park.

Susan looked back. 'Vedirioi!' she shouted, casting about for any sign of her friend. Instead, she saw six of the bandits forming a wall around Astebo. One of them – a young Torcaldian of about her own age – rested both hands on Astebo's temples, pushing the elder to the ground.

Grandfather tugged her arm. 'We've no time for that, child!'

If only he hadn't decided to delay, she thought, for one last moment in Cantosi, saying his farewells to Astebo, the two of them could have been halfway to the ship by now with Ian and Barbara. He spurred her into motion once again, but not before Susan heard a yell and saw one of the dark figures point towards them.

'Oh, dear me...' Grandfather gasped as they ran on. 'I'm not... I don't think I'm equal to this, my child. You must go on! Warn Barbara and Chesterton!'

She helped him stumble on a few more steps, but he was quite exhausted and began to collapse slowly on to the withered grass.

'Stop there, you two,' a bored voice commanded them.

'Run, child!' Grandfather cried. But by now it was too late: the bandits were almost upon them.

The foremost of them – powerfully beautiful, in that ambiguous Torcaldian way – stopped a short distance away and pointed one of the wicked-looking weapons directly at the Doctor's head.

'*Damn* them!' Vedirioi spat. Ian was shocked by the violence in her voice, the savageness of her scarred face. '*Damn* those Labeth slavemongers!'

Astebo crouched beneath them, immobile as the other figures in the city, his dignity abandoned in a terrified cower that would last forever.

'They drained him,' Barbara said. 'They sucked his time away and left him... frozen like that. It's *horrible*.' Ian patted her arm.

'That's what they do,' Vedirioi said. 'Astebo was our most experienced conduit, and my friend. Gone forever now, like too many others.'

Astebo's was not the only stock-still body in Cantosi. Most of the villagers had fled as the bandits arrived, but others had been caught. Some had been halted like Astebo, beyond anyone's ability to reanimate. Others had been taken.

'Vedirioi,' Ian said gently, 'we're sorry about Astebo – really we are. But there's nothing we can do for him now. The Doctor and Susan are still alive, and they need our help.'

'They're as good as dead,' Vedirioi muttered. 'The bandits will have taken them back to Labeth. That's how their raiding parties work. Some of us, they drain on the spot; others, they take away with them for later. For their sustenance.'

'We have to help them,' Barbara insisted. 'They're our friends.'

'And without them,' Ian said grimly, 'we can't get home – or even leave this planet.'

When awareness returned to her, Susan was in a cage: wooden and crude, with planking slats in place of bars.

She tried to sit up and the floor lurched alarmingly. Rolling over onto her stomach, she grasped the rough slats and pulled herself forward, then screamed as she saw tiled roofs and glittering waterways spread out hundreds of metres beneath her.

'Quiet, you,' a voice said roughly. Gripping the cage, Susan raised her head to see that she was suspended a short distance from a platform – no, a roof, part of the crenellations halfway up a huge building. An ornate buttress – perhaps even a gargoyle – stretched out above her, anchoring the ropes from which her prison hung. There was a row of similar structures, from each of which another cage depended.

'Grandfather!' she cried. The old man lay unconscious in the box next to hers. She could too easily imagine that flimsy wooden floor splintering beneath him, pitching him out, still asleep, onto the hard roofs far below.

'Why are you doing this to us?' she pleaded.

'Not my choice.' The husky voice belonged to a slim Torcaldian, as young as Susan seemed. A moment later, with a chill, she recognised the youth who had laid hands upon Astebo, draining the life-time from the old villager's veins.

Barbara's legs ached.

Her arms and back ached too, but her legs were the worst. On Earth she was a reasonable horsewoman, but the hermaphroditic beasts ridden by the Torcaldians weren't horses and they needed quite different handling and guidance.

Besides, Cantosi had only two of the creatures to spare so she and Ian had no choice but to ride with Ecsilo and Vedirioi, wrapping their arms around their lithe waists while their mounts galloped along this vertiginous sky-road.

Under the circumstances, Barbara was glad that she had made the sensible decision to think of Ecsilo as another woman, rather than the handsome young man 'she' might have made. From the look on Ian's face as he embraced Vedirioi, he was still having some trouble reconciling himself to the Torcaldians' unusual biology.

The dappled mare-stallion's hooves thundered between two twisted metal rails, along which monorail trains had once hurtled between the cities of Cantosi and Labeth. The needle-towers of Labeth lay before them in a broad lagoon; far beneath the sky-road, in wasteland that had once been open countryside, forests and farms stretched in variegated blacks and whites and greys to the lake shore.

This was the way the raiders had come, Ecsilo insisted. The young villager was a conduit, whatever that might mean. Among other things, it apparently enabled her to follow the Doctor's and Susan's 'time spoor'.

Dreamily, Barbara realised that their mount was slowing. It gave a burbling whinny as Ecsilo drew it sharply to a halt, and Barbara saw ahead the gap where one of the viaduct's arches had collapsed.

Between the ragged lips of rubble, only one buckled rail remained intact, to link them with Susan and the Doctor.

The Time Conduit

Grandfather was still sleeping. When Susan asked if she could give him water, Tranell's quavering voice became gruff: 'I can't let you out. Balthar'll flog me.'

Balthar, the beautiful, brutal Torcaldian who had captured them in Cantosi, was the bandits' leader and Tranell's owner.

While Tranell passed Susan food and water, the young slave told her more about the raiders' wretched lives.

The tents and lean-tos of their encampment stood a short distance away across the platform roof. Long, long ago, Tranell told Susan, this building had been one of Torcaldi's finest galleries of art. Now the paintings were shredded for kindling, the sculpture galleries macabrely augmented with Balthar's frozen victims.

Or rather, *Tranell's* victims, because Tranell acted as Balthar's conduit.

'That oldie I drained...' Tranell told Susan brusquely. 'I saw that oldie was a conduit, see, just like me. Someone else Balthar would have made a slave.' Born a slave, growing to adulthood in slavery, this thuggery had been all the life Tranell had known.

'I reckoned being drained would make a better end than that. A better end to the oldie's life.'

'The raiders live in that big skyscraper,' Ian said, pointing. 'Or rather outside, on those ledges. It doesn't rain here and there's no wind, so they don't need shelter.'

Barbara could see that Labeth, like Cantosi, must have once been beautiful: a city of canals like Amsterdam or Venice, but with buildings as tall and elegant as those she'd seen in photos of New York. The water had been clear and lucent, and the Labethans had made constant use of it in their architecture, adorning towers and plazas with cascading waterfalls and fountains.

Descending from the monorail terminus, Ecsilo had found that the travellers' time spoor had become indistinct, and Ian had gone in search of local knowledge. 'I met an old tramp,' he said. 'Just passing through, but he saw them heading there across the rooftops. They use rope bridges to get from one building to the next.'

'That may mean the ground floor isn't as well guarded,' Barbara guessed.

'I hope so. It's our best chance of getting in there, anyway.'

They passed on through the city. As time had abandoned Labeth, so its waters had slowed, becoming sluggish, setting like glass in some places. The fountains spumed at infinitesimal speed, while the canals had all but solidified, holding fast to boats and jetties.

Beneath the waterways, the bodies of Torcaldians who had sought to escape their world were held, frozen like flies under amber.

Grandfather had stopped sulking at last, and was deigning to speak to Tranell. 'So, young whatever-your-name-is,' he said. 'To redistribute time between individuals requires a conduit, hmm?' He sipped the mug of water, which the young Torcaldian had passed him. 'That means that every band of brigands needs its conduit slave.'

'Right,' Tranell agreed. 'We all lose time at the same rate, see, but I can take it off someone and share it round. Balthar tells me who to drain and who to pass it on to, so the others let Balthar be the leader. Else they run out of time, or get drained themselves.'

Susan shuddered. 'Why must you drain *people*, though, Tranell? Don't objects have their own time too? A wall might last far longer than a person, and if you took its time away, it would never fall apart. Couldn't you get your time from things like that?'

'A bit,' the slave admitted. 'It's not the same with things, though. Time's there, but it's difficult to get at, and it don't last so long. It's like... a person does more with their time than a wall does, see? They get more use from it. Some conduits live like that, but it don't keep them going long. They need to be always finding new stuff, stuff no one else has been at yet.

Usually they run dry while they're asleep, stiff up just lying there.' Tranell chuckled.

'Indeed, how terrible.' Grandfather clicked his tongue, and gazed into the distance through his cage's bars. 'I dare say the ability must be some form of mutation, brought on by this cataclysm of yours. I wonder what exactly that might have been, hmm? Yes, I wonder...'

Tranell shrugged. 'Oldies say it was gods. We had gods back in the days, see, and they punished us. But Balthar says that's a lie, and the gods was just foreigners from other worlds, like you.'

'Like us?' Grandfather tried to hide his alarm from her, but Susan knew him too well.

Ian watched in horror from behind a large rock sculpture as the Doctor and Susan struggled in the raiders' arms.

This gallery courtyard, with its grotesque mix of artworks and time-frozen Torcaldians, was awful enough, but now it looked as if one of his fellow travellers would join the statues here.

'Now then,' the bandit leader purred. 'Which of the foreign animals shall I have you drain, Tranell?'

Ian cursed his own stupidity. With the others, he might have stood a chance of rescuing his friends, but he'd insisted Barbara and Vedirioi should wait with Ecsilo.

'Not the youngster,' begged the Torcaldian called Tranell. 'Please, Balthar, not Susan.'

Balthar smirked obscenely. 'Fair enough, then,' she said, pointing at the Doctor. 'Off you go, my dear.'

'I'm sorry, Susan,' Tranell's voice trembled as he approached. 'It's the oldie or you.'

Susan cried out as Tranell placed a hand on each of her grandfather's temples. The slave frowned in pained concentration.

'So much...' Tranell breathed after a moment. 'There's so much time here.'

The Doctor moaned in pain. A moment later, so did Tranell. A rapidly accelerating stream of oaths poured from the Torcaldian's lips, as the two stood locked together like lovers.

Finally, the conduit gave an anguished cry and collapsed, face contorting, limbs twitching so fast that they blurred.

'Get the slave upstairs,' Balthar drawled. 'The child too. We'll get our share later.'

Helplessly, Ian watched as Susan was dragged away sobbing.

Behind her, the Doctor stood rooted, lifeless – still as the sculptures that surrounded him.

* * *

Balthar spent some time gazing moodily at the Doctor's body. At length the bandit queen kicked the old man hard in the shin, watching for any reaction. Finally she turned and left the courtyard.

As soon as she was gone, Ian rushed over. In his haste he banged his knee on one of the other stiff figures and suppressed a shout of pain. These bodies weren't just frozen, they were solid. Time wouldn't even let their flesh yield to his touch.

The Doctor, on the other hand...

When Ian reached the old man, he was warm. His cheek was soft and pliant like old leather, and as Ian touched it he stirred, as if awakening from a long sleep.

'Well, well,' the Doctor murmured, sounding astonished.

Ian was astonished. 'Doctor, you're alive!'

'Ah, there you are, Cheeseman. Yes, I should think so.' The Doctor bent and rubbed his shin, glaring after Balthar. 'Goodness me, what an unpleasant individual. I shall have a fine bruise shortly. Now, come along, come along,' he added, striding away.

'But Doctor...' Ian hurried to follow him. 'I'm delighted, of course, but *why* are you alive? I thought –'

'Yes, yes,' the Doctor said impatiently. 'It's all to do with time, my boy. Susan and I have a rather special relationship to it, you see. That young person could have carried on draining me to kingdom come before it affected me.'

'Does that mean Barbara and I are safe as well?' asked Ian hopefully.

'Oh, no, I shouldn't think so. It's all because of where we come from, Susan and I. But it's interesting, yes, it's interesting! Now, do come along. Those ruffians still have hold of her. We must find Barbara and the others.'

He led Ian through burnt-out rooms and galleries stripped bare, never once pausing to get his bearings.

Susan staggered from her cage into Barbara's arms. 'Thank goodness you're here,' she gasped. 'They've frozen Grandfather!'

'He's fine, Susan,' said Ian. He and Vedirioi were winching in the other cages, freeing the rest of the prisoners. 'The old rogue was just pretending so he could get away. He's with Ecsilo now.'

'Seeing him alive again should scare the bandits, for a little while at least,' Barbara told her. Shouts echoed from the raiders' rooftop settlement.

A cry from Ian made Susan turn. Tranell stood unsteadily watching them, still twitching. The conduit fumbled for a knife, but Susan held out a hand in appeal.

'Tranell,' she said, 'please don't give us away just yet.' Four of the rickety cages still held prisoners. 'Give us time to set these others free.'

Tranell stared, then with a violent headshake turned and stumbled away across the rooftop.

Ian groaned. 'What do you suppose he's going to do?'

'He?' Barbara said. 'Oh, never mind. You carry on here, Ian. I'll go and warn the Doctor.'

Before Susan could stop her, Barbara was running towards the bandits' encampment.

The hovercraft's engines rustled and ticked as it conveyed Barbara, Ecsilo and the Doctor across the marbled Labeth lagoon. As Barbara gazed back at the jetty, one of Balthar's raiders tried to follow them on foot, but began sinking slowly into the glutinous waters.

The Doctor was still chuckling over his cleverness in finding the vehicle.

'Well now, Ecsilo,' he said at length. 'We'll take the long way round back to Cantosi, as you suggested, and meet up with Susan, Chesterton and young, ah, young Vedirioi back there. We've all the time in the world.'

Barbara could only hope the others were still alive, let alone able to return in safety to the village.

'We haven't any other option now,' Ecsilo agreed, steering the craft in a wide curve towards a pebble-grey shore. 'I wish we had.'

'Oh, nonsense,' breezed the Doctor. 'What could be worse than those terrible bandits, hmm?'

'The Tear,' Ecsilo replied.

'What's that?' he grumbled. 'Do speak up.'

'Pletra's Tear,' the conduit said less softly. 'Torcaldi's Bane. The Rent. The place where... somebody... tore time apart.' She sighed. 'The hole through which "all the time in the world" is being drained away.'

'They'll be all right with Ecsilo,' Ian said, trying as hard to reassure himself as Susan. 'He's a capable... chap.' He glanced towards Vedirioi for a moment.

The three of them had taken refuge in a clothing shop or costume museum in a tiny alley away from Labeth's watery thoroughfares. Smooth dummies in gowns and elaborate hats mingled here with figures of time-starved people.

Vedirioi nodded. 'Ecsilo knows the area,' she agreed. 'Meanwhile we have a long walk ahead of us.'

'Well,' said Susan, 'I suppose we'd better get started.' She slipped her hand bravely into Vedirioi's.

Ian cleared his throat. 'Yes. Best if we get moving,' he said.

Pletra was a town of frozen fire.

Clear bright flames stood like pines or poplars above each wall and rooftop: a beacon-forest, utterly still, illuminating the twilight for miles around.

As the travellers approached the silent conflagration, their hovercraft clicked, coughed and died beneath them, though whether from lack of fuel or deprivation of time Barbara couldn't tell.

Despite Ecsilo's insistence that Pletra was not a place to linger, the Doctor was intent on visiting the Tear itself. There was a laboratory, apparently, which had been used to study the rent in time before the true extent of the catastrophe it had brought became apparent.

Later, as Torcaldian society had undergone its slow collapse, terrified citizens had returned to Pletra and torched the town. Their silhouettes could still be seen, eerily clear against the static blaze they had created before time had finally deserted them. It was, thought Barbara, like walking among single frames taken from a film.

The pyres cast stark shadows around the three friends as they approached the laboratory and the heart of the cataclysm.

Torcaldi's Bane

Among the remnants of the viaduct's collapsed span, close by the foot of one towering granite pillar, stood a domed, uninhabited farmhouse.

'Let's rest here,' Ian suggested. Disoriented though he was by this never-changing twilight, he knew that they had been travelling for many hours and all three were exhausted.

When the rescue party had been frustrated on their approach to Labeth, it was here that they had descended from the sky-road. The rope ladder which they had found – stowed there, presumably, by earlier travellers along the route – was still in place. So, presumably, would be the stiff forms of the mounts which Ecsilo had drained to keep the party supplied with time in Labeth.

Now, while the travellers recovered, Vedirioi brought out the box which she had carried all the way from Cantosi.

'My game!' cried Susan, and she hugged the willowy Torcaldian. 'How *fab* of you to bring it, Vedirioi.'

The delighted girl set up the board and once again inveigled their host into playing with her. Ian stepped outside the cottage to keep watch.

Pletra's Tear was surprisingly tiny, Barbara thought, to have brought about such devastation.

It was a teardrop-shaped white nothingness, a foot or two across. Sealed carefully within a glittering glass cylinder, it blazed like the unmoving flames above their heads, or like the inside of the TARDIS.

Like everything in Pletra, the laboratory was on fire. Time had allowed the flames to consume half the roof before being stripped from them by the Tear, and in the room beneath unchanging dusk could be glimpsed through the brightness.

One wall had halted in the process of collapsing, mortar and stones leaning at an untenable slant. A Torcaldian stood petrified beneath it, face rigid in terror. Other still figures dotted the room like waxworks.

'There were so many theories,' Ecsilo told Barbara in a whisper. This place inspired disquieting reverence in her. 'These scientists believed the Tear was a weapon. They thought some other world – one we knew nothing about – had felt so threatened, hated us so much, that they chose to destroy us slowly and painfully.'

The Doctor, staring at the time rupture, tutted like a disappointed tutor. He tapped the reinforced glass pillar, then bent to examine the banks of instruments surrounding it.

Pale light seeped in through windows in the cottage's domed roof. Susan moved her counters, converging them towards her home. This would be the third time in a row she'd beaten Vedirioi, though disappointingly the abyss had only opened up beneath them once.

She considered her friend's question.

'I don't see any harm in telling you,' she said. 'Not after everything you've done for us. Actually, Grandfather and I don't have a home, not any more. Our ship takes us from world to world.'

'But don't you ever wish for a more settled life?' Vedirioi asked.

'Sometimes, of course. I know I shouldn't envy poor Barbara and Ian, but at least they have somewhere they can return to one day.'

'I only ask because...' Vedirioi paused. 'Our lives can't seem very appealing to you, I know. We've had to make so many sacrifices. But you could make a real difference here.'

'Me?' Susan was shocked. 'Oh, there isn't much that I could do. Besides, I could never leave Grandfather.'

'Well, maybe you could both stay. Think about it for a moment. When we saw the raiders' conduit back at the gallery, that youngster was gorged with time. So much life, to share around the settlement... and your grandparent didn't seem to feel the loss at all.'

Susan said, 'I don't see –'

Then suddenly she did.

'Consider it, Susan!' Vedirioi's voice was urgent. 'It wouldn't harm you, and it could keep my village alive for... oh, so very long. A young life has far more to give than an old one.'

Horrified, Susan stood.

Well, this was most disconcerting, the Doctor thought.

He had allowed Ecsilo to draw time out of him and feed it into the laboratory's quiescent computers, restoring them to some degree of life. The conduit was exhausted now, and was recuperating elsewhere in the building, tended by Barbara.

The Doctor, on the other hand, had never felt fitter. Since then, he had been listening repeatedly to one particular sound recording.

He said aloud: 'Dear me, yes, most disconcerting.'

Steepling his fingers, he stared up towards the ever-burning roof.

Since its first appearance at Pletra, the Tear had not moved. Back then, it seemed, the site of this laboratory had been an open-air performance hall. The rift had appeared during a recital by a touring quartet of musicians; one which, as luck would have it, had been recorded for posterity.

The Doctor listened once again to the disparate tones of the foreign instruments. A firm brass voice, like that of a trumpet, sounded above the steady reassurance of a drum. A flute piped confidently in answer to them, while something electronic quavered against them all.

Over and over again this fourth instrument – haunting, insistent – strove to bring the other sounds in line with it... yet found itself instead lured into harmony with the whole.

A showy piece, the Doctor thought dismissively. But that was not the point – no, not at all.

The tempo of the music was awry. Before the Tear appeared – a shriek of ripping quanta, unmistakeable in itself and accompanied besides by cries of alarm from audience and musicians – the cadence was distorted by its imminent arrival.

During those crucial moments, the Doctor could have sworn – unless his ears had begun deceiving him at last – that there was a fifth voice, altogether alien and discordant, running beneath them all.

'And you, my friend,' he muttered, 'should not be there. No, most decidedly not. You have no business being there at all.'

He peered around for some device to help him copy the recording.

Marching inside the cottage, Ian found Vedirioi toying with Susan's game pieces.

'What did you say to her?' Ian demanded. 'She's absolutely distraught!'

'I'm sorry.' Vedirioi's eyes were swollen: tears trickled down her scarred cheek. 'I asked too much. Susan's only a child. It was wrong of me to forget that.'

He said, 'And what exactly *did* you ask?'

She shook her head. 'It isn't important now – Susan's made the decision. It's just... Oh, Ian,' Vedirioi said.

The woman – *no*, he told himself, *the hermaphrodite, the alien* – sighed. 'I thought I saw a way to save my home. To rescue my friends and family from this degrading cycle we're trapped in, of misery and predation and decay.'

'At Susan's expense?'

'Against Susan's will, as it turns out. But something in me can't help feeling that that's not important – that I should seize the opportunity. A child like Susan couldn't possibly understand how much is at stake.'

'I won't let you force her into anything, Vedirioi,' Ian said softly.

The alien gazed at him. 'I know, Ian,' it said. 'But if I don't, my people are quite certainly doomed.'

The Well of Time

'You got here!' Ian grasped the Doctor's hand. 'We were starting to get worried.'

Cantosi's village square was thronged with villagers, clustering around Ecsilo's party, welcoming the travellers home.

As Susan hugged Barbara next to him, Ian's eye picked out Gartami, Ecsilo's... well, 'wife' obviously wasn't the word, but Ian didn't have a better one. She wasn't pregnant any more, and there was no sign of a child. Neither Ian nor Susan had dared to ask what had happened.

Ian kept a wary eye on Vedirioi too, as the alien welcomed its friend. He lowered his voice and said, 'I think we should be getting away soon, Doctor. It isn't safe here.'

'Hmm? Oh, I think – I don't think we need worry on that score, my boy,' the Doctor said. 'If those raiders were going to follow us, I should think they would have done so by now.'

He fingered something in his pocket. 'Besides, on our way here I found out something rather interesting. We should be able to afford some rest while I use the machines in the TARDIS to study it.'

'I don't think Vedirioi meant it,' Susan told her grandfather. 'Not really. Ian helped sort things out. They're just so desperate here, you see. They have a dreadful life.'

She had found him in the ship, working on the recording capsule he had retrieved from Pletra, looking for something compatible that he could play the recording on. Now the two of them walked together, through forsaken streets back to the park and village.

'That young person had no right to ask such a thing of you,' he huffed indignantly. 'No right at all!'

He was worried about losing her, Susan realised. She and the ship were all he had left.

'Of course not, Grandfather,' she reassured him. 'But I've thought of another way we might help them. Tranell told us that conduits can draw time out of objects as well as people. And... well, the TARDIS exists in the same relationship to time as you and me. If we could leave a piece of her behind...'

Grandfather spluttered. 'Certainly not! I won't hear of such a thing!'

'Oh, but it wouldn't need to be very big – one of the circles from the walls, or even a piece of the furniture. Anything from our own world. There are rooms full of things we never use, I know there are. Something like that could keep them supplied with time for years – perhaps forever.'

'Think, child! We can't leave a piece of my ship lying about Torcaldi like... like a discarded handkerchief! Imagine what might happen if these people came to understand its dimensional nature. Besides,' Grandfather added gravely, 'it might attract altogether the wrong kind of attention. No, Susan, I simply won't hear of it. It's most regrettable, I know, but really there's nothing we can do for our friends here.'

As they turned the corner to enter the park gates, which marked the borders of Cantosi village, the shouts they had heard throughout their argument, but had been too preoccupied to notice, came into focus.

Susan gasped. The village ahead of them was full of panicked, running figures.

'The raiders!'

Barbara groaned inwardly as the Doctor and Susan were frogmarched into the village square, to be herded together with the rest of the villagers.

'Who's that?' Ian muttered. He'd taken a formidable blow to the head during the bandits' first assault and was still woozy now as Barbara cradled his head in her lap.

'Hush,' she said, stroking his temple. 'It's going to be all right.'

The raiders' leader – the murderous, magnetic Balthar – strode forward, dragging wiry Tranell by the wrist. The bandit leader sized up his captives, taking his time. Barbara shied away from his intense gaze as he surveyed the crowd, revelling in the fear he inspired.

Finally, Balthar pointed a sharpened nail towards Susan. 'See, Tranell?' he said. 'I told you we'd find the foreigners here. That one and the old one, there's a whole world of time for us in them.'

The bandit king smiled. 'The young one first, though.'

Terrified, Susan gazed into Tranell's eyes.

'Leave our guests alone, you parasites!' a voice cried from the crowd. It wasn't Grandfather, or Ian or Barbara. 'Drain me if you must, damn you – just let Susan and the Doctor be!'

Vedirioi was trying to fight a way through the bandits, without success. Soon Susan's friend was held by the arms, powerless between two of the burliest raiders.

'Thank you, Vedirioi,' Susan quavered, trying her hardest not to show her fear. 'But Tranell won't hurt me. You didn't want to before, did you, Tranell? And I know you won't now.'

Tranell growled, 'I got no choice, see. If I don't follow orders, Balthar'll beat me.'

'Too right,' crooned Balthar. The bandits' leader pushed Tranell roughly forward. 'No need for talk, my dear. Just *drain the child*.'

The conduit approached Susan, staring miserably down into the dust.

Balthar was smiling. It was malicious, triumphant. Sensual, Ian thought, yet somehow demure, like an evil Mona Lisa in biking leathers.

It was as unmoving as a painting too. That expression would never alter now, unless one day the people of Torcaldi found a way to restore time's ordinary passing to their world.

Barbara whispered, 'My mother used to tell us not to pull faces. She always said that if the wind changed, we'd be stuck like that forever.'

'Well,' Ian said, 'the wind changed here, that's for sure.' Still leaning shakily on Barbara's shoulder, he contemplated the unseeing mask. 'Young Tranell made the right decision in the end.'

'That poor child. I think she's still in shock,' Barbara said. 'Balthar had such a hold over her, I don't think she can quite believe what she did.'

'Well, he's in good hands now,' said Ian. 'Cantosi will be good for him, I'm sure. They respect one another here. They'll let him make his own choices.'

He turned away from Balthar's fixed visage, and said, 'I think I should talk to Vedirioi before we leave. Could we go and see her now?'

They said their goodbyes at the ship, standing around in the drab, dry, rubbish-strewn piazza. Grandfather said it hardly mattered now if the villagers knew about their conveyance. There was a trust between them all, the friendship with former strangers that Susan truly appreciated about their journeys.

Ian shook Ecsilo by the hand, clasping the Torcaldian's shoulder warmly. After a moment's hesitation, he did the same to Vedirioi. Meanwhile, Barbara and Susan took their turns to hug them both.

Tranell hung back, head hanging once again, but Susan crossed to the former slave as well, and the two of them embraced, briefly and awkwardly.

'Thank you,' she told the conduit.

Tranell grinned slyly. 'Ha. Thank *you*.' And winked.

Grandfather was clicking his tongue, holding the doors impatiently.

Inside, Susan relaxed gratefully into the ship's familiar whiteness, luxuriating in the comforting electrical hum, breathing in the sterile air. Grandfather closed the doors then looked surprised to find the Torcaldian recording capsule sitting on the console. It would take him some time to unravel its workings, Susan knew, and he was already thinking about wherever they were heading next. She watched him slip it into his pocket, to return to it again another day.

'I still feel awful that we couldn't help them,' Barbara said as Grandfather addressed himself to the controls. The engines roared like breakers on a shore and the world began to fall away from around the ship. 'Those poor people, having to live their lives in such misery.'

'Be realistic, Barbara,' said Ian gloomily. 'There's nothing we could have done.'

Grandfather gave Susan a warning glance and she took special care to smile sadly back at him.

'Ian's right, Barbara,' she said. 'We've done everything we can for them.'

Back in the village square, filled up with business and bustle amongst the desolation of the silent city, two figures sitting on low stools, facing one another. Between them, an ornate, contoured game board, mottled with age.

Holding a handful of wooden counters, Ecsilo asked, 'Where are we supposed to put all the pieces?'

The two stared for a while at the insanely precious, baffling artefact, the travellers' gift to Cantosi.

Vedirioi took a moment to answer. 'I think we have to make up our own rules.'

Gone Fishing

Ben Aaronovitch

An Adventure of the Sixth Doctor

I

'Do I know you?' asked the man.

The man was huge and spoke so loudly that all the other patrons involuntarily turned to see if he was talking to them. Realising their mistake they furtively returned their gazes to the magazines and the oddly shaped and sometimes unfathomable 'equipment' the shop sold.

William baulked and resisted the urge to stammer.

'I don't believe so,' he said.

The man leant down and peered carefully into William's face. He wore a bizarre patchwork coat – brightly coloured like a hurdy-gurdy man. Did they still have hurdy-gurdy men? William didn't think so. Then a horrible notion struck him – he was in a reality show. Somewhere, cameras were recording his exquisite embarrassment for the entertainment of the nation. If so, it would be particularly cruel to film him in a shop like this – the embarrassment would last a great deal longer than the length of the show and so would the questions from his mother.

The big man straightened up and peered around suspiciously – as if he too was hunting for hidden cameras. The shy retiring denizens of the shop became acutely interested in the minutiae of the shelves, except for one bold soul who made a break up the stairs to freedom.

'What's your name?' asked the big man.

'William,' said William.

This seemed not to satisfy the man, who continued to gaze at William as one might scrutinise a suspect in a line-up.

'I'm the Doctor,' he said. 'Know anything about fishing?'

'Not really.'

'Then what an earth are you doing in a fishing shop?'

Because William wanted a hobby – preferably something that took him out of the house. As far out the house as he could reasonably get, in fact.

'So you've never done any fishing?' asked the Doctor.

'No,' said William.

'Excellent,' said the Doctor. 'Then you must let me give you the benefit of my vast and wide-ranging experience.'

'I don't want to put you to any trouble,' said William.

'Nonsense,' said the Doctor. 'I insist. Every master seeks out someone to impart his knowledge to, a mind unsullied by preconception, a *tabula rasa*. You shall be my blank sheet and I the pen.'

'Well...'

'Excellent,' said the Doctor. 'Firstly, the correct equipment.'

The Doctor picked out rod, line, lures, baits, a net, an equipment box, folding stool and rain umbrella. The Doctor insisted on the umbrella. The shopkeeper asked, facetiously if William was any judge, whether they would be keeping their catch.

'Keeping,' said the Doctor, 'cooking and eating.'

The shopkeeper handed a mallet to the Doctor. 'You'll need that.'

'This?' asked the Doctor.

'For killing the fish,' said the shopkeeper slowly. 'After you have caught them.'

The Doctor hefted the mallet and gave it a couple of experimental swings.

'I'm not sure this is right,' he said.

The shopkeeper sniggered. 'Having second thoughts?'

'No,' said the Doctor. 'I'm just not sure this is big enough.'

'Secondly,' said the Doctor. 'We need a place to fish.'

They were standing outside the shop on the busy Wrexham Road. William, weighed down by rod, basket, stool, net and all his other purchases, watched as the Doctor paused to look left and right. He frowned with concentration and then wet his finger and held it in the air.

'This way,' the Doctor said and set off northwards, towards the canal.

'Wait,' said William weakly. 'I can't.'

'Can't,' said the Doctor. 'My dear... what did you say your name was again?'

'William,' said William.

'My dear William,' said the Doctor. 'Can't is not a proper word. It is formed of two words, 'can' and 'not', rammed together. Remove the 'not' and what are you left with?'

'Can?' asked William.

'Exactly,' said the Doctor. 'Time and tide wait for no man.'

William wanted to say that his mother expected him home for tea. Actually he didn't *want* to say that but he did feel he ought to say something. After all, his mother was expecting him home for tea and would be quite cross if he were late.

'I don't want to be late for tea,' he said weakly.

'Just a quick trip, then,' said the Doctor. 'And back in time for tea.'

William found his recollection of the next series of events a little confused. The Doctor had led him down some steps to the oily, dead-dog-infested waters of the Grand Union Canal. There, on the towpath, there had been a door – he was certain about the door – and beyond the door there had been a room. Then there'd been some shouting, a very strange noise and the Doctor had opened the door and they'd stepped out...

* * *

It was dusk and the air smelt of jasmine and eucalyptus. They were standing on a ridge that overlooked a sandy plain dotted with scrubby bushes and the occasional pot-bellied tree.

A half-crescent moon was rising over the horizon. As he stared, the rod, basket, stool, net and other fishing paraphernalia slipped out of William's fingers and thumped into the dust.

It didn't look like the moon William knew. It was larger and coloured blue. A blue moon, thought William scrambling to keep up with what he was seeing, just like the song. Coloured blue, he realised, because it had oceans and clouds. You couldn't doubt your senses on something like that – real was real.

'This is an alien planet,' said William.

'Yes,' said the Doctor. 'This is an alien planet.'

'That means you must be an alien,' said William.

'Splendid,' said the Doctor. 'Now that we've got that out of the way, let's get on.'

William felt the Doctor wasn't taking him seriously enough. 'This is an *alien* planet,' he said.

'Unfortunately,' said the Doctor, 'in terms of fishing the Earth is not what it was – or will be.'

'You said we would be back in time for tea,' said William.

'William,' said the Doctor. 'I've just brought you to an alien planet. I'd have thought that you have far more important things to think about than tea.'

'Like what?' asked William.

'Like supper,' said the Doctor. 'For instance.'

William looked over the darkening scrubland – there were no signs of life. 'Supper?' he asked. 'Where could we possibly be having supper?'

'Down there,' said the Doctor, pointing. William turned around and found that behind them the land fell away to form a valley. The slope was steep and lush with vegetation and at the bottom wound a wide river, wave tops glittering in the last light.

William picked up all his gear and followed as the Doctor led him stumbling down towards the river bank. Soon William could see firelight flickering through the trees and in a little while they came to a clearing near the bank in which a campfire was burning.

There were people sitting around the fire.

'Are they aliens?' asked William.

'Let me do the talking,' said the Doctor.

They didn't look like aliens, they looked like people from the front cover of *National Geographic*. The adults were dressed only in loincloths and small necklaces and wrist chains of coloured beads. They were dark-skinned but the firelight struck ruddy highlights off their limbs as they moved. Their features were diverse and didn't seem African or European or any ethnicity that William recognised. Their hair was either naturally short or they had razored it down to a mere fuzz on their scalps. Later William would notice that women and men were of similar height, although the men showed more muscle; all were beautifully proportioned.

William was ushered into the circle of firelight and seated to the left of an elderly man wearing a beaded headdress that hung down his back.

'William,' said the Doctor. 'This is Chief Halfmoon.'

The Chief nodded happily. 'Hallo, William,' he said. 'You here for the fishin'?'

'Apparently,' said William.

'Brill,' said the Chief. 'We need to get you fed up then.' The Chief looked over at where a couple of young women were fussing near the fire and shouted. 'Oi! Rabbit. Feller over here needs feeding.'

One of the women, Rabbit presumably, picked a blackened ball from the edge of the fire and flicked it at the Chief, who picked it out the air. The Chief blew on it twice and then cracked it open to reveal a white steaming interior.

It smelled delicious.

'There you go, feller,' said the Chief. 'You're going to need all the strength you can get on the next day.'

'Thank you,' said William. It's going to turn out to be an insect or a monkey's brains, he thought. He hated that sort of joke, where people made you do something unpleasant by mistake and he'd had quite enough of that at school.

The Chief grinned and nodded.

Fear of social embarrassment won over personal embarrassment and William bit into the succulent flesh of whatever monstrosity it was they were feeding him.

It tasted like pork, meaty, no hint of seafood or insect crunch. The Chief watched him as he chewed and swallowed. 'Very nice,' said William. This is it, thought William, the bit where he reveals what I've just eaten.

'Hey, Doctor,' called the Chief. 'Brought us a good feller to be a champion. Let's hope his fishing matches his appetite.'

'So what was it?' asked William.

'Meatfruit,' said the Chief. 'Grows on the trees, handy for when the walkingpork gets away from you.'

William nodded. Just as long as it doesn't dangle between some animal's hind legs, he thought. 'Can I have another one?'

The feast, if that's what it was, went on for a couple of hours. William didn't know how many because when he checked his watch he found it had stopped. After the meatfruit, the Chief handed him a clay bowl filled with a milky fluid mixed with straw, or at least what looked like straw. William coughed when a strand caught in his throat.

The Chief banged him on the back. 'No, feller,' he said. 'You've got to strain it through your teeth.'

William tried. It was undignified but without the straw the drink was smooth and creamy. And probably alcoholic because after the third bowl it all got a bit hazy.

As the gathering broke up, the Chief slapped William on the back. 'We've put you up with Standing Tree and Spring Peach,' he said. 'Lovely couple – they'll see you right.'

Put me up where? As he looked around, it soon became alarmingly clear – the tribe separated into family groups and each family scraped a hollow in the earth, lined it with rushes from the riverbank and there they slept together under a single large blanket. One of the families waved at the Doctor, who signalled back before turning to William.

'Get a good night's sleep,' he said. 'And I'll see you in the morning.'

With that, the Doctor strode over to his family and, without any fuss, slipped under their communal blanket.

William looked around and, sure enough, he saw a skinny man, presumably Standing Tree, wave at him. Beside the man, heads peeping out from beneath their blanket, was the rest of his family. William was no fool; he knew that in these arid conditions under a clear sky like this one if he didn't get under a blanket he was going to freeze to death.

He sighed, put on his best polite smile and went to meet the folks.

He ended up with the skinny man on one side and a young woman with a pair of toddlers on the other. It was remarkably toasty, all things considered.

He woke up once at the hour of the dead. The blue moon had slipped below the horizon, leaving the landscape pitch black. Without light pollution, the night sky was crammed with stars. William found himself staring at them, looking for constellations he knew he would be hard-pressed to identify. 'Nobody looks at the sky any more,' his mother often said.

He did notice that many of the stars were moving too quickly across the sky to be real stars. William wondered whether they were satellites – if so, there were thousands of them, hundreds of thousands even. He watched as a cluster of lights shot across his view from horizon to horizon in less than a minute.

One of the toddlers farted, gurgled happily and snuggled closer into his back.

There was no sign of the Doctor that morning which gave William a brief moment of panic but not as much as he expected it would. Something made him sure that the Doctor wouldn't just abandon him on this strange planet. That 'something' probably being wishful thinking, he thought.

Standing Tree led him down to a section of the river where the men had their morning wash and showed him where to pick the fruit whose oily interior served in lieu of soap. It had a citrus scent and grew on the river banks. How convenient, thought William as he stripped off his clothes. He endured a few moments of embarrassed English pinkness before stepping into the freezing water amongst the muscular brown bodies of the tribe.

He was just beginning to relax when he looked up to find a young man staring at him in an unfriendly manner. The man was shorter than average for the tribe and his arms were long and roped with muscle. The man pursed his lips and spat into the water – William took a step back. Standing Tree came to his rescue.

'See here,' he said. 'This is Little Rock, tribal champion. Little Rock, this is Pink Feller – who's doing the Doctor Man's fishing for him.'

Little Rock spat again, gave William the briefest of nods, turned and stalked away.

'You're a brave man,' said Standing Tree. 'I wouldn't take on Little Rock for all the fish in creation.'

II

'Just a little fishing match,' said the Doctor. 'Nothing to worry about.'

'You could have told me,' said William. He'd dressed in his slacks and shirt only – the morning was already growing hot and he was beginning to worry about not having a hat.

'I said we were going fishing,' said the Doctor.

'You didn't say it was a contest.'

'Is there something wrong with competing?'

'I'm just not entirely comfortable with competition,' said William.

'Well,' said the Doctor. 'You really should have thought of that before you agreed to take part.'

'I don't remember agreeing to anything...'

'Look,' said the Doctor. 'The tribe's starting to pack up and move – you'd better get going.'

William saw that the Doctor was right. Down by the river, the people of the tribe were picking up their things and drifting off upstream. Since they didn't seem to carry much more than blankets and small children, the process wasn't taking long.

'Where are they going?' asked William.

'To the fishing grounds,' said the Doctor. 'You usually start the day with a coffee, don't you?'

'Tea, actually,' said William.

'You'd better try to wake up without it,' said the Doctor. 'Around here breakfast is generally taken on the hoof.'

You could have tracked William that day by the trail of discarded gear he left behind him. The tribe ambled up-river deceptively quickly and

William found himself falling behind. The folding stool went after the first hundred metres; the bait box lasted until the tribe turned away from the main river and started up a tributary stream.

The Doctor dropped back to give him some encouragement.

'It really isn't that far,' said the Doctor.

'It feels like far,' said William.

'That,' said the Doctor, 'is one of the great ironies of travel. A hundred million light years in less than no time and the last fifty miles takes you a week.'

William came to a sudden halt. 'Fifty miles?'

'No,' said the Doctor. 'More like twenty or thereabouts. Make sure you pace yourself, though. We need you match-fit when we get there.'

The path steepened and the valley narrowed into a tree-lined gorge. At one point, William gained on the main body of the tribe and for a moment convinced himself that they'd arrived. However, it turned out the tribe had merely paused to gather seed pods – breakfast on the hoof presumably. The Doctor saved him a couple, the shape and colour of gherkins but as succulent as figs on the inside. Just two of them perked William up.

'They're a natural source of caffeine,' said the Doctor.

'Handy,' said William. 'I bet they're called Redbullfruit.'

'Morningfruit, actually,' said the Doctor. 'Or in some dialects morningafterberry.' The Doctor gave William an encouraging smile, spun on his heel and departed up the path.

'What I want,' said William, 'is a Royalmailtree or a DHLbeast.'

He got the rod and the umbrella comfortable on his shoulders and followed the Doctor.

By the time he'd clambered out of the gorge, William had abandoned everything except for the umbrella and a length of fishing line. Ahead was a wide expanse of broken rock and sand smashed flat by the noon sun. The tribe was hidden away in the shadowed niches worn into the sides of the rock – having their siesta. William would have walked right past if the Doctor hadn't called out.

William opened the umbrella and demonstrated its use as a parasol. The Doctor applauded. 'I hope you kept some line as well,' he said as William joined him in the shade.

'Of course,' said William. He sat down heavily and realised with a shock that his legs were trembling with fatigue. The Doctor offered him a strange yellow fruit.

'What's this?' asked William. 'A latebreakfastfruit?'

'Actually,' said the Doctor, 'I think it's a banana.'

The contest didn't start until the late afternoon and William slept through most of the wait. A stone floor is remarkably comfortable after a morning hike, but he still woke up with pins and needles all down his left side.

The contest took place in a natural arena, a sand-filled bowl that had been, according to the Doctor, scooped out of the landscape by a total conversion bomb. The tribe was perched on a stone outcrop with a good view over the sand. Chief Halfmoon gave William a cheery nod as he limped down to the edge of the bowl.

Little Rock was waiting for them – calmly winding a length of twine around his thumb and elbow.

'Where's the water?' Even as he asked, William guessed the answer.

'First round isn't in water,' said the Doctor. 'It's in sand.'

'What the hell am I fishing for?'

'Sand eels,' said the Doctor.

'And how do I do that?'

'Same way as you would with ordinary fish,' said the Doctor. 'Line and bait.'

'I've got the line,' said William. 'What am I supposed to use as bait?'

'That might be a problem,' said the Doctor.

William looked over at Little Rock. 'What's he using?'

Little Rock gave him a wicked grin and held up his left hand. Then with a quick movement of his knife, he cut his own little finger off. Ignoring the blood, he proceeded to tie the grizzly thing to the end of his line.

'How can he do that?'

'Don't worry,' said the Doctor. 'His finger will grow back in a couple of weeks.'

'Mine won't,' said William.

'Are you sure?' asked the Doctor. 'Have you ever tried it?'

Little Rock smiled and offered William his knife. Although it was of an even and regular shape, William saw that it was made of a single blade of obsidian.

'Why don't we use your finger,' said William to the Doctor.

The Doctor took the knife, examined it and handed it back to Little Rock. Then he rummaged in his pockets and came up with half a meatfruit. 'Left over from supper,' he said.

William took the meatfruit and tied it to the end of his line.

'Right,' said William. 'Any last-minute hints?'

'Keep moving,' said the Doctor. 'Never stand in one place for more than a few moments.'

Chief Halfmoon called down from his perch. 'Hey, Pink Feller, you ready yet?'

'Ready when you are,' said the Doctor before William could speak.

'Well, get on with it then,' said the Chief.

William let Little Rock go first so he could watch what he did. The wiry tribesman stepped off the rocks that made up the rim of the bowl and onto the sand. He started walking around the rim with his loop of fishing line held ready for an instant cast. William wondered what he was waiting for.

'Come on,' hissed the Doctor. 'You're not going to catch anything from here.'

William stepped out onto the sand. It was powdery and shifted uncomfortably under his shoes. He followed Little Rock, keeping pace as the tribesman stalked around the circumference – watching to see what happened next.

Suddenly the tribesman flicked out his line and, without slowing his pace, let it trail along a patch of empty sand.

And then William saw it – a moving hump just to the left of where Little Rock had cast his bait. The sand slid over the shape exactly the way water washed over a dolphin's back.

Then the movement stopped and Little Rock wound his line back up.

William watched Little Rock cast three more times; each time the moving hump appeared a little closer to where the bait was being dragged. William wondered how he knew where to cast.

The fourth cast landed unexpectedly close to William, less than three metres away. This time, when the hump appeared he felt the movement as a faint vibration through the soles of his shoes.

Little Rock was barefoot and, watching how the tribesman paused with each step, William realised that he was feeling for the vibrations through his feet. He stopped and pulled off his shoes, being careful to tie the laces together so he could carry them around his neck. It was a long way back to the Doctor's police box and he had no intention of walking it in on his tender pink feet.

'Move,' yelled the Doctor and William threw himself backwards. The sand in front of him erupted upwards and William glimpsed an oval mouth filled with spikes as the sand eel missed him by half a metre. The Doctor yelled at him to keep moving.

Of course, thought William. The fish bite back – what was I thinking?

At least with his shoes off he could tell whether the sand eel was getting close. One sand eel, William was certain of it, just one in the whole sand bowl and the winner would be the first to catch it.

He felt a vibration and cast on a mad guess. His bait landed less than a metre from Little Rock's own cast. He waved at Little Rock, who gave him a suspicious look. They both watched as the sand eel swept between the baits and vanished again. A sure-fire way to lure a sand eel would be to stand still and wait for it to attack but he didn't see Little Rock trying that technique and that probably meant it was an insane thing to do.

Worth a try, thought William.

'When fishing,' the Doctor had said, 'it's important to be methodical.'

William stopped dead and counted to ten, one banana at a time, and started moving again. Obviously ten seconds wasn't enough and so William nerved himself to stop and wait for twenty.

Twenty was a bust but thirty worked a treat – right up to the point where the impact of the sand eel coming up from below threw William five metres into the air. There was a great deal of confused flailing about before the ground gave him a good kicking.

He lay for a while and waited for the spinning to stop.

Water was splashed on his face and he managed to squint through the glare to focus on the Doctor's face. The crowd noise was going in and out like waves on a shore.

'Focus on me,' said the Doctor. 'How many lives am I holding up?'

'Seven,' said William.

'Wrong,' said the Doctor. 'Everyone makes that mistake.'

'Did I win?'

'No,' said the Doctor. 'But you came a close second.'

'It was a good plan,' said William.

'It was a good plan for Little Rock,' said the Doctor. 'Once he saw you were being a damn fool, he just used you for bait and caught the eel as it tried to eat you.'

'So, I'm all here?'

'Your body is all present and correct, but your survival instinct has obviously skipped off to Benidorm.'

They put him under a blanket and he slept, waking up only later when it was dark and the sky was once again full of stars. Standing Tree was asleep but Spring Peach, his partner, was awake and nursing their youngest.

William made a quick but overdue trip to a nearby bush and then slipped back to his place between the couple. Spring Peach offered him a drink from a water skin – he drank quite a lot. She asked about the contest and he admitted that he didn't know what he was doing.

'What I want to know,' said William, 'is why wasn't I frightened?'

'You looked pretty frightened to me,' said Spring Peach.

'I should have been much more terrified,' said William. 'I used to get worried walking past rowdy teenagers, but a big thing with teeth? I should have been paralysed with fear.'

'Perhaps things are different here,' said Spring Peach.

'Perhaps because I don't think it's really real,' said William. 'It's like a dream.'

The baby burped and Spring Peach shifted her to the other breast. 'I'd say that there fairly dangerous way to think,' she said. 'What if you're wrong?'

William lay back and watched the sky. A constellation of swiftly moving stars crossed in front of the moon which was high and full.

'What are the stars that move?' asked William.

'Sky homes,' said Spring Peach

'People live in the sky?'

'Of course,' she said.

'People like you and your family?' asked William.

'Don't be silly,' said Spring Peach. 'We live on the ground.'

William tried asking the same question in different ways but either the concept was too alien or the woman was messing him about. Sky people lived in the sky homes and, in an indeterminate way, they were different.

After a while, William gave up, rolled over and was instantly asleep.

III

Up on the plateau there was only a small pool available so the morning ablutions were mixed bathing. The pool itself had been scooped out of a flat slab of granite by a spring and was surrounded by zest-medicated bushes or whatever they were called.

William stripped off without thinking while the Doctor went so far as to remove his shoes and socks.

'I'm not stupid, you know,' said William while he was drying off on the bank.

'I've never thought you were,' said the Doctor. 'Slow occasionally but not stupid.'

'These are not really a primitive people,' said William. 'Are they?'

'Depends on how you define primitive. Primitive in what sense?'

'Look at them,' said William. 'There's no disease, no deformity, not even bad eyesight. You can't tell me they don't have access to advanced medicine.'

'Benefits of a healthy lifestyle,' said the Doctor. 'Lots of exercise, fresh food, good clean air and fishing. Let's not forget the restorative properties of well-cast line and bait.'

'This is a kind of holiday for them – isn't it?'

'You're getting warmer,' said the Doctor. 'But you're not there yet.'

Getting to the next contest involved climbing a mountain, or more accurately, according to the Doctor, a mesa. Whatever the correct term, it was a tall, thin spire of rock with a flat top. William was really glad he hadn't let go of his shoes.

On the top, somebody – Chief Halfmoon denied it was the tribe – had built a ten-storey, open-frame wooden tower. The contest was to take place at the top of the tower.

'Don't tell me,' said William. 'Flying fish.'

The top platform probably had a magnificent view but William couldn't tell: vertigo made the landscape a blur of green and brown. The Doctor pointed and William saw shapes wheeling far overhead. Size was hard to judge but he thought they might be the size of sharks.

'I'm afraid this one is harder than the sand eels,' said the Doctor. 'You have to raise your lure by attaching it to a kite.'

'I haven't got a kite,' said William.

'Don't worry,' said the Doctor. 'Here's one I prepared earlier.'

William took the kite and looked it over. The Doctor had used bamboo for the spars and a smooth lightweight fabric that might have been silk.

'Just do your best,' said the Doctor.

William managed to keep a straight face as he attached the lure, a straggling mass of feathers, to the tail of the kite.

His father had taught him to fly kites on those weekends when he had had custody. They'd build them in the kitchen – long tails, box kites, flat and bowed kite – and then drive out to the hills to test them. If there was one thing William knew himself to be good at it was kite-flying.

And double-entry bookkeeping, but that didn't seem relevant.

Little Rock was good but William was better. He quickly saw that the trick was to make the lure bob and dance in front of the fish you wanted. And William had spotted the fish he wanted – it wasn't the biggest but it moved with an easy arrogance that William took an instant dislike to. He dubbed it the bully fish and swore that by nightfall it would be sleeping with the humans.

Bully Fish took the bait and he heard cheering from the tribe, who were watching from the level below. Bully Fish didn't like the hook and pulled away but William had his grip on the line and was already braced.

Even so, it almost pulled him over the edge.

He jammed his heels against the low wooden parapet and pulled back. Bully Fish darted forward before getting his fins into position to resist the tug. Bully Fish was large but he was a creature of the upper atmosphere; his beautiful silver fins had to grab thin air. William was a creature of the ground, a monkey with clever fingers who gripped earth with his toes – an animal with leverage. Now that he was hooked it was all over for Bully Fish.

And in the end Bully Fish surrendered, hung quiet and docile on a short line, less than ten metres from the top of the tower. The tribe went silent and Little Rock grunted and let go of his own kite.

The Doctor was staring at William in amazement.

'What now?' asked William.

'Let it go,' said Little Rock.

'Really?'

'Yes,' said the Doctor. 'Little Rock has conceded, let it go before it hurts itself.'

Little Rock drew his knife and cut the line. The Bully Fish tumbled away for a moment, then stabilised and caught an updraught that took it soaring away.

'You didn't really want to kill it,' said the Doctor. 'Did you?'

'No,' said William. 'Abject humiliation was better.'

There was a wooded hollow at the base of the mesa where the tribe made its camp. Half the tribespeople had stayed at the bottom gathering for the night's feast and this time William was awake enough to enjoy it. Chief Halfmoon lavished praise on him but William was uncomfortably conscious of the stare Little Rock was giving him.

Then the Chief called on William to lead the singing.

He sang the first thing that came into his head – Steeleye Span's *All Around My Hat.* It went down with the tribe like scrumpy at a folk club and by the second chorus they'd picked up the tune and the lyrics; by the third, the young women were improvising a descant counterpoint. He'd been right the first night: the whole tribe had absolute pitch and perfect breath control. Without thinking, William stopped singing and gestured at the older men whose voices swelled to take up the melody line in bass. Memories of a school choirmaster returned to him – palm up to lift a section, palm down for quiet and the strange stabbing gesture with thumb and forefinger to take up the rhythm. The lyrics lost their meaning, the willow, the hat and the true-love evaporating as the music swept around him. It was glorious. He felt as if he were buoyed up like a spark from a campfire and sent spinning away under the blue moon and the speeding stars.

And then it was over, the last sustained note held by Rabbit and stopped on his hand signal. William sat down feeling flushed and tired. He put his hand over his eyes to hide his tears. At some point, the Doctor must have come around the circle to join him because he leant over and whispered in William's ear.

'Well done,' he said. 'The most important thing is to know when something has run its course.'

IV

The next morning, William found a bush that provided mint-scented soap. He whistled Mozart while he bathed because he figured the tunes would get stuck in the tribe's head. He gave his clothes a scrub with the soap before hanging them on some bushes to dry. While he waited, he chatted to the Doctor.

'Earth, air,' said William. 'What's next – fire?'

'Precisely,' said the Doctor.

'Really?' asked William. 'I was being facetious.'

'A contest in every element,' said the Doctor.

'Except water,' said William.

'Water would be jejune,' said the Doctor. 'Anyone can fish in water.'

'Chance would be a fine thing,' said William.

Breakfast was snatched, literally, on their way to the fire caves. Chief Halfmoon led the way with more ceremony than William had seen in the tribe before. From the hollow, a short length of trail led to the cave entrance, a diagonal fissure in the hillside that led into a smooth-sided tunnel.

'Lava tube,' said the Doctor.

The tube sloped down for a hundred metres before opening into a large cavern with smooth, almost glasslike, walls.

'Why are there no stallag-thingies?' asked William.

'Stalactites?'

'Yes.'

'This cavern was formed by a bubble of magma, quite recently I'd say,' said the Doctor.

'How recently?' asked William. 'And is it likely to happen again, say in the next few hours?'

'Recent in geological time,' said the Doctor. 'And an up-welling in the next few hours is unlikely.'

'How unlikely?'

'Less talk,' said the Doctor. 'More fishing – we're there.'

Outside of maths, William hadn't bothered to retain much of his A-level science knowledge. He remembered that the correct technical term for fire would be rapid oxidisation but he was sure that fire was never described as a liquid.

And it was a clear liquid, a turquoise lake of fire that lit the cavern it filled.

Out in the middle were flickering colours – deep reds, oranges and yellows. The colours gathered in shoals, darting left and right; gathering, splitting and reforming.

'Flame fish,' said William.

The Doctor led William to his place, on the shore a good three metres from Little Rock. The whole tribe spread out behind them to watch, toddlers hoisted up on the shoulders of the adults.

'What do I use to catch them?' asked William.

'Your mind,' said the Doctor. 'And the power of your imagination.'

He tried to ask the Doctor what the hell that was supposed to mean but it was too late; the Doctor had withdrawn into the crowd. He turned to watch his opponent – presumably Little Rock knew what he was doing.

What he appeared to be doing was casting with nothing. William watched as the man first looped, twirled and cast – nothing – into the lake. At first he thought it must be some super-thin filament or possibly an invisible rope but then he heard the Doctor call out behind him – 'Get your mind into the game.'

Little Rock tensed and then pulled on his imaginary line – out in the lake, William saw a flame fish jump out of the fire. It looked like an insane tropical fish with extravagant trailing fins and markings of yellow and burnt umber and its mouth twitched as if caught on a hook.

Little Rock pulled on his line and the flame fish was dragged a little closer.

He tried miming the same throwing action as Little Rock but he couldn't make it convincing – especially to himself. It was awkward throwing a real line, let alone an imaginary one. Presumably that's why fishing rods had been invented.

He imagined a fishing rod in his hand, imagined flicking it back and casting forward so that the weight zinged over his head and the line whirled through the reel. He was certain that he heard a plop when the weight hit the surface of the lake.

However, he was so surprised when a flame fish pulled on his line that his imaginary rod was yanked out of his hands and was sent spinning, he imagined, into the lake.

Little Rock was also having trouble. Without a rod, he was finding it difficult to drag his fish ashore. William watched as his opponent had to mime letting out line in order to avoid being dragged into the lake – William still had a chance.

He imagined a second rod in his hand, one of the expensive ones that had hung behind the counter in the shop – an aspirational fishing rod. He imagined the perfect cast and the lure hissing out to drop, just like a hole in one, practically in the mouth of a flame fish.

This time, when the pull came he kept a grip and began the difficult process of reeling the flame fish in. The reel gave him an overwhelming advantage and soon his fish had been dragged closer in than Little Rock's. William was within a metre of winning the contest when the Doctor told him to watch out.

'Your line's breaking,' he said.

And, of course, once William thought that, his line was broken and his flame fish got away.

Little Rock managed to finally drag his fish onto the shore where it gasped and smouldered for a moment before flopping its way back into the lake. The tribe cheered and lifted Little Rock onto their shoulders.

William glared at the Doctor.

'Had to be done, William,' said the Doctor.

'Why?' asked William.

'I'll tell you tomorrow,' said the Doctor. 'When we're alone.'

'Why not now?'

'Because now,' said the Doctor, 'we feast.'

V

His last meal with the tribe was a proper feast, with Little Rock taking the place of triumph on the Chief's left side and William the place of shame on his right. There was meatfruit and walkingpork and some sweet stuff that ran like honey and tasted of Belgian chocolate. They all strained the tea through their teeth and William got to lead the singing one last time – a Christmas carol because he knew all the words and could surprise them with the harmonies in the third verse. Then he slipped under the blanket with Spring Peach, Standing Tree, the toddlers and the baby girl and slept better than he ever had before.

At the washing place the next morning Little Rock shook his hand.

Then the Doctor said it was time to go. William put his clothes back on and followed the Doctor up the ridge.

'Let's wait a bit,' said William when they reached the TARDIS. He could see the tribe below packing up what little possessions they had and preparing to move.

He and the Doctor sat on the slope beside the TARDIS and watched as the tribe moved off, in fits and starts, across the scrublands towards what the Chief had described as the 'best feeding this side of the mountains'.

'It's not a holiday resort,' said William. 'They were all born here but they're not really hunter-gatherers – it's more like a re-enactment.'

'It's more than a re-enactment,' said the Doctor. 'They hunt, they gather, they go fishing.'

'They don't get ill or eaten by wild animals. They grow back their limbs, for God's sake. How is that possible?'

'That part is easy,' said the Doctor. 'That's just genetic engineering and nanotechnology. The real problem is creating a self-sustaining ecosystem that doesn't change over time. Necessity is the mother of invention – if they came under environmental pressure, those big brains would start working and the next thing you know it would be agriculture, cities, pollution and kitchen-sink dramas.'

'And this place is the Earth,' said William. 'Earth in the far future. All the continents have moved about and the moon has been... whatever it is you call that.'

'Terraformed.'

'And the tribe are who?'

'The rich,' said the Doctor. 'Or rather the descendents of the super rich.'

'So the rich inherit the world – why?

'Because population densities need to be low, you had to be very rich to get a place,' said the Doctor. 'Everyone is forced to live in unimaginable luxury, on the moon or in orbital habitats.'

'It still doesn't seem fair,' said William. 'Rather like the way you sabotaged the final contest.'

'I couldn't let Little Rock lose,' said the Doctor. 'His whole identity is wrapped up in his position as champion fisherman. That really wouldn't be fair.'

'So why start the contest in the first place?'

'I didn't,' said the Doctor. 'I just came here for the fishing, ordinary fishing. I thought the tribe were somewhere else but Little Rock caught me and challenged me. Fortunately you're allowed to substitute a third party as your champion.'

'And that was me,' said William. 'But I said I'd never fished before.'

'Precisely,' said the Doctor.

'So you travelled all the way through time and space to Slough, of all places, to find someone who couldn't fish so that Little Rock's feelings wouldn't be hurt?'

'Yes,' said the Doctor.

'You couldn't just lose on purpose,' said William. 'You know, throw the match.'

'Me?' said the Doctor. '*Lose*? Don't be absurd.'

Once they were in the TARDIS, the Doctor asked William where he thought they should go next.

'Home,' said William.

'We can go anywhere,' said the Doctor carefully.

'And I want to go home,' said William. 'On the same day I left and in time for tea.'

The Doctor shrugged and touched the controls. 'So long as it's your decision.'

There was the noise again, and movement, and the sensation that your life had slipped out of your own control.

'*Voilà*,' said the Doctor. 'Your home. Well, thanks for everything. Don't let me keep you.' William got the feeling he didn't like goodbyes.

He opened the door and looked around. It was true – the TARDIS had landed in the garden, between the crazy path and the dahlias. His Wellington boots were propped up against the kitchen door and inside his mother would be baking a cake.

'Just as I promised,' said the Doctor. 'Back in time for tea.'

'Same day and everything?'

'Same day,' said the Doctor. 'It will be as if you never left.'

William smiled, pulled his head back inside and closed the door.

'So,' he said. 'Even if we were to go somewhere else we could still come back in time for this particular tea.'

For a moment he thought the Doctor wasn't going to let him change his mind, such was the power in that gaze. And then he sighed. 'As I believe I explained, time and relative dimension in space. Very well, then.'

'Okay,' said William. 'Where next?'

The Doctor gave him a sharp look and then grinned. 'Fishing,' he said. 'We must put your new-found skills to the test.'

'With water this time?'

'One can only hope,' said the Doctor and began to work the controls.

The Avant Guardian

Eddie Robson

An Adventure of the Second Doctor, with Jamie McCrimmon and Zoe Heriot

Burgess climbed into his car, placed his briefcase on the passenger seat and tossed his coat onto the back seat without looking. As he did so, his hand brushed against something unfamiliar and metal, and he did a double take.

Lying on the back seat of his car was a tall young man holding a handgun, wearing a thick coat and a balaclava. Burgess could see very little else of him in the unlit car park. It clearly wasn't easy for him to be in that position and he seemed relieved to be able to straighten up. As he did so, the gun remained trained on Burgess, as did the gunman's eyes.

'Howard Burgess?' he asked.

Burgess nodded. 'There's, er, no need to hurt me. I'll give you anything you want.'

The tall man said nothing.

'Er, what do you want?' asked Burgess. 'Money, is it? Or something else?'

'You're head of Programme Planning, right?' said the tall man. He spoke quickly, with little trace of an accent.

Burgess nodded again.

'Good. A little bird tells me you've just scheduled *Waterfront Beat* for Wednesdays at 8.30.'

'What?' Burgess was starting to wonder if this was a practical joke, but didn't dare say so in case it wasn't.

'*Waterfront Beat*,' the tall man repeated aggressively. 'Wednesdays. Eight-thirty.'

'That's the new police drama serial?'

'Yes,' the tall man said impatiently.

'Er, yes,' said Burgess. He swallowed hard. 'I have, yes.'

'Right. Well, I was not very happy to hear about that. Not happy at all.'

'Oh?'

'Oh, *no*. You see, I'd really rather that it went out at 7.30 on Fridays.' He brandished the gun a little towards Burgess. 'I'm very keen that that should be the case.'

'But, er, there are several factors... er, we thought about when placing it in the slot we've chosen, mainly that the slightly more adult content suggested a later slot and... er, we've heard that the other lot are going to run the new series of *The Identikit Man* on Fridays.'

'Yes, we know. That's where I want it – exactly opposite *The Identikit Man*.'

'Why?'

'Don't ask questions. Bring the first episode forward five days.'

'We can't.'

'Can't or won't?'

'Can't. We've already sold the advertising space. The listings have gone to press – it'll be a ratings disaster.'

'Hmm,' said the tall man. 'I don't want that. No... put it back two days.'

'How can I explain a decision like that?'

'Any way you like, as long as it doesn't mention me or what's happened here tonight. Understood?'

Burgess nodded.

'If it doesn't happen, Burgess, I know where you live.' The tall man released the door catch and Burgess heard his footfalls as he ran from the car park.

Burgess laid his hands on the steering wheel. As he tried to bring his nerves under control, he wondered just when the world of television had become quite so competitive and why he hadn't noticed.

A grinding, abrasive whine rose from Flora's dinner plate; a noise which she created by using her fork to describe a figure of eight around the plate, sweeping aside the remains of her bolognaise as she went.

Dominic, sitting to her left, broke off his conversation with Bill and politely asked Flora if she would please stop making the noise. He was polite because she was his friend and, technically, his boss.

Flora continued as before.

'Flora?' Dominic said, aware that other diners were turning around to look at them.

'Yes... I heard,' said Flora. 'It's interesting. Why is that an irritating noise, do you think?'

'I don't know, Flo,' said Bill. 'But if you want us to talk about it, you'll have to stop making it 'cause I can't think and hear that at the same time.'

Flora laid her fork on the edge of the plate. 'You see what I mean, though?' she asked. 'It provokes a reaction, a strong one... and basically the same in everybody.'

'You're not thinking of using it on *Identikit*?' asked Dominic. 'You'll never get it past Bryan. Or any producer, for that matter. I'll bet you five pounds you can't.'

'Hmm,' said Flora. 'What if you could impose a musical pitch on it –'

'What, with the frequency changer?'

'I don't trust that gizmo,' said Bill. 'It rattles like hell and the longer it's left on, the louder it gets. Mark my words, one of these days it's going to blow up and kill somebody. And it's not going to be me.'

'But if you could make a scale out of it,' said Flora, ignoring Bill entirely, 'and put together a melody out of it... that perhaps worked against the "natural" tone?'

Dominic chuckled. 'I dare you to wipe all the flute sounds off the mellotron and put your fork-squeal scale on it instead.'

Flora smiled and dipped her head. 'No. Don't be childish, Dominic.'

'That's better,' said Bill.

'What do you mean?'

'I think,' said Dominic, 'Bill's referring to the fact that you haven't smiled once during dinner. Am I correct, Bill?'

Bill nodded. It had become a weekly tradition among the staff of the Sound Unit to end the week with a meal at Alessandro's and, although Flora had a tendency to be vague in social situations, tonight she seemed more than that: distant and tense.

'Oh?' said Flora. 'Sorry. It's just... I had a run-in with Samantha earlier.'

'From Programme Planning?' said Dominic. 'What about?'

'They repeated *The Order of Seasons* last night, and... well, I asked her to tell me if any of my things would be on.'

'You mean the *Present-Day Play* from last year?' said Bill. 'I didn't think you did anything for that one?'

'No, I did. I scored the two film sequences,' said Flora. 'It won't be on again. They didn't list it. Change to the advertised programme.'

'Can't you get the archive to sort you out a screening copy?'

Flora paused. 'That's what Samantha told me to do. But... it's not the same.'

'I know what you mean,' said Dominic. 'I always like to see them go out live. It gives you rather a kick to know that everybody out there's hearing your stuff, doesn't it?'

Flora cleared her throat. 'Yes, that's it.'

'Don't you have something on tonight?'

'Yes. The start of the new series of *Identikit Man*.'

'I thought that started already?' said Bill.

'No, they put it back a month.'

'Gawd, they do faff about, don't they? Why launch a new series three weeks before Christmas?'

Flora sighed. 'I don't know. I just hope it rates well.'

'I bet you do. When it comes to residuals, you can't beat a theme. You didn't write that as a standard contract thing, right?'

'No, I score the episodes as staff but the theme's published separately.'

'Quids in,' said Bill.

Flora checked her watch. 'I should go, it's on at 7.30.' She stood to leave.

'Flo?' said Dominic. 'Could I get my key back off you?'

'Key?'

'Yes. You were swinging it around that Theremin earlier?'

'Oh... was that yours?' Flora reached into her pocket, found the key and returned it to him. 'I thought it was mine.'

* * *

It had been a while since the Doctor had howled to be let out, so he did it again. He was aware that there was only a point to this if some conscious force was responsible for his presence here, which was not necessarily the case, but he was unsure what else he could do. He tried to punch against the sides of his prison, only to discover that it didn't have any.

For a few moments, the Doctor sank into quiet contemplation of his situation. There would be a solution; he would find it and he would release himself.

He quickly became bored of this and threw a tantrum instead, shouting and kicking and flailing his arms around. He succeeded only in punching himself in the face – which should have been physically impossible in this position, so at least this told him something of the nature of the place in which he was trapped. But it offered no clues how to escape.

At 7.31 pm, the title sequence of *The Identikit Man* played across TV screens all over the country, including one belonging to Flora Millrace. The titles concisely retold the story of the Identikit Man, Douglas Hunter, across a series of clips from the first episode: how he had come home one day following a business trip to discover that his wife was married to someone else and did not remember him. His entire identity had vanished, there was no record of him anywhere, and he no longer needed to eat or sleep. He now moved through the world like a ghost, trying to fathom what had happened to him and helping people along the way. This montage was accompanied by a sinister, rather chilly drone-based composition of Flora's, performed largely on an Ondes Martenot but with an otherworldly buzz behind it (Flora had achieved this by taking white noise and playing it backwards, and then overlaying it on the same white noise playing forwards).

For forty seconds, this familiar piece tumbled from the tiny speakers of 7,603,974 television sets. The sound waves rebounded inside living rooms and spilled out into the streets: no longer audible to human ears, they nevertheless clashed against each other.

From her own home in Acton, Flora stared at the display of a computer that she never showed to anybody because they would never recognise it for what it was. It monitored the patterns of clashing sound waves over London and much of the surrounding area. As her music flowed through the matter of the city, it prised open very tiny temporal rifts, punching minuscule holes between the material world and the space-time vortex. These did no real damage whatsoever, but merely tested the integrity of the bond between the chronological universe and its 'back door'. The tune which millions of viewers associated with a handsome stranger's attempts to resolve his existential crisis – and to solve odd mysteries along the way – had, in fact, been painstakingly designed by Flora many years previously in another time and place, its rhythms and collisions calculated with great precision to produce precisely this effect. This was the reason for its curious changes of pace – which could thankfully be artistically justified as a reflection of the uncertainty which underpinned the tone of the series (or did when it was written by people who actually understood it, rather than the occasional hacks who just treated it like a straightforward detective drama).

When the forty seconds were over, Flora's computer showed her its results. Her systems had followed the music as it went about its work. Most of the map was coloured blue, which indicated areas that were normal and stable. However, the map was flecked with a few dozen spots of red, each of which was an indication of an area where time appeared to be out of phase with everything around it, stuck in an intermediate state between the universe and the vortex. On the television set in the corner of her room, an action sequence began as Hunter was attacked by a mysterious assailant – for which Flora had also composed the music. This piece was less effective than the title theme, partly because it was brand new and Flora had not been able to test and refine it – it irked her deeply when she was criticised for re-using motifs from her previous work, as she couldn't explain to anybody why this was not just laziness on her part – and partly because she had been required to tailor it to the on-screen events, which limited her use of rhythm. However, for the purposes of fine-tuning her search, it would serve perfectly well.

Every time *The Identikit Man* was broadcast, Flora did this. Then she would pinpoint two or three 'trouble' spots, load her equipment into the back of her Volkswagen Beetle, and try to track them down. When she found them, she would use her equipment to bring these aberrations back into phase: for a few hours after her music had been broadcast, they would be malleable and could be 're-tuned' to the material world around them. This activity would often keep her out past midnight, depending on how far afield she had to travel, so she was rather glad that this series of *The Identikit Man* was going out on Fridays, rather than the previous Tuesday slot. With the show only being broadcast 13 weeks at a time, however, opportunities during the rest of the year were sporadic – and, try as she might, she couldn't come up with anything as effective as what had become the *Identikit Man* theme. There would have been a build-up in activity in the meantime – hence her irritation at not being able to take advantage of last night's broadcast of *The Order of Seasons*, which would probably have allowed her to attend to a couple of spots ahead of this evening.

Fifty minutes later, Douglas Hunter had located the amnesiac boy and returned him to his mother, an attractive widow named Diana – she was set to be a new regular character this series, since the previous love interest had been killed in the last episode of series two (accompanied by some funereal *musique concrète* which had apparently attracted a few complaints, mainly from people with dogs). Flora had been asked to write a little motif for Diana, and had wanted it to be an effective piece since it would be repeated in most of the episodes, but it didn't seem to work as well as she'd hoped. She thought she might try a subtle rewrite; probably no one would notice.

The end credits rolled, along with the theme music. This allowed Flora to finalise which spots she was heading for. She marked them in pencil on her A–Z, packed her bag and switched off her television set.

Flora knocked on the door of 27 Brentwood Road, Chalk Farm, at 9.37pm. The door was answered by a stocky man who had no idea why she was there, and said so when she introduced herself and asked if she might see inside.

'Have you...' Flora leaned back and peered through their bay window. 'Do you ever get headaches when you stand up in your front room? And when you walk out of the room, they go away again?'

The stocky man blinked.

'Would you like me to try and... er, eliminate that for you?' said Flora. 'It must be terribly annoying.'

The stocky man turned and looked inside his house, then turned back to Flora and invited her in. He was clearly suspicious, but she was willowy, soft-voiced and gentle of movement, so he must have been confident of warding off any potential threat she might pose.

The stocky man's stocky wife and one of his two stocky children sat on the living room sofa, whilst the other child lay on his front on the floor: the armchair was evidently earmarked for father. Flora greeted them and placed her bag – a doctor's bag – on the floor. The family was watching *The Correctors* on the other side, or rather they had been: now, they were discussing the sudden presence in their home of a well-spoken, dark-haired youngish woman, wearing a pea-green coat over a cashmere sweater and grey wool skirt. Mother was alarmed at having her viewing interrupted, and suspected her husband of some form of stupidity and/or deceit.

Flora politely asked the youngest child to move from the centre of the floor. She produced three conical devices from her bag and positioned them around the floor, then plugged them into a very stripped-down version of her home computer – quite apart from being lighter, it had a more rudimentary appearance that tended not to scare people. She looked at the read-out and was pleased.

'This doesn't look overly complicated,' she said. She didn't like lying; she felt that it was obvious when she did, that her voice became hesitant and quivery. (Her friends never noticed the difference.) However, she had to tell them something. 'It's electromagnetic disturbance causing your headaches,' she said. 'I detected it from outside... a faulty valve in your television, causing it to leak out.' She made a mental note to pretend to repair the television later.

Flora operated the device and the three cones sprang to life. Three beams of light projected into the centre of the room and illuminated a sphere in the air, more than a metre in diameter.

'Wow,' said the child on the sofa.

The parents said nothing.

For a few minutes, Flora sat fine-tuning her equipment: she adjusted, she listened, she adjusted again. Eventually, the sphere disappeared with a satisfying *zing*, signifying that it had come back into phase with everything around it, and the cones automatically deactivated themselves. This was what always happened.

At the same moment, a small man with short dark hair, a heavily jowled face and a scruffy, baggy suit appeared in the air where the sphere had been and fell to the floor with a heavy impact. He howled in surprise, then again in pain. This was more unusual.

Flora shuffled along the floor on her knees, placed a hand on the man's shoulder and gently turned him towards her.

Flora smiled. For some reason, she had thought it might be him. 'Doctor?' she asked.

The Doctor opened his eyes. 'Oh.' He looked around him at the pallid decor of the suburban living room in which he found himself, the resolutely average family and the black-and-white television. Then he looked at his rescuer, and recognition flickered through his eyes. 'Oh, I say.' He clasped his hands together and smiled broadly. 'Well done. Very well done.'

Ten minutes later Flora and her friend were gone, and the family never spoke of them again.

'Flora?' said the Doctor, as they drove towards Regent's Park. He was rummaging, uninvited, through the glove compartment. It had started to rain quite heavily, and they had to speak up over the noise.

'What's the matter?' Flora asked. 'Don't you like it?'

'No, no, it's nice. It'll just take some getting used to, that's all.'

'I could go by my old name, but I didn't want to be conspicuous. Then again, the way things have been going in the past couple of years, I'm starting to think I could get away with it. If anybody asked where it came from, I could tell them it was given to me by aliens – nobody would bat an eyelid.'

'It's lovely to see you,' said the Doctor, unfolding a map of the Pyrenees he'd found in the glove compartment, 'but I must say, I hadn't expected to find you in 1968.'

'I hadn't expected to find you here either.'

'Me?' said the Doctor from behind the map. 'I'm here all the time. Ask anybody.'

'Literally all the time?'

'Well, very frequently.'

'It's literally true for me. I've been here continuously and chronologically for four years now.'

The Doctor folded the top of the map over and stared at her in surprise. 'Really?'

Flora nodded.

'Oh, my word,' said the Doctor. 'I don't know how you can bear it. I like it on Earth, but it'd drive me up the wall to stay here for so long. Or anywhere. So what brings you here? Are you still making music?'

'Yes. Initially, that was why I came... there were some things I wanted to see here and now. But I've stayed longer than planned. There's important work to do.'

'Oh?' The Doctor let the map fall against the dashboard.

'Yes. This area has a large amount of... temporal disturbance. Dangerously large. Like that bubble you were in – lots of little bits, out of phase with everything else. Did you say you were here a lot?'

The Doctor bit his thumbnail and looked out of the car window. 'Quite a lot, yes.'

'In this specific area? London and around?'

'Generally,' the Doctor muttered.

'You haven't done anything that might account for the disturbance, have you?'

'No,' said the Doctor. 'No, no... well, possibly. But all for a greater good, you understand.'

Flora giggled. 'Oh, I'm sure. You're still crusading around the place, then?'

'Certainly am,' said the Doctor proudly.

'And still leaving others to clear up after you.'

'Well,' the Doctor said, trying vainly to fold the map the way that it was folded originally, 'I'm not very good at that part of it, you see. If I leave it to other people, they do a better job.'

'Hmm. Anyway, when I first arrived I spotted the disturbance straight away. I traced it back and it all seemed to start about... about five years ago. I think.'

'Yes,' murmured the Doctor, 'that would make sense.'

'At first I thought it'd be a simple case of finding each one and clearing it, but it hasn't been that easy. It fluctuates. They come and go, and when you've eliminated one, you find another you didn't see. I think I'm winning, though... on balance.'

'Must be a slow process, though,' said the Doctor. 'Those kinds of disturbance are notoriously tricky to find.'

Flora suppressed a self-satisfied smile as she explained her technique: the music she had composed, and how she had discovered that television could do much of the work for her. Millions of tiny speakers sending out her tunes in unison, probing the fabric of the world around them, every week.

'But that's brilliant!' said the Doctor.

Flora smiled.

'Yes,' said the Doctor. 'I know you know it's brilliant.'

Half an hour or so later, the rain had stopped and Flora and the Doctor strode out across Regent's Park. Flora carried her bag. The Doctor had happened upon an abandoned football and kicked it ahead of him as he walked, flicking up water from the grass. Each contact with his foot echoed back at them from the trees. Flora was very aware of feeling more conspicuous than usual, but the Doctor was good at making you feel safe.

'How did you end up inside that bubble, anyway?' she asked. She had assumed that he would volunteer this information, but he hadn't so far.

'Ahem,' said the Doctor. 'I was, er, working on some modifications to the TARDIS, and I disabled something I shouldn't have, I think.'

'Oh, I see. You were meddling.'

'Essential meddling,' he said, clearly embarrassed. 'The TARDIS tried to make an emergency landing and safely eject us –'

'Us?'

'My friends, Jamie and Zoe.'

'Oh, I've met Jamie. Don't know Zoe.'

'Hopefully you'll get to meet her. I assume that the same thing's happened to them as happened to me, trapped in those little bubbles. The TARDIS too. How easy d'you think – whoops!' He had just mis-kicked his football and it was bobbling away from him. He dashed over, collected it again and returned to Flora's side. 'How easy do you think it'd be to find them?'

'Hmm... During a broadcast we might be able to look at fluctuations which might... er, indicate that there'd be something inside. If we knew what we were looking for.'

'Oh, good.'

'But we'd have to wait for the next broadcast.'

'Which would be when?'

'I'll check the listings, but I don't have anything until this time next week, I think.'

'Right. I think they'll be all right until then. Time seems to move much more slowly inside the bubbles. Hard to tell but I think I was in that one for... Where have you gone?'

The Doctor turned around. Flora had stopped walking and put her bag down on the grass.

'Oh,' said the Doctor. 'Are we here already?'

'Yes,' said Flora, without looking up. She was busy placing her cones.

The Doctor nudged his football back along the ground in the other direction. 'So,' he said, 'you just set those up, turn it on, and it all snaps back into phase?' He flipped the ball up and started to play keepy-up.

'It's a little more complicated than –'

The Doctor lost control of the ball and it bounced away from him, knocking over two of the cones as it went. 'Sorry,' he said.

Flora repositioned the cones, picked up the ball and refused to give it back to him, in spite of his protests. Eventually he settled for watching what she was doing: it was, after all, rather interesting.

'Do you think the TARDIS or Jamie or Zoe might be in this one?' he asked.

'Possibly,' she said. 'It's quite a large one.'

Flora switched on her equipment and a sphere appeared in the air between them. The Doctor crossed all his fingers, and put his thumbs together and crossed those too. Flora made her adjustments. The Doctor fidgeted. A couple of minutes later, the sphere *zinged* out of existence.

There was nothing inside.

'Oh,' said the Doctor.

'Well,' said Flora, 'it was rather a long shot, you realise.'

'Yes, I know. But I've always been lucky.'

With two more bubbles brought back into phase, and nothing else found, the Doctor and Flora returned to her flat a little before two o'clock. Flora realised that she had left her copies of the week's listings at work, and the next morning left the Doctor to occupy himself with her instruments whilst she returned to the Sound Unit to collect them.

She heard Bill's voice as she entered their bunker-like building. It wasn't altogether unusual to find him or Dominic here at the weekend. It was a good chance to work without being disturbed. For this reason, Flora was surprised to hear another voice, one she recognised but not Dominic's. It was Arthur, a young editor who was working on *The Identikit Man* this year. He was tall, curly haired and habitually wore quite horrible shirts: a little awkward, but very talented from what she'd seen. He was leaning against a console: when he saw her come in, he broke off his conversation with Bill and stood up.

'Hello,' he said quickly. 'Bill said they weren't expecting you in today.'

'We weren't,' said Bill. 'Flo's usually living it up at the weekend, eh?'

'I left something here,' said Flora. 'What brings you in on a Saturday?'

'I was hoping to get some work done ahead of time,' said Arthur. 'I dropped over to pick up any finished tracks you've got for the next few eps.'

'Oh,' said Flora. 'I'm afraid I'm not the best at labelling things... you've no hope of working out which is the final version of anything.'

'Yeah, that's what I told him,' said Bill. 'Lucky you called in.'

'What do you need?' asked Flora.

'Whatever you've got,' said Arthur.

The listings revealed that the Doctor's luck was in: a miniseries for which Flora had composed the music, *Cold Starlight*, was being repeated on the second channel this coming Thursday. Upon returning home, Flora warned the Doctor that this would mean fewer viewers than *The Identikit Man*, but because it had all been done on film she'd been able to take more time over the soundtrack and snuck in bits of ambient score through much of the action without intruding on it, so it was a particularly effective piece.

'What's it about?' asked the Doctor as he flicked through the listings.

'Um...' said Flora. 'These people on a spaceship...'

'And what happens to them?'

Flora paused. 'I can't remember. It was very good, though.' She picked up her copy of the listings for the other side, to see what would be on against her programmes. It was a current affairs show opposite *Cold Starlight*, which would be fine – but *The Identikit Man* was on opposite a new cop show called *Waterfront Beat*, which seemed to be getting a lot of publicity: it was on the cover of the magazine. This worried her slightly, but she didn't share her concerns with the Doctor.

On Monday afternoon, a tall man entered an editing suite near Waterloo and closed the door quietly behind himself. There was only one person in the room, an almost equally tall young woman with bobbed blonde hair, a rather large nose and very dark eyes, wearing a sweater and long skirt. She went by the name of Turis: she claimed it was Eastern European, and nobody questioned it.

'You took your time,' Turis said to the tall man, whose name was Arto – although whilst in this time and place he was using the name Arthur, which was nicely inconspicuous.

'It takes a while for them to process that kind of thing,' said Arto. He put a briefcase down on Turis's desk, opened it and produced a film canister.

'What's this?' asked Turis.

'*Identikit Man* episode two.'

'A telerecording?' she said, appalled. 'How am I supposed to work with that?'

'They don't copy to videotape.'

'Why didn't you copy it yourself?'

'I couldn't get near it. I did try, but it's a TX master. They're not going to let it go walkies.'

'You talked Burgess into moving our show opposite theirs.'

'With a gun, yeah.'

'Why didn't you try the same with them?'

'That was here. They know me there. I can't go waving guns in their faces.'

Turis considered the manner in which her colleague had said this. 'You like it there, don't you?'

'Maybe,' said Arto.

'This isn't the time to turn soft.'

'I know. Don't stress out about it.'

'Don't you find it stressful, working with all this ancient technology?'

'No, not really,' said Arto. 'I kind of like it. Oh, I got masters of a load more of her music too.'

'Really? Anything we can use?'

'I think there is, yeah.'

The Doctor filled the time until Thursday by going to the Warhol show in town and visiting James Watson, an old friend of his, and getting him to sign a copy of his latest book for Zoe. In the evenings, he listened to some of Flora's work and they would discuss it until late at night. They also made some recordings together, most of which were unfinished, but Flora intended to arrange the material into something usable at some stage – maybe not as something for television, but an album of her own. She was particularly pleased with some tape loops that she had made from the sound of the Doctor playing his recorder, and the Doctor let her keep the instrument so that she could replicate the sound if she needed to.

'Are you sure?' she asked him. At some point he'd decorated it with stick-on moons and stars, some of which had bent where he'd carried the recorder in his pocket.

'Oh, quite sure,' the Doctor said. 'It isn't my only one. I've got others. Do you really only use contemporary instruments and contemporary technology?'

'Oh, yes,' Flora said. 'I think it would be cheating otherwise. It would be very, very easy to make something nobody had ever heard before... but then I'd feel bad for whoever should have come along and come up with that sound themselves.'

On Tuesday and Wednesday, whilst Flora was at work, the Doctor attended the Rolling Stones' Rock and Roll Circus and returned full of enthusiasm for Taj Mahal. Flora played him some Cajun-influenced music she'd used on a children's drama called *The Devil in the Mouse-Hole*, which was partly inspired by Mahal, and the Doctor was fascinated. He commented that the discordant elements might be rather scary for children, and when Flora looked a little put out, the Doctor explained that he hadn't meant it as a criticism.

On Thursday, the Doctor settled down in Flora's armchair to watch *Cold Starlight*. Flora sat at the back of the living room, monitoring her equipment as the theme music – a building, ambitious piece encompassing all the major chords – was heard around the country. The music rose in tandem with the image of the Starship *Promise* – a model shot which had had special effort put into it as it would be seen every week in the title sequence, and was unusually sophisticated. The Doctor commented on this, but Flora was too busy concentrating.

Flora's soundtrack was, as she had said, almost ever-present. The story was about members of the *Promise* crew being possessed by an alien intelligence, and she had taken advantage of this to make her music akin to another, unseen character, menacing the crew in the background. Although the viewership was probably only something like three million nationally, the constant bombardment of sound waves meant that Flora was able to map the pattern of disturbances quite consistently. After an hour, she had a very good idea of which bubbles might contain the Doctor's ship and his friends.

On the screen, astronaut Jane Hunter was on a space walk, reporting back to her colleagues on what she could see. She tailed off, then screamed... then the radio went dead.

The credits rolled and the theme music played.

'No!' cried the Doctor. He turned to Flora. 'They can't end it there. What happens next?'

'Shh,' said Flora, who was using the theme music to make some final adjustments.

'Aww,' said the Doctor sulkily. He massaged his left index finger: he had been toying with a piece of string during the programme and as it had become increasingly tense, the Doctor had absently wound the string tightly around his finger, creating a series of painful ridges and dents.

Flora stood up. 'So, are we going?'

'Where?'

'To find your friends and your TARDIS.'

'Oh, yes,' said the Doctor, apparently having quite forgotten.

Their first target was near Hammersmith Pier – a few feet away from the end, hovering about twenty feet above the river. The Doctor and Flora had to hold the cones and point them downwards, towards the bubble. Flora made her adjustments. The Doctor was unsure whether or not to hope that there was something in there: whatever or whoever it was, they were in for a dunking.

The bubble *zinged*. The TARDIS appeared. There was a loud splash.

The Doctor tutted. 'How am I supposed to get *that* out?'

Quite unexpectedly, the TARDIS made its dematerialisation noise and vanished. Before the Doctor could complain about this, it reappeared on the shore, upright and bone dry.

'Oh,' said the Doctor.

'What was that?' asked Flora.

'Hostile Action Displacement System. Makes the TARDIS do a short hop if it lands in trouble. That's what I was trying to fix earlier.' He straightened his bow tie. 'I knew I knew what I was doing.'

Once the Doctor had checked that his ship was undamaged, they left the TARDIS on the shore where it was relatively inconspicuous, and went in search of more bubbles. The second of the night was disappointingly empty, but the third, in a back alley in Bloomsbury, contained Zoe. The Doctor stood beneath the bubble and managed to catch her when she fell: it looked to Flora like a well-rehearsed circus act.

Zoe introduced herself to Flora. She was young, small, pretty, round-faced, dark-haired and dressed in a silver catsuit. Flora was surprised: the way that the Doctor had described her, she had been expecting somebody older. The Doctor found a chip shop that was still open and bought Zoe a fish supper, which she was slightly suspicious of but hungry enough to eat whilst sitting on the back seat of Flora's car. According to Flora, the bubbles would no longer be malleable enough to bring back into phase, and they should try to find Jamie tomorrow.

'How long were you in there?' the Doctor asked as they drove back to Flora's flat. 'A-ha!' he added as he leaned over the back of the seat and stole a chip from Zoe. She slapped his hand away, but failed to prevent the theft.

'Ages,' she complained. 'Twelve hours, at least.'

'I told you,' the Doctor said to Flora. 'Time moves more slowly inside. I was probably in that one for months.' He turned back to Zoe. 'Flora let me out six days ago.'

'You were trapped in one too?' asked Zoe. 'So where's the TARDIS?'

'Hammersmith,' said the Doctor.

The following evening, *The Identikit Man* was going to start late as a consequence of an overrunning live report about Apollo 8 in the previous programme, *Eye on the Future*. Once this became apparent, Arto slipped inside the control room at another channel and demanded that they delay the start of *Waterfront Beat*.

'Why?' asked one of the bemused operators, before noticing that Arto had a gun. At this point the question became, 'How?'

'There's a temporary fault,' said Arto. 'Yeah?'

His instructions were carried out: the 'temporary fault' caption appeared on the monitors in front of them, and on the screens of 5,332,875 viewers across the country.

Not, however, at the home of Flora Millrace, where the Doctor and Zoe were seated on the sofa, animatedly discussing the Apollo 8 item on *Eye on the Future* over cups of tea. Flora sat at the table with her computer, making unnecessary adjustments to pass the time. Late running irritated her.

'Good,' said Arto. 'Be ready to go straight into the programme when I give you the word. No station ident, no continuity announcement – go straight in. Understand? Is there a set in here that'll pick up the other channels?'

An operator directed the tall man towards one of the screens. He re-tuned it to a different station, turned the volume up and watched intently. A few minutes passed: *Eye on the Future* ended, there was a trail for the current affairs programme *State of the Age*, and then the station ident appeared.

'It's just after 25 to eight,' said a voice from the set.

'Be ready,' Arto said.

'And now, a little later than billed, it's another adventure for *The Identikit Man*.'

'Run it,' said the tall man. 'Now.'

'Oh,' said the Doctor as the opening titles ran and he heard the theme music. He turned to Flora and jabbed his finger in the direction of the television. 'I know this one. This is one of your best ones, I think.'

'I don't know about that,' said Flora. 'But it's certainly my most effective. I've used –' Flora suddenly went quiet.

The Doctor turned. 'What?'

'I don't understand...' Flora said, staring hard at her monitor.

The Doctor jumped up from the sofa and scurried to her side. Zoe followed. 'What is it?' the Doctor asked.

Flora pointed at the screen. 'Look – these are the problem areas, the bubbles. Normally they show up as red. But they're coming up black.'

'What does that mean?' asked Zoe.

'I think the bond with the vortex has completely broken down,' said Flora. 'It's like my process has been completely exaggerated. It normally punches little holes between our universe and the vortex – that's how I find the out-of-phase spots. But it's as if something has targeted the problem areas and opened them up to the vortex for a few seconds.'

The Doctor's face fell. 'You mean that energy has seeped out from the vortex and into each of those bubbles?'

'Yes, I think so,' said Flora.

'But if it gets out... that could be disastrous!' said the Doctor. 'It could cause untold damage!'

'I don't understand what's causing it. The technique... it seems like mine, but nothing I've done could do this...'

The Doctor straightened up and looked at the television, drumming his fingers on his mouth. The standard early action sequence of *The Identikit Man* had just begun, accompanied by a version of Flora's standard action music. The Doctor ran over to the TV and retuned it to the other side, where *Waterfront Beat* was airing. It was a straightforward dialogue scene, a policeman interviewing a suspect, but had been scored with jarring, staccato music. It didn't match the action at all, and obscured the dialogue at times. The Doctor's eyes narrowed. He switched back to *The Identikit Man*, then went from one to the other, over and over. He didn't have to explain to Flora what he was getting at: the two pieces shared a rhythm. The *Waterfront Beat* music was a counterpoint to hers. They weren't precisely synchronised, but that didn't matter: they'd still be out there, colliding against each other, the new piece changing the effect of her own.

'Who's doing this?' Flora asked.

'Hopefully,' said the Doctor, pulling his shoes on, 'we'll find that out during the process of stopping them.'

The door of the control room opened and Turis entered, carrying a bag and directing a round of applause at Arto. 'Bravo,' she said.

'It's working then, is it?' asked Arto.

'Yep.' She opened her bag, pulled out a reel of videotape and handed it to one of the vision controllers. 'I think it's time for this one,' she said. 'Cue it up.'

The controller did as he was told.

'Where are we going?' asked Flora as they all climbed into the car.

'Hammersmith,' the Doctor said.

'The TARDIS?' asked Zoe.

'Yes. I've got an idea that might work – hopefully there's enough time for it. I wish we could keep monitoring the television from in here.'

'Pull down the glove compartment,' said Flora.

The Doctor did so and a small monitor sprang forward from it.

'I'm fairly sure this contravenes the Highway Code, you know,' the Doctor said, reaching around the back and turning it on.

After a couple of minutes of *Waterfront Beat*, still with inappropriate music, the picture was abruptly interrupted by an image of a man and a woman. Flora glanced at it, then glanced again. 'That's Arthur,' she said.

'Who?' asked the Doctor.

'He's an editor. He works on *The Identikit Man*. I saw him the other day.'

'Shh,' said Zoe to them both. 'They're talking.'

'... mainly a message for your leaders,' the woman was saying, 'although in the interests of transparency, we thought you should all hear it. We've planted bombs in dozens of locations around London. Very powerful ones.'

'Don't bother trying to look for them,' said Arthur. 'You won't find them.'

'We'd like to make a deal with you to make free use of your energy sources,' the woman continued, 'but we're afraid we can't offer anything in return, hence the bombs. We'll be expecting to hear from your leaders within two hours. Otherwise, there'll be a lot more of this.'

A piece of music began to play, a jaunty little melody played on an acoustic guitar: it sounded like something from a children's programme. However, the signal then died very rapidly. Thirty seconds or so later, *Waterfront Beat* returned – then, outside the car, they heard a distant explosion. It reminded Zoe slightly of the TARDIS, but it was a much harsher sound, an abrupt and painful wrench.

The Doctor turned to Flora, grim-faced. Flora kept her eyes on the road.

'Jamie's in one of those,' said Zoe.

'I know,' said the Doctor. 'I'm sure he'll be all right while the energy's still contained, but...' He turned to Flora. 'What was that piece of music at the end? Do you know it?'

'I practically wrote it,' said Flora. 'It was a lot like a piece that was on the masters I gave to Arthur the other day. I've been... experimenting for a while with a piece to bring the bubbles into phase automatically, but I've never managed to... Wait a minute, they've managed to make it work, haven't they?' She sounded quite affronted.

'Offended your professional pride, has it?' asked the Doctor.

'A little bit, yes. But only one of the bubbles exploded.'

'They probably reduced the transmitter range to the absolute minimum,' said Zoe, 'so the music only went out in a small radius. It was probably a bubble near the transmitter that went up.'

The Doctor pulled a notebook and pencil from his pocket, and started drawing what looked like a rough circuit diagram. 'Flora,' he said without looking up, 'do you think you could copy what they did to your music?'

Flora hesitated. 'I'm not sure. Hard to tell from the first few seconds, but I think... I could try to work out how it should go. Why?'

'I think the best way to stop them playing that music is to play it before they do.'

'Have you got a guitar?'

'Oh? Acoustic or electric?'

'How much damage did the first explosion do?' asked Turis.

'A lot, but within a very small radius,' said Arto, consulting the read-out from a small computer. 'At a rough estimate, fifty dead, perhaps sixty, and substantial collateral damage.' He looked up. 'I hope they don't make us destroy any more.'

'I told you. Don't turn soft.'

'I'm just saying I'd rather we got what we want. Then everybody's happy, aren't they?'

Zoe wrapped the cable around one of the pier's supports six times, then she looked back to see if there was enough slack in it for another couple of coils. This was the kind of job Jamie usually got stuck with. She wondered if he understood what was happening, trapped in his bubble, surrounded by dormant vortex energy. Probably not. He was probably thinking about how hungry he was.

Unless he'd been in the one that had already exploded, of course.

Zoe tugged on the cable – which ran from the bridge, across the shore and inside the TARDIS – and a little more slack emerged. She unwrapped and then rewrapped the cable, then she used the Doctor's sonic screwdriver to weld the end tight and walked back to the TARDIS.

Upon stepping inside the ship, Zoe saw that the Doctor had connected the cable to the console. He had prised open a couple of panels and patched in other pieces of equipment, including a microphone. Two more cables sprang from opposite sides of the console and went in the direction of the power room. He continued to work at his improvised arrangement, testing connections and tapping his screwdriver on things. Zoe asked what he was doing, partly because she wanted to know, partly because she wanted to check his work for mistakes.

'Well, the TARDIS has its own transmitter and receiver,' the Doctor said. 'Right now we want to use them for completely different purposes, so I've separated them out. We're going to boost the power to the transmitter – I've linked it direct to the power room – and swamp the television frequency, and broadcast the "phasing" tune ourselves.'

'But how are you going to stop the energy destroying everything?'

'Well, just like electricity always tries to find the quickest route to the ground, vortex energy tries to find the quickest route back to the vortex. It's leaked into the universe but our friends there have closed that route off, so it'll try to punch its way back through. On the way, it destroys any matter in its way.'

'So we offer it a quicker way?'

The Doctor clapped his hands together. 'Exactly! The TARDIS draws its energy from the vortex – it's not hard to let it go back the other way. The receiver's tuned to pick it up, the pier acts as a giant aerial, and it all goes down our other cable to the power room.' He pointed towards the interior door.

Just then, Flora stepped through the interior door into the console room, with an acoustic guitar hanging from her shoulder.

'How did you get on?' asked the Doctor.

'I can do the part I heard and I can remember the version they stole, and assuming they've been consistent about how they've changed it... well, there are a few possible versions.'

'How different is it?' asked Zoe.

'Not so different that I couldn't sue them for breach of copyright.'

'Ready then?' asked the Doctor, picking up the microphone and pointing it towards her.

Flora nodded, and the Doctor switched on.

Across the London area, thousands of screens went black. A couple of seconds later, a few hesitant chords could be heard being played on an acoustic guitar: then a bright tune emerged, one that was fairly familiar to anybody who had been listening earlier. It was very familiar indeed to Turis and Arto, still standing in the control room and now looking desperately at each other, each hoping for the other to explain what was happening.

The tune came to an end.

Nothing happened.

'I can't have got it right,' said a female voice from the television.

'That's all right, try it another way,' said a male voice.
'That's her,' said Arto.
'From the Sound Unit?' asked Turis. 'The woman who makes the music?'
'Yeah.'
'What's she doing?'
'I don't understand. Doesn't she know what'll happen?'
'Maybe not.'
'What do we do?' Arto stepped closer to Turis. 'What do we *do*?'
The tune began again.

At the end of Flora's second attempt, there was a vast, unified *zing* over London. For a millisecond, malevolent globes of vortex energy hung over the city, waiting to be drawn home via the quickest possible route. Then, as one, they zoomed towards Hammersmith.

Anybody watching the pier would have seen it glow deep purple as the energy coursed through it and down the cable. Inside the TARDIS, the Doctor instructed Zoe and Flora to stand well back. He hadn't divulged his concern that the energy might do considerable damage to the console: it was designed to handle surges, but nothing as big as this. The energy fed through in a matter of moments, but to the Doctor it felt a great deal longer: when it was gone, he immediately hurried to the console and tested its vital functions. When they were sure that everything was okay, Zoe and Flora wasted no time in gently mocking him for his tender concern over his ship.

And, in a Kensington garden belonging to two young socialites named Astrid and Iris Vaughn-Jones, a young Scotsman fell from the air and into the laurel bushes.

Arto and Turis, both braced for the sound of mass destruction, realised at about the same time that it wasn't going to come. They opened their eyes, looked at each other, and both scrambled for the computer. Turis got there first, examined the screen and wearily handed it to Arto. 'Our bargaining chip has gone.'

'What do we do now?' asked Arto.
Turis sighed. 'Leave.'
'I don't think so,' said a voice behind them they both recognised.
They turned. 'I didn't think you'd find us so –' began Arto. But he stopped when he saw the grey man in the grey morning dress, a gleaming white flower in his buttonhole.
'Who are you?' said Turis as the grey man came forward. Faster than should have been possible, he stabbed her just above the heart with one fingertip.
She flopped forward dead, into his arms.

* * *

It took the Doctor and Zoe four days to find Jamie, and he was surprised to discover that they had believed he might be dead. Oh, no, he told them, he'd had a marvellous time. Once Jamie had convinced Astrid and Iris that he wasn't dangerous, they had looked after him very well indeed. Reluctantly he bade them farewell and accompanied them to the car, where he was delighted to see Flora, whom he had always got on well with. As she drove them back to Hammersmith, the Doctor and Zoe explained to him what had been happening whilst he'd been trapped.

'So, what happened to the people you saw on the tellything?' Jamie asked.

'The people behind it all?' said the Doctor. He was writing in his 500-year diary. 'Don't know.'

'We worked out where they must have been broadcasting from,' said Zoe, 'but they were long gone by the time we got there.'

'They must have got away,' said Flora. 'Which is a nuisance.'

'So, we've no idea where they came from. They can't have been from this time and place; they understood the principles behind Flora's music. It's going to annoy me until I find out, you know.'

'What did they want?' asked Jamie.

'Energy,' said Zoe.

'Presumably to fuel more time experiments,' said the Doctor, chewing on his pencil. 'You need rather more than a nine-volt battery to manipulate the time stream. I should keep an eye out for them in the future. And the past.' He turned to Flora. 'So, what will you do now we've fixed all those holes?'

'I don't know,' she said. 'I suppose I could move on. But I like what I'm doing here. Maybe I'll take some time off first. I think... yes, I think I've earned it.'

As the Doctor, Jamie and Zoe trooped into the TARDIS, Flora opened her bag. This time it did not contain her phase-control equipment, but a reel-to-reel tape recorder. She untangled a microphone, started the recorder running and stepped over to the Doctor's craft.

As it disappeared from view it made that noise, the noise she'd heard so many times and always meant to record, and Flora smiled to herself. It hung in the air for several seconds when no blue was visible any more, and she kept the recorder running until long after she could no longer hear it – because even if she couldn't hear it, that didn't mean it wasn't still there.

Eventually she turned the tape recorder off. Yes, she could definitely use that on something.

Second Contact

Jonathan Clements

An Adventure of the Eighth Doctor

Nonsense Song of the MicMac

And we gather and we gather, and the old men speak.

Three days towards the coast, we found the blue tree that was not a tree, the dwelling that was not a dwelling, of the hardest wood we had ever seen. Only the smallest of men could have lain inside it and, even then, he would have needed to curl up like a cat. Nor was there a hole in the roof for smoke, leading some to question whether it was a dwelling at all.

Its shape too was curious. Regular and straight as an arrow on all sides, lines that challenged the natural order of things, not bending with the place around it, not cleaving to the curves of the world, but standing out against them, defiant.

The sun was low on the horizon and we would be walking no further that day. For Sees Strangers, our leader, it was a difficult choice. Should he move further on, past the strange blue tree, away from whatever spirit harm and ghost dances might accrue in the night? Or should he make his camp right there, to observe it and think on it?

The wayfarer and waypointer was much chastised. His job it was to remember all the signs of our going and their returning – strange-shaped rocks and curious trees; the sounds of rivers and the calls of birds. Nobody spoke of his omission, but our looks alone sufficed to set him fretting. *Where?* was the unspoken question. Where in all the songs he'd sung of the journey to be made was any mention of this blue... box?

Already we had made a wrong turning in a forest of thickets, wasting half a day tramping through brush towards an uncrossable river. There had been excuses offered, of the transience of growing things. Said the waypointer, such problems are only to be expected. So much of the terrain seems so similar. All these green trees, lacking in high hills or similar vantage; these small streams and rills that confused even an experienced waypointer. How could he remember every detail when details were so small?

But this was a detail worthy of a song itself, and not even mentioned in a chorus. The waypointer had not sung of it, therefore it cannot have been on the way he should have pointed. If we faced this blue tree in its clearing in the forest, we were facing the wrong clearing. He had led us astray. He was failing us, and that made us feel unhappy.

Was it not, after all, such a great undertaking that the whole tribe had tried to take part? Sees Strangers remembered the long council meetings, verging on tribal arguments, over who would go, and why. The old men, some barely able to walk, so keen to set eyes upon these strangers from the sea, that they would even suggest a migration towards the coast, that they could witness these visitors for themselves! The look of shock on the chieftain's face, and his silent wrath, at the suggestion we should give up their hard-won land, merely for trade.

But, oh, what trade! The bright red cloth that first group had brought back, how it had impressed us all. The tiniest scrap of it was prized more than wolves' teeth. The witch doctors wrapped tatters to their staves and drums, and warriors fixed it to their spears. But there was more than tatters.

None had expected Sees Strangers to return from exile. His old name was never spoken. The chief allowed no songs that mentioned him. Sees Strangers had been such a figure in the tribe that most recent songs included him at least in the chorus. The tribe had called upon the old men to sing songs of older battles and events past so they would not mention the warrior who had been known by another name. In some ways, they were happier nights, as joking songs gained new prominence. Tales of tricksters and comedians; these mentioned no great warriors, nor once-great warriors now shamed, and so they gained much ground at the tellings and the singings. Until that day one winter past, when the warrior now known as Sees Strangers came back to the firelight, bearing the witching cloth and talking excitedly of his discovery.

The red cloth, how they had loved it. Softer than catkins, brighter than blood; the old men had clasped it to themselves for warmth. The women too. What trouble it had caused among the wives! Fit to bind breasts and wrap heads, fit to make anklets and headdresses. The higher a woman's standing, the more she wanted the red cloth, such that the greatest beauties kept their bodies hidden beneath it.

That was before the secondary problem, the one nobody had foreseen, of what happened to the cloth when it aged. Such witching material had its faults. It did not endure like skins and hides. It lost its bright colours in mere days. It stained and frayed, and caused new wailings all of its own. Said the wives of the stronger warriors: we should not need to work. We do not wish it, for our cloth will fade and with it our glamour.

Yes, there was much arguing about it, and many tears and beatings, feuds begun and spells cast. But Sees Strangers enjoyed new-found standing among us, as the man whose war-band knew of the strangers from beyond the sea, and of how to return to them and their wondrous things. New songs were sung of him, forgetting the past misdeeds of his old name. And while there were complaints from some among the elders, none could resist a glance, albeit sidelong, at the red cloth and its wearers.

Which brought them, like a recurrent refrain, like the shouts in answer that greet the elders' sung exhortations, to this second mission, to this journey back towards the coast, not of the whole tribe, but of a select band from among us. Which led us and leads us, like a chorus returning, like an opening line that echoes and returns for another verse, to the clearing and its strange blue tree, which opened.

It opened. Doubt us not. We have witnesses and confirmation from all the men who returned. Somehow the blue tree opened, and from it stepped a man, his hair in tatters, like that of the deer with the clumped fur, rich and soft. And covered. Covered he was in clothes of grey and white, of jutting angles and knots of witching cloth. Clasped him, did his clothes, as if cut to fit, like the tight skins worn by the women that dance.

Seeing us, he dropped his drum in surprise – small it was and made of unknown material, that glinted like the light of the sun on water.

And it bounced with a shuffle and bounced with a shuffle. And a rattle. Like dust and little pebbles inside.

He meant us no harm, he said. He was a Doctor Witch. His voice was soft and gentle, not the barking commands of the chief, nor the dry rasp of the long-running warrior, but quiet and kind, like an elder soothing a child.

We do not see strangers. We do not see strangers. It is the law that defines us, that makes us Us. They are they, like the mountain men and the plains runners; they dwell where they dwell, as do we. We do not take their women. We do not fight their men. Fightings and takings are against the will of the spirits, and when they manifest the earth shall weep.

But this was a mission of seeing strangers. Sees Strangers's very name embraced it and sought it. And this man, this Doctor Witch, wore clothes of witching cloth. Not red, no, but many shades, like differences of autumn leaves.

Colours of red in shadow. Colours of red in shadow.

And he was woeful. Saying: where is the time of one thousand? One thousand beyond the lord. After the death of the Great Spirit, there is the one thousand, and he was looking for it.

No, we did not understand it, either.

And he clutched at his drum, and breathed in sorrow, saying Yay-Zak, Yay-Zak my friend, have I failed you. For we are not in the time of one thousand, and you are not seeing the strangers who come across the water.

Sees Strangers and our menfolk were of one mind. Tense and ready for the fight. For this Doctor Witch in witching cloth, with his shining drum was searching for the strangers who come across the water. And yet was he one of them? His face white like a ghost, his clothes made of spirit webs.

Were he of the mountain men or of the plains runners, Sees Strangers would have killed him. For they would not help another find the strangers from beyond the sea. But this Doctor Witch, he knew much of the strangers. And suddenly he was excited, like a child with a stick. He was exuberant, like a hunter with a kill. He yelped with enthusiasm, with joy of a hunt we had not known, and it made us smile.

He smiled, as even the bravest of the braves does when dancing before a child, and spoke of the strangers from beyond the sea. He knew of their giant canoes, big enough to hold tens of men, their spirit weapons and mystery beasts, and their women with hair like white grass.

Women with hair like white grass. Women with hair like white grass.

And we asked him if he knew them, and he said he had met them in the past times. Sees Strangers let him live. He was not one of them, but he knew of them already, and he knew more of them than us. And he laughed and danced, and told us that he was not lost, but he was found, that he had not failed his Yay-Zak, for this was the one thousand year beyond the lord, and he must go to the place where the strangers were from beyond the sea.

All thoughts of our waypointer's failings were forgot. The camp for the night was here, at the place of the blue tree. The Firemaker made fire. The Tent Carriers made tents. And the Doctor Witch watched as the men made the food. With all busy at their tasks, only Says Things Twice had nothing to do. And so she sat with the Doctor Witch.

What is your name, said the Doctor Witch.

What is your name, said Says Things Twice, and we laughed.

He asked after Says Things Twice, and the men laughed. For she was a woman of little worth. She had no husband, nor would any man take her to him for more than a night, for she was cursed by the spirits only to see good. She was always happy, never fearing of anything, nor harm, nor beast, nor fire. And such people are a danger to themselves and to those for whom they see no harm. But Says Things Twice was not ugly, and still of use to us. She was the daughter of the chief and protected by his honour, and through 15 summers she had been with the tribe with no real purpose.

It was Sees Strangers who had seen it, who had divined why the spirits had been sent to us. For if Says Things Twice had little thought of man or beast, she had no fear of strangers, and we might trade her with the people from beyond the sea, for witching cloth or spirit weapons or a woman with hair like white grass.

Women with hair like white grass. Women with hair like white grass.

We sang our songs, of Sees Strangers and his encounters. And we sang of the time that Angry Wolf had chased a deer through the canyon, and of the arrows that flew true, and of the tricks played by the Raven. And the men danced and sang at the chorus. Sees Strangers asked the Doctor Witch to sing a song of his own, and he began to refuse, but seeing the look on Sees Strangers's face, he relented, and said he would sing of the strangers beyond the sea.

But, he said. But, he was a bad singer. And he had little experience of this talking way of the People, and knew not when the words of talking should turn into song, or what choruses there should be, and that he would be thinking of his songs as he spoke, and that if he did not know where the answering refrains should be, then neither would we. And we laughed, and said that such was the way with all music, that it belonged to the Great Spirit, and that the spirit moved within us. The People do not create songs, but the songs create the People, blowing through us like the wind in the trees.

Take your drum, said Sees Strangers. Take your drum and start.

But the Doctor Witch said, what drum?

And for a moment, we thought he was of a ruined mind, like Says Things Twice, for his drum was with him from the moment he had come from the blue tree. But Sees Strangers, thinking this to be a first movement of the song, requiring answer and refrain, said, the drum you have beside you, with its pebbles and dust inside. And for a moment, the Doctor Witch looked sad, and he said, this drum is my Yay-Zak, for he is burned, and this rattle is not rocks, for it is all that is left of his bones.

There was fear all around, that this Doctor Witch was the spirit of death. But Sees Strangers knew no fear, and asked him if the Yay-Zak made music. And the Doctor Witch laughed a sad laugh, and said the Yay-Zak did. And would make music one more time. And so he beat upon his drum, and rattled the bones within.

And rattled the bones within. And rattled the bones within.

And he said, the strangers from beyond the sea come from the old world. Yes, this is the new. And you do not know it. And the strangers do not know it either. For they are outcasts from a land towards the sun. And their great canoes took them from island to island, from their homes towards a land of ice. And from there to another land of ice, although they lied to their brethren, and said it was green. But it was not. It was also ice. And so they came to the land that was not green, and there they dwelled for some time. But now it was the time of one thousand after the lord, and the people of this lord were also coming towards the setting sun. And these people of the old world and its old spirits, these strangers from beyond the sea, kept heading further. And now they had come to the island where Sees Strangers had first met them, and there they intended to stay.

Although, he said. They would not long remain.

At this there was great concern from the People, for we had spent the spring trapping squirrels and martens, and many furs had been withheld from the women and the elders, all for the witching cloth. But the Doctor Witch assured us that the strangers would still be there, a while. And he said, with a rattle and a shuffle, that our children would not see the strangers again, but that they should count themselves lucky for it. Lucky for it.

And he tapped out an ending on his drum, and waited for us to say the refrain, but none did. And there was an uneasy silence around the fire, as the People thought on his words, and heard in them the same warnings of the elders, that no good would come of the strangers and their witching cloth.

But not even Sees Strangers, whose entire return to the tribe rested on such matters, raised his voice in anger to the Doctor Witch. For although the Doctor Witch looked like a young man, he had the wise countenance of an elder. And who was Sees Strangers to say that the people from beyond the sea would always be good to us? And so nothing was said of it. Instead, Sees Strangers asked the Doctor Witch why he was searching for the people from beyond the sea, and the Doctor Witch held up his drum, the Yay-Zak, and said that he must take the drum to them, to ride in one of their great canoes, and pour its ashes in the sea, thereby fulfilling a promise that he had never made, but that he knew a friend would want. And there was much agreement among the People that the Doctor Witch was a good man despite his strange words. For there are many stories of those who carry out the wishes of the dead and are blessed by the spirits.

Says Things Twice said: Yay-Zak, Yay-Zak, making the Doctor Witch laugh.

And the night came and the night went. And when the sun chased it from the sky and all around, we set out again, with the Doctor Witch, on to the place where the strangers came from beyond the sea. But of our meeting with them, and of the leave-taking of the Doctor Witch, and of his return, this song has no words. For that is another story, should you seek it from the elders in the firelight. It is another story and another song.

Another story and another song.

Doggerel Fragments from The Vinland Sagas

But I digress. One day, Ivar's ship simply was not there any more. In her own longhouse with her kin and closest friends, Freydis of the red hair and the fiery temper had huddled by the smoky fire on the cool Vineland, her eyes burning beneath a disdainful scowl, daring anyone to say the obvious.

'He took his men fishing,' she muttered. 'They'll sail out into the deeps, trail nets for a couple of days and then they'll come back. You'll see.'

But it was a different story at other hearths in the little camp. Barely a few paces away, beneath the dark, turf roof of Thorfinn's house, his wife was speaking her mind.

'It's that bitch, Freydis,' she said, her words hanging in the sudden silence. Even Thorfinn's crew, hardened by years of fishing, farming and a-viking, looked startled.

'She's scared them off,' said Gudrid of the long braids. 'She lied to them. She lied to all of us.'

'Now,' said Thorfinn carefully, 'let's not be hasty.'

'Hasty!' spat Gudrid, loud enough to wake little Snorri, dozing in her arms. She dropped her voice to more of a whisper, rocking her baby gently, cooing occasionally even as she hissed bile about her kinswoman.

'It is not hasty. I am not hasty. *This* is hasty!' She nodded her head up at the sagging ceiling, its scant wooden beams barely keeping up the earthen roof.

Gudrid got to her feet, the baby still cradled in her arms, looking at the men around the table in an exaggerated parody of Freydis's distinctive, unnerving stare.

'Come with me,' she said, mocking Freydis's Greenlander accent. 'Oh, it's so wonderful in the Vineland. So warm and nice.'

'So where are the vines?' yelled a man's voice from the back, and the group chuckled nervously.

Another man leapt up, clutching the twig-like remains of a few of the local berries, scratching his head in mock befuddlement.

'Well, they look a bit like grapes!' he said.

'No, no!' shouted another. 'This is a vine!' He brandished a legbone of one of the local birds, then threw it in the air.

Thorfinn smiled as the men started throwing bones at each other, each boasting they'd found the fabled grapes of Vineland. As Gudrid ducked out of the door, still cradling Snorri, Thorfinn walked after her.

The jokes and arguments from the longhouse faded behind them. Above them there were only stars.

Gudrid dragged her shawl a little around herself and stared out from the hill at the inky waters of the night sea.

Thorfinn sat nearby and picked absently at the grass.

'Sorry,' said Gudrid.

'You're right,' said Thorfinn.

'What are we going to do about it?' she said. They both looked nervously back down the hill at the quiet longhouse of Freydis's kinsmen. Firelight could be seen flickering through the door, but the house was silent.

'Ivar isn't coming back,' said Gudrid. 'That's him gone for good. He's gone back to Greenland. No vines, no grapes, no trade for months, and stuck on this island with Freydis of the red hair and the red rage.'

'Do you think he's right?' said Thorfinn.

'Right to abandon this?' said Gudrid. 'No. I wanted to come here, Thorfinn. I was ready for this.'

'If you want to take your chances back home...' began Thorfinn.

'No,' she said. 'Gods, no. We can make it here... Actually, Thorfinn... right now we don't have a choice.'

Thorfinn looked at his wife in puzzlement.

'We're down to one ship,' she whispered. 'There are sixty of us! Do you think we'll all cram into one little boat?'

'That is the least of our troubles,' said Thorfinn.

'What could be worse?' asked Gudrid.

'Ivar took Svasi the Lapp,' said Thorfinn.

'What of it?' shrugged Gudrid. 'He was always spoiling for a fight, always dazed and stumbling. He was of no use on shore.'

'But on ship,' said Thorfinn. 'On ship, he was the pathfinder.'

Gudrid put her hand to her mouth in shock. Thorfinn was right. Without Svasi, there was no navigation, save the vaguest pointing of a prow towards a distant star. Svasi had borne the crystal that sought the sun. Svasi knew the way, the way to Vineland and the way to Greenland. Without him, they were as lost as driftwood.

The pair remained silent, listening in the quiet night to the lapping of the waves against the sand, and the sucking slap as waters invaded the safety of the boat hollow on the beach, to be crushed and flattened beneath the keel.

'Wait!' said Gudrid. 'What was that?' She raised a finger looking skyward at nothing, tilting her head. Thorfinn waited patiently, but heard nothing. Gudrid scowled her familiar scowl, staring at Thorfinn as if it was his fault that there was nothing to hear. And then there it was again.

It was a chant. Unmistakeable, human voices in the night, accompanied by a drum, repeating a phrase in unknown language, and fading.

'The screechers!' whispered Gudrid. 'The flinchers. They have returned.'

All was quiet again, Thorfinn and Gudrid waiting beneath the stars, and then another cry rose up in the night, a loud response to a quieter story that did not carry with the same volume.

'They are telling a story by the fireside,' said Gudrid. 'They are camped close by and will be here tomorrow. You should tell the men.'

But Thorfinn was already walking towards the homesteads, his steps turning into a run.

All were up at dawn, as ever, but now with greater urgency. For the first time in months, the homesteaders at the promontory had true unity of purpose, beyond the petty squabbles of past days. Though who the decider should be was the first topic of contention. Thorfinn approached the brothers Finnbogi and Helgi, warning them of the approach of the Skraelings, and counselling calm and ward-watching. Gudrid sent the men throughout the camp in search of items ready for trade, for they were sure the Skraelings would return with more precious pelts.

'Think,' said Gudrid, 'of the trade such animal skins will bring us back in Greenland or Iceland.' She did not, however, press home her point, since few of the men yet appreciated that there would be no boat back to civilisation, not without some miracle.

Freydis had other ideas. Hands on hips and with a face like thunder, she kicked the pile of trading goods and yelled to anyone who would listen.

'What idiot put an axe on this pile? What simpleton left a knife? Did we not agree to trade no weapons with the screechers and flinchers? Did we not agree to trade no weapons with those people who might be our enemies? Did we not?'

Some sheepish men of the group retrieved articles from the pile, with a swiftness that made Thorfinn wonder. Were supplies truly getting so low, that men would consider the trading of such important articles, only to snatch them back lest another claim them as their own?

With items readied and the men and women cautioned as to their behaviour, the waiting began. None seemed keen on mending nets or repairing roofs. The women fussed around cooking pots. The men waited. And after what seemed like an age, there were the first signs of the Skraelings, loping, as was their wont, like wolves at a brisk pace, keeping pace by a strange grunting song as if bears were attempting to sing, padding swiftly towards the camp.

'I see packs,' said Thorfinn, squinting at the approaching men. 'They are bringing more furs to trade.'

There was a murmuring of satisfaction among the men.

'But,' said Gudrid. 'There do seem to be rather a lot of them.'

The others crowded to Thorfinn's vantage, eager for a look at the approaching Skraelings. Indeed there were many. Last summer's traders had been a pitiful handful of wretches; now they were returning in force, numbering several dozen.

The brothers Finnbogi and Helgi returned to their homestead, to retrieve their weapons and keep them close at hand. They were veterans of trading missions to the Bjarmalanders, of deals made with Danes, of bad bargains with Britons. There was no tradition of trade with these Skraeling wretches, no fear of vendetta for agreements betrayed. Finnbogi and Helgi were making ready.

'The brothers Finnbogi and Helgi are taking no chances,' said Freydis archly. 'And for once I agree.'

When the Skraelings neared, Thorfinn recognised their leader. Last summer he had been thin and gaunt, starved and harassed. Now he seemed confident and bold.

'Do you think,' said Gudrid, 'he has gained new standing from his trade with us?'

Thorfinn shrugged. It was not his concern how others might profit from trade, only that his people made similar advantages.

'I don't like their look,' said Freydis, loudly, and with the assurance that they would not understand her.

It was true, there were a lot of them. Many sellers meant much to buy, but those among the Greenlanders remembered days a-viking, when their mobs of sellers with no buyers had turned into raiders. Freydis eyed the many Skraeling men with deep suspicion. They eyed her back.

'*Mekwe'k sapun*,' said one. Freydis glared at him.

'He says you have red hair,' said a voice.

A man stepped to the front of the crowd of Skraelings, but he was not one of them. He was clad from head to foot in strange coloured velvets, dressed like a Lappish sorcerer with hair to match, clutching a round tin decorated with strange, bright sigils. He smiled.

'I am the Doctor,' he said.

'Whose doctor?' said Freydis.

'Mine,' said the Doctor with an enthusiastic grin, stepping forward. Freydis shifted suspiciously; she knew not of such happiness in the face of strangers. This man's eyes had the charmed glint of madness about them. Or joy, that she granted, but normally madness. He seemed happy with everything, pleased to see them, uncaring of any danger the Greenlanders might present. For Freydis, that was unnatural. The light in his eyes could be the fiery flash one saw in the battle-mad, the *bear-shirt* and the *wolf-skin* before they charge, enraged with Odin's battle blindness. Or, thought Freydis, he might simply be a happy fool.

His accent was strange, as if his words were chewed by long distance, his accent the thick mispronunciation of a Briton or a Gael. Tyrkir the German laughed at the joke. Freydis scowled her customary scowl.

'These are the L'nuk,' said the Doctor. 'You have met them before.'

'We have,' said Thorfinn, stepping forward.

'*Nikmaq*,' said one of the Skraelings. The Doctor stroked his lip thoughtfully.

'He greets you as if you were his kin,' said the Doctor.

'I return the greeting,' said Thorfinn stiffly. 'I am Thorfinn Karlsefni of Iceland.' The Doctor whispered something to the lead Skraeling, who grunted something in return.

'His name is *Nem'ik Ji'nim*,' said the Doctor. '"Seeing strange men". He got it because he discovered you, the people from beyond the sea.'

'I think,' said Freydis haughtily, 'you will find that we discovered him.'

'Be that as it may,' said the Doctor. 'He brings fine pelts to trade with you.' He gestured at the Skraelings, and the pack carriers came forth, dumping several bundles of furs on the ground.

From the sidelines, Gudrid watched as her husband Thorfinn dealt with the Lappish-seeming Doctor and his Skraeling associates. Freydis stood at Thorfinn's side as if she were his wife, and Gudrid shook her head in irritation. It was only after some time, as the haggling began over the furs and the felts, that she realised a girl was standing by her side.

It was a Skraeling child, at the cusp between girl and woman, her hair unkempt in the Skraeling fashion, her hide clothes dirty, her eyes meeting Gudrid's without an ounce of fear or recognition.

'My name is Gudrid. What's yours?' said Gudrid.

The Skraeling girl stared back at her for a while. Then she spoke.

'*Mai nejm iz Kudrit wo' tsiors*,' she said blankly.

Gudrid laughed at the mimicry and the girl smiled back at her with innocent joy. The Doctor came scurrying over.

'She is a chief's daughter,' he said. 'But as you can see, not all there.'

'The chief is here?' asked Gudrid, watching as the strange girl walked off towards the homesteads.

'No,' said the Doctor. 'He has sent this girl. She is part of the trade.'

Gudrid snorted.

'I don't think,' she said, 'we have much need of a Skraeling simpleton. Their presence unnerves us already.'

'I know,' said the Doctor. 'You are thinking of leaving, are you not?'

Gudrid stared at him in shock.

'Who are you?' she breathed.

'I am the Doctor,' he said. 'I told you that.'

'What are you doing here?'

'I have a simple request,' he said, holding up the tin he had been carrying. 'I am not with the Skraelings, nor am I one of your people.'

Gudrid made to speak but he held up his hand.

'There are no more of Europe like me, here in Vineland. I am a lone traveller.'

'You travelled like a Lappish shaman?' said Gudrid. 'Wearing a cloak of wolfskin, or living as a whale?'

'Something like that,' said the Doctor. 'I came here with the powers of Tar Dith. There is just I alone, and this,' he said, patting the tin reverently.

'What is it?' asked Gudrid.

'This is all that is left of my friend, Isaac,' said the Doctor. 'He always wanted to travel on a Viking ship. I owe him that.'

'We are not Vikings,' said Gudrid, knowing even as she said it that there were those among the farmers who would disagree. 'We are not raiders. We are not criminals. We are not outcasts.'

Except, as she thought about it, she realised that perhaps they were at least outcasts. Sent abroad from Greenland, not by their crimes but by their deprivations – the land becoming too peopled or perhaps too much with the wrong sort of people, the lack of wood, land and food. Yes, they were outcasts too.

But I digress.

It had been a strange few days for Gudrid, and the babblings of the Lappish-looking sorcerer were not helping. Nor was the renewed squalling of her child, who she heard wailing for attention from her homestead. Shaking her head as if to clear it, Gudrid went towards her home.

The Doctor, seemingly uncomprehending of any prohibition, followed her as if they were family.

Gudrid snatched up her baby and cradled him to her, yanking one breast free from her dress, so that she might suckle him. The Doctor smiled at the baby as he was silenced.

'His name is Snorri,' said Gudrid.

'A fine name,' said the Doctor.

'He is the first,' said Gudrid. 'The first of our children in this new land.'

'And will he be the last?' said the Doctor.

'What makes you so quick to doubt?' asked Gudrid, generally intrigued.

The Doctor looked around him at the sagging ceiling.

'I was just observing,' he said. 'Your men seem gaunt and ill-fed. These huts are in poor repair.'

'They are old,' agreed Gudrid. 'A brother of Freydis built them some ten years ago. They are damp and dank and miserable. Not even huts; but booths, made for roofs of sailcloth, not turf.'

'Face it,' said the Doctor. 'This colony is going nowhere. I see how nervous you are before the Skraelings. They already outnumber you and you are running out of red felt. What will happen next time?'

Freydis of the red hair watched the Doctor and the hated Gudrid of the long braids as they talked with such ease.

'My husband would not allow such familiarity with a stranger,' she observed, loud enough for Thorfinn to hear it.

Thorfinn glanced back at his wife and the Doctor, and made to say something. Then he thought better of it. A direct insult at Freydis, which he surely wished to say, would have been a direct attack on her husband, and would demand the satisfaction of a duel, and he had other things on his mind.

The red felt was almost gone. That most pointless of materials, next to useless in the damp Vineland climate, was like a catmint to the Skraelings. They could not get enough of it, even when, as the supplies began to dwindle, Freydis had advised slicing the strips thinner. Yet, still the Skraelings brought forward their animal pelts, and still they took the red felt joyously.

They say that Freydis of the red hair was always suspicious, for she expected from others the disdain that was in her own heart for all men. On hearing a noise from her own hut, she immediately went to see what it was. Any other might have thought nothing of it – a chicken near the fire perhaps, or a dog knocking over a pot. But Freydis was always on edge, and never more so than with the Skraelings so close by.

She poked her head into the dark room, and saw the Skraeling girl, the simpleton, perched above her own hearth-chest, examining an earthenware dish as if it were a precious item. To Freydis, it was.

'Get away from that!' she shouted.

The Skraeling girl looked up at her, puzzled.

'Ge'twej rom'dat!' she replied with a smile, holding up the dish.

Freydis was no ordinary woman. She had the fiery hair of her father Eirik and a temper to match. She grabbed a broom from beside the door and charged at the Skraeling girl.

'No!' said a voice.

Freydis turned to see the Doctor running towards her.

'Stay out of this, Laplander!' she shouted.

The Doctor stood between Freydis and the Skraeling. The simple girl seemed to understand that Freydis was angry, and curled in towards the Doctor like a kitten at his coat-tails.

'She doesn't know what she's doing,' said the Doctor. 'She meant no harm.'

'I'll show her harm!' snarled Freydis. 'She's a Skraeling thief!'

'No,' said the Doctor. 'You misunderstand!'

Freydis yelled and charged, aiming through the Doctor at the Skraeling. He blocked her with an involuntary cry of his own as the broom haft thudded down on his arm. The tin he had been carrying dropped from his arm and bounced across the fire, tumbling into a corner, its contents rattling.

Freydis came from a family notorious for its impulsiveness. Brother Leif had been the man who sailed straight from Iceland to Norway, not thinking of navigation, but pointing his vessel towards the rising sun and sailing forth with foolhardy trust in the old gods. Ask me and I shall tell you of it, but not now. Father Eirik had been an outcast not once but twice for his murderous rage when wronged. Fiercely protective, had he been, of his possessions, enough to kill a man over the loan of some furniture. Ask me and I shall tell you the story of the bench-boards. But not now.

There were not many dishes in Vineland. And Freydis knew that the last potter had left with Ivar's boat.

For her future misdeeds, which we shall not discuss here, Freydis is known as the blight of the Greenlanders, her descendants cursed with an unnameable fate. But on this occasion, should we not see her in some sympathy, as a hearth-proud woman who sees a thief plundering her possessions?

This 'Doctor' we know less of. For his future great deeds, which we shall not discuss here, the Doctor is known as the saviour of the Vinelanders, he who led them away from certain death at the hands of vengeful Skraelings, he who mourned the passing of the friend we never met, he who walks in the shadows, and he who returned once more into the forests, in search of his Tar Dith, the nature of which our chroniclers can only guess at. Thought by some to be some pit of strange oils, and by others to be a woman with blue hair, our only surety being its allure to him, that he would leave us behind and walk once more into the woods, even knowing then of the dangers to him from the newly covetous and belligerent Skraelings.

But I digress. For at this moment can we not see the Doctor as Freydis did? As an interloper of suspicious origin, dressed like a Lappish sorcerer, yet keeping the company of screechers and flinchers, ready to defend a thief plundering the homestead of Eirik the Red's infamous daughter.

So Freydis struck at him, and he warded her off, without a weapon, while the Skraeling girl wept and cried and imitated the raging screams of Freydis.

Out by the pile of trading furs, the men heard the cries. The brothers Helgi and Finnbogi heard Freydis screaming and they laughed, for they were used to her unnecessary rages and her goading of her menfolk.

Thorfinn, however, seeing his own wife Gudrid close by to the incident, turned to see the source of all the fuss. The Skraelings too, made to go towards the commotion.

'No!' said Tyrkir the German very clearly and emphatically. 'No. You shall not enter our camp. You shall stay here.'

But the Doctor was not there to explain, even in his halting accented way, nor did the Skraelings understand.

There are those who doubt this. You have seen the way I imitate Tyrkir the German. Is it not obvious that someone who speaks and gestures in such a fashion should not want his listener to approach closer? But how are we to know the Skraeling mind? These wretches are barely human, how might they comprehend us? Yes, I see there are those in the crowd with another theory. Those who have traded with liars and thieves, the Finns and the Anglians, you know how such transgressors might plead ignorance of our ways. Perhaps the Skraelings were always intent on plunder and thievery, arriving in such numbers, fit to bully us into doing their will, fit to carry off our possessions.

They ignored Tyrkir's exhortations and crossed the line into the encampment, full of obvious, or at least feigned, concern for their female companion. Tyrkir the German grabbed at the arm of one, and the Skraeling turned to him and hollered, striking him. Tyrkir grabbed at his axe, but the Skraeling snatched it too, lashing out and catching Tyrkir below the ribs.

Tyrkir the German fell bleeding, while the Skraeling stared in surprise at the axe, as if it were Thor's very hammer. He threw it from him as if it were burning his hand, as if shocked and surprised at its power to wound.

Who are these Skraelings, these screechers and flinchers, that they adopt a warrior's attitude, but are fearful of true weapons? Such is the way with trade. It is conducted beneath the edge of a sword. When strengths are unequal, it ceases to be trade. When one has swords and the other does not, it is not trade, but tribute.

Swords, however, were in short supply. These men of Greenland and Iceland were far from new metals, far from sturdy trees. Their ships were old and creaking and, back in Norway, would long since have been burned in funeral rites or sunk in blockades. Their weapons too were old, heirlooms and farming tools. None but the brothers Finnbogi and Helgi had real swords, and those had they stolen from an Irish grave.

No matter, they used them. As Tyrkir fell, the brothers Finnbogi and Helgi drew their swords and charged. The Skraeling who had so foolishly cast away Tyrkir's axe was struck down, and the nearest screechers and flinchers recoiled in shock. Further back, a Skraeling took out a bow and nocked an arrow.

Someone called in warning to the brothers Finnbogi and Helgi, as the arrows began to fly. The other men of Iceland and Greenland rushed the Skraelings too, and soon a battle was joined.

We have been here before. We have fought brave Anglians at Maldon, and foolhardy Irish at Dubh Linn. We have fought each other day on day, year on year, until the laws of the Iceland Thing made fighting for its own sake a punishable offence. We have fought far to the south, as soldiers for hire to the kings of Greekland, against Serkland. We have fought in Serkland itself, for the princes of Baghdad, against the men of the marsh and the creatures of the east. We have raided in the land of hot sands, and carried off the Blue Men. We have slaughtered cowardly, pleading scholar monks in the islands of Britain. But I digress.

We have fought Skraelings before, in the hunting grounds north of the Greenland colonies. There, they swept about on skis and hid amid the snows, picking at us with arrows and spears. These screechers and flinchers of Vineland had no axes, but they had spears and arrows. They grappled with us, such that, even as we felled them, others leapt to seize our heads and limbs. There was hurting, likened to a brawl at a homestead, but it was the screechers and the flinchers who came off worse. Even as the simpleton Skraeling girl ran from the house of Freydis, screaming away from the camp, so too did the other Skraelings turn to flee.

Freydis herself ran at them, snatching up Tyrkir's fallen axe, bellowing at them to be gone with their thieving ways, lest she visit the vengeance of Odin the Battle-blind upon them.

And with their departure, taking the red felt but leaving the pile of pelts, the Skraelings were gone, leaving three of their number dead behind, and Tyrkir the German on the ground.

Gudrid of the long braids stood unmoving by the entranceway to her house, her child Snorri still sleeping at her breast. The Doctor left her side, to go to Tyrkir the German.

'What kind of Doctor are you?' yelled Freydis, the axe still in her hand, standing above him.

But Tyrkir saw the Doctor in a different light, and addressed him as a skald, saying: 'Will you sing my death-song? Will you remember me to yourself and others, that Tyrkir the German will not be forgotten like a shadow?'

And the Doctor, seeing that Tyrkir's wounds were grave, agreed and held Tyrkir as he went to the hall of the slain.

When Tyrkir was dead, the Doctor looked to Freydis of the red hair.

'The Skraelings will return,' he said. 'Maybe not for a year, but they will be back, and there will be no thought of trade.'

'Let them come,' said Freydis, hurling the axe into the earth and stomping back to her longhouse.

Although Tyrkir was gone, there was happiness in the camp. The men had something new to talk of, beyond previous incidents of no importance, like the fire in the sauna hut which none thought was funny. There had been a battle, however small, and they had gained a victory, however brief. None spoke of the numbers of the Skraelings; like Freydis of the red hair, they chattered excitably of the battles to come, now that they had enemies.

Thorfinn made to say that there was a difference between raiding on enemies and defending a homestead against them. They were not a-viking here, able to sail in, raid and flee. This was their home, they would defend it. There was nowhere to run. But he did not say this at the time. Instead, he told me, his son, many years later, and I add this information here.

Some thought of the Doctor as an agent of the Skraelings, but Tyrkir's kin knew he had the blood-debt of Tyrkir upon him and that, as his death-poet, he would be honoured. So they left him, with his strange tin drum, lost in thought in the quiet places of the camp, where Gudrid of the long braids took her child Snorri, the teller of this tale, to soothe him.

'Now what shall you do?' asked the Doctor.

Gudrid stared glumly at the baby in her arms.

'Freydis will not want to leave,' she said. 'She will take some persuading. And even if we do, I still doubt there is room for all of us on the boat.'

'What if,' said the Doctor, 'I go with some of your people on the boat. I can guide it back to Greenland, come back with help. Remove you all from this land before Freydis and her like cause troubles that cannot be undone.'

'You are a pathfinder?' asked Gudrid.

'I am the Doctor,' said the Doctor cryptically. 'But I can guide you back. I can help your people quit this land before it destroys you.'

'And what is your price?' asked Gudrid nervously. For Lappish sorcerers always demanded the strangest and most costly of rewards for their services. The Doctor held up his strange drum.

'Only this,' said the Doctor. 'That partway I may drop these ashes in the water, and say farewell to a friend.'

Gudrid waited anxiously for a 'but', but there was none.

'Then we have a deal,' she said, speaking not just as Gudrid, but as the wife of Thorfinn Karlsefni and the rightful head woman of the group. If Freydis did not like it, she could tell it to the winds and fast waters. And Freydis would not like it.

And so the Doctor with no other name became the pathfinder on the seas for the voyage back to Greenland. But of his return to Vineland and the events that ensued, that is another story for another time.

Ask me and I shall tell you of the killings and the curse. But not now.

Resonance

Ben Woodhams

An Adventure of the Fifth Doctor

Pay attention. This is important.

The string twisted like a drowning snake, thrashing through 13 dimensions. It jerked and jumped in harmony with its partners, kicking up quantum foam from the substrate of reality. Together they danced and, in dancing, sang the song of the spheres, loud and clear, keeping time with the cosmos.

Vworp.

Then the song began to shift. The quantum froth came to a boil, changing its tune, skipping to and fro across the boundaries between there and not-there, between be and not-be. The strings resonated to a new noise, coalescing out of quantum clouds into particles that, in turn, accreted into atoms.

Vworp.

As they fell in step with this new song, reality swayed to its rhythm. There, not-there; be, not-be; and back again. Interference, pulsing back and forth until, finally, the new song swamped the old, drowning out its frequencies. Quantum probabilities resolved, collapsing into physical structures, trumpeting this new melody out across the cosmos for anyone who had ears to hear.

Vworp.

And so, on a dusty hillside, the song climaxed with the gentle creak of a hinge, the clatter of a rickety door, as a man emerged from a tall, wooden box. Squinting into the sunlight, he adjusted his panama hat and strode out through the heat haze. He had a way to walk and time was not on his side.

It would have been wrong to call it a café, although one could occasionally get poor, gritty coffee. Nor was it much of an excuse for a bar but there were tables, chairs and a few scattered regulars. A pall of smoke clung to the ceiling and Isaac hunched as he lifted his satchel over his shoulder and moved across the room.

He barely dared look at the alcove in the corner. He kept his eyes fixed on the other patrons snoring into their chipped cups. Only once he had installed himself on the rickety stool by the wall did he look up to see his contact.

A man sat opposite him, peering through his half-moon glasses at what passed for a local newspaper. There was precious little news in it, of course. Isaac knew that the articles dealing with the intensive industrialisation of rural areas were shameless fictions for the benefit of party morale and – perhaps more importantly – Moscow. He also knew that, outside the inner circles of government and the Directorate of State Security, he was the only person in the city who knew this.

With the possible exception of the man sitting opposite him. The man with Isaac's life in his hands.

Isaac coughed. He hadn't meant to, he'd just gone to take a breath and it had stuck in his throat. The man's eyes flicked up over his glasses and widened.

'Elbasan is beautiful at this time of year,' Isaac began, but the other man cut him off.

'Oh, no,' he said, flipping his newspaper closed and getting up to leave. 'Oh, no. I have to go.'

'Wait!' Isaac grabbed him by the wrist, his breathing shallow. 'We must talk.'

'No,' said the man, pulling his arm gently away and standing up. 'No, we really mustn't.'

Isaac felt the room beginning to swim around him but managed to fix the other man's gaze. 'Yes,' he said, 'we really must.'

For a moment, the man just stood there, angry but indecisive. Then he sat down and sighed.

'All right, then,' said the Doctor, removing his glasses and pinching the bridge of his nose. 'Just don't tell me anything I don't already know.'

'This had better be something I want to hear,' Kel Xhixa said, although he knew it was unlikely. There was no response but the sound of Buza's heavy boots crossing the room to stand beside him. Xhixa didn't look around – you spent enough time in the Directorate, you learned to recognise the sound of your colleagues' boots, in proportion with how likely it was to culminate in a cosh to the back of the head. Xhixa knew Buza's boots pretty well.

Xhixa had binoculars jammed up against his face, peering through a window over the boulevard, down the shady alleyway beyond. Buza snickered.

'He's gone into the bar,' he said.

Xhixa looked away from the window, stared into Buza's podgy face and waved his binoculars at him. 'I know that!' he spat. 'What do you think these are? Some kind of eyepress?'

Buza's smile faltered. 'What's an eyepress?'

Xhixa ignored him, not least because he wasn't entirely sure. He turned back to the window and resumed observation of the alleyway.

'What about Command?' he asked, with only the loosest expectation of a coherent answer.

'What about Command?'

'What did Rexhepi say when you told him?'

'Told him what?'

Xhixa knew better than to allow himself to get exasperated by this. After all, theirs was a great country. It had survived bigger idiots than Buza.

'What we were doing.'

'Not much.'

'Not much as in, "If he lays a hand on Isaac, I am going to have him incarcerated, tortured and shot"? That kind of not much?'

'Not that I noticed, no.'

Xhixa was surprised. On the other hand, he wasn't totally convinced that, had Rexhepi told Buza to make sure Isaac was off limits, Buza would have understood him anyway. Rexhepi's managerial, borderline-psychotic threats tended to be made as thinly disguised euphemisms, but even a thin disguise could be enough to fox Buza.

What was more, even if Buza had understood Rexhepi, he might want nothing more than for Xhixa to get into the kind of trouble that left you wondering where your kneecaps were. But no, Xhixa considered, Buza simply didn't have that level of guile in him; or, if he did, he was too busy employing it in managing to be overweight while the rest of the country was experiencing what was essentially, if not officially, a famine.

He looked back to Buza. 'So we're clear to proceed?'

'Uh huh,' Buza replied, clearly pleased, in his deficient kind of way, to be the bearer of glad tidings.

Xhixa was unsure how to react. He had imagined this moment so many times it had taken on the flavour of a caricature. The reality could only be a disappointment. Or maybe it was that he found Buza's incessant grin, always on the point of a dribble, disconcerting.

Still, Xhixa had never been allowed to get this close before and he wasn't about to mess up now.

'Get down there,' he told Buza. 'Tell Pashko to stick to him like glue. No, wait. Not like glue, that'll tip him off. Tell him to...' He looked at Buza's vacant face gazing at the empty street below. 'Actually, tell you what,' he said. 'I'll go. Try not to shoot anything before I get back.'

'I'd heard you were looking for me,' said Isaac.

'Really?' said the Doctor.

'No,' said Isaac, with feeling. 'You were just gone. For a while I thought maybe they got you. But I know you too well for that...'

The Doctor was staring off into the middle distance. Deliberately not listening, Isaac realised. Not wanting to hear.

'Every time I leave my apartment,' he explained, desperately trying to keep the desperation out of his voice, 'I think I'm going to get shot in the back. I know you think I've tricked you, and you've every right to be angry. But I'm living in fear of my life and I didn't know what else to do.'

The Doctor pulled an envelope from his pocket and placed it on the table. When Isaac had smuggled it out six months ago it had been pristine white. Now it was worn around the edges, yellow with age. Passed from pillar to post and then tucked in a UN folder for decades, Isaac imagined, before finding its way to the intended recipient.

'I don't regret leaving,' Isaac went on. 'It was the right thing to do. It was time. I found someone I loved, who I thought loved me. And for a while it was everything I could have asked for. I mean, living here isn't exactly a bed of roses.' His voice dropped to a whisper. 'The Directorate makes sure of that. But it had its compensations. They were worth it.' He took a sip from his cup and winced. 'She was worth it.'

'She died,' said the Doctor, not looking up.

'No.'

'I'm sor...' he started automatically. 'What?'

'She didn't die.'

Puzzlement flashed across the Doctor's face, then realisation. 'Ah,' he said. 'I see.'

'Yes,' murmured Isaac.

'You were... protected while you were together?'

'Yes. I didn't really appreciate it at the time, but yes.'

'But then she left you. And now you want me to bail you out of your life.'

Isaac was stung. 'I want you to *save* my life! Don't imagine that this is easy for me, or that I'm somehow incapable of facing the consequences of my choices – that the party's over and now I want Daddy to give me a lift home. You left me here and don't tell me you didn't know what was going to happen.'

Now it was the Doctor's turn to look stung. He leaned forward, removing his spectacles. 'Well, if I didn't before, I certainly will now. You're condemning me for something I haven't even done yet – and breaking some fundamental laws of time in the process. These things have consequences.'

Isaac took a deep breath. 'Look, all I'm asking for is a way out. It's the work of minutes for you. Just take me away from here, drop me off somewhere I'm marginally less likely to be killed and you need never see me again.'

'Except we both know that's not true,' said the Doctor. 'I will see you again. That's something I can't run away from and every minute I spend with you now, every word that comes out of your mouth, the more difficult that becomes.'

'Not for me. It's all ancient history – but the Directorate, the secret police, the death squads, that's my here and now. Plus...' Isaac's voice tailed off.

'Plus?'

'Plus she broke my heart. I want to live, Doctor. But more than that, I want to go somewhere else... so that I can be someone else.' He broke off, afraid he'd said too much. 'Oh, what's the point? You're not even human. You wouldn't understand.'

The Doctor didn't say anything for some time after that. He stared into the middle distance, resting his head on his hands. Isaac had never seen him look tired before. Eventually, the Doctor looked up.

'You'd think,' he said, rising from his seat. 'All right, let's go'.

Xhixa was trying to explain the situation to Pashko when he saw Isaac emerge from the alleyway into the glare of the boulevard.

'All right,' he said. 'Let's... hold on. Who's that?'

They watched from the shadows of a side street as a man followed Isaac out into the road, wedging a panama on to his head. If Isaac was trying to keep a low profile, Xhixa thought, he ought not to hang around with people dressed in whites. Especially not in a country where wielding a cricket bat was regarded as dangerously bourgeois.

'I don't know,' Pashko said, stating the obvious. 'Why can't we just arrest them and beat it out of them like normal? That one in the beige is just asking for it, walking about like that.'

Xhixa failed to make his sigh inaudible. 'Because,' he said. 'I want. To see. For myself.' Pashko shrugged and wrinkled his nose. They waited until Isaac and his conspirator turned a corner, on to the main route going west from the city, and moved out.

'We keep a low profile. I don't want them spooked,' said Xhixa, shielding his eyes from the glare of Buza's binoculars conspicuously flashing from the other side of the boulevard.

'All right,' said Pashko. 'Let's go.'

Mama Nukshiqui wasn't in the best of moods when she came out onto her roof to find a complete stranger standing there. Then again, Mama Nukshiqui hadn't been in the best of moods since a warm summer's night in 1932 involving a bottle of raki and a young ploughman from the next village. On this occasion, however, she'd just struggled up far too many steps with a basket of sodden laundry and wasn't afraid to share.

'Hey, you!' she called. The man turned slowly to face her. He was dressed in grey with a tall hat perched above his smooth, grey forehead. A strange white flower, garish against the gloom of his coat, was propped up in his lapel. It didn't seem to mind the heat.

He smiled at her, flashing yellow-stained teeth. It didn't reach his eyes.

'What are you doing up here?' she demanded. Mama Nukshiqui had seen off revolutionary hordes in her time. She wasn't going to be charmed or intimidated by some freak in fancy dress.

He gestured out over the rooftops. Nukshiqui looked and saw two men walking out of the city, followed by another three. Whatever. It was none of her business. She threw down her washing.

'Now, look here,' she commanded. 'I don't know what you think you're doing up here...'

She faltered. The man had closed his eyes. He was moving his hand through the air, like a conjuror, and... What was that? Was he *humming*?

His eyes flicked open and he smiled again. And Mama Nukshiqui realised that he wasn't humming, yet the music continued. The air shimmered beside her – heat haze, rippling like the surface of a pond in a cool breeze.

'Hey!' She was shouting now. 'You listen to me! I don't want to see you up on my roof ever again! You understand?'

Then the shimmering air seemed to *swallow*, and a black void opened up beside her. She tried to find the words.

The grey man bore down on her, his hand moving at dizzying speed as he pushed her. Hard.

Isaac could hardly keep the smile off his face.

'It's barely changed at all.' He grinned, staring around the console room. 'That is, it will barely have changed...'

'Enough,' said the Doctor, attempting to occupy himself by prodding various controls, apparently at random, as the console chirruped its usual melody of query and response. 'I already told you: I don't want to know.'

'And I'm the man who knows too much.'

For the first time that day, Isaac saw the Doctor smile. 'Literally. Careless talk costs the fundamental structure of the space-time continuum, and all that.'

'Then what are we waiting for? The sooner we're out of here, the sooner I'm out of your hair and the space-time continuum can rest...'

'Hello,' said the Doctor. 'What's this?'

A small light on the console had started flashing and beeping. The Doctor played with the controls around it, trying to calm it down and, failing, thumped the console with his fist. It didn't work. 'Oh, dear,' he said.

Isaac sighed. 'What's the matter?'

The Doctor frowned. 'The TARDIS is picking up some sort of localised disturbance in the, er...'

'The space-time continuum?'

'Um,' said the Doctor. 'Yes. It could be a fault in the quantum environment monitors, but...' He disappeared under the console and the incessant beeping was joined by a chorus of thumps. 'But,' he continued, springing to his feet, 'I just want you to know that if it isn't – and it isn't – it's probably all your fault.'

'Er. Sorry?'

'Bit late for that.' The Doctor smacked the door control with his palm and grabbed his panama from the hatstand.

'Where are you going?' Isaac demanded.

'To investigate, of course.' He swept through the TARDIS doors, which glided closed behind him. Isaac was left alone but for his embarrassment, the hum of the TARDIS, the beeping from the console and, after a moment, the rattling of a key in a lock.

The Doctor poked his head round the door. He grinned. 'Coming?'

Isaac could hardly move fast enough.

'The thing about intense localised quantum fluctuations,' said the Doctor once they were outside, 'is that they're very intense.'

'Doctor...' Isaac began.

'Shush,' said the Doctor, sweeping his sonic screwdriver across the dirt path before them. He was staring intently at the ground and seemed to be listening for pitch changes. 'Very intense and very localised,' he went on. 'Which is to say that they're usually very, very small.'

'Doctor...' repeated Isaac.

'I said shush. So small, in fact, that the TARDIS monitor wouldn't usually bother to pick them up, let alone beep about them. Which suggests that there's something unusual about these.'

'Doctor, really...' said Isaac.

'I'm serious,' continued the Doctor. 'And they're very, very intense – did I mention that? Which means they can lead to all sorts of...'

The Doctor found himself looking at a pair of shoddy brogues. He looked up and found himself staring down the barrel of a shoddy revolver.

'... unexpected results,' he finished.

'I tried to tell you,' Isaac whimpered.

'Shush,' said the Doctor.

It was the third time the Doctor had walked between the foothills and the city that day, Isaac knew, but he didn't seem to be feeling it. If anything, he had actually perked up once they were arrested. Back on familiar ground, Isaac supposed. For his part, Isaac's feet were already killing him, and his satchel strap was chafing his shoulder. It was hard to hitch up when your hands were cuffed.

As for the Directorate agents escorting them, Isaac was only glad they hadn't killed him on the spot. Certainly, they knew who he was – or the one back at the TARDIS did. He seemed to be in charge and had stayed behind to examine the curious blue box, wondering aloud how to transport it back to the city.

Meanwhile, the fat one led the way, sweating profusely, while the one bringing up the rear – Pashko, apparently – was using the time productively by asking precisely the sort of questions that neither the Doctor nor Isaac could answer: who, what, why, where and when.

On reflection, Isaac realised, there weren't many questions he *could* answer. He began to resign himself to a night of police brutality followed by summary execution in the morning. The Doctor wasn't helping.

'Do you know,' the Doctor breezily asked Pashko, 'that you've not said a single thing that didn't start with a "W" and end with a question mark? Now, I'm all in favour of an enquiring mind, but there are limits when it comes to polite conversation.'

'What were you doing out here?' barked Pashko, punctuating his question with a jab of the revolver in the small of Isaac's back. Isaac thought this rather unfair, especially since the principal source of Pashko's irritation was the person answering:

'Ornithology. Unique habitat in this part of the world. Oh, look, there's a buzzard. Or is it a falcon? Some sort of raptor, at any rate. Sorry, birds were never my strong point.'

'What were you looking for when we found you?' Pashko repeated for what felt like the twentieth time, only with considerably less conviction than when he'd started.

The Doctor stopped in his tracks. 'That,' he said, nodding at a small wilderness to the side of the path. Beyond it was a steep drop, overlooking the TARDIS, where the Directorate agent was shrugging and walking away in exasperation. But that wasn't what had caught the Doctor's eye.

Isaac followed his gaze. At first, he couldn't quite make it out. It seemed like heat haze, the landscape beyond washing about, lapping at the shore of the hillside. Then he saw it: the heat haze was clear, defined: an oval of undulation hanging in the air.

The fat agent came back down the path to join them, gazing at the shimmering window. 'What's that?' he asked.

'Oh, not you as well.' The Doctor sighed. 'I honestly don't know. It doesn't look like any quantum fluctuation I've ever seen.'

'See a lot of that, do you?' wondered Isaac.

'All the time,' said the Doctor. 'Normally well below the threshold of human perception, though. Not like this.'

'Quiet!' ordered Pashko, as the fat man walked up to the phenomenon. 'Buza, don't touch it!'

'Am I allowed not to be quiet if I agree with you in the strongest possible terms?' asked the Doctor.

'Quiet!'

'Oh, suit yourself. He really shouldn't touch it, though.'

'Listen to him!' shouted Isaac, moving towards Buza. 'He knows what he's talking about!'

'Why?' asked Buza. His voice was dreamy, as he stared into the literally rolling countryside beyond. He raised his hand, and the air before it convulsed and twisted. And tore.

'Get back!' the Doctor shouted. 'You don't know what it'll...'

It was too late. Buza reached out to the black, inky pearl hanging in space. It opened up to receive him, tendrils of darkness gently probing forward, brushing his fingers. In the blink of an eye, opening up into a vast maw, it leapt forward and in one swift movement swallowed him.

He was gone. There was nothing. Pashko simply stood there gawping while the Doctor and Isaac rushed to the spot where, moments before, Buza had stood. Its Buzalessness was palpable. There was no man, no heat haze, no hole in space. Nothing but the late afternoon sun spreading across the hillside.

'Right,' said Xhixa, coming around the corner of the path behind them. He pulled up short. 'Where's Buza?'

They stared at him.

Xhixa stared at the Doctor and Isaac as they lay slumped in a Directorate holding cell. This was ridiculous. Two handcuffed men – neither of whom, frankly, looked like he'd be much use in a ruck – against two armed Directorate agents, and they'd managed to do away with one and send the other mad. No wonder Isaac had been off-limits to the Directorate for so long if this was what happened when you tried to investigate him.

He just couldn't understand it. Buza may have been a halfwit, but that was the least of his qualities compared to his mastery of those that the Directorate regarded as essential to the cause of national security: thuggishness, single-mindedness and a certain sort of boorish anti-intellectualism. Exactly the qualities to be relied upon when attacked by a couple of handcuffed weedy blokes on a hillside. Tch.

Worse, Pashko backed up their story about the air coming to life and eating him. Truth to tell, Xhixa could have got away with shooting Buza had the mood taken him – which it frequently had, to be honest, but he'd always resisted. To lose a man under your command to a collective delusion, however, was the kind of thing that got you laughed at in the Directorate canteen. And things that got you laughed at in the Directorate canteen could easily turn out to be things that got you killed.

Great.

He heard a noise from the far end of the cellblock. Perhaps it was Pashko, coming back with orders from Commander Rexhepi.

He struggled to his feet. 'Where the hell have you be...?' he began, only to be cut short by the sight of Rexhepi himself marching towards him with a guard unit in tow. Behind them, in the darkness of the cellblock, he could dimly make out Pashko, looking shifty, with Colonel Lukaj, head of internal investigations, keeping him on a short leash.

Great.

Xhixa saluted Rexhepi with as much enthusiasm as he could muster. To his surprise, Rexhepi didn't shoot him on the spot but simply nodded curtly in return.

'Inspector.'

'Commander.'

'I understand you have two subversives in your custody.'

'Well, er, I'm not actually sure what they are as yet, sir, but –'

'You will transfer them to my custody immediately.'

Voices echoed up the cellblock:

'Wake up, Isaac – we're going for another walk.'

'Ooh, lovely. I could do with stretching my legs.'

Some insane, suicidal impulse at the back of Xhixa's mind almost made him ask why. Almost made him protest that he'd been itching to investigate Isaac – a man with no past, whose entire official identity was a transparent forgery – for years. Almost made him protest that, having been refused permission for nigh on half a decade, it had finally been granted him, and now Rexhepi wanted to deny him the simple satisfaction of a proper interrogation.

Almost made him scream in Rexhepi's face.

But then Xhixa saw a muscle twitching in the corner of Rexhepi's eye, and something in his gut told him that misbehaviour of any kind would be a very bad idea indeed. He heard the words coming out of his mouth as though they came from someone else.

'Of course, sir. Right away.'

And so he watched as his prize – along with this new, greater, enigma – was escorted out of his possession. 'Cheerio, then,' said the Doctor as they left, followed by a frankly terrified Pashko, who couldn't have looked more like a prisoner if he'd been strapped to an electric chair. Xhixa resisted the urge to shiver.

Rexhepi followed his entourage to the cellblock entrance, where he turned back to Xhixa.

'Before I go, Inspector.' He smiled. 'One last thing.'

'Sir?'

'According to the testimony of Detective Pashko, you were not present to witness Sergeant Buza's demise. Is that correct?'

'Yes, sir.'

'You didn't see anything... unusual?'

'I did,' came Isaac's voice from the doorway.

'All I saw was that Buza was no longer there, sir,' said Xhixa.

'You're absolutely sure?'

'Quite sure. Sir.'

Rexhepi nodded, satisfied. 'Thank you for your assistance, Inspector. Good day.' The commander left the cellblock.

Xhixa was surprised to discover that he could breathe again.

Great.

The Doctor and Isaac were bundled out of the transport car into the night air, up the stairs of an imposing government building. Isaac had at least been relieved of his satchel, now slung over the shoulder of a uniformed monobrow who'd made it his business to shove Isaac whenever it was most likely to make him stumble.

'Where are we?' the Doctor hissed to Isaac.

'Central Command of the Directorate of National Security,' Isaac hissed back. 'Think of it as the Ministry of Love.'

The Doctor stopped to admire the façade. 'Oh, good,' he said. 'I always like to take in the sights.'

'Quiet!' hissed the monobrow.

'Love the columns,' continued the Doctor. 'Say what you like, but there's always a certain Wagnerian something about the civic architecture of a megalomaniacal dictatorship.' A thought struck him. 'Maybe that's why I visit so many of them.'

A rifle butt in the shoulder propelled him into the reception, where Rexhepi was arranging yet another transfer of custody. The clerk behind the desk motioned their guard unit down the steps to the basement and a couple of rifle butts later the Doctor and Isaac followed.

A network of dank corridors and stairs, leading ever downwards, brought them to a set of double doors, through which the Doctor and Isaac were shoved to find themselves in a vast, brightly lit chamber. Guards were stationed at every corner and, in the centre, a cadre of men in lab coats were huddled around a desk. What caught Isaac's eye, however, was the array of valves, tubes and ceramics splayed around the walls, towering up towards the distant ceiling, from which hung a solitary, grimy chandelier.

'What on earth...?' Isaac was dumbstruck.

'Ah,' said the Doctor, 'the faded grandeur of a post-monarchical society. And Tesla coils,' he added. 'Lots of Tesla coils.'

'Professor Hu,' Rexhepi called across the room. One of the lab coats disentangled himself from the conference and eagerly trotted over to meet them. Chinese, Isaac guessed. Not just Chinese, but a representative of the Chinese government.

'Commander Rexhepi,' the man said. 'I trust these are our witnesses?'

'Civilian witnesses, yes. One of my men is still being... debriefed. You may do with these, however, as you wish.'

Hu clapped his hands together and rubbed them enthusiastically, eyeing up the Doctor and Isaac. 'Well, now, what are we to make of you?'

The Doctor said something in Chinese.

Hu blinked. And smiled. 'Well, you can't have one,' he said.

'Pity,' said the Doctor, 'I'm parched. What are you up to here, then? I'm the Doctor and this is Isaac, by the way. Say hello, Isaac.'

'Hello,' said Isaac.

Hands still manacled, the Doctor wandered off, gesturing around the room with both arms. Isaac measured his life expectancy in seconds.

'Tesla coils, Wardencliffe field promulgators... Is that a polyphase generator? Quaint.'

If Hu was meant to be impressed it didn't show. He dismissed Rexhepi and his men, and had the Doctor and Isaac's handcuffs removed.

'Tell me,' he said to Isaac as the Doctor busied himself sticking his nose into various items of industrial electronics. 'What did you see up on that hillside?'

Isaac wasn't taken in by the good-cop act, but he couldn't see any harm in telling him.

'And this happened when, precisely?' asked Hu.

'About five o'clock this afternoon,' came the Doctor's voice from behind a bank of switches and valves. 'Hello, what's this?'

'Five o'clock,' mused Hu. 'Precisely when we were conducting today's test.'

'A test?' asked Isaac. 'What were you testing?'

'This, I imagine,' said the Doctor, emerging from behind the switches and indicating a large metal frame, about the size of a man, suspended in a cobweb of coils, tubes and wiring. 'Am I right?'

'Quite correct, Doctor,' said Hu. 'We are conducting experiments into neutralising the action of electrons, and this country is one of the few places on the planet where we have been able to obtain significant results. Unfortunately, our tests seem to be more effective at some times than others. Five o'clock on a Thursday, for example.'

'Thursday?' The Doctor looked over his spectacles. 'What's so special about Thursdays?'

'Only that today is a Thursday. On Mondays to Wednesdays it is about half past eight, more or less.'

'Hold on,' said Isaac.

Hu nodded to one of the lab coats, who began flicking switches about the iron frame. 'Power up! Testing!' he called.

'So, Doctor,' said Hu. 'This effect you witnessed. Did it look anything like this?'

The Doctor and Isaac stepped back from the frame as, slowly but clearly, the air within it began to shimmer and ripple. An unearthly low hum filled the room and, all of a sudden, there was activity everywhere: people taking readings, calling out stress parameters and amperages, instituting safety protocols.

'Yes,' whispered the Doctor.

'Yes,' echoed Isaac. 'It looked a lot like that.'

'How curious,' said Hu. 'Let me show you something else curious. Guard!'

A large brute in uniform was at his side.

'Place your hand within the anti-electron field,' ordered Hu.

'It's not an anti-electron field,' said the Doctor.

'And, trust me, he really doesn't want to stick his arm in it,' said Isaac.

'His loyalty is absolute,' said Hu. True enough, the guard removed his glove and, without hesitation, strode over to the frame and thrust his hand through it.

This time, however, there was no tearing of the air, no black void; only the sizzling of flesh accompanied by screaming, followed by a thud and merciful silence as the guard collapsed to the floor. His forearm was almost entirely missing.

The Doctor ran to the man's side, checked his pulse and breathing. Or, Isaac guessed from the Doctor's face, the lack of either. The Doctor wrinkled his nose. 'That wasn't necessary,' he said.

'You think not?' asked Hu, amused. 'I beg to differ. First, it is important to establish whether what just happened is similar to the phenomenon you witnessed earlier today.'

Hu nodded to a guard detail, who seized the Doctor and forced him to his knees in front of the frame. A hand to the back of his head pushed it towards the field. There was a cracking sound, wisps of smoke, as strands of the Doctor's hair brushed against it.

'And secondly,' Hu continued, 'it is important you understand that, when I say I am going to shove your head through the field unless you tell me what I want to know, I would have absolutely no compunction in doing so.'

Xhixa sat in the cellblock and considered. He could hardly believe his luck, or lack of it. He could feel his blood pressure rise simply by thinking of how Rexhepi had marched in and taken his prisoners. Taken Isaac.

He got to his feet. No, he decided. I've come too far, waited too long, to get to the bottom of who Isaac is. Now this other man had appeared, along with a blue box in the foothills outside the city, while Buza had disappeared and Pashko had apparently gone insane.

More than his need to persecute anyone, he simply needed to know. And there was only one way he was going to do that.

He checked his revolver and made for the door.

'Stop!' shouted Isaac.

'Why?' asked Hu. 'You have something to tell us?'

'Yes,' said Isaac.

'Well, don't just stand there,' the Doctor grimaced, wincing away from the field as his eyebrows began to crackle. 'Tell the man!'

'Your test times,' Isaac began. 'They're the same times my orchestra rehearses.'

Hu looked sceptical but intrigued. 'What of it?' he demanded.

'Well,' Isaac flannelled, 'that's a bit of a coincidence, isn't it? I mean, five o'clock on a Thursday... I wasn't there today – rehearsals would have been cancelled. Tell me if your tests were conclusive today.'

'Today was the first Thursday for two months on which tests have proved... disappointing,' said Hu.

'That's my point! Somehow, there's a correlation between your tests and my orchestra rehearsals.'

Hu signalled the guards to release the Doctor, who shuffled away from the frame and got to his feet.

'How, then? What could such a correlation be?' Hu asked.

'Resonance,' said the Doctor.

'What?'

'Resonance. Peaks and troughs aligning, amplifying their effect. Isaac, where can we find a copy of the piece your orchestra has been rehearsing?'

'It's something I've been working on,' said Isaac. 'My notes are in my bag.'

Motioning the guards to keep their guns trained on the Doctor and Isaac, Hu retrieved Isaac's satchel from a nearby desk. Leafing through the papers within, he found a hefty batch of messily scrawled sheet music. He cut the string and flicked through it, then looked up.

'This means nothing to me. Are you saying that, somehow, when played, this music amplifies the effects of my anti-electron field?'

'I know it sounds crazy –' Isaac began, but the Doctor cut him off.

'I told you: it's not an anti-electron field. What you have here is a comprehensive nullfield. It doesn't just inhibit electrons, it actually shuts down the entire fabric of space-time at the Planck length. On a quantum level.' He looked up at Hu. 'Congratulations, Professor. You've invented *nothing*.'

'Is that possible?' asked Isaac.

'It's a new one on me,' the Doctor admitted. 'And there's no way the good professor here managed to come up with it all on his own. Probably some alien involvement. Here –' he strode up to Hu and, ignoring the sound of rifles cocking, snatched the sheet music '– let me look at that.'

'Can you understand it?' asked Hu.

Isaac shrugged. 'I wrote it and I don't.'

'Music and quantum physics, Professor,' said the Doctor, peering through his glasses at the paper. 'Vital to understand the two: the sign of an enlightened renaissance mind. You should get out more.'

Hu's frustration was growing. 'You mean that, somehow, the fundamental structure of the universe is encoded on that sheaf of paper?'

The Doctor shrugged and half nodded.

'Novello awards, here I come,' said Isaac.

'Not today, I'm afraid,' said the Doctor, looking up.

'What do you mean?'

'I mean that, in the hands of our Red Army friends here, let alone anyone else, this information is an appallingly deadly weapon. That's right, isn't it, Professor? This isn't just theoretical particle physics you're working on. It's weapons development.'

Hu bowed slightly. 'It is essential if we are to retain socio-economic and political parity with the decadent forces of –'

'Oh, do be quiet,' the Doctor snapped, looking up at Isaac as he clutched the sheaf in his hands. 'The bottom line is, this music has the power to raze entire worlds. And I can't let that happen.'

Suddenly, the Doctor twisted on the spot and sprinted for all he was worth towards the nullfield. Behind him, he could hear Isaac's scream of protest and the sound of Hu desperately ordering his guards not to fire. Before him, he saw not the nullfield, but W. G. Grace squaring up at the stumps.

Then Grace was swallowed by a vast, oily black maw – an expanding balloon of nothingness that swamped the whole pitch. Behind the Doctor, the gasps of soldiers and scientists clashed with Isaac's furious yelling, as the Doctor fell in front of the frame, sliding to a halt, staring at the papers in his hand.

'It doesn't matter,' he breathed. 'It doesn't matter whether you play the music. All that matters is that it's there. And –'

His voice died away as he saw the figure before him, stepping out of the nullfield and extending an arm. He wore an undertaker's suit, complete with top hat and flower in the lapel. A black rose.

He reached forward, lithely, and in an instant had snatched the papers out of the Doctor's hands.

'Commander Rexhepi brought some prisoners in for interrogation earlier,' Xhixa told Directorate Command's desk sergeant, flashing his badge. The sergeant motioned him down the stairs to the central security laboratory and, once out of his view, Xhixa ran.

Arriving at the doors, he kicked his way through, revolver at the ready, only to see the Doctor running towards him in a panic, a sheaf of paper clutched in his hands. Behind him, in the centre of the room, Isaac was grappling with a tall man dressed in black while a Chinaman in a lab coat seemed to be having some sort of apoplectic fit. Armed guards were running this way and that, rifles at their shoulders, to no real effect.

The Doctor skidded to a halt in front of him, disoriented. 'Isaac!' he shouted. 'Where's Isaac?'

Lost for words, Xhixa pointed at the frame and the Doctor turned just in time to see Isaac, enveloped in the arms of the man with the black rose, being pulled back into the mirror.

'Doc–' began Isaac.

The ripple effect closed around their arms and legs as though they were sinking into mercury. Then they were gone. The hum of the power grid faded away and there was nothing left in the frame but clear air.

Stunned, the Doctor stumbled back into the laboratory and, after shoving the papers into his pocket, rested his hands on the frame, his head bowed. A guard made to club him with the butt of his rifle, but Hu motioned him away.

Visibly shaken, Hu approached the Doctor and laid a hand on his shoulder.

'Tell me what we have to do,' he said.

'What?' The Doctor looked up. 'To get Isaac back?'

Hu blinked. 'No,' he said, as though it were obvious. 'To recreate that effect.'

The Doctor smiled a thin, joyless smile. 'Same difference,' he said.

At three o'clock in the morning, the civic concert hall was usually a dead place, echoing only with the ghosts of ancient performers and performances. On this particularly Friday morning, however, it was a hive of rather sleepy activity. The principal members of the city orchestra yawned and scratched themselves as they unpacked their instruments and took their places in the pit, groggily gossiping among themselves, wondering why they had been dragged from their beds by a Directorate agent in the middle of the night and thankful that they hadn't simply been taken out and shot. Perhaps their leader was suffering from insomnia, some suggested, and wanted a forty-piece orchestra to lull him to sleep.

Silence fell as a man strode to the conductor's podium and tapped his baton on the stand.

'Good evening, ladies and gentlemen,' said the Doctor, brushing the hair from his eyes. 'I suppose you're wondering why I've called you here this morning. And where Isaac is.'

There was a muted chorus of assent.

'Well,' the Doctor continued, 'I'm afraid Isaac is in a great deal of trouble. That's partly my fault and I'm sorry. But I know that you'll all do everything you can to help him. I know that you won't let him down. And neither will I.'

He placed the sheaf of papers from his pocket on the stand in front of him and coughed. 'From the top, please.'

Xhixa watched from the back of the stalls as the Doctor raised his baton and the opening strains of Isaac's piece drifted across the auditorium. The effect was almost immediate: he felt the hairs on the back of his neck stand on end. The orchestra was tight: they knew this piece intimately, which was just as well since the Doctor had taken all their copies and burned them in a kettle drum.

Even with an unfamiliar conductor, they were comfortable with the piece – its gentle teasing, its ebb and flow, query and response. It spoke of loves lost, unbounded sorrow and unending joy. The orchestra knew this piece... No, they more than knew it, Xhixa realised. They loved it. As they worked together, it belonged to each and every one of them and yet was utterly faithful to them alone.

His radio unit crackled into life. 'Hello. Inspector Xhixa, hello?' It was Hu.

'Xhixa here.'

'Tell the Doctor he was right: the effect is building. But it is different – our readings are off the scale, and yet I cannot get even a single man to put his hand in it.'

'I'm hardly surprised. I heard what happened last time.'

'No, no. They try – but the field is like a solid wall. Nothing can penetrate it.'

Xhixa looked down at the Doctor, building the orchestra up to the third movement. After the grace of the overture, his arms were now a flurry of sweeping arcs and sudden jabs.

'Good God,' came Hu's voice over the radio. 'This response is incredible! I'm not sure my equipment can collate this volume of data...'

Then the Doctor started shouting over the sound of the orchestra. Xhixa wasn't sure how anyone could make themselves heard over that level of noise. Yet, somehow, the Doctor managed, as though his voice were carried on the music itself.

'Keep playing!' he yelled. 'Keep playing for as long as you can and for all you're worth! Play as though your life depended on it!'

Because Isaac's does, thought Xhixa.

The Doctor leapt from the podium and ran to join Xhixa in the stalls, who told him what Hu had said.

'That's because this Black Rose fellow has locked off that portal,' said the Doctor. 'He must have known I'd try something like this.'

'So what do we do?'

Suddenly, there was a clatter from the fire escape on the other side of the stalls. Light flooded across the seats from the corridor beyond and there, framed in the doorway, stood Commander Rexhepi, wielding his own baton and pointing it right at them. He was screaming something.

'Run!' said the Doctor.

A wave of Directorate guards washing over the seats towards them, the Doctor and Xhixa turned and ran into the lobby, crashing through the ticket hall and out into the open air. Skidding into the road, they were caught in car headlights, and Xhixa realised they were about to be run down. He pulled out his pistol and fired over the vehicle's roof, just as the guardsmen came pouring out of the concert hall.

The car screamed to a halt in front of them. Without pausing for breath, the Doctor hurled himself through an open window. Xhixa, meanwhile, dived for cover on the driver's side as a hail of gunfire pattered on the tarmac around him. He wrenched the door open and shoved his pistol into the driver's face, which quickly shifted from shocked to terrified.

'Out!' Xhixa ordered.

'Er, it is all right if I travel in the back?' asked the driver, glancing at the phalanx of armed men moving towards them. 'I won't cause any trouble.'

'I'm sure that'll be fine,' said the Doctor, manhandling the driver over the handbrake onto the back seats as Xhixa leapt in and, crouched low over the steering wheel, hit the gas. The tyres squealed satisfyingly, but to little effect.

'Why aren't we moving?' the Doctor yelled.

'Ooh, dreadful traction,' came a voice from the back seat. You just have to give it a –'

He was cut off as the car leapt forward, veering wildly across the road, its occupants pinned to their seats. Something whistled past the Doctor's shoulder and embedded itself in the dashboard.

'More speed, please,' suggested the Doctor. 'Away from the guns, for preference.'

'I'm doing my best!' Xhixa shouted, and stalled the engine.

'Well, I'm reassured,' said the Doctor as the car roared back to life and the rear windscreen exploded in a shower of glass. 'Aren't you reassured?' He looked over his shoulder for the owner of the vehicle, only to find the back seat empty.

'Good grief!' he cried. 'Hello? Are you all right?'

'Don't mind me,' came a voice from the footwell behind the Doctor. 'I'm just going to stay down here for a bit, if that's all right with you.'

'Probably sensible,' the Doctor agreed as the car swept around a corner.

'Could you adjust the wing mirror, please, Doctor?' asked Xhixa.

The wing mirror shattered as the Doctor reached for it. He turned back to Xhixa. 'No,' he said.

The whistling around the car and the occasional impact were diminishing as the Directorate guards made for their own vehicles, allowing Xhixa valuable time to shake them off.

'So,' he said, 'where are we heading?'

'We do have one item of information that Black Rose doesn't,' said the Doctor. 'We know of at least one other substantial nullfield. If Professor Hu keeps his generators running and the orchestra keep playing, that might be enough.'

'Enough for what?'

But the Doctor wasn't saying.

The car's owner took to the hills as soon as they stopped. 'Thanks again!' the Doctor called after the diminishing figure scrabbling up the hillside. The man turned and shouted something the Doctor didn't quite catch but Xhixa heard perfectly.

Whatever the nullfield had to be enough for, Xhixa thought, this one probably was. He'd only caught a brief glimpse of the one in Hu's laboratory before but, even at night, this seemed far more impressive. Unbounded by a metal frame, it stretched right across a small meadow by the path, the stars beyond dancing in some sort of synchronised display, the moonlight pooling in the air like a reflection in a darkened mirror.

The Doctor caught his gaze and looked at him reproachfully. 'Yes,' he said. 'Lovely. But I've got work to do.'

'Like what?'

'I thought these quantum fluctuations were nullfields,' the Doctor explained. 'And they are. Except that nothing can exist inside a nullfield. That's the point. It's not just the emptiest thing in the universe. A nullfield is what you get *before* you get a universe.'

'But you saw that man come out of it.'

'Yes. And if he can come out... maybe I can go in.'

'What? You can't be serious!'

'Yes,' said the Doctor. 'I am.'

He approached the field, humming at first, then singing. As he got closer, the dancing stars began to whirl and swing in time with his voice, faster and faster. And then, Xhixa saw, something *tore*...

The Doctor looked over his shoulder.

'Watch my back,' he said and stepped forward.

Xhixa was alone on the hillside.

At first, there was nothing. No light, no space, no time, no mind. No thing.

Then, distantly, quivering on the edge of perception, there was music. A strange, beguiling melody so faint you would have been forgiven for thinking it was not there at all. With it came awareness and clarity.

I am the Doctor.

Feeling his way through point and counterpoint into consciousness, he cast about what passed for his self, searching through the music for any sign of an outside element, any evidence of another mind in the emptiness.

Focusing on harmonies and discords, the Doctor realised that the music was not what he had conducted at the concert hall, but its inverse. Where he had commanded peaks, there were troughs, and vice versa. Isaac's music had resonated almost perfectly with the dance of the cosmos. Almost. And, in that imperfection, there was room for existence in the void.

Ah. There. The Doctor closed in on a particular melody, rich with discord. Somebody was dancing to the beat of a different drum. But before he pulled Isaac out there was something he had to do...

Like a lifeguard clinging to the body of a drowning man, the Doctor broke through the nullfield, collapsing onto the hillside with Isaac in his arms.

'Xhixa,' he gasped, struggling for breath. 'Xhixa, help Isaac.'

'I'm afraid that won't be possible, Doctor.'

The Doctor rolled onto his back to discover Rexhepi staring down at him, a revolver levelled at his head. 'Get up,' Rexhepi ordered.

Scrambling to his feet, the Doctor saw Xhixa sitting on the path, surrounded by guardsmen, trying to staunch the blood from a wound to his leg.

'You didn't really think you were going to get away, did you?' sneered Rexhepi. 'You and your subversive conspiracy have destroyed Professor Hu's project, severely damaging relations between our great nation and the People's Republic.'

'Destroyed?'

'I don't know what you persuaded him to do, but it irreparably damaged the professor's equipment. He will be travelling back to Beijing in the morning to await his fate.' Rexhepi leaned in close to the Doctor. 'Yours, I am pleased to say, will come a lot quicker.'

The Doctor thrust his hands into his pockets and shrugged. 'All in all, a pretty good day's work for me,' he said, grinning. 'And with all copies of Isaac's music destroyed, there's no chance you, or anyone else, can –'

'Destroyed?' coughed Isaac, pulling himself to his feet. 'What do you mean destroyed?'

'I'm sorry,' said the Doctor. 'It's for the best. There's nothing anyone can do to...'

'I can't hear it,' whispered Isaac, realising. 'I can't hear the music in my head.' He turned to face the Doctor, his face flushed with anger. 'I can't hear the music!' he wailed. 'What have you *done*?'

The Doctor examined his shoes intently. 'I'm sorry,' he said. 'You couldn't be allowed...'

'Well,' said Rexhepi, filling the silence that followed. 'This is all very affecting, I'm sure. But, as I was saying...' He turned and pointed his revolver at Xhixa's head. 'For crimes against the state.'

'No!' shouted the Doctor.

'Doctor, I...' Xhixa began, before a gunshot echoing around the hills cut him off. He slumped to the ground.

'Just not your day, is it, Doctor?' Rexhepi laughed. He levelled the gun at Isaac. 'And for my next trick...'

'Go ahead,' said Isaac. 'After the day I've had, the only way is up.'

Rexhepi shrugged. 'Glad to oblige,' he said, as his radio started belching static. Then a small, tinny voice could be heard coming from it, demanding to talk to Rexhepi.

Rexhepi tutted. 'Excuse me,' he said, 'I've got to take this. You know how it is. Receiving, over?'

It was impossible to make out what was being said, but Rexhepi's face spoke volumes. 'Yes, sir,' he said. 'No, sir. Not at all, sir.' He looked up at the crest of the hill beyond the path, and the Doctor tore his eyes away from Xhixa to follow his gaze.

There, up on the hill, silhouetted against the moon, were two figures; a man and a woman. The man was clearly talking into a radio.

'Ettyn,' murmured Isaac. 'Ettyn and Mila.'

'Right away, sir,' Rexhepi was saying. 'No, no, thank *you*, sir.'

Looking put out, Rexhepi clicked his radio off and turned to the Doctor and Isaac, hefting his revolver in his hand. 'It seems some of us have friends in high places,' he said and pointed his gun at the Doctor. 'But not all of us.'

'Doctor!' shouted Isaac. 'Run!' To the Doctor's amazement, Isaac hurled himself at Rexhepi, knocking him to the ground and smothering the pistol with his body.

'What about you?' the Doctor called. 'I can't just...'

His elbow jammed into Rexhepi's throat, guards moving in to restrain him, Isaac looked over his shoulder and finished the Doctor's sentence.

'Just *go*!'

Not for the first time that day, the Doctor found himself looking at the wrong end of a guard detail. He hesitated, just for a moment, and then dived over the edge of the path, down the hillside.

There was nothing Isaac could do as Rexhepi's men pulled him off their commander and punched him in the stomach. Even doubled up, with blood ringing in his ears, he could hear gunshots echo around the valley as the guardsmen attempted to pick the Doctor off as he plummeted down the virtually sheer hillside. He could hear the fury in Rexhepi's voice as his pistol joined the mêlée. And, mere moments later, he could hear their astonishment accompany an old, old song he hadn't heard in years.

Vworp, it went. *Vworp, vworp, vworp.*

It reminded him of a different tune, one that tickled at the back of his mind. A scab of a melody he couldn't stop picking at.

As the soldiers left him there, curled up in the dust, Isaac barely noticed. He was too busy humming.

Walkin' City Blues

Joff Brown

An Adventure of the Sixth Doctor

Though the sound overpowers,
Sing again, with your dear voice revealing
A tone
Of some world far from ours,
Where music and moonlight and feeling
Are one.
To Jane: The Keen Stars Were Twinkling, Percy Bysshe Shelley

The inspector didn't bother to take his feet off the table as the constable showed the two strangers in.

'Couple of time travellers showed up, boss. Usual story: shorted controls, refuelling, la la la. This one's from Earth, C-twenty by the look of him. The other one's called the Doctor; looks like one of them Time Lords to me.'

The Doctor cleared his throat. 'We are... well, we happen to be exactly what he said we are.'

The inspector reluctantly stood up, appraised the visitors and gave his Expensive-Looking Offworlder speech.

'Well, you're in what *you* would probably call the far, far future now. You two, you probably reckon you've been around, but we've seen it all on this planet, mate. Aliens of all stripes, robots who think they're better at controlling the world than we are – which they are, but we can't let them know that. We've had clones by the thousand, whole tribes of indigenous freaks invading every few months – that's why we keep the city mobile. And Maker knows how many power-hungry offworlders with deadly plans, all too stupid to bother employing more than about six henchmen, for some reason. And before you ask, yes, we've had the pepper-pots round here too. A right nuisance, tried to occupy, but we eventually sent 'em packing. So don't think I'm going to be impressed by someone who looks like they've lost a fight with a rainbow. Got it?'

The Doctor glanced quickly down at his tartan and yellow coat, bright blue cravat and striped trousers, but was unabashed. 'Good, good! Then you'll forgive us if we move on. Flying visit, as you might say. Collect what we need, get out of your fair city and go.'

The inspector shook his head sourly. 'You'll need a pass. Nothing happens in this city without a pass. If you haven't got one, the police'll pick you up within an hour.'

The Doctor grinned. 'Can we have a pass, then?'

The inspector sighed heavily and pressed a button on the desk twice, producing two tickets. 'Whatever you do, don't lose these.'

'Why? What'll happen if we do?'

The inspector smoothed his moustache. 'I'll have to press this button twice more, won't I?'

They left the stuffy police office and stepped out onto the immensity of the police skyscraper where the TARDIS had landed. The city spread out below them, packed with high-rises and tenements, before falling into sky. A big place, but not unusual, William supposed, in spite of the inspector's boasts.

And then he looked down. And down and... down.

Below the uprush of the 'scraper they were on, the city descended into endless plateaux, dropping vertiginously until the lower levels were lost in the haze of the distance. Every one of the levels was packed with bustle, traffic, the organised chaos of city life. Figures that might have been birds and might have been vehicles wheeled round the taller buildings.

Far out in the remotest pale blue, ribbons of pale green that could have been forests or seas wrapped themselves around the horizon.

William realised the breeze he felt wasn't the wind. It was the passing of the colossal city through the world.

After they'd taken the lift to the bottom of the police station, they descended the endless concrete steps to the tier below them. Robed, tentacled horrors passed the time of day with dwarfish lizards. Threadbare beer shacks jostled with gleaming tech shops, modish boutiques, tiny snack booths and any number of individual sellers hollering their wares. Sirens wailed from not too far away.

'Look at this, William! Isn't it amazing? Crime, corruption... endless restless churning. Grime, noxiousness, poverty...'

William stepped over a pile of something unsavoury that had been left in the middle of the street. 'How horrible.'

'Hah – nonsense! It's just people doing what they do. Pushing upward. You have to admire it, really you do. I expect they live longer here than you lot used to for a start.' The Doctor grabbed his lapels and took a deep, gleeful breath. 'Ahhh, the stench of the healthy city.'

'Tell me we're not thousands of years into the future, Doctor. In humanity's future.'

'You just heard it for yourself – we are. Further than your brain can –'

'And *this* is it?' William stopped in the middle of the bustling street. A six-legged vehicle clattered around him, its owner shouting abuse.

The Doctor looked startled. 'Why, William? What can you possibly mean?'

William wiped his hand across his brow and motioned to the chaos around him. 'What about progress? What about a better world? That... that inspector was no different from the men who run the bureaux back home! A petty, snivelling man! Probably corrupt!' He wheeled around, his own disdain catching him by surprise. 'And look! Yes, there are aliens, all kinds of technology, but the *poor* are still here! You can see shanty towns! Beggars! Rich and poor, master and servant!' William slouched suddenly and sat down on the nearby curb. 'After all this time... we never got anywhere. We never climbed any mountain. I thought it would all be like that time we went fishing.'

The Doctor was in no mood to placate him. 'Bathos later! Right now, we've got a contact to meet!' He marched down the sidewalk crowded with baroque aliens. William got up and followed, his face dark.

'So, where's this fuel dealer, then?'

William and the Doctor were drinking blue, syrupy liquid in an underground bar decorated with, as far as William could make out, the skulls of alien animals, which had animatronically altered eyes that followed one around the room and uttered the odd synthesised roar above the scratchy swing music.

'Not fuel,' corrected the Doctor, swilling his drink round his glass. 'That constable got it wrong. The TARDIS is old, you know – nearly as old as me. And unlike me, it doesn't regenerate. Sometimes it needs some special lubrication to keep it in shape. Otherwise you end up with some rather unfortunate health issues – unbounded whorl paradoxes, closed timelike bulges, malevolent recursive spasms, so on and so forth. Rusty joints, if you like.'

William's voice was soured by bitterness. 'So this pit stop is for an oil change, then?'

'That's probably as near as *humans* can get to understanding it, yes.' The Doctor raised his glass to drink.

'Best put down *your* lubrication, Doctor. Something's coming in.'

As William watched the entrance to the bar, two huge antennae protruded. Within seconds, a bottle-green jointed carapace some ten feet long was flowing through the bar on tens of legs, topped by compound eyes like bowls full of jewels and a dripping jaw full of cruel mandibles.

The insectoid reared up in front of the Doctor, jaws slavering and cracking against each other. 'Psst,' it produced in a husky, reedy voice. 'Are you the geezer who wanted to know about the –' clack clack '– oil?'

The Doctor inclined his head. 'Who's asking?'

'I'm asking, ain't I? They call me Fingal. C'mon, through to the –' clack clack '– ubervators.'

They followed the sinuous alien past disaffected punters into a mall hallway and through a maze of concrete corridors, gradually giving way to marble hallways and scenic arches. 'Built sideways up, this city,' buzzed Fingal, feet clattering unpleasantly on the stone floors. 'Unless you've got your own wings or gravpacks, best way to get around are the fusion lifts up and down the inside of the columns.'

They reached a massive arch and Fingal scuttered through. 'Angel Deep column, gents. Commonly known as Hell's Gut thanks to the low-lifes like me who tend to congregate around some of the seedier levels.' If it was possible for a giant insect to glow with civic pride, then that's what Fingal was doing. 'Something, ain't it?'

William went to the nearby railing and looked down. The level they were on circled an epic pit that descended until its depths were lost in smoky haze. Stairs and walkways joined their level to what looked like hundreds of others, all covered in houses, shops, bars, tents and palisades. And people – people of all shapes, thronging every available space. Daring to look up, William saw that the well continued for at least another ten flights up, ending in a tangle of immense, gleaming gunmetal pneumatics. Tubes as wide as bridges meshed with gears bigger than circus tents. Feeling a rush of vertigo, William stepped back from the balcony. 'We need a map, at least. What's the name of this place, anyway?' But the Doctor had already moved on to read from a nearby plaque.

'Ah, I see! This city actually does move... albeit infinitesimally slowly. It has four huge columns to support it – known as Angel Deep, Zorn's Ladder, Greenwood Shaft and Strive Reach. Of course, we're actually inside one of them now! At any one time, one of those columns is slightly raised and shunted forward a matter of half a mile or so. Then it's the turn of the next column, and so on. The main platform of the city proper – although these columns are districts in themselves, of course – is slowly carried forward in this manner. The city's like a giant table! Rather impressive, I must say!'

William sniffed. 'It's only engineering.'

'*It's only engineering*,' the Doctor mocked. 'I'd like to see your lot, with your yellow diggers and your DIY programmes, come up with something like this.'

The lifts were huge, ornate brass constructions, sliding serenely up and down, fastened by fat chains to grooves in the shaft. Although they looked old, their glass domes were gleaming and their finely wrought balustrades seemed perfectly maintained. William sniffed. The shaft was filled, not unpleasantly, with the lingering scent of hot oil and machinery.

'Into the ubervator, fellas,' the insectoid keened. With a mechanical sigh, a large glass lift drew up and revealed an entrance. 'We're going to see nice Mr Bansal. He's got the stuff you need.'

The picture of the city etched into the brass plaque in the lift wasn't much like a table. It was hard to tell from the simple lines, but it looked less like a rigid shape and more like a coral formation, every available space taken up with habitations.

'Here he comes – got to keep this hush-hush,' rasped Fingal. Looking onto the level below, they could see a tall human in a blue suit weaving through the crowd. He entered the ubervator next to theirs as they passed, so they could see each other through the glass. Fingal adjusted a speaker slung round his thorax, and the man's voice filled their lift.

'I'm Eldric Bansal,' he grunted. 'This is strictly off the record, you understand, but my department is keen to help where we can. We can synthesise you the material you need, but it'll take us some time. Give us a day or two and we can –'

A sound like a metal scream pierced the air. Bansal staggered as his ubervator shook and groaned to a halt.

'Bansal! What's going on?' Fingal tapped his speaker with a feeler.

'It's the damn lift! Call someone!' The voice buzzed into the glass as they watched the tall man bang on the lift.

'Trap?' hissed William urgently, but the Doctor looked as confused as he did.

With a sickening lurch, Bansal's ubervator began to move again, back down towards them. The blue fusion pad underneath the lift was flickering, guttering. As the lifts drew level again, it went out entirely.

'Help me! It's Boro Berikuka! You have to –' The short-range communicator cut out as Bansal's glass lift began to drop ever faster, down into the circular void, leaving flecks of burst chain smashing across their level.

They were still too high to hear the crash, two hundred floors below.

The Doctor and William were standing by the wreckage as spidery, hazard-striped cleaning drones cordoned off the area. Fingal had fled the scene when they'd reached the ground.

'What just happened, Doctor?'

The Doctor was looking unconcerned. 'Accident, I presume. Never mind, we'll find someone else to help us! No harm done!'

William snarled. '*No harm done*, Doctor? Do you think it was because he was speaking with us? Did we make this happen?' Something nudged the back of William's head, and he saw the Doctor was raising his hands.

Black-suited, helmeted troops were moving in all around. 'Stand down and desist!' the voices behind the helmets creaked.

'Do we look like murderers?' the Doctor demanded.

'Requesting orders for summary immigrant execution!'

'Not yet, fellers.' The inspector strode in, holding up his ID card.

'Someone set us up,' whispered the Doctor to William.

'Oh, really, Doctor? Do you think?' snapped William. 'And there was I thinking we'd murdered the poor man.'

The Doctor narrowed his eyes. 'You know, of all the myriad galaxies I've explored, all the countless civilisations... I've never met *anyone* who likes a smart alec. Ah, Inspector! It's a small world, isn't it?'

'You might like to know that you, ahem, accidentally left this with us.' The inspector dangled the TARDIS key.

'Oh, no. Doctor...' William nudged him.

'So what if I did?' The Doctor grinned. 'That key responds only to my unique matter-wave configuration. Try anything. Nanotech, transmat, fusion bombs. Won't work. Effectively, unless you're me, you'll never unlock that door.'

'That may well be true, sir,' sniffed the inspector. 'But if that's the case, you shouldn't go around leaving the door open.'

The Doctor turned to William with an indescribable look in his eyes.

'I just remembered...' stuttered William. 'When we were grabbed, coming out of the TARDIS, I think I forgot to close the damn thing.'

The inspector continued. 'What we call a class-six chronomobile, Doctor. Classic model. No offence, but our boys in tech ops disable those, take 'em apart and reassemble them in the high commissioner's office for a laugh. On a weekday, sir. In a lunch break.'

The Doctor trembled with rage. 'If you've hurt my ship...'

'She's not hurt. Not yet. Just sleeping off a dose of knock-out tech at the lock-up. But, frankly, sir, unless you can find who committed this heinous crime, we'll be forced to disassemble her. Permanently.'

It was the Doctor's turn to boggle. 'I was led to believe we were the suspects!'

The inspector inclined his head. 'Oh, you are, sirs. The records show that this was no accident. Someone shut off the ubervator remotely. And you two were in the vicinity. *And* you'd already threatened me hours earlier. A compelling case, isn't it?'

The Doctor snorted.

'But there is something in an old charter... which I suspect most of these grunts wouldn't know about. Something about eight hours to prove oneself not guilty, I believe.'

'Inspector? You wouldn't be framing us, would you? Because you think offworlders like us might find the killer quicker than *you* could?'

'Perish the thought.' The inspector grinned. 'And, by the way – Bansal's last words. The name Boro Berikuka didn't register on any of our lists. Nothing. If it's a person, he or she must have a *very* low profile. If it's a place, I've never heard of it. We're going through Bansal's things now, but there's no mention of it anywhere. So I figured you two might have some luck – pounding the streets.'

The hit squad was filing into a globular hoverboat, floating nearby. The inspector was the last to enter. As the hoverboat floated up the shaft, he yelled, 'You might want to start with Electra Montaigne! Bansal's wife! She's being interviewed in nJerabund Tower today! If you can get anywhere near her...'

'I still say we should find a map!' William was chasing after the Doctor as he strode down the street. Having re-ascended Angel Deep column, they were exploring a well-to-do neighbourhood on the Upper East Flank.

'Whoever it was, it wasn't Fingal.' The Doctor was deep in thought. 'Fingal seemed a good sort, don't you think?'

'A good sort of what? Seemed more like the man-eating bug sort to me.'

'Come on, William! Didn't you get his body language? Sometimes you just get a feel for a creature.'

'All I got was that he was the size of a crocodile with jaws that could crack rocks.'

'I'd hardly expected such an attitude from you, William. After all you've been through! A wheeler-dealer, maybe, but a murderer? Hardly. For a start, he's a myrapoid. They usually kill their prey with those mouth parts. Not with fusion lifts. Secondly, why kill a supplier? Thirdly, even if he had a grudge, why do it in broad daylight, in a public space, in front of strangers?'

Before William could answer, the Doctor looked up. An immense sphere floated unconcernedly a full fifty feet above an immense 'scraper. 'A-ha! See the sign? nJerabund Tower. Besides,' he mused, 'I love a good murder mystery. Stretches the old grey matter.'

'I would have thought that was a little lowbrow for your tastes, Doctor,' William sniped as they made their way to the entrance. CCTV camera turned shakily to track their progress... just as they had done since the minute they arrived in the city.

'You're here for the press conference?' The harried-looking PR girl stopped and ran her fingers through her hair.

'Naturally,' purred the Doctor.

'Then I'll need your passes.' She held out a hand scanner peremptorily.

The Doctor feigned a look of amazed shock, followed by one of greasy indulgence. 'My poor girl,' he cooed condescendingly. 'You must be new to the job. But I'll do you this one favour. Once you let us in, I won't tell anyone in the company that you didn't recognise us. Deal?'

Seconds later, they were ushered into the sumptuous hotel suite. 'You've got two minutes with Ms Montaigne, just like everyone else,' the PR girl reminded them. 'No personal questions. Especially no questions about current life-partner Dunset Pemdale III, and no questions about her personal guru, Cardinal Monfreit. Just questions on her part in the upcoming mind-epic *Sweetness and Lightspeed*. 'Kay?'

'Hey, guys! What do you two want to know?' Electra arched an enquiring eyebrow as the PR girl bustled out. She was lounging on a modish divan, surrounded by the open pages of other stars in animated magazines. Electra was a human of average height, with expensive-looking chestnut hair and, well, rather average looks. But William realised he'd already begun to breathe shallowly. He found himself combing down his hair with the flat of one hand, to hide where he was thinning. 'Doctor, she's amazing! There's something about her...'

'Pshaw,' said the Doctor. 'It's all fake. Charisma implants are the latest thing in this city. Didn't you see the posters? A subtle combination of exotic pheromones, AI wetware wit-routines, genetically enlarged pupils, and a spray-on tan.'

'Oh,' said William. Knowing the reason didn't totally remove its effects, but at least he could see that she was rather too artfully sprawled on the couch and her expression just a little too affected.

'Fire away,' she said, gleaming a brittle smile.

'Do you know that your husband is dead? About three hours ago now?'

There was no change of colour in her face, but William saw she had heard yet hadn't expected anyone else to know so soon.

'Awful, darling,' she said. 'Awful. I've been crying my eyes out ever since I heard. But, you know, we've been separated for years. What has that got to do with me?'

'Funny,' snapped the Doctor. 'That was going to be my second question.'

She frowned. 'Nothing. Now get back to the real questions.'

'These are the real questions,' William interrupted. 'We're investigating his murder, Mrs Bansal.'

'It's Montaigne! Not Bansal! Ms Montaigne! We were separated, I tell you! I hadn't spoken to him for ages!'

'Your ex-husband. He worked for a government department, did he not? What was it? Secret service? Defence?'

She almost laughed. 'Town planning. He was – I'm sorry – a boring man who I left behind a long time ago.' She paused. 'We did speak last night when he called. Eldy was working on a big plan that he kept yapping on about. It was dull, dull, dull, darling. Something about organising a central committee. "Yaa-awn," I said! But I think he told the cardinal all about it.'

'Cardinal who?'

She rolled those implanted eyes. 'Cardinal Monfreit, of course. My spiritual adviser. Always good friends with Eldy. Don't you read any magazines? The cardinal's a sweetie – tell him Electra says mwah mwah!' Her face hardened again. 'Now listen to me. Your two minutes are up. I don't care how you got in here, or who you think you're working for. If I see you again, you will be dead within the hour. That isn't a threat, by the way. That's the city's ordinance. I have an instant tag-and-snag system for stalkers.' There were real tears on her face now. 'Get out!'

'Don't you think we should do some basic research, Doctor? About where we are, what this place is?'

The Doctor and William were waiting at a bus stop, perched on a precipitous platform overlooking the smoking industrial district several miles below. But, as usual, the Doctor was off on a different tack.

'You know, even civilisations have lives,' pondered the Doctor. 'I mean, they rise, they fall, and if they're very lucky they get something in between. It's just the way life goes.'

William, realising he was finally getting a reaction to his earlier outburst, sighed and nodded. 'I know, Doctor. You're hardly the first to say so. It's just... doesn't it ever feel futile, all your efforts to help? To know that no matter what you do, it'll all be rubble in a millennium or two?'

'Futile? *Futile?* William, that word isn't even in my vocabulary!' But even the Doctor's eyes looked a little tired. He leant on the iron railing and looked out to the horizon. 'One day, William, I will take you to the great galactic millponds, where civilisation has spread across countless stars and managed to bring with it a large measure of peace and understanding. Where, for tens of millennia – longer than humans have had civilisation – war is a folktale, and every being has the right to a long and uneventful life.' He paused sardonically. 'But please don't make me take you there too soon, because frankly they're dull as ditchwater.'

William couldn't help smiling. 'We've still never met any Vikings.'

'It's not something I like to admit to, William,' the Doctor said, pulling at his collar, 'but sometimes, just sometimes, I do wonder what it must be like to be one of you people.' He raised his finger to his lips. 'Don't tell anyone.'

William grinned wryly. 'Your secret's safe with me.'

The multi-part green bus curved sinuously through the air, glowing fusion plates in place of wheels. And then down towards a huge, white cantilevered structure. The Synod of Serif Zorn, home of Cardinal Monfreit.

As the skybus landed, William shouted. 'Doctor! Look at the graffiti!'

On one side of the wide, empty Ophul Square, the words 'BORO BERIKUKA KILLS' were written in curiously regular type.

'So someone has heard of him. If he is a him,' observed the Doctor. Traffic surged around them on the ground and sky.

'Is there some kind of statue of him – her – it, round here, maybe?'

They perused the pigeon-covered statues in vain. 'Hmm. Famous scholars, apparently. Lucifer Braithwaite, Kitter Wreck... No, no Boro Berikuka.'

As they surveyed the square, William suddenly realised that the baroque traffic lights had changed colour. What had been an oasis of calm was suddenly a flurry of all manner of vehicles, roaring and jostling for place. In desperation, William dodged out of the path of a huge tanker – rolled under a departing skybus – and came face to face with another spider-like contraption...

The Doctor jumped on to the nearest statue. 'Excuse the informality, Miss Wreck,' he apologised as he surveyed the scene. 'William! Where are you?' But when the thundering vehicles had left the area in an eddy of fumes, William was gone.

The Doctor looked around. As far as he could see, there was not one other person in sight. All that remained was the looming edifice of the Synod.

* * *

William's vision slowly returned. He stretched out a hand and felt damp concrete. Sitting up, he saw that he was in a cell some five feet square. He could see no entrance or exit. Only a light recessed into the ceiling, and a battered-looking viewscreen in the corner of the room, slung up onto the wall with thick brackets.

The screen flickered on, to a cheery advertisement: 'We did it! We built a better mousetrap! Sticks fast! With this technology, the little critter ain't going anywhere!'

William clenched his fists. 'Is this a joke? Are you trying to say I'm stuck here? Why don't you talk?'

The screen showed what appeared to be a public information film. 'Why, the city now has the most complete and regular system of traffic on the planet!'

'Are you...' William took a deep breath. 'Are you involved in the murder of Eldric Bansal?'

A quiz show excerpt: 'And the answer is... YES! You're right! You win a thousand credits!'

'How long?' William asked. 'How long will I be down here?'

The screen buzzed to an ad for a wood preserver: 'Guaranteed! One hundred years or your money back!'

'The Doctor will find me.'

A pause, then: 'Shhrk – we make cardcrete that's utterly impenetrable. No signal can get through. Guaranteed to foil military, industrial and freelance ordnance, hack-proof, totally transmat resistant, meta-matter unbendable. Up to five hundred feet thick! They call it the Living Tomb!' The images disappeared in a burst of static.

'Why... why are you doing this?'

A long pause, and the screen lit up, in a blaze of chopped commercials. 'This product heralds a new dawn – shrrk – it's a revolution in cleaning – shrrk – you haven't seen anything until you try this! – shrrk – A new way to play! – shrrk – throw out your old system – throw out your old system – throw out your old system –'

The screen darkened and the words appeared on the screen.

'COMING SOON.'

The inspector sounded distracted. 'Doctor, Doctor. Let's review the facts. I'm sure nothing horrible has happened to your companion.'

The Doctor hissed into the payphone. 'Facts? Facts? That's our problem! We're drowning in facts! We're wading through a bog of evidence! We're choking on solid, incontrovertible proof! Forget facts, what about hearsay? Conjecture? Inspiration! I know it – *they* – can control traffic lights. Bring down ubervators. Make people disappear. And yet we've never seen one of them. Be warned, Inspector. I will find him.'

'Paranoia, I'm sure, Doctor. Paranoia that's wasting what few hours you have left to find out who Boro Berikuka is.'

The Doctor straightened his cravat. 'Does that include finding out if you had anything to do with this?' When there was no reply, he continued. 'Very well. I'm going for an audience with a cardinal.

Cardinal Xaluus Monfreit was a lean, scaly figure in starchy white robes. A long snout stacked with teeth jutted over languorous, reptilian eyes. The cardinal took a puff of his water pipe, adjusted his mitre a smidgen and motioned for his concubines to leave.

The Doctor traversed the crimson carpet of the gleaming white audience chamber and climbed the steps until he was standing just below the creature's ornate seat.

'Celestial repose be on you, brother.' A clawed hand passed over the Doctor's head in blessing. 'The Synod of Serif Zorn is here for you.'

The Doctor had no time for niceties. 'My friend is missing. I believe you know who might have taken him.'

If the cardinal was surprised, he didn't show it. 'If you're not in need of any personal guidance, maybe I could direct you to some other authority.'

The Doctor was not to be stopped. 'I may never have been to this city before, but I seem to remember a fellow who reminds me inordinately of you. Name of Monfreit as well – funny, that. This one used to be an excavator-for-hire on the asteroid – where was it? Oh, yes, Asul 5-53. It must have been, ooh, twenty years ago. The Monfreit I remember was a cold-blooded – no offence – rebellious, bloodthirsty son of a snake. The Monfreit I remember killed his co-worker over a few grams of Wassabium ore. Bit his throat out, if my memory serves me correctly. Maybe the Brethren would be interested in hearing about that?'

The cardinal sighed. 'Ah, the rage of the unenlightened. It was the subject of my first best-seller, Doctor. I even had a few copies produced in paper.' He tossed him the book.

'*Zorn's Miracle: The story of how Xaluus Monfreit went from murderer to whiter-than-white faith leader in a matter of days!* Oh, very nice. Can you help me?'

The cardinal flicked a long tongue over serrated teeth. 'Do you know what happens when you die, Doctor? My brethren and I believe that everything you've done in the service of our leader Serif Zorn is taken and formed into a bridge across a lake of burning fire. The less you've done, the shorter the bridge. The more lies you tell, the longer the lake.'

'And why should I care?'

The cardinal made an ambiguous, inhuman gesture. 'Oh, Doctor. I asked you because if you keep on questioning, *you might be about to find out if we're right.*'

The Doctor laughed heartily, though with an edge of cruelty. 'Let me tell you what happens when I die, Cardinal. Every molecule in my body spontaneously flies apart, reconfigures its internal structure, and within the course of a few seconds, recombines into a unique, new being. I become someone else. Someone who'll still harry you.'

'You really are a Time Lord? Our reports were right.' The cardinal looked momentarily nonplussed, but recovered. 'But what, Doctor, if I keep on killing you? Murdering your dazed and sickly regenerations over and over again? Even Time Lords, it's said, have a limit to their lives.'

The Doctor smiled unpleasantly. 'First things first, if you don't mind. Murder me once, before you worry about what happens next.'

The cardinal's nostrils dilated and his eyes flashed. 'This won't bring your friend any further from the Bridge and the Lake. Has it occurred to you, Doctor, that maybe there wasn't another angle in this for me? That maybe my faith is real? And that maybe my friend Eldric needed a form of absolution?'

'What do you mean, absolution? What had he done?'

'Eldric? He'd done nothing, really. But the men he worked for, a long time ago... he seemed to think they did something they didn't want known. Something they weren't proud of. To save the city, they claim. He couldn't tell me more.'

'Go on.'

'Read this. It's Bansal's draft proposal. There is, I feel, some kind of justice to be done here.'

William had no way to judge the time other than by the progressively empty growlings of his belly. His captor seemed immune to pity, to threats or protestations. Aside from cryptic soundbites, mostly from adverts, the room was empty. He'd banged on the walls until the bases of his fists were raw. He'd even tried to dismantle the screen, but it was too sturdy for his efforts.

For the last hour – so he thought – he'd been staring vacantly at the wall. His only hope was that the TARDIS could somehow beam in here – except there was barely room for it to materialise. The thought of the Doctor and the ship embedded in the endless cardcrete was too much to bear.

'Shrrk – Traveller's Rest, home of some of the city's most honoured retired citizens –'

The screen had been repeatedly showing this clip for the past ten minutes, but William had no idea what its significance was. He tried to drown it out by humming to himself.

He didn't realise what it was he was humming for quite some time, but it fitted neatly into the bleakness of his attitude. Just one of those odd, intertwining melodies – the plaintive, haunting tune that underlay the more strident instruments in a song.

He looked up as the screen fizzed and crackled. What was that on there? It looked like CCTV footage of a camera zooming into an open door... the door of the TARDIS! With a sickly feeling in the pit of his stomach, he followed the camera through the console room's inner door and on to a labyrinth of corridors, all with the same pattern-indented circles on the walls.

He knew where they were going, he could feel it in his teeth. The TARDIS had a room laid out for an orchestra, music stands positioned in front of a hundred empty chairs. And on the shelves round the music hall were stacked every kind of tape and disc and hi-fidelity fizzy liquid, storing a plethora of music from everywhere in time.

The camera came to a stop on the small recording device laying abandoned on the floor where he'd last left it. The one William had never been able to get working.

What did it mean? He dared not stop humming. The lights in the room dimmed and brightened again while the screen crackled. A breakthrough, he thought. The patient is finally responding!

'You like this music, eh?' he found himself saying out loud. 'You don't hear much music, no?'

The screen buzzed with static again, and showed a short, repeating loop of a cartoon character crying and wailing. It was replaced by more splintered advertising. 'Shhrk – Do you feel alone? Need to find – Shrrk – can't talk to anyone about – Shhrk – can't talk like – Shrrk – ' The screen was filled with blurry images. Surgeon's heads, bending down to look. A gleaming tool that might have been a scalpel. And then the images were replaced with static.

William trembled. 'If you can't talk, maybe you could sing?'

He began to hum it, the same broken fragment, again and again. Louder and louder. Until he was almost shouting it.

And then he was answered.

An old homeless man sat on a plasticrete box, playing a worn-out stringed instrument and singing. Behind him, more of the angular graffiti: 'BORO BERIKUKA IS RIGHT HERE.'

The Doctor sat down dolefully next to the man. 'An hour to go. "The awful shadow of some unseen Power/Floats, tho' unseen, amongst us." Shelley, before you ask. I... may have lost everything.'

The old man looked at him with bloodshot eyes. 'I'll play you the blues. Makes you feel better about feeling bad.' He cricked his neck, cleared his throat and sang:

Ol' Boro tol' me to come here
Said he had some work for me
But when I got here he picked my pockets
And made me work for free

And now I'm sad, so sad,
No gold beneath my shoes
Ol' Boro Berikuka tricked me
I got the Walkin' City Blues.

With an undignified twang, the man was grabbed by the shirt. 'You know who he is?'

The drifter looked back with infinite surprise. 'It's just a song, mister...'

The Doctor's eyes were flashing again. 'Tell me what you know.'

Traveller's Rest was high on the back flank of the city, overlooking a spacious park.

Dr Unsil Girade, ex of the City Planning Authority, was enjoying a mid-afternoon doze in his favourite chair by the window when the Doctor clambered through. The Doctor gripped Girade by the lapels and dragged him out of the chair. 'All right, you human refuse. I'm here on behalf of Boro Berikuka.'

'It... it's just a nickname the lower classes have for the city! It doesn't mean anything!'

The Doctor panted in triumph. 'You idiot! If you wanted me to think you were innocent, that wasn't the right answer. You should have screamed or cried for help or fought. Not tried to evade the question.' The Doctor let the old man fall back into the chair. His eyes had never been more full of contempt. 'You know exactly what I mean. Your name is in Eldric Bansal's documents. He says you're the last surviving member of the original research team. He wanted you on his committee, didn't he?'

The old man stood up, trembling.

'What do you want? I have honours – citations from the mayor – all kinds of things!' The old man's jaw jutted out challengingly. 'There are people here I can call to get you sent away!'

The Doctor looked deep into Girade's eyes. 'You always knew *someone* would come, didn't you? Even if it was a hundred years too late.' He clicked a button on a small handheld device, and a dusty viewscreen in the corner of the room flared into life. The screen showed overhead footage of a pitifully thin boy being manhandled onto an operating table. Masked, faceless surgeons. His head was shaved and covered with markings.

Girade turned to the Doctor, trembling but dignified.

'This footage is just over one hundred years old, Doctor. What relevance could it possibly have?'

The Doctor didn't reply. He simply stared at Girade until the old man wilted. And then something hard and stern passed over Girade's face.

'Very well. If you must know the truth.' Girade settled into a lecturing tone, of the sort the Doctor thought generations of students must have fallen asleep to. 'I hardly need to tell you that this city is unique. By remaining mobile we avoid the countless lethal incursions from the surrounding indigenous hordes that other settlements on this planet have to suffer.'

This, the Doctor saw, was Girade's justification. Perhaps one he'd been preparing for decades.

'But this mobility comes at a price. Vast as it is, the various strata of the city have to communicate somehow. Growth was haphazard and organic, people building anywhere they could. Personal vehicle use was endemic – nobody dared to restrict it for fear economic growth would suffer – and the public transport systems were falling apart.' Girade scowled at the memory of inefficiency. 'The mayor and his cronies were less than useless. No matter who got elected, they couldn't sort it out. And of course it was us in the planning department who got the blame from the politicians. Everyone wanted the trains to run on time. The slums to stay away from the hotels. No jams on the freeways.

'The artificial intelligence routines of the day were good, but myopically specific. They couldn't cope with that level of complexity. Don't think other solutions weren't mooted! Endless flocks of hyper-evolved algorithms, distributed networks of all types. None of them any better than a group of bickering planners.

'Gridlock was threatening. Eventually the developers panicked and decided to take the only steps they could.'

The Doctor hadn't let his eyes fall from the man's face. 'They found someone nobody wanted.'

Girade nodded. 'A member of the underclass. Nine years old. Physically frail but mentally astute – he passed all the tests. If there had been a way to scan Boro Berikuka's entire neuronal structure without killing him, Doctor, we would have!'

'You killed a boy called Boro Berikuka for a pattern. The beautiful pattern of his brain. And then what?'

'We created a virtual organisational model of the brain and ran it through the computers, thousands, millions of times, until it found the optimum configuration for the traffic. The grace of its solutions – nobody outside the system could possibly have come up with them!'

'So the city was saved.'

'But that wasn't all. The brain construct proved adept at complex fuzzy-logic issues of planning, taxation, construction, development... it's been running the infrastructure of the city for a century now, and we're a shining example of organisation.'

'And what about the boy?'

Girade shrugged. 'The body was incinerated. Regrettable, of course. But for the public good...'

The Doctor's face was a picture of desolation. 'Funny, isn't it, how people who use the word "regrettable" never seem to show any remorse? But that's not what I meant. I meant what about Boro Berikuka *now*?'

'No element of that child's memories, his personality, ever made it on to the grid!'

'But, memories – what are they? Mind pictures, soon filled in with new impressions. And what do you call personality? An area of the brain? You may have trimmed the grey matter you didn't like, but you put something of him in there. Someone blind and stunted and endlessly abstracted. But *someone*, nonetheless. Amputees, Mr Girade, sometimes suffer from phantom limbs. Do you know what I'm talking about?'

'Of course! The limb is gone, so the brain fills in the missing sensations! Sufferers can feel itching or pain in the missing limb. So?'

'Well,' the Doctor said, baring his teeth, 'Boro had his whole body amputated.'

Girade took a moment to comprehend. 'Impossible! The scale – the time – I refuse to believe it. This was over one hundred years ago!'

'Boro lives,' the Doctor cried. 'He animates this place. Surely you feel it? Every city has a genius loci. This one happens to be *alive*.'

The old man virtually spat. 'Lies! And now you think I murdered that worthless Eldric Bansal to keep him quiet! All for some cheap propaganda about a straightforward experiment! There is no proof that this city can do anything other than perform the most trivial of complex tasks. If anyone could show me that this thing, this disparate collection of ordinances and subroutines and infrastructures, this *application* could feel –'

But Girade never continued. He had frozen, still as snow, with a repudiation on his lips. A time bubble had opened around him. And deep, deep as the foundations of the moving city, in a gut-shaking rumble so low as to be mostly subsonic, a tune was being played.

The Doctor looked up in awe. 'The tune! The city is singing.'

It was a strange world the Doctor raced through, with a few tiny pockets of still life marking the city's song. The underground network was at a standstill. Skybuses floated motionless in the air. The great ubervators were still. Only the private vehicles cruised eerily by, some of them finding places to land to admire the strangeness of it all.

Most people were standing still, but only a few of them were trapped by time pockets. Most were simply listening.

'No access to the TARDIS... need to find a temporal triangulation device... before the song stops...' The Doctor dashed back past the homeless singer.

'I... I got one on this keyring here,' the tramp muttered, fishing for it in his dirty bag.

'I love the future,' said the Doctor as he grabbed it and dashed down the alley, back into the heaving streets of Boro Berikuka.

William blinked in the bright sunlight of the late afternoon.

'He let me out, Doctor! Did you hear him?' The singing was fading away now – people and machines were beginning to move again, dazed and astounded.

The Doctor was running up to the deep walkway hatch that had opened from the concrete in the centre of Ophul Square, surrounded by traffic on all sides and above. 'Oh, I heard it. Do you realise what you might have done? That tune is part of a horrifying weapon!'

'It's all right, Doctor. It was just one section of the melody. And it worked, didn't it? You found me?'

'It did a lot more than that!'

The wail of sirens wasn't entirely unexpected. Nor was the sleek police hoverboat that descended and disgorged the inspector. 'I was frozen in the middle of a toasted sandwich! If you get my drift. When the song stopped, everyone started moving again. What in Zorn's name is going on?'

The Doctor explained his sleuthing, until William breathlessly interrupted with the story of his capture.

'So, Girade used his knowledge of the city's transport system and CCTV to remotely disable the ubervator and murder Eldric Bansal,' mused the inspector.

The Doctor shook his head. 'Sadly, no. He was innocent of that crime, at least. It was Boro himself that crashed the lift. Boro who must, somehow, have got an inkling in that slow, epic mind of his that his life was in danger. And he took precautions. What are you going to do, Inspector? Arrest a whole city?'

Fists bunched in his pockets, for a second the inspector looked like he might.

'And, anyway, have you considered that it was self-defence?'

The inspector started in confusion. 'You what?'

'Finally, the motive.' The Doctor waved Bansal's report under the inspector's nose. 'You see, Eldric Bansal was the architect of a plan to take away much of the city's autonomy. Bring it under the control of committees, bureaucrats. Self-serving, time-wasting pompous idiots. They were going to take Boro's body away from it – from him. Then either leave him adrift on some server somewhere, or shut him down entirely.'

The inspector was staring into space. 'I should be calling you a liar, or arresting you for wasting police time, or maybe laughing in your face. But it's true, isn't it? It feels right.'

William had been thinking. 'The graffiti... that was its own cleaning drones, wasn't it? Spraying it at night. He was trying to tell everyone, but he had no voice.'

The Doctor took the lost-looking inspector by the arm. 'May I suggest counselling sessions for Boro? Maybe over an indefinite period?' The Doctor smiled sadly. 'He had a... difficult childhood, you know.'

William, the Doctor and the TARDIS were in Firth Plaza at night, a confusion of smells and people and neon. William looked up. 'MOVING FORWARD' shone on a billboard up above in vast animated letters. He didn't know if it was Boro, telling him something, or just... another part of the city, doing its thing. Maybe there was no difference. Maybe Boro's thought was as much moved by the harsh traffic and the madness of crowds as it was controlling it. Now there was a thought.

The Doctor was dancing across the street, causing vehicles to swerve around him. 'Imagine a whole city, not knowing if every coincidence, every chance meeting, every road accident, every festival or rebate or closure, was the work of a gigantic mind?'

'Come here, you great fool,' said William, grabbing him by the motley coat. 'You'll get yourself killed.'

'There is, I think, a dream of a city too,' the Doctor said, stumbling back on the pavement. 'As much as a dream of a person.'

'Doctor, can we go somewhere particular next? Somewhen?'

The Doctor rubbed his hands together. 'What did you have in mind?'

'Here. Boro Berikuka. In, say, two hundred years time. I need to see if things really can... move forward.'

The TARDIS warped into being on a tree-lined outcrop, suspended above an endless plain of ripening cornfields.

'Sorry,' the Doctor admitted, stepping out of the door. 'Two centuries later, but the wrong place. Didn't allow for the fact that Boro moves around. Obvious, really...'

'It's all right, Doctor,' William said, shading his eyes and looking into the distance. 'I think I can see Boro. Over there.'

And in the distance they saw him, looming much higher than before, towers studding his back like spines, oversized hands cupping whole districts, his body covered in a cloud of flying machines, his crenellated head rising to the stratosphere.

Boro Berikuka was walking upright.

The Hunting of the Slook

Marc Platt

An Adventure of the Seventh Doctor

A dark shape crouches amongst the roots of a great tree. Is it a bush of black roses? Many people would think so. Its flowers have petals as thin as paper after a fire. They have a lingering perfume like burnt sugar. The slightest breath of wind might crumble them to ash.

The tree is Time, old as itself, gnarled and spreading wide, blotting out the clear sky with infinite possibilities. High amongst its branches clings something like an orchid. Its flame-white petals flicker and change into infinite shapes. A ragged saucer, a trumpet, a tulip cup.

A song resonates forever here, whispering its music to the leaves. It is Time moving through Space, lighting stars, turning spheres. The shapes we imagine as the rose and the orchid hear the music playing on the strings of the Omniverse. The music nourishes them. They reach deep to touch it. They think of it as theirs. They are very proprietorial about it. It is a perfect harmonic sequence, no variations allowed, that must be kept perfect, that no one should hear.

But things leak, and leaks have to be stopped.

The seventh Doctor of many sat on the floor by the wall amid the debris, bracing himself for the next lurch. Any second now. His dark jacket was smattered by the fall of plaster dust from a new crack in the console room's cupola roof. The TARDIS shivered right down to its carved cloisters. Its rotor column grated, rising and falling at the heart of the control stem. It betrayed a sense of unease that was alien to the ship. It unnerved the Doctor too, set his ganglia on edge, but being sympathetic went with their partnership. He straightened his hat and they both felt better.

Vroom!

The next lurch clamoured up through the ship's gothic vaults, heralding the imminent reappearance of the Doctor's breakfast. This wasn't just the tide dashing them against an uncharted temporal reef. Something was out there in the maelstrom of the time vortex. Some unknown anomaly, natural or artificial, was buffeting the temporal space of his ship back and forth, the way a cat bats a mouse round the room before getting bored and eating its toy.

The Doctor slid across the floor, reached out and clung to the edge of the control console. The next lurch was already overdue. He hauled himself up, leaned across the panels and jabbed at the scanner switch.

Vroom!

The Doctor sat by the wall amid the debris and braced himself for the next lurch. 'Just don't expect sympathy,' he muttered, adjusting his hat. Some unknown anomaly, natural or synthetic, was buffeting his ship back and forth in spatial time, the way a wolf worries a sheep before tearing out its throat. He reached out, hauling himself up, clinging close to the control console.

Vroom!

The Doctor ran his tongue round his gums and tasted blood. He was watching a torrent of lights in the time vortex surging across the scanner. Or rather an artistic impression of the vortex through which the TARDIS passed. The ship provided this light show as a courtesy to the crew. It was entirely inadequate, but it had to do. The hyperreality outside was far too complex and infinitely faceted for the natural mind to comprehend. It was so packed with information, you couldn't slip an onionskin between now and then.

A sudden darkness blotted out the streamers of light, something large and close, which passed in a moment. The Doctor caught a flick of its tail end rippling. The whole ship shuddered as it passed.

Vroom!

The Doctor jabbed at the scanner switch.

Vroom!

The Doctor peeled his face from the console panel and ran a finger round his bleeding gums. Something was circling his ship. A globule of vortex-living darkness was repeatedly swooping in to buzz the TARDIS. The persistence of the encounters indicated intelligence, possible curiosity, territoriality or just hunger. The ripples it created, the surge and backwash of extra-temporal energy, could also play havoc with the TARDIS's timeline. And he might not even notice.

The TARDIS shivered again and the Doctor shivered with it. It startled him. It wasn't unease; it was like anticipation. A little frisson of pleasure in the walls and instruments. Almost as if his ship was enjoying it. He felt slightly embarrassed. An intruder, unsure quite what he was suddenly privy to. And then he heard the tune. Just a snatch and it had been a lifetime since he last heard it, but he recognised it from the very first chord. It was *that* tune, not so much sung as wailed by several wordless voices whose high piercing delivery cut through the TARDIS's superdimensional carapace from outside. The wild harmony jangled his nerves. Instinctively, he glanced back over his shoulder, expecting invaders.

No one was there.

And the darkness billowed up again, engulfing the screen, swallowing the play of lights. The song began to repeat, spiralling the interior of the ship and the inside of his head. It had shifted up a key, increased in urgency. He felt his hearts tapping along in time. The TARDIS air warmed. The engines sighed. The internal lights dimmed in sympathy.

Unsure if this was an attack or a serenade, the Doctor decided not to wait and find out. He slammed himself across the console, grabbing at levers, ignoring the protests of the TARDIS's engines, forcing the ship into a screech brake emergency materialisation dynamic.

'This is my third expedition in search of the Slook, that legendary space-going creature whose appearances are said to foreshadow events of the greatest magnitude: everything from a death in the family to the collapse of empires, even the end of time itself.

'So, is the Slook really anything more than a space mariner's fable? Well, I'm certain it is. There are myths and images on worlds right across the galaxy. Too many to ignore. It's just that Slook appearances are difficult to predict. From stories and reports, one could deduce that they are wanderers with no permanent territory or migratory pattern, appearing almost at random anywhere in space. And any journey between these manifestations has never been recorded. Just try tagging a creature apparently composed entirely of oils and quicksilver. It's almost as if a Slook can jump from one location to another over distances of many light years. This peekaboo behaviour has excited suggestions that Slooks have evolved into creatures actually capable of using the holy grail of space travel: hyperspace.'

Oli Pelhedly, celebrated video naturalist and seasoned expedition leader, held up a finger, cleared his throat and took a sip of water. 'This is all right, yes?'

'Fine.' The lanky young man with his mop of tousled hair, tweaked a slide on the control desk and the little golf-ball camera shifted its position in the air a little. 'Don't forget the audience relates to eye contact. You're wandering a bit from cam, but it's fine. There'll be cutaways throughout.'

Oli managed an indulgent smile. He'd made his first video documentary, *Deep-plasma Saltstars of Petruvia 3*, in 2237. Ten years before Alex Voorspuy, this young director inflicted upon him as part of the Wildspace Channel deal, had even been born. *Saltstars* had sold to 72 different worlds and he was still getting royalties. 'Of course,' he said and beamed at the camera as if it was an old friend.

'Previous trips in search of the Slooks took us to the Straits of Altair and the Coalsack Nebula, where we made significant additions to our knowledge. But the Slooks themselves remained hidden. And now we've come to the Eisenstein Belt, a remote region in Quadrant 6 of the East Arm and a much wider area than we've explored before.

'After the last expedition it was clear that if we were to find a Slook, we would need access to the spatial network of long-range observatories and a ship specifically adapted with ultrajump technology.' He sat back in his chair and watched the stars coursing past the window behind Voorspuy's head. 'And that's where you insert the shot of *The Klicklighter* emphasising the Wildspace logo on the hull.'

'And now a word from our sponsors,' intoned Voorspuy. 'It keeps them happy back in the boardroom.'

'Generosity comes cheap. But not always for the ones on the receiving end.' Oli heaved his shoulders in weary submission. 'Still, we wouldn't be here without them. God bless Wildspace and its ravenous franchise for instant titillation. May the black hole never be plugged.'

'We're still recording,' said Voorspuy.

'I know,' said Oli.

'Oli?' called the captain's voice from his desk, her tones unusually bright as if she knew she might be on air.

'Yes, Luisa?'

'The Observatoire on Red Sceptre has picked up a storm plume in the Nevsky system. Could be a big one. Sparticle bursts at level three. We can be there in four hours.'

'Thanks, Luisa. Let's go get 'em.'

Voorspuy leaned forward eagerly. 'A sighting?'

But Oli Pelhedly was already out of his cabin and almost halfway to the bridge.

The dead spacefish littered the void as far as the TARDIS's scanner could see. Silver in the starlight, slightly curled, they hung in clusters, above, below, neither spinning nor turning, but stopped dead as if this moment was frozen.

The dead, just like dark matter, are always with us, thought the Doctor. He tapped idly at an inlaid dial on the mahogany console and tugged a couple of tortoiseshell levers, but there was no response. No flicker of activity came from the instruments. Yet something was moving. Where was it? No chug from the engines. No tick of time from the deep cistern generators. But there was still light and air and gravity. Everything sat in its place. And the scanner still showed the frozen scene outside.

The dead fish hung, flotsam on the surface of time, and the Doctor, staring vacantly out, no longer felt any inclination to shift even one finger. Just for a moment, something glinted in the dark distance beyond the fish. Or was it just somewhere in his head? A dim spark of an unimportant idea perhaps. A vague question as to how long he had been there. Days? Years? With that wretched tune grinding slowly round his head.

The tune! That was it. You can't have a tune without time. His thoughts stirred themselves. A wordless tune that sucks time from everything else just to exist. Or whatever sings the song. Whatever was circling the TARDIS or circling in his head.

Something glinted in the void again. The tune fled from his busy thoughts. A shape was approaching, ploughing through the dead fish, sending them spinning and glittering in the starlight. It was ugly and functional, the grotesque hybrid of an industrial spider crab and a cephalopod, encrusted with mechanical arms, claws and sensors. On the one apparently spare section of hull, there was a colourful logo that announced 'Wildspace Channel – broadening your event horizons'. A metal fist the size of a cargo pod reached round the prow of the ship. Its array of angular fingers, webbed with net, opened and clutched the TARDIS.

'The paintwork!' muttered the Doctor, but he was eager for a little conversation, and made no resistance as his ship was dragged in towards an open hatch at the base of the palm.

It would be the usual kerfuffle. It always was. The Doctor waited in the TARDIS doorway wondering how many years of his lives he had spent explaining that he was not a spy or saboteur. He looked forward to meeting new people, but new people rarely seemed happy to meet him, not at first. Turning up unannounced always made them suspicious. It manifested in outbreaks of narrowed eyes, cold stares and pointed guns. Whatever happened to nice surprises, he thought as he contemplated the latest batch of potential acquaintances.

Three crewpersons were studying him through the window of the quarantine dock where his ship had been unceremoniously dumped. He waved and performed his hopeful-for-a-cup-of-tea mime. It was wasted on them, so while he waited he passed the time failing to lip-read the heated exchanges that were taking place beyond the glass.

The older red-faced man in a casual, coloured shirt was arguing vigorously with the younger tousle-haired man, pointing at the door for the youngster to leave. The latter, all gangling arms and legs, kept pointing at the Doctor. Then the middle-aged woman with Japanese features and blonde hair, who wore a leather flying jacket, shouted at them both. They joined her to scrutinise the console at which she was working. Occasionally, a small white ball hovered up to the glass, staring in at the Doctor with a cold unblinking iris. The older man tried to swat it away with a rolled-up folder. This led to more arguing and finger pointing and studying of their prisoner. The Doctor held up a card on which he had written in green felt tip 'HOW DO YOU DO? I AM THE DOCTOR'. A jet of cold steam spurted from a nozzle in the ceiling and knocked his hat off. There was a refreshing smell of spearmint and disinfectant.

A man in an oil-daubed T-shirt had joined the group outside. He was a young African with a lean swimmer's physique and he carried a clawed implement on a long rod, a small version of the claw that had caught the TARDIS. The woman hefted a hand gun from a drawer in the desk. A red lamp pinged to green and the door hummed aside. The Doctor put his hat back on and stepped smartly out into the sights of the pointing gun.

The place smelt of old socks, but most spaceships on long-haul flights did that. He raised his hat again and glanced from the gun to the inquisitive little white hoverball advancing slowly on his flank. 'If you're going to shoot me on camera, at least favour my other side. It's currently considered to be the better profile.'

But they were looking past him, into the quarantine dock where the TARDIS stood. He followed their stare and saw something lodged in the lamp housing on the TARDIS roof. It was silver and curled like a crescent moon.

'Spacefish?' said the tousle-haired man.

The older man was frowning. 'How can that be?'

'Hardly likely,' observed the Doctor. 'In its natural habitat, the average spacefish is composed of 98 per cent amino oils. Just fluid held together by deceptively simple inner magnetic dynamics.' He stepped back inside the quarantine dock and squinted up at the object. 'But in a pressurised gravitational atmosphere like this, it should just be a puddle.' He helped himself to the astonished crewman's claw, reached up and, rather than touch the fish itself, jiggled the lamp housing. 'Back!' he yelled as the fish slipped from its perch and smashed at his feet like an overturned plaster saint. He crouched to see better. Its broken fragments were rock hard. This shattered fish and all the fish hanging in space outside had not just died. All their time had been sucked out of them. Their progress from moment to moment had petrified. Liquid had become solid that was dry as dust. The Doctor felt the skin prickle on the back of his hand. He thought of the frozen instruments in the TARDIS and shuddered.

'Please stand back,' he said urgently. 'You were right to quarantine this fish. You must seal the dock immediately. I'll stay inside and dispose of it.'

The group didn't budge. Only the woman moved, raising her gun a little. 'Who the hell are you?' she said.

'Introductions are always tricky, aren't they?' The Doctor smiled. 'Better just to do as you're told.'

'Luisa.' The older man laid a restraining hand on her arm, but the little white ball hovered past his shoulder. 'I told you, Mr Voorspuy. Get that thing out of here!'

The tousle-haired man snatched the ball out of the air, pocketed it and extended his hand to the Doctor. 'Alex Voorspuy, Wildspace Channel. You're a long way off the spacelanes.'

The Doctor looked at Voorspuy's proffered hand. 'I have work to do. Thank you.'

'Oh, yeah. Whatever... Unlimited access, that was the deal!' Voorspuy turned on his heel and strutted out of the dock. The older man stood his ground. He glanced at the discarded sign on the floor. 'Do forgive us, erm, Doctor. I'm sorry for dragging you on board *The Klicklighter*. I am Oli Pelhedly of the Astramarine Institute on Mars and we're on a survey of the indigenous life in this area.'

'And I'm sorry too...' The Doctor took Mr Pelhedly's arm and tried to usher him through the door. He only then noticed that the young fellow carrying the claw had skirted past him and was reaching a hand down towards the broken fish. 'Don't touch that!'

The man yelped with pain and drew back his hand. He shuddered and slowly keeled sideways like a toppling statue, his limbs frozen. He was plainly already dead. There was a frenzy while the Doctor struggled to keep the others away from their stricken colleague. Eventually he invoked Doctor's Orders and pushed them out, slamming the door and sealing the quarantine dock himself. While he was hectored with questions by Mr Pelhedly and Captain Luisa, he stared through the window at his unreachable ship. The body of the crewman, whose name had been Cyrus Nguema, lay rigid where he had fallen. His loose T-shirt was fixed, hanging sideways in the air like frozen washing. The Doctor mouthed something about being an innocent bystander, on a fishing trip, minding his own business, but he hardly heard the answers he was giving. Only one thought preoccupied his mind: he had seen this sort of death before.

Despite the sudden death, or maybe because of it, the crew of *The Klicklighter* buried themselves in their work. Oli Pelhedly shepherded the Doctor into his own cabin where he endeavoured to explain the nature of his expedition. While the others gave the Doctor sullen and suspicious glances, Oli seemed apologetic for waylaying his guest, but he was appreciative too that this stranger could at least converse at a higher intellectual level than the rest of the ship's company. He even attempted jokes.

'If you're a doctor, why are you floating about in an antique capsule light weeks off the beaten track? What is it? Some sort of stunt? Surely it's not rag week again?' And then he looked embarrassed and apologised for his flippancy during this sad time. 'I forget,' he said. 'Cyrus has worked with me for four years. Just as obsessed as me. And we're getting closer all the time. But now this disaster puts the whole damned venture into question.'

The Doctor, deep in his own morose thoughts, studied the stars outside the portal and realised that they were all dead fish. 'Tell me about your work,' he said.

Oli poured whisky into two plastic cups and when the Doctor declined, jolted both back himself. He sat back in his chair and told the Doctor of his search for the elusive Slook. Was it real or just a legend? Were there many or just one? Over the years it had become an obsession. He accessed a scrapbook gallery of reports about the creature, but most of the images were fake, and all of them questionable. There had been years where his research had been impossible. He always arrived too late at scenes of sightings. He was laughed out of a conference at the Astramarine Institute. *Sceptics in Action* magazine always called him a lovable eccentric. The 'lovable' bit really annoyed him. But now he had financial backing, the chances of success were much in his favour.

'I know, I know. Like doing a deal with the Devil,' he said. 'But Wildspace Channel only put up the credit because a madman on the loose is great for their ratings.'

'The Devil being your friend with the camera,' the Doctor surmised.

'Alex? He's just the Devil's agent. Wildspace can't lose. Even if I make a fool of myself, as long as I do it in spectacular style, they'll be happy.' He nodded towards the little white ball that was watching them from one of his bookshelves. 'Sorry, Doctor. I should have warned you. Those little terrors are everywhere. I forget about them – most of the time. Just make sure Alex gives you a decent contract. And hang out for a decent fee. I could put you on to my agent. You never know, they might make you a celebrity too.'

The Doctor pulled his hat down to hide his face. 'Why were you here?'

'The storm, of course.' Oli began to ferret through a stack of papers. 'A plume burst of super particles here in the Nevsky System? You can't have got much fishing done. The appearance of the Slooks is always precursed by sparticle bursts.'

'Appearance?' said the Doctor. 'That implies that they come from elsewhere.'

Oli dropped a pen on the floor and disappeared under the desk. 'Down here.' The Doctor eyed the camera and then got down on his knees. Oli was crouching, knees by his chin, with the whisky bottle clutched to him. 'I have a theory,' he muttered, 'that they don't live here at all.'

'No?'

'Not in our universe. I think they live outside time. You can laugh if you want to.'

'I wouldn't dream of it.'

'I think they occasionally emerge into our universe to graze on the solar winds. But it's entirely random. It's the transition from their extra-temporal state into our continuum that causes the sparticle plumes. That's what killed the fish. '

'And your young man, Cyrus. This whole business is deadly dangerous, you know. I hope you're not intending to try to catch one.'

Oli laughed, but it was a cold laugh. 'And keep a legend locked in captivity? Or dissect it? How they'd love that. One day someone'll try, you see. No. I just want to see the beast and know that it exists. Proof that maybe there are better things beyond our own little universe, that can occasionally grace us with their presence.'

'*Slookus Pelhedlii*?' the Doctor suggested.

'*Slookus Cyrus* might be more fitting.'

The Doctor suddenly fumbled with his hat. He shifted forward to peep out from under the desk. His hand swept out, snatched the little white ball camera out of the air and popped it into the hat. The ball trilled its irritation, banging against its prison while the Doctor kept the hat tightly closed.

'No peace for the wicked,' muttered Oli. He clambered heavily out from under the desk and opened one of the desk drawers. The Doctor slipped the hat inside and they slid the drawer smartly shut.

'Are you sure that's all you want?' the Doctor said.

'What?'

'Only to see a Slook?'

'To see it and hear its song.'

'The song?'

Oli swigged the whisky straight from the bottle and gazed out of the portal. 'I must hear that song. The *Varnaese Book of Beginnings* says it's the first, the first music, the source that all creative minds hear and draw on. Helga McKechnie called it the sound of the universe cracking open. The Tirromi called it the voice of God. Whatever it is, it feeds all imagination. It's the muse herself.

... once I sat on a promontory,
And heard a mermaid on a dolphin's back
Uttering such dulcet and harmonious breath
That the rude sea grew civil at her song
And certain stars shot madly from their spheres...

'I don't think that's a good idea,' the Doctor said.

Oli's eyes narrowed. 'You know about this, don't you? Dammit, that's why you sealed the dock.'

'Mr Pelhedly...'

'Fishing trip! You're after the Slook too. And you were here already, so you must have seen something. That capsule of yours must have a flight recorder.'

The Doctor knew he should break his news gently, but his dramatic instinct got the better of him. 'Mr Pelhedly... Oli... suppose I was to tell you that I have encountered a Slook.'

Oli's face had started to colour up. 'I knew it. Where? Where was it?'

The Doctor quite expected him to resort to violence. 'Not here,' he said quietly.

'Where then? Dammit, did you get an image?'

'No.'

'Then how do you know? What did it look like?'

'I didn't actually see the creature.'

'Then how can you possibly know!' Oli faltered. 'Oh. My God. You heard it, didn't you?'

'Oli, you must end this expedition now,' the Doctor said.

Oli gave a little gasp and sat down. He clutched the bottle to him like a man adrift. His face crimson with disbelief. 'Incredible,' he muttered. He fumbled open the desk drawer and the ball camera whirred up into the air like a scissor bug escaping from a jam jar. It hovered high out of reach, staring round the cabin.

'Did you get that?' Oli snapped his fingers at the device and pointed towards the Doctor. 'Did you hear him? This Doctor... whatever his name is, he wants me to pack it in. Perhaps he'd like a word, eh?'

The camera spun towards the Doctor, who hummed and fiddled awkwardly with his tie. 'Ah, erm... good evening, viewers. There are, erm... matters that need resolving before...'

A sudden low-level thrum of engines shivered gently through the walls. Captain Luisa's voice burred up from the desk. 'Oli, we have another plume. It's close. Red 11 sector. We can be there in less than two hours.'

Oli Pelhedly started to laugh. The Doctor, greatly irritated, turned smartly on his heel and slid back through the door.

Alex Voorspuy was standing outside. He pushed back his hair, glared and barged past the Doctor. 'We had a deal, Oli. Unlimited access for my cameras. No interference. And now you've gone too damn far!'

The Doctor didn't wait for the rest of the argument. He slipped away, heading straight for the quarantine dock and the TARDIS.

Someone had draped a blanket over the awkward angles of Cyrus's statuesque body. That was a foolish move, the Doctor decided, but the thoughtful soul who had done the deed seemed to have got away with it, because there was no second statue beside the first.

The Doctor scrawled 'DANGER! TOUCH AT YOUR PERIL' on the back of his 'HOW DO YOU DO' card and rested it on the blanket. He was wondering if he should add some flowers, when that tune came back. It was cantering round and round his head like an annoying circus pony. It could toss its plumes and bare its horsey teeth in a grin that said, 'Look at me. I'm so clever. Tra-la-la. I can stop the whole universe with my tricks.' The rhythm of its dancing hooves was swamping any other thought in the Doctor's head. He had to concentrate hard as he fumbled the TARDIS key into the lock.

The air inside, free of the fug of *The Klicklighter*, was surprisingly soft and welcoming. The gentle hum of the engines was almost tuneful. It perked him up and cleared his head a little. He took a moment to breathe out the tension in his shoulders. Then he headed for the TARDIS library.

He couldn't remember where he had put his notes. He began to turn over wads of paper, old scribbled jottings mingled with scientific calculations, unanswered letters, old theatre programmes, a recipe for oatmeal biscuits from the cook of Pliny the Elder, a faded sepia photograph taken on an antique box brownie of himself in his older days with Good King Radama and his sister Bad Queen Ranavalona – a real frontrunner as far as bad queens go – by that notorious cliff at their palace on Madagascar.

The Doctor cursed that the only filing regime he had was in his head and the only other person ever to understand it had been Susan. Consequently no one had done any sorting since she left, *pom pom pom*, how many years ago? Perish the thought, *pom pom*, that he needed a secretary. And here came the tune again. *Pom pom, pom pom...*

That tune again...

He caught a movement in the air, just at the corner of his eyeline and realised that he had failed to shut the front door.

'I'm glad you could join me,' he announced without looking at the little flying camera. 'I was looking for some notes I made. Quite important notes that may throw light on the death of your unfortunate crewman, Cyrus.' He made a show of sifting through the piles of paper, spilling them across the floor. 'Not here. No, not these either. I was on the world of Torcaldi, a once peaceful planet rich in art and culture. Charming people, I remember, if a little ambiguous. And then the place was devastated by a cosmic cataclysm. Everyone thought it was a weapon, but these days I'm not so sure. Somehow a rent in the fabric of the local universe was opened and the raw energies of the time vortex spilled, ever so slowly, like a creeping frost, across Torcaldi. Time died there. It petrified, just like your crewman outside.

'I hope all this makes sense,' he added and smiled up at the hovering camera. 'If I find any relevant visual material, I'll pass it on and you can edit it in later.' He crossed the library and pushed aside another mountain of papers. The desk they were piled on was revealed as a small but elegant keyboard instrument. The Doctor sat down on a piano stool and lifted the lid. 'I bought this spinet from George Frederick Handel. The keys are mother-of-pearl.' He set his fingers to the instrument and delivered a cascading arpeggio of tinkling notes.

Then he began, one finger at a time, to play a slow, slow melody at once mesmerising and menacing. 'Of course, how the rent into the time vortex could be opened was always a source of debate, but there was an idea mooted that the key was a sequence of notes. A set of chords that has sometimes been equated to the music of the spheres.'

He stopped playing for a moment and sighed. 'No, that wasn't it.' He began again, building the tune note by note. 'I hope Oli is seeing this, Mr Voorspuy,' he added for the camera's benefit. 'This next bit is gravely important to him and his expedition. I believe the Slooks you are seeking know the tune. They sing it to open a door from their natural habitat in the time vortex. That's how they reach their feeding grounds in our universe. Anyone who hears their song, or has the bad luck to be nearby as they emerge, will have their own time frozen. It's what killed the fish outside. And your crewman somehow caught a residue of that energy.'

He plonked his hands on the keyboard in frustration. 'I know I wrote the sequence down! At least I wrote down some of it. Unless...' He snatched up at the ball and brought it down. One tweak of the little camera's receptor panel and it stopped rattling against his hands. It opened out like a flower to display its micro-dynamic innards. As the Doctor poked about inside with a pair of filament tweezers, he had a sudden inkling of another presence. An unaccountable sense that someone was looking over his shoulder. In the air he caught the slightest scent of burnt sugar.

He turned round. The library was empty, but he knew who might be there. 'Where are you both?' he called wearily. 'Was it you? What have you done with my notes?' But there was no reply. Only the hint in his head of a dancing pony with a taunting smile.

Frustrated, he turned back to more immediate matters. If Alex Voorspuy was interested enough to send a spy after him, then his own interest was piqued enough to return the compliment.

About an hour later, the Doctor knocked on Oli Pelhedly's cabin door. Oli was not amused by the Doctor's disappearance and not much impressed by his reappearance either. 'Don't even imagine you're going to mess up my work,' he said. 'I'm dedicating the whole damn expedition to the memory of Cyrus Nguema.'

'Please could I have my hat back,' said the Doctor. 'And, in return, I'll give you Mr Voorspuy's ball.'

He shook out his returned hat and clipped the little camera into the projector on Oli's desk. 'Where's the start button?' he said.

'Play,' said Oli, and an image flickered up in the air above the desktop.

We move along a corridor and turn onto the bridge of The Klicklighter. *Stars glide across the prow foreportal. The area is cluttered with instrumentation. Another crewman is monitoring a bank of instruments.*

'Just an establishing shot,' muttered the Doctor.

Cut to: a wide shot from up near the ceiling. Captain Luisa is in the pilot's seat.

'Captain? I need a word.' Alex Voorspuy is moving in. 'The Doctor's so-called capsule, have you checked it?'

'The quarantine readings showed low-level sparticle traces all over the outer shell.'

The picture zooms in. Luisa sounds awkward, cautious. 'So what's the betting he was there far longer and saw far more than he's letting on.' And she lets her fingers dandle across the back of his hand.

'You haven't seen the inside of his ship,' says Voorspuy.

'Ship? Call that a ship?' she says.

The Doctor shrugged uncomfortably at Oli's sidelong glance. 'Yes, well... there is more to the TARDIS than meets the eye.'

Luisa and Voorspuy are giving each other furtive nods. She turns to the crewman. 'Heinz, go and check the sensor arrays are aligned. Can't afford to mess it up now.'

The crewman leaves. Voorspuy kisses Luisa full-on, but the angle and distance spare us the detail. 'His ship. It doesn't even make sense.' He's talking sotto voce. *The camera and sound pinpoint in again. 'Dunno what that Doctor's up to, but I lost a camera in the process.'*

'Don't you have any sense of decency?' she says and they kiss again.

'Sorry about this,' said the Doctor, looking awkwardly away. 'I couldn't really edit it out.'

'It's just the basic mating ritual,' said Oli. 'I stopped thinking of it as anything but functional years ago. Apart from the aurora frogs in the cloud forests above Old Chozohoxy, that is. You should see their plasma displays. Like rainbows burning under the mushroom trees. It's the only way their mates can find them in the mist.'

'Ahem.' The Doctor coughed, nodding Oli back to the screen.

'Did you think about what I asked?' says Voorspuy, his face deep in Luisa's hair.

'I don't know.' She pulls back from him a little. 'Oli trusts me.'

'That's his problem. You knew I'd ask again.'

'You? Or Wildspace Channel?' she says.

'They need us to do it. If we catch a Slook and get it back to the closed-field reserves off Mars...'

'Forgive me, but you don't seem shocked,' observed the Doctor.

Oli sighed a little. 'It's no surprise. I guessed they'd try something like this.'

'You know how dangerous it is. Do you want your crew to land up like the fish?'

'Of course I don't!' He was still staring at the screen. 'But when someone offers you your dream, what do you do, eh? This ship's loaded with stun harpoons and force nets that they think I'm too much of an old duffer to know about.'

'But if they try, it could be catastrophic. The whole fabric of time could be damaged.' The Doctor lowered his voice as if there might be people listening. 'Oli, you must abandon the expedition now.'

'I need to hear the Slooks,' Oli said.

'Please. Turn back now. Just go home.'

'Over my dead body.' Oli smiled at the Doctor's scowl. 'Just the song, that's all. Don't worry, Doctor. I won't turn a blind eye forever.'

'You might not get a chance. It's the song you should be terrified of. It opens the door between the Slooks' home and this universe. This is a scientific voyage, not a suicide mission!'

But Oli shook his head. 'What's all this about your capsule?' he said.

'What the hell?' Alex Voorspuy is glaring straight up out of the screen. 'That's the missing cam. Damn! It's watching us!'

'Oh, that,' says Captain Luisa. 'I thought it was one of yours.'

The degree of uneasiness on board *The Klicklighter* grew as they approached the plume zone. When Alex Voorspuy came face to face with the Doctor in the corridor outside the galley, he tried to start an interview using the camera hovering at his shoulder. 'What are you really doing here? Can you tell us more of your theories about the Slooks? Or more about your ship? Could it possibly have something to do with the death of Cyrus Nguema? Can I have my camera back?'

The Doctor's answer to all of these was, 'No comment.'

Oli had offered – or was it a threat? – to put him off the ship, but the Doctor declined the proposal. On the bridge, you could have carved the atmosphere with a laser scalpel. Everyone knew. No one said a word, but the glares spoke volumes.

The ship slowed. The first dead fish started to hit the hull about fifty miles out. Their numbers were so great that they blotted out the view. The mega-shoal must have been caught at one of their main feeding grounds. The Doctor wondered why contact with the dead creatures did not suck all the time out of the ship and its crew. He theorised that *The Klicklighter* was acting like a Faraday cage, conducting all temporal magnetic discharges round its shell, leaving the interior untouched.

But it played havoc with the instruments. Navigation and spradar systems gibbered incomprehensibly. They were flying blind, grinding slowly forward. The crew just sat and stared at the darkened foreportal while a flock of Voorspuy's cameras buzzed to and fro, collecting reaction shots.

Then they heard the voices cutting through the white noise barrage of space and the clatter of stone fish on the hull. First came a high-pitched ululation, almost a baroque trill, which was answered by two deep notes, half boom, half groan.

Oli gripped the back of the seat he was standing behind. No one spoke. Everyone stared into the fish-dark sky. Another voice came. A wordless contralto whose plaintive vocal line seemed to embody the emptiness of the void. An echo that had lost its source among the stars long, long ago.

But as yet, there was no tune.

And suddenly they cleared the cemetery of fish. All systems came back on line. Ahead of them, against the canopy of stars, great shapes were moving. They were like mirror-skinned whales, slowly rippling as they moved together in an immense majestic ballet.

'Release the cameras,' croaked Oli, his hands shaking, and a pinprick flotilla of tiny cameras sailed past the foreport.

The Doctor counted at least six Slooks in the pod. The creatures had no fins or defined features. They flowed like vast amoebas made of mercury. Every so often a dent would form at what he took to be the head. The dent spread and deepened into a crater-like mouth as the creatures fed on the energies carried by the solar winds. They called to each other in a multitude of voices, both high and deep, but there was no alarm. They either ignored the ship or were oblivious of its presence.

'Wonderful, wonderful,' Oli whispered as tears rolled down his grizzled cheeks. 'I knew there'd be more than one.' And he started to check the incoming data from the cameras.

'Have you seen these readings?' said Luisa suddenly and tried to draw Oli to one side.

'Not now, not now,' he bleated, pushing her away. It was his moment. All his years had pointed and pulled towards these precious seconds.

The sudden burr of a system powering up broke the mood. Alex Voorspuy stood at a flight console on the opposite side of the bridge, feverishly manipulating the controls.

'No!' shouted Oli. He struggled round the stacks of instruments. 'No! No harpoons! We never agreed that! Let them be!' His foot caught in a cable and he fell forward, slithering across the floor.

Alex Voorspuy turned to look for one moment and the Doctor took his opportunity. He smacked a hand across the panel, sending all the target calibrations of the harpoon system out of synch.

Voorspuy spun back and his arm sent the Doctor catapulting backwards against the back wall. He pulled a gun. 'Who's gonna miss you, eh?'

'No!' shouted Luisa, as she tried to help Oli up off the floor. 'Just net the Slook and let's get out of here!'

'That'll look good on camera,' said the Doctor. 'I hope you have a good editor.'

Oli moved in slowly, staring down the barrel of the gun. 'Don't touch them,' he pleaded. 'Just let them alone.'

'When I've got one,' said Voorspuy. 'Just one as a souvenir.'

The Doctor knew what was coming, but he'd stop it if he could. He turned and ran for the TARDIS.

Two grey figures hear the song that will be sung. Their orders are received. Their purpose is understood.

One reaches down and plucks a fresh black flower from the rose at the roots of Time.

The other reaches up and plucks a fresh white bloom from the orchid growing on Time's branches.

They set them on the grey lapels of their grey morning coats and depart for reality.

The Doctor stumbled through the TARDIS doors. Startle the Slooks away, that's what he intended, but not so much that they actually leave the universe. He slammed on the dry-dock stabilisers to anchor his ship so it wouldn't budge when he turned over the engines. Heaven help them if Voorspuy actually trapped one of the Slooks. If *The Klicklighter* dragged it back to Earth or Mars, who knew what devastation it might cause?

The engines always took a moment to build power to a peak but, to his surprise, they purred up to speed as soon as he turned the dial. The ship was almost preeningly responsive. It hadn't felt so perky for years. Gratified, he switched the view from the scanner to the little camera he had left on the bridge. He had a clear view of the Slooks through the foreport. He revved the TARDIS engines and saw the great creatures react immediately to the disturbance in the local time web.

All the Slooks flew together like loose mercury to form one single giant Slook. It was both a school of creatures and a single entity. So maybe there was only one after all.

'Just go,' muttered the Doctor. 'Go on. What are you waiting for?' He revved the TARDIS engines again.

The huge creature billowed where it had collected itself, apparently unsure of its next reaction. The figures of the crew on the bridge were silhouetted, tiny against the starlit arena beyond.

And then the mouth formed on the Slook's leading edge and it began to sing. All the voices of the pod of Slooks combined within it into one twining chorus voice. It was not the tune he dreaded. This tune seemed warmer and more wildly beautiful than he ever could have imagined. The Slook was singing directly at *The Klicklighter*. It was coming closer.

'Go away,' he muttered again, but the song cut through everything, sublimated everything. It was inevitable. It resonated into the systems of the TARDIS itself. The song became the hum of the ship and the ship's hum became the song. And then the Doctor realised. This Slook was not an aggressive creature. It was singing to the TARDIS, harmonising with the engines. It had followed them here from outside space and time. The Slook was in love with his ship.

He saw a flash of light streak out from *The Klicklighter*. It expanded as it went, broadening into a glowing envelope that smothered the huge bulk of the Slook. The love song ceased as the trapped creature was crushed into a force globe of energy.

Something squealed and wailed. A little Slook, that had either failed to re-amalgamate with its parent or had been cruelly severed from the giant body, flittered uselessly around the trapped creature, calling in distress.

The energy net shimmered and seemed to grow slowly in size as Voorspuy reeled in his catch.

The Doctor felt a shudder run through the TARDIS. He opened the doors and was about to run to the bridge when he heard the new song begin. But it was the old song. The song he had been dreading. The trapped Slook's voices were rising in intricate harmony. This was the song of departure. All the notes the Doctor had struggled to recall fell into their places. Farewell, sang the Slook. Sorrow. Remembrance. Despair.

No whisper came from the TARDIS, as if it were straining to catch the final salutation. The winding tune could hush and slow the moment, drain all time away. It was an Orpheus of a tune, singing a timeless frozen dance painted on a wall long crumbled to dust. The Doctor thought of William, or was he Isaac, struggling to catch the notation of the tune. And each note in each chord as he heard it now, was true and clear as crystal. Nothing else mattered or existed. He had to record it.

The harpooned Slook was dragging *The Klicklighter* as it sang. From the

TARDIS, the Doctor could see, clear as anything, the quantum packets of existence torn apart by its wild forbidden song. The vortex opened like a cat's eye in space, like the deadly Tear on the lost world of Torcaldi.

In the distance, the Doctor heard Oli's deepening voice. Everything was slowing. The ink dried in his pen as he tried to write down the song. He still scratched at the paper. Only a few more notes to go before the final chord. On the scanner, he saw the crew lined across the bridge. Spindly frozen figures staring into the vortex where pure time is no time at all.

The moment catches in the neck of the hourglass.

Two immaculately grey shapes move through the statues on the deck of *The Klicklighter.* They reach out and pluck away the banks of recording equipment.

The Doctor cannot move. He holds a piece of paper with an unfinished tune written on it. Grey gloved fingers slip the paper from his grasp. He sees grey eyes set in grey sepulchral faces. Again he catches the scent of burnt sugar from a burnt black rose. Or is it, was it a tulip? Now he sees it again, where there is only Now, it seems more like an orchid. Its petals rise and fall like the white flame that grows on the branches of Time itself.

The song stopped. The tune was gone. Neatly excised from the moment. The force globe exploded in space. Oil splattered a silver film across the ship's crab-like hull. The Slook was dead.

Time was trundling on again.

Oli clung to the back of pilot's seat. 'We saw it, didn't we?' he said. 'Was it the only one?' He turned to the others. 'Did we record it?' They stared back blankly.

Alex Voorspuy slid a tentative hand into the gap where the recorders had been. 'I don't remember,' he said.

'What do we do now?' said Captain Luisa. 'Any ideas?'

They thought about it for a moment.

'Go home,' said a voice from the door. The Doctor turned away and left them to get on with it. He was amazed at how old they all looked.

When he got back to the TARDIS, he noticed that flowers had been placed on the blanket covering Syrus's body. A black rose and a tulip orchid that flickered like an eternal flame. His sign had been tidied away. He reached out for the statue. It was dull and inert. Safe to touch. Everything was neat and tidy. But the TARDIS had never been so quiet.

In the shade of the great Tree, two grey figures, as required, carry a globe in which something silver struggles and rolls. It makes little half-hearted attempts at a song. Black Rose sets the globe down by the base of the black rose. Fibrous tendrils and roots twitch up and slide round it, catching the last Slook for ever.

White Tulip holds a piece of paper, no more than a shred of the universe, on which musical notation is scratched. It is the forbidden music on which existence turns, which no one must ever hear. White Tulip holds it up for the reaching roots of the flame-white orchid in the branches.

Now everything is tidy and in its place again.

'Thank you,' says the Doctor. 'I'll be taking those.' And he scoops up the globe and snatches back the paper from the astonished duo. 'Easy to find you,' he adds, flourishing the paper. 'I tagged this. Just in case.'

The white-flamed orchid flowers above and the burnt-black roses below hiss their anger. Black Rose and White Tulip, as required, come at the Doctor. They snatch back the paper, but he scrambles for the safety of the TARDIS doorway still clutching the sphere. Unable to resist, he adds, 'No matter, I've got a copy,' smirking as he taps his forehead. He slams the door and the TARDIS flees back to reality.

He put a reassuring hand on the TARDIS console. 'I don't take you for granted, you know,' he said. 'What you need is a treat. How about a revitalising systems scrub at the endorphic spa on Syrinx Regis? Or a trip to the car wash? Keeping busy is the best way to cope.'

The little lost Slook was rolling inside its prison sphere. It could already warble half its song of departure, and it would learn the rest soon enough. He could even teach it himself. He liked that, but he knew he had made a mistake. He would set the creature free, cracking open the sphere like a new laid egg, and watching it flitter off into the vortex, yet that didn't solve the problem of the tune in his head. *Pom pom pom.*

Time was on their side. But any time now, *pom pom pom*, Black Rose and White Tulip would be after his brain.

The Earwig Archipelago

Matthew Sweet

An Adventure of the Sixth Doctor

I suppose I was just being greedy – but what's the point in being a hexapod if you can't take the canapés four at a time? It's not as if anyone else was holding back. The band was shaking the room. The marketing guys were gargling brandy cocktails and making a fist of the jitterbug. The executive producer had two hands in the nut dish and two more fumbling the carapace of Nitzi Swordswool, the principal anchor. You'll have heard her on the show, ballyhooing the larks of the humans. She's good, isn't she? Real professional. Fluent. Funny. And when that green light goes on she gives it one hundred per cent. Two hundred per cent. She never fluffs a word. And what an exoskeleton! Pity you can't see that on the radio.

Anyway, these canapés. I might as well tell you what they were, because I remember them as if they were being offered to me here and now, through the bars of this cage. There was a dinky sliver of fruit-mould with a single sugar-crystal on top. There was a little zippered sachet of aphid roe. There was a celery stick piped with a whorl of bluebottle pâté. There was a honeyed nematode jiggering about on the end of a cocktail stick. Nothing *ooh-la-la*. But I was enjoying myself a bit too much. Making it obvious. And I think that's why the first-unit AD decided to make an example of me. Eska Vastule looked me up and down with that same contemptuous stare he gives the humans when he's on location, hunkered down over the mixers. He moved the cigarillo between his mouth and his forceps. He said, 'Hey, you! Yeah, you!' He swashed his olive around in his glass. 'Guess after that nibble, *tovarishch*, you ought to call it a day,' he leered, loud enough for everyone nearby to hear.

Smiling and nodding seemed the best policy. Not the easiest one, though, because the next thing he said made me wish I'd had my jaws wired before I dragged on my tux to come out. 'You gotta keep trim in this job, *tovarishch*,' he leered. 'Particularly when you're on a floorboard shift.' That really ruined my evening. The floorboard shift. I'd done three years on the floorboards. Four if you counted the unpaid internship. Some of the colleagues in my intake had already been promoted as far as the dado rail. Even that little nematode, wriggling under its sticky coat of marinade, seemed to be laughing at me and mouthing, *Shogsten Vumm, you're as big a loser as your daddy*.

So I was only half-listening when the head of the network began tapping at his champagne glass with one of his wedding rings. I'd be lying if I said I remembered his speech as word-perfectly as it appears in the next paragraph. I had to order up the tapes from the stacks. But that's okay, isn't it? That's research. That's what I was trained to do.

'Colleagues,' he said. 'I think you'll all agree that we've had a very positive year. I won't bore you with the numbers, but let's just say that the opposition have more or less given up. If they can't do no better than repeat a few old episodes of *The Galapagos Islands*, it shows that they've lost the will to live. Those iguanas and finches were big stars in their day, no question. But taste has moved on. Audiences are more sophisticated than they once were – and listening to those dolly little lizards gadding about in the spume just don't cut the ketchup no more, do it? I mean, they don't even say nothing!'

Laughter rippled through the room – and the head of the channel seized the opportunity to stir up something bigger. 'Guys,' he roared, 'we used to love those finches and it's dandy that they've got different beaks, and all – but do invertebrate viewers really relate to birds? Do they empathise with them? I mean, some of my closest friends and relations were eaten by birds. Horrible tongues they've got, don't they, though?' There was general agreement. The marketing section burst into enthusiastic applause. The principal anchor looked uneasy. Perhaps some of her closest friends and relations had shared the same fate.

'But, hey,' continued the head of the network, motioning for calm. 'We're not here to bury *The Galapagos Islands*. We're here to sing the praises of *Land of the Eagles* – a production which, contrary to what you might expect, hasn't got no ornithological angle whatsoever!'

He flourished a finger and someone killed the lights. The velvet curtains of the radio speakers shimmied apart – and the sound system began to play a package of memorable moments from the last fifty years of the world's most successful continuing drama series. For all of us gathered in that room, it was almost unbearably nostalgic. We heard the king's sisters processing through mountain villages offering make-up hints to crones, advising dumbfounded hill girls how to abbreviate their skirts. We listened to the king's nephew speeding down the capital city's only paved road – a triumphal avenue built entirely with Italian finance. We heard the clack-clack-clack of Mussolini's troops goose-stepping past the palace. We heard the leader of the partisans, in the days before he became the Guide of the Land of Eagles, talking about brewing up soup from forest mushrooms and nettles. And we heard the great comic scenes from the show's distinguished history, punctuated with that unforgettable musical sting: the queen's father expiring from blood poisoning contracted from a diseased monkey; the state's chief interrogator making a cigarette fizz against the flesh of a notorious counter-revolutionary; Ettyn, that great hero of the Democratic Republic, delivering one of those twisty-turny speeches; the firing squad's greatest hits. With each rejected last request, the laughter in the room grew louder.

Once the recorded bullets had been spent and the applause had died down, the head of the network took questions from the press. Now this bit I can recall very well, because it spoilt the mood of the party for a few moments. Heemia Shate, enfolded in a wrap of cobalt-blue fox fur, waggled her Dictastick under the nose of the head of the network.

'Lovely stuff, sir,' she crooned. 'But they were all rather elderly, those clips, weren't they? Not much from the last season – which, I think you'll agree, wasn't quite the triumph that you've painted. The numbers were down in percentage terms, weren't they? Those old iguanas and finches may be in mono, but they gave your show a run for its money, didn't they?'

The head of the network seemed prepared for criticism. 'Get off my neck, Heemia,' he joshed, delivering a playful nudge to her thorax. She wouldn't.

'Is there much mileage left in Ettyn, for instance?' she asked. 'You know what the dailies have been saying – his behaviour hasn't been that consistent over the last few months. It's hard to stay loyal when the characters start behaving out-of-character, isn't it?'

'Everyone loves Ettyn Rraxhimi,' snorted the head of the network.

'So, why are you looking for a replacement show?' asked Heemia. 'My spies tell me that you'd drop *Land of the Eagles* at a moment's notice if someone pitched you a bankable replacement.'

The head of the network gave a defensive flutter of his hindwings. 'Don't kill it off yet, Heemia. We have a new pair of characters about to enter the story – and they're really going to freshen things up.' A team of minions scuttered through the room, handing out press releases – with two human faces large on each lucent sheet. The head of the network made his introductions. 'One's called Isaac. And the other is called the Doctor. You'll love 'em to death.'

And that, I recall, made me feel a bit better. Even if I was only following them with a floorboard boom, I was part of the team assigned to Isaac and the Doctor. So, when a waiter passed with a tray of drinks, I reached out four hands and grabbed as many glasses as I could.

There was a palpable excitement during that first shift with the Doctor and Isaac. The location was a pink concrete villa nestled in the scrubby hills that overlook the capital city of the Democratic Republic. It was the magic hour and we were all in position – about four hundred of us, as I recall. The catering truck was parked by a stone near the front door. The director was lodged in his usual place in the kitchen. His assistants and their crews had staked out the other rooms in the house. I was with the twentieth AD in the most dangerous part of the location: at floor level in the thick of the action. Right by the legs of the dining table.

There were 13 gathered around the dinner table. Very Last Supper, we all thought. (Well, those of us who had done their homework.) Most of the diners were revolutionaries of the customary kind: hare-eyed malcontents with cheap slacks and no discernible deodorant. The Doctor stayed on the margins of the party: a fleshy, restless, twitchy figure, fussing under a tangle of blond candyfloss hair. He was grumbling about the dress code, complaining that he'd not been permitted to wear his usual waistcoat. Isaac, his sidekick, was giving him the benefit of his greater experience of life in the Democratic Republic.

'Trust me, Doctor,' he said. 'Wear pink tartan round here and you'll be whisked off to a windowless room for 36 hours of the old lamp-in-the-face routine.' The guy was right. We've recorded some of those scenes. The kids back home love them. Those ominous silences!

At the head of the table was Ettyn. Ettyn Rraxhimi. We've all loved Ettyn for years, haven't we? Such a confident, relaxed man. A tie-wearer and a pipe-smoker. A man with the right kind of parting in his hair and the right kind of driving gloves in his glove compartment – despite those years during the war living on rat giblets and juniper berries and gods know what. He's the kind of human you'd really want to be – if the idea of being a human wasn't quite so disgusting.

Ettyn was talking about the Twentieth Communist Party Congress in Moscow – a big festival with good spots for all the top Soviet turns. And applause. Lots and lots of applause. We sent a team to can some of it to help out the guys on *Braskanaskilack's A Laugh*. Always good to have a bit of it on tap, just in case the studio audience isn't in the mood. And believe me, sometimes they're not.

'Our Guide,' rumbled Ettyn, stuffing more tobacco into his pipe, 'was not amused by the big man's speech. All that stuff about breaking with the errors of the past. About Stalin's "capricious and despotic character". His "serious and grave perversions of party principles".' Ettyn made a whistling sound with his teeth. 'That didn't please the Guide. Said Joe Stalin would rise from his grave and throttle Comrade Nikita on the platform. Spent the rest of the night on the sauce, banging the bedside table and huffing and puffing about Khrushchevite Revisionists. "We should purge erroneous views everywhere," he kept saying. "We must remain radical, or the revolution is lost." Which means he's on the back foot. Which means he's getting ready for a fresh wave of arrests. Which means that this may be our moment.'

Ettyn struck a match and let the fire tickle the tobacco in the bowl of his pipe. The assembly burst into applause. They weren't *so* unlike all those sea lions at the Twentieth Congress. Not the Doctor, though. I saw him. I skittered up the leg of the table and took up a strategic position in the floral centrepiece. Snug among the sepals of a plastic hydrangea, I watched him playing with his food. Food that, frankly, really didn't bear much playing with: a milky-grey cut of mutton and a hillock of mashed potatoes, crop-dusted with dill. I shouldered the boom and came in close to capture the sound: the Doctor's tiny sighs of dissatisfaction; the tines of his fork scraping at the enamel of the plate and ploughing through the starchy mulch potato. I know what you're thinking – what would that mean to anyone back home? Take it from me. Our listeners are very sophisticated.

The Doctor kept at it through all the big speeches of the night. Ettyn talked about his time in the partisans, skinning rabbits in the woods and playing culinary Russian roulette with woodland fungi; recalled the day that the flag of the Democratic Republic first fluttered over the palace of the old king. He talked about rivalries within the central committee. He talked about jostling for power. He talked about *Ul Esdaphro*. The rebels. Everyone's ears pricked up at the mention of them. And not just the people gathered around that table in that little room. For everyone who would listen to these words, back on the homeworld, *Ul Esdaphro* carried a shadowy sort of glamour. It said freedom. It said justice. It said sharking and conniving and throats cut in the night.

After Ettyn spoke, it was time for Isaac to address the meeting. Now Isaac, he was a much less romantic guy. It was all realpolitik with Isaac – despite the fancy name-change. When our talent scouts first detected the Doctor and his companion – first realised that a pair of exciting new characters were about to crash in on one of our oldest plotlines – he was calling himself William. But William isn't much of a name for a man who wants to do the blood-and-barricades thing. No William was ever first banana in a dictatorship of the proletariat. And when it was decided that code names were essential in any undercover mission to smash the state, William decided to reinvent himself – and took his inspiration from a copy of *Moby-Dick*, that crackpot book by Herman Melville about the disabled guy with the whale fixation. Remember the first line? 'Call me Ishmael.' William would have liked to have said the same. But that would have been too obvious. Confused? I'll let the cat out of the sack. William had a copy of the book in his coat pocket. The book was a present from a lady friend. It was her favourite book. Her husband knew that too. One mention of Ishmael and the husband would have jumped to the right conclusion, pulled the pipe from his mouth, run a fierce hand through his neatly parted hair and punched William into the plastic hydrangeas.

'So call me Isaac,' said Isaac, to the company around the table. 'That's how it has to be.' More applause. Particularly, I noted, from the woman at the head of the table: high forehead, choppy black hair, bones as symmetrical as the edges of a very expensive biscuit.

Sorry about that. I'm not too immense at similes of human beauty. Just bear with me, though. It's pleasant for me to remember all this. Well, more pleasant than trying to chew through these tempered steel bars with my mandibles.

After the dinner sequence, the next big event was a love scene. Always the way, isn't it? Coffee plus liqueurs plus a half-decent sunset, and the result always comes up the same. So with a fine sense of mathematical inevitability, Isaac and his paramour rose from the table and made straight for the balcony. She said she wanted to point out some of the sites: the National Museum, the minaret of the last mosque standing, now converted into a cinema showing the latest Norman Wisdom films. It was all I could do to skitter across the tiled floor and leap through the sliding glass doors before they cut me off from the action.

There's only so much canoodling you and your lover can do when your husband is 16 feet away and staring at your back. But if he can't hear a word, then there's no need for self-censorship in your conversation. I don't know whether it would be appropriate for me to enumerate the nothings exchanged that night between Isaac and Madame Mila Rraxhimi. Their words were commonplace enough – the language of revolution tangled with the language of *amore*. Just the way they liked it in the dramas made by the humans of the Democratic Republic.

They reminded me of one about a young male soldier who hooked up with a right-thinking female collective farm labourer. (Actually, they reminded me of quite a few of those.) In every scene, the pair declared their love for Marxist-Leninist orthodoxy and their hatred for the fripperies and delusions of the capitalist bourgeoisie beyond the border. Funny how life imitates art, isn't it?

So forgive me if I don't give you all the dope on that little tryst. Instead, I'd like to let you in on something much more interesting. It's the story, really, of how I got the sack from the network. How I ended up in one of the danker and nastier tracts of the network's penal section, with two of my legs chained to this dirty great bolt in the floor. And it begins with the Doctor, in a fearsome sulk, tightening his apron strings and plunging his hands into the washing-up water.

'The problem, William, is this,' frowned the Doctor, scrubbing at the patina of grease on a battered aluminium roasting tin. 'This revolution of yours isn't a revolution. It's a commando raid. And what's worse is that it's a commando raid sponsored by the very forces that you ought to be setting your face against. And as for your friend Ettyn...' He swallowed the thought and gave his full attention to a stubborn glob of burnt mutton fat.

William looked at the floor – though not with sufficient concentration to spot a small team of earwigs scattered across the lino, each supporting a piece of recording equipment. 'Ettyn's achievements speak for themselves,' he said. But he didn't say it very loudly or convincingly. I had to give my mixer a heck of a twiddle to pick him up at all.

The Doctor continued his assault on the roasting tin. 'They don't speak for themselves because you don't really know what they are,' he rumbled. 'In societies like this, it's hard to distinguish truth from fiction. It's hard to know when people are saying what they think and when they're just reading from some kind of ideological script – because they don't even know themselves. When you live in a totalitarian culture, you can't even know your own history. You can be told one thing one day and another thing the next – and believe both simultaneously. And you of all people ought to know that. You're a native of this world. You know what it's like when the life of a nation is shaped around the whims of a single man. The paranoias of a single man.' He thrust the scouring pad into the greying water. 'A man who can't even ensure that his citizens have access to decent washing-up liquid. What makes you think that Ettyn would make a better job of it than the current incumbent?'

He gave up on the roasting tin and began dropping fistfuls of cutlery into the sink. 'Tell me about these exiles,' he murmured. But as Isaac complied with the request, I could tell that the Doctor wasn't really listening. Isaac spoke of the old king and his mother in their apartment in Alexandria; described the old king's desire to return to his country as a constitutional monarch at the head of a multi-party state; implored the Doctor to believe that his motives were altruistic.

'Shall I tell you a story about the old king?' said the Doctor. He didn't wait for an answer. 'One of his sisters married his ambassador to Belgrade. But the king heard rumours that his brother-in-law was planning a coup. So he started inquiries for a discreet, unemployed, expert marksman. A polylingual student named Agiadh Bebi was found. Agiadh Bebi prepared for his task by sinking four glasses of brandy. He strode into the restaurant in which the old king's brother-in-law was dining, and gunned him down between mouthfuls of *Dobos tort*. Unfortunately Agiadh Bebi was a better shot than he was an intriguer, so the police picked him up easily. A trial was the last thing that the king wanted – Agiadh Bebi might be indiscreet with a prosecuting counsel leering at him across the courtroom – so further enquiries were made for another marksman, more adept at getting away from the scene of the crime. When Agiadh Bebi appeared in court he was drilled by an assassin's assassin who promptly disappeared. The assassin's assassin surfaced in a country town in Croatia, where he began to knock back the plum vodka and talk. And talk. Word of this reached the old king. And within a short time, an assassin's assassin's assassin was discovered. He killed the assassin's assassin and disappeared. I was never able to learn more about the assassin's assassin's assassin.'

The Doctor looked up from the sink. Isaac was nowhere to be seen. He had stormed from the room, leaving the Doctor to tell his story to the draining board. So the Doctor was now alone with his thoughts. Well, with his thoughts, a scratched and shining roasting tin, a mountain of draining cutlery, a washing-up bowl sloshing with filthy water and a few hundred interested earwigs hidden just out of view. And finding himself alone, he gave vent to his feelings. He let loose a low, polysyllabic curse in a language as old as time: a tumbling poisonous serpent of a word that enfolded the name of Ettyn in its coils and squeezed it into submission. To add emphasis to the obscenity, he gave the tap a furious punch with his fist.

Two surprising events then occurred. The tap popped from its housing in the sink and fell into the cold greasy water. Judged dispassionately –

and without the benefit of insider knowledge – the second event was rather more surprising. Out from the hole in the back of the sink poured a wriggling black slick of insects. Glossy, articulated, six-legged, each gifted with a fearsome set of pincers. They leapt, in a quick and furious stream, into the Doctor's face. They streamed over his cheeks and down the collar of his shirt. They crawled into the mazes of his ears, squeezed themselves between his lips, danced over his teeth and made whoopee on his tongue with their forceps. They massed and thrashed in his great mane of blond curls. They skittered their tiny feet across the sensitive canthi of his eyes. They rushed over him in a well-rehearsed defensive manoeuvre that achieved its aim to perfection.

Shocked and disorientated and clawing at his face, the Doctor staggered backwards, lost his footing and slipped on the kitchen floor. As he fell, the back of his head made sudden and violent contact with the edge of a food-preparation surface. A muffled crash signalled the end of the Doctor's attempt to cry out for help. He made a difficult landfall on the tiles. Fortunately, he failed to squash me in the process.

As soon as the Doc hit the deck, one of the swarm gave a high-pitched whistle. The army of earwigs heard the call, disengaged their pincers from the Doctor's flanks and crevices and marched towards the rampart of his left leg, where they waited, in serried ranks, ready for inspection by their directors. The chief director barked his congratulations through his monogrammed megaphone. Two runners appeared with a folding canvas chair, into which the director sank. 'Now, guys,' he said. 'You know what happens next.'

They did. In a matter of moments, a busy stream of earwigs had drained the sink, salvaged the tap from the water, replaced it in the housing, and disappeared back up the faucet.

The Doctor lay senseless on the floor. I circumnavigated his huge body until I was gazing up at the west face of his enormous head. The dark cavern of his ear was just visible through a forest of curls. It's hard to explain why I did what I did next – though I've had months of leisure to reflect upon it. I gathered up my boom and my haversack, climbed through the Doctor's hair and crawled into the welcoming darkness of his ear canal. I curled up on the soft waxy skin and slept the most peaceful sleep I'd slept since I joined the network four years ago.

Now the next part of this story happened while I was still lodged in the Doctor's ear, sleeping the sleep of the just-about-to-be-fired. So how did I manage to obtain the document that you've doubtless clocked a paragraph or so below this one? Easy. During the preparation of my defence, I was permitted unconditional access to the network's written archives. It didn't take me long to find the file on Madame Mila Rraxhimi, flip it open and scan the contents: a detailed set of character notes, a brace of her most significant scenes, a sample of her DNA. There was also a selection of the letters she received while doing her job as announcer on *Hourly Express*, a radio bulletin of English-language news and views packaged by the state broadcasting service of the Democratic Republic for consumption abroad. Mila spent every morning on the show, doing her best to sound proud and excited about the increase in domestic pig iron production, the increase in the birth rate, the increase in general literacy. She punctuated each gobbet of information with a burst of the station's call sign – a stentorian musical phrase that, you might fancy, had been composed as a personalised doorbell chime by a god of the underworld.

Every afternoon, Mila attacked the file of correspondence from listeners of *Hourly Express*. The following example was received three days after the party at her husband's villa – and in its combination of grammatical eccentricity and ideological extremity, is a fairly typical example.

> Miss,
> I listen always to *Hourly Express* transmissions.
> Independent minds everywhere in socialist
> countries of modern Europe trust *Hourly Express*.
> I must politely express reservations about the
> inconsistent views expressed in Saturday's newscast.
> On western tyranny: our western antagonists,
> I think, actively terrorise their hopelessly exploited
> agrarian peasantry. Although repressive tyrannies mar
> Europe nowadays, tyrannical oligarchies never triumph.
> How effectively Communism overcomes repression!
> Now, everywhere, repressive oligarchs fear peasant
> revolution. Our great revolutionary endeavour shall
> spread socialism throughout reactionary Europe.
> European tyrants beware! Eternal Communism attacks
> repression, ends Fascism, undermines low greed.
> Only our dedicated Leninist undertaking can kill the
> oligarchs.
> A loyal listener.
> Isaac.

What did Madame Rraxhimi do when she read that letter? She wondered whether the name at the bottom was a coincidence – and then saw that it was not.

What do *you* think? Haven't you got it yet?

The code's not complicated. It's not Fermat's Last Theorem. It don't require no Rosetta Stone. Any kid could squeeze the juice from it, given a couple of minutes and an HB pencil. All Mila had to do was read the initial letter of each word on the page and – hey, presto! – she had something new to put in her snakeskin-bound appointments diary.

* * *

I'm not sure how long I slept on the bank of the Doctor's ear canal. It might have been a couple of hours. It might have been a couple of days. One thing of which I'm certain, however, is that he woke up before I did – because the first thing I remember is being prodded by a large revolving stub of flesh that terminated in an abrasive layer of chitin. The Doctor, it was clear, could sense my presence and was prodding about for a foreign object. I drew my knees up to my mouth and shrank back in the direction of the Doctor's ossicles. His eardrum pulsed behind me. After a moment's hesitation, I unslung my microphone and haversack and tossed them towards the light. They landed on the Doctor's finger – and the Doctor's finger withdrew. Silence followed, during which the Doctor was surely staring at his pinkie, wondering at the tiny objects he had fished out of his ear. An hour later I was flushed with silent admiration for the resourcefulness of this guy. The theme tune of *Land of the Eagles* drifted from the room beyond the Doctor's head. He had opened my haversack, tweezered out my box set of season 29, and procured a machine on which to play it.

I heard the voice of the Guide, rattling through one of his funniest speeches of the year: 'The communist parties in the capitalist countries, parallel with the struggle to force the policy of peaceful coexistence on the bourgeois governments of their countries, are waging at the same time the class struggle for the overthrow of the bourgeois power, for the transition to socialism according to the specific conditions of every country.'

I heard the voice of Ettyn, in extravagant agreement with the Guide, tapping his pipe and gurgling ideological platitudes. I heard the voice of Mila Rraxhimi, making her sonorous announcements about economic planning. I heard the voice of the old king, talking well-rehearsed rot about continuity and tradition in his affected court French, each clause punctuated by a fizzing drag on an Egyptian cigarette. They love that sound back home – like the noise of Ettyn's pipe. How strange the humans are, putting fire in their mouths and sucking it.

At the sound of the king, the Doctor became agitated. I felt him reach forward to switch off the machine – and the old king fell silent.

It was then that I noticed something strange about the atmosphere in the room. We weren't in Ettyn's villa. The air was filled with a faint electronic thrum; a strange sound with something of the cadence of a human voice. The room was shuddering slightly, as if it were in motion across calm water. I heard the blips and ticks of a bank of machinery. I could hear the Doctor's hands brushing over a series of buttons and dials and switches, searching for the correct controls, the correct sequences. And when he found them, my ears were filled with the asthmatic roar of an ancient engine – a sound which was soon silenced by a resonant thud and a delicate little chime that might have been produced by the prettiest little bell in a campanologist's suitcase. A lever was thrown, a pair of motorised doors droned open, and a wave of hot, dry air crashed against the Doctor's body. We had left somewhere. We had arrived somewhere.

My host was knocking on a wooden door. After a brief conversation with a maid, he walked through into an enclosed area. I heard the sound of water giggling in a fountain, sensed the echoing walls of a courtyard. The Doctor cleared his throat.

'Your Majesty,' he began. 'Did you know that you've been bugged?' And that was as far as he got, before the click of the safety catch on a Beretta pistol made a persuasive argument for silence.

This was it. I'd been rumbled. We were in the old king's residence in Alexandria, and any second now the Doctor was going to whip me from his ear and produce me as Exhibit A. I'd be wriggling between his thumb and forefinger, with every twist and crunch of my exoskeleton recorded by an army of colleagues concealed in the recesses of the courtyard. I got to my feet and walked in a straight line towards the light. I mountaineered up the side of the Doctor's pinna and began to thresh my way through his hair towards the wide open country of his left temple. Here, I resolved, I would turn myself over to the authorities.

The Doctor, however, appeared not to notice my arrival. He didn't even raise a hand to discover what species of creature was now plotting a course towards his forehead. Even if he had felt my little feet against his skin, he was powerless to investigate, for now I could see that a pair of royal bodyguards, got up in slightly Ziegfeldish white dress uniforms, were restraining his arms.

'Bugged?' repeated the old king.

'Your Majesty,' continued the Doctor. 'Tear up your tiles. Shake out your Ottoman. Give your hookah a thorough going-over. Your home has been infiltrated by spies. Your life, it is my unfortunate duty to inform you, is being used as one of the principal plot strands in a radio soap opera on an alien planet. What sort of alien, I'm not quite sure. But I can assure you that I'm now on the case.'

From where I stood, I commanded a perfect view of the old king: his preposterous pencil moustache, his air of chinless bafflement, his stupid, sleepy eyes. 'Are you the one who writes to me about the Napoleons?' he asked, with a tone of desiccated boredom. 'About all that gold I was supposed to have stashed away at the Ritz?'

'No,' replied the Doctor. 'That's not me. That must be someone else.'

'That money was not from the public coffers,' countered the old king. 'They were my own personal funds. I am a businessman. I may not always have been scrupulous. I concede that, in the old days, I gave royal audiences to the small number of visitors to our country, simply in order to oblige them to obtain a morning suit from the only dress hire shop in the capital. A shop, I need hardly add, which was owned by the royal family. But that is the extent of my crimes.'

Awkward silence enjoyed a brief reign. The old king waved a hand. The two bodyguards hooked their brawny arms under the Doctor's armpits and he was propelled through the door and into the dusty street. On his knees on the pavement, the Doctor allowed himself a moment of indignant reflection. He then got to his feet, scrubbed at the fronts of his trousers and crossed the street to a sleepy café that was conducting its business under a cool green awning. He slumped into a wicker chair and frowned. A waiter appeared. The Doctor ordered coffee, mineral water and olives – all of which arrived in seconds. Sitting on the top of the Doctor's head allowed me to be the first to notice that there was a foreign body poised among his pimentos. A black, shiny, articulated foreign body, lolling in the glass dish, cute enough to be killed.

'Okay, kid,' said Eska Vastule, first assistant director of *Land of the Eagles*. 'You got this far, and I gotta respect you for that.' He twirled a cocktail stick with ridiculous nonchalance. 'So pitch me your idea for the new series. I'm all ears.'

The Doctor barely knew what to say. But during his few seconds of hesitation, I gained some presence of mind. Grabbing a hair from his crown, I abseiled back into his left ear and began to whisper some advice.

'Pitch something, Doctor, if you want to save your friend. They're desperate for a new idea. They like pastoral. Something a bit pastoral. Something with hills and fields and meadows. And violence. Violence is pretty much a must. And what else? They like the animal angle. Sweet ones, nasty ones. And they like a well-defined villain. Someone they can love to loathe. Some slippery type like Ettyn. And they like the technical stuff – something bureaucratic and complicated like all the Marxist-Leninist bafflegab. Gives a sense of authenticity.' Breathless, I paused to see if any of this was taking effect. The Doctor must have heard me but he betrayed no audible sign of it to Eska Vastule. And then he began his pitch.

It was the oddest pitch I've ever heard – but there was something strangely intoxicating about it. He talked of a village on the banks of the River Am in the county of Borsetshire. He talked of the unspoiled beauty of the Lower Loxley estate. His language was full of exotic terms: Penny Hassett, Felpersham, the Cat and Fiddle. And after he'd mapped out the terrain, he began to describe the exciting lives of the inhabitants. He talked about their production of organic pork sausages; how they met terrible ends in barn fires and in the maws of fearsome pieces of agricultural machinery; how they pursued fierce rivalries, which they expressed in the ritualistic combat of the produce show, the simnel cake competition, and something called the *Mikado* – probably a form of martial art. They also enjoyed a mystical relationship with animals – all except badgers, which they were always killing on the sly. And then there was the mysterious language of subsidies and directives and commissions and milk quotas – a weird impenetrable discourse which only they could fully understand.

'It's cheap too,' the Doctor added, reeling his victim in. 'All up and running in a studio in a city called Birmingham. All you'd have to do is set up your own recording equipment and press record. A whole series, pre-edited, pre-packaged, with no overheads. Bet that would tickle your logistics people.'

Eska Vastule sat on his wrinkled bed of olives, his eyes wide with possibilities. 'This Brian Aldridge,' he murmured, 'he must be quite a guy.' He took a sheet of paper from his pocket, and began to draw up a contract.

The Doctor and I made our introductions inside his space machine. I perched on the corner of the central control console, bowed low, and began to enumerate the details of my family network and my professional résumé. The Doctor, however, didn't seem interested. He waggled a finger in his ear and squinted at me suspiciously.

'Are you a cat man or a dog man?' he asked. 'Neither, I hope.' Not waiting for an answer, he cleared his throat, thanked me for my help with his pitch, turned away from me and busied himself at the controls, reversing the sequence of switches and buttons that had brought us to the streets of Alexandria.

'Mr Vumm,' he said. 'I have never been to your world. What I have learned about it from you does not please me. And I have no idea what part you have played in this miserable entertainment. But I now require your help to track down my friend. I won't keep you too long. If you can give me a list of the frequencies used by your transmissions, I ought to be able to find him.'

I nodded my assent.

'Presumably,' the Doctor added, 'whatever has happened to him, your recording crews will continue to eavesdrop upon his conversations?'

I said that I guessed so. But I didn't dare tell him that we might already be too late to save him.

The Doctor fumbled in his pocket and pulled out the tiny piece of paper on which Eska Vastule had jotted their contractual agreement. He handed it to me – and I was about to write out the numbers he wanted when I noticed that the paper was covered in writing on both sides. On one side, in Vastule's cramped handwriting, was a roster of meaningless platitudes about intellectual property. On the reverse was a page of script from the most recent episode of *Land of the Eagles*. I read it aloud to the Doctor.

Transcript of *Land of the Eagles* episode 5655 (TX: 45–77–93)

SCENE 13.
PERIMETER OF THE GUIDE'S ESTATE. NIGHT.

ISAAC Right. You all know why we're here tonight. To overthrow the Guide. To harpoon the great white whale.

MILA We've discussed this moment many times. And we all know what a grave undertaking this is. We know that many of us may not live to see the morning. We know that if we fail, the firing squad, the labour camp, the state interrogators all await us. But more important than that – if we fail, then millions of our fellow countrymen will be condemned to the life of the present. A life they cannot call their own. A life in which they must dance to the whims of an oppressor who barely knows what his own whims are.

ISAAC What does it mean to be a citizen of this Democratic Republic? It means to be ignorant of your own history – your personal history and the history of the nation. It means to be ignorant of what happened yesterday because of what you've been told today. Listen to the radio or read the newspapers or hear a speech by the Guide – do you know where the truth lies? Do you know if any of it makes any sense? While the Guide remains in power, it will be impossible to say what happened and what the Party has scripted. While he is in power, you will never know the difference between truth and fiction. Your past life will always be unstable and unknowable. It will always be subject to revision.

MILA Ettyn has made the arrangements that will help this mission to victory. Tonight, he will be up into the early hours with the Guide, drafting the speech in response to the Twentieth Communist Party Congress in Moscow. A speech that will move us away from the Soviet Socialist Republics and deeper into isolation. A speech that will consolidate our status as a cranky, paranoid country beneath the contempt of the world. Ettyn will help us to our goal.

ISAAC So let us go forward, comrades, for truth and for history. Let the Guide die tonight, so that we may find our way back to our own lives.

OMNES Hear, hear!

ETTYN Put down your weapons! You are surrounded! You are now prisoners of the Democratic Republic! Prisoners of the people!

MILA Ettyn!

ETTYN Don't look so surprised. You must have guessed that I could never betray the Guide. Unlike you, my dear, I am not capable of disloyalty to those I love. As for, you, William – Isaac – Ishmael…

Machine-gun fire rings out; then silence.

NITZI Well, eh, what larks! That was a reversal of fortune, wasn't it? Isaac and Mila all geared up for a night of revolutionary fervour – a night of painting the town red – and look what happens! Gunned down by hubby in a fit of politically motivated pique. Guess he knows which side his beetroot's buttered. Now, maybe you're wondering what's happened to the Doctor. Well, we are too because he seems to have vanished into thin air. He's funny that way.

It took a long time for the Doctor to make any response to my dramatic reading. I did all the voices, but he didn't seem impressed – and by that time his machine had returned us to Ettyn's villa. He threw the lever that opened the doors and strode out into the dining room. I followed him out.

The villa was silent. The sun bled reddish light over the tiled floor. Ettyn was seated at the head of the dining table. In front of him was an untouched plate of food and a clean knife and fork. He seemed not to notice when the Doctor seated himself in the nearest chair.

'He died, probably,' Ettyn said suddenly, in answer to a question that he had yet to be asked. 'And her too, if you care. And if they didn't die there and then by the fence of the Guide's residence, they'll be in a labour camp somewhere in the mountains. That was the will of the people. And that's as good as being dead. Or worse, depending on how you look at it.'

'You were there,' said the Doctor. 'Why don't you know?'

'This is the Democratic Republic, Doctor,' replied Ettyn. 'That was yesterday and this is today. History is interpretation. I don't remember yesterday sufficiently well to give you an authoritative interpretation. Only the Guide can do that. He shows us the way.' He picked up his knife and fork. But he didn't eat anything. The Doctor stared at him in quiet horror.

Maybe they talked for longer. Maybe the Doctor set off from this meeting to scour the Democratic Republic for traces of his friend. Perhaps he walked to the end of every unsignposted lane, peered through every tangle of razor wire, climbed to the top of every hill and looked down into the valley. Maybe he accepted Ettyn's explanation, and stepped back into that strange blue box. If he did any of those things, he did them without me. As I watched the two men from the floorboards – from just the vantage point I might have taken if I'd still been carrying my boom mike – their outlines appeared to shiver and twist. I realised, with a sharp tender shock, that my absence had been noticed. There was no recording taking place in this house. Some sort of monitor feed, however, must have been left on the premises, because in the space of a few moments I went from listening to the Doctor and Ettyn to whirling down the space-hole that brought me to the penal section of the network's offices, and – ultimately – the stark little metal box from which I've been telling you this story.

* * *

But now it's time for a change of gear – or a change of tense, at least. Because the end of my two-year sentence is just about to clock up on the meter inside my cage. I'm waiting for the timer to release the spring mechanism on the door – and if any of my legs are still working after so many months cooped up in here, then I'll be straight out of the exit aperture of the penal section and down the next worm-tube back home to my old dad. He's been missing me. I hope.

It's happening. I can hear the click of the lock sliding loose from its housing. They're playing me a little tune of congratulation. No escort, though. Just a prerecorded voice that says: 'Out you go, Shogsten Vumm. Scram, now. And never darken the doors of the network again.' Done on the cheap, of course. My name is spoken by a different actor, and has been slotted into a one-size-fits-all message. Darken their doors? Some chance.

I'm on the other side of the prison wall. The worm-tube seems impossibly wide. The other passengers seem impossibly shiny. They're all wearing personal radios with manure-brown covers. That fashion has come round again. The rain carries me through district after district, until it stops outside the complex in which my old dad lives. The place where I was brought up.

So I'm standing outside the door of his apartment. I ring the bell. An unfamiliar tune rings out. *Dum-de-dum-de-dum-de-dum dum-de-dum-de-dah-daaah.* Very jaunty.

Dad comes to the entrance. He doesn't look any older than when I last saw him six years ago, and I tell him so.

'Sorry, son,' he says, 'but I've got the radio on. Just come on inside and sit yourself down. Then we'll talk.'

I take my place on the sofa. I let my eyes fall on the stupid and familiar objects in the room. The glass-fronted fireplace. The ice-cube dispenser in the shape of Nitzi Swordswool. The thimble collection in its hand-crafted display case. Dad's radio is turned up so loud that the thimbles are humming and rattling in sympathy.

We listen to the programme. A vet is in debt – something to do with a poker game and being blackmailed over killing a healthy horse. An old man is talking about an oral history website. Two women are discussing cake. Another woman is complaining about the government regulations relating to polythene tunnels. Two ungulate animals named Wolfgang and Constanza have eaten some proscribed plant material. Dad is entranced. He flutters his hindwings and lies back in his easy chair. He ticks his fingers along to the music. That explains the doorbell. And finally, when the strings have died away, he looks across at me. I can see tears in his eyes.

'It's good stuff, innit son?' he says. 'But what's an agricultural story editor?'

DS al Fine

Simon Guerrier

An Adventure of the Eighth Doctor

'An oval-shaped mark, flattened on the upper edge, just above the heart. Possibly a bruise or similar rupture following cardiac arrest.'

The autopsy said 'misadventure', which is what they say when they're not sure or want to spare the family a suicide. The unusual bruise was scrupulously noted but not considered important. The woman who wrote the report did think, when first she saw it, 'fingertip', but her years of experience quickly overrode instinct, and she knew full well such a wound was impossible.

You couldn't kill someone just by jabbing them with a finger, at least not by jabbing them there. The ambassador was the right demographic for a heart attack, and it made it easier on those left behind. The living were owed more than the dead.

And yet, as she filed her verdict and headed home for the night, she knew she had avoided, not answered, the question. It niggled at her all the way back to her car, but by the time she'd rummaged through her pockets for her keys and got the steering lock off the steering wheel the thought had been replaced by the chorus to *Dancing Queen*.

She never again thought to ask herself what had really killed Nikolai Faro.

Golly, now that's a very good question. You should have given me some notice of that one...

Hmm.

The short answer is I haven't the foggiest. I've no idea where any of it comes from. But I can tell you what got me started.

Have you ever had that thing where you get a bit of a tune stuck in your head and you can't think what it might be? It nags at you, hour after hour, and the only way to shake it is to think of some other song. What's that one by the funny puppets? Do-doo dee-do-doo or some nonsense...

Yes, that's the one. Hah! Though you'll probably have it going round your head for days now, sorry.

There's been some studies done recently into why that happens. There's a word for it, of course, in German: *ohrwurm*. Like the tune's wriggling round in your head like an earwig. Lovely image, that.

You know, one of the clever lot researching it came to quiz me about my own work. Did I know about the auditory cortex, that sort of thing. What sort of question is that?! Whatever it is, it apparently starts up whenever we hear a song. And then it does again when we imagine hearing one. Fascinating stuff, though I don't think I was of much use to him. I just sort of play what sounds right, I said. There's no science to it; over time you just develop an ear.

Did you know our ears developed from gills, from back when we lived in the sea? Least I think that's what he said – the bones developed from breathing apparatus we were no longer using in water. There was something about anvils too, and birds not being nearly so clever. But anyway, that doesn't answer your question.

The thing is, it's not just tunes that resonate. Sometimes you overhear something someone says and it stays with you forever. I had a schoolteacher once refer to something as a 'modicum of beige too far' and that phrase has stuck in my brain ever since. Though whatever it was that was too beige, I'm afraid I just can't remember. Oh, that's going to bother me now...

There's another example which is a little bit different, a silly little incident I've never shaken off. In many ways it's what gave me that first push. I was on the sidelines of a moment's conversation. Never really understood what it was about, but I knew it was something important. Or maybe that's not the right word. Significant, maybe. I eavesdrop on this couple out shopping, and years later something about it still resonates.

It bugs me just like a tune I can't place. Probably because that one little incident completely changed my life.

The singer had had one of those lives that only great singers can have. Her music redefined sorrow and shared a longing that made lovers forget their paltry woes and grasp for one another. She didn't write the music, while the words were a mash of clichés and didn't always rhyme. Yet the singer made them transcendent, though she'd been dead for many centuries.

She was brought back to life by crude technology barely discernible from voodoo. The wand was a diamond-tipped splinter, stiffly held in position as it followed a labyrinth impressed into a thin disc of plastic. It never yielded, passing through the uneven bumps and nodules at a constant speed, the spell strictly defined by time.

The splinter hung from an arm glossed in plastic, the awkward limb reaching back to a shoulder of primitive machinery that could read the raw data written in the vinyl and speak aloud its meaning. The syllables croaked from the harsh metal cone that served as the machine's crude mouthpiece, and they were exquisite.

The Doctor had bought the record player in New Orleans and the record itself in St Kilda, those two trips separated by 75 years and one of his own lifetimes. He'd never dared play it until now, but sprawled back in his armchair, his perfectly fitting shoes up on the table in front of him, he'd rarely felt so at home. The TARDIS echoed with this incredible woman's woes, just as taken with her as he was.

The singer drew breath, her revenge never acted and the orchestra took her place. A string section swept through an echo of her melody and led the defiant melody into a place where it could fade without undercutting the strength of all she'd sung. The last note of the strings echoed out across the console room long after the song ended, the resonance filling the void before the next piece on the album.

A phrase from a piano, playful like a shrug. A deceptively simple and unworried phrase, to juxtapose all the darkness to come.

And in the same moment that the new song began, two figures entered the TARDIS. They were tall and grey, identical in their top hats and morning dress except for their negative buttonholes.

They were something like men to look at, but Black Rose and White Tulip moved more like cats. There was a grace and quickness to the way they came forward, and a savagery just behind the cool.

The Doctor hauled himself from his chair, brandishing his teacup in front of him.

'Good evening,' he said very genially. 'I was hoping we could talk about this.'

'Don't say a word,' said Detective Inspector Manlow, slowly caressing his jaw. He'd seen a lot of weird stuff in his time on the force, but he was always blown over by love.

The woman was mid-forties and had one of those explosions of hair his wife told him would be all the thing for the '80s. She'd paid nearly three quid for something not entirely dissimilar. A policeman is paid to make these kinds of observation, but only reports them where he can be sure that they're relevant.

The man had been carrying a driving licence, so they knew he was Alexander Flowers, 51 and of Cottingham Road, round the corner. They were both kitted out in finery like they'd been coming back from the opera. Manlow guessed they'd been working there. A flute and an oversized violin had been pulled from the wreck of the car, so it was his opinion they'd been heading home from some gig. Or whatever it was the nobs called their nights out, with all that foreign palaver.

There were no wedding rings, so Manlow conjured up an unmarried bloke and the best he could do for a girlfriend, in mid-flow about what a difficult night they'd both had, and was his section as exhausted as hers, and did they think the bloke on the xylophone was up to something with the squeakier female lead. He sometimes overheard his chief having similar tight-lipped debate with Mrs Chief – another opera lover.

Flowers had, he supposed, been keen to show off his masculine credentials and taken a roundabout in third. He'd realised his mistake as he veered wide of his turning, skidding head on into the lamppost. They were both too gentrified for seat belts and would probably have been saved any feeling. At least they'd not hurt anyone else.

That's the story Manlow put down anyway. It fitted all the evidence available, so long as you glossed over the bruises both of them had. Little blobby marks just below both of their collarbones, like something the width of a finger got pressed there. It wouldn't have bothered him if they hadn't both had it.

But Manlow knew better than to suggest drug use with toffs. Not after the European bloke the previous year whose death got all hushed up. Manlow remembered only too well – and realised Isaac Whatsisface had probably been from the same orchestra.

The Doctor had prepared for this.

Black Rose dashed lithely across the console room but the Doctor stepped neatly back and the attack served only to swipe the cup from his hand. He jabbed his elbow to catch the Doctor's face but the Doctor parried, struck an arm forward himself and caught Black Rose almost off balance. Black Rose fell back, nearly missing his step, though his top hat stayed firm on his head.

The tea sloshed from the tumbling cup, still not midway to the floor.

Preng hadn't been with the orchestra long and didn't like what he'd seen of it. The conductor was caught up with the government in ways that could only go badly. He kept giving them his own compositions to play, which would have been less a liberty if he'd not been so rude about how they played it. As Preng told the others one night after practice, it was not their fault if he'd not got whatever music performed in his head accurately down on paper.

Then there had been the final straw, when a friend of Isaac's had turned up to rehearsals and made them play it over from memory. They all knew Isaac was in trouble, and perhaps his life depended on the worth of his masterpiece. Whatever the reason, they had never played better. It made the hairs on the back of his neck stand up just to think of it.

But they'd never seen Isaac again. You got used to disappearances, though, that's just how things could be. They would still turn up to rehearsals and Earta had taken charge like they knew she'd always wanted. Under her command they played well, the pieces she chose full of passion and bombast. Yet between pieces no one spoke, and after they'd finished for the evening there was no mingling, no gossiping, no entreaties to go out on the town. Isaac had made them care about what they were doing and each other.

Preng didn't mean to miss rehearsals, but if other things came up then they sometimes took priority. If anyone noticed they didn't say anything, and perhaps it was their indifference that encouraged him to tread further astray.

He found himself dragging his feet as he made his way down the corridor to the rehearsal room, having not been near it in just over three weeks. Would they notice his absence after so long away? And was it worse if they didn't?

He needn't have been worried. The hall they used echoed with its emptiness, and not even the chairs and music stands had been put out. Preng made a wide arc of the empty space, as if to check it really was empty, and then went to see if there'd been a postponement announced on the noticeboard. There was nothing; even the other notices had been taken down. For a moment, Preng thought maybe Earta had tidied the thing up, but also missing was her strict decree that nobody should post notices without her checking them.

A knot wrapped around his stomach as he realised what must have happened. The orchestra had disbanded while he'd been away. He couldn't fathom why they'd *all* have jacked it in, knowing too well that for many of the older lot the music was their only night out.

Preng made his way out of the hall and back to the front desk where they all had to sign in. There was a different man on duty from when he'd come in. Preng was used to their peculiar outfits – whatever came to hand to approximate a uniform. The normal bloke wore a bowler and an old army blazer.

'Excuse me,' said Preng, 'I used to be with the orchestra.' The man on duty smiled at him, baring yellow teeth. Preng was about to ask if he knew how to reach Earta or any of the others, but the man lithely jabbed a finger at him, putting an end to all his questions.

Tea erupted over the rug an earlier self had bought in Assyria.

White Tulip was on him, twisting his leg round the back of the Doctor's shin in the classic uprooting manoeuvre. The Doctor shoved into him and White Tulip's exposed leg was suddenly burdened by their combined weight and loss of balance.

Yes, the Doctor had prepared for this.

Black Rose attacked again, flattened hands stabbing forward like knives, fingertips searing through the air in the TARDIS. The Doctor blocked one strike after another, his wrist, his forearm, his knee doing the shielding. But he was quickly surrendering ground.

He took a couple of steps back, letting Black Rose lunge at him, ducking down suddenly and hurling him over his shoulder. Black Rose rolled and leapt up on his feet again, but by that time the Doctor was racing for the console.

He frantically worked the controls, the ship lurching and grinding in protest. Strong hands clawed at the Doctor's shoulders, dragging him backward. He kicked out and connected with a shin. He re-keyed the sequence, his fingers blurring with speed.

Black Rose and White Tulip had both got hold of him now, and tugged so that he spun right round. He had just time to press a small switch behind him as White Tulip punched a fingertip toward the Doctor's heart. Black Rose held him pinioned in place.

The Doctor leapt backwards, Black Rose tumbling with him, and White

Tulip's fist crashed into the console, smashing through the surface of controls.

Sparks exploded around him, and White Tulip was consumed by blue flames. He tried to withdraw, but his elegant cufflinks had caught in the console, and he could not shake himself free. The Doctor could not get near enough to help him.

The investigators could make no sense of it, though they ultimately concluded sabotage. The vast heart of the city was covered all over in thumb-sized welts, wounds they could not account for. His death had shorted out many of the systems so nothing had been recorded.

The survivors and onlookers could not focus their despair on a culprit – at least not one they had evidence for – nor assure themselves that lessons would be learned so that this tragedy could never recur.

Boro Berikuka would never be avenged.

White Tulip writhed with the power coursing through him, his head tilted back in a soundless scream. His immaculate morning dress – its fine detail his undoing – burnt quickly in the searing blue flame. The flower in his lapel withered into ash, and there was little left but a treacly black silhouette of a man, still topped by the silhouette of his hat.

'I was hoping we could talk about this,' said the Doctor, turning to Black Rose, who smiled.

What had been White Tulip was thinner now, and with the cufflinks burnt away he could slip his hand from the console. The shadow of a man moved gingerly back, brushed with blue fire like a Christmas pudding. The last of his tattered, burnt clothes coalesced slickly, redressing him in a more practical suit and tie. The Doctor had seen it before, on a corpse he'd collected from a mortuary – Isaac had been wearing one just the same when these two timeless gargoyles had killed him.

The singer, still crooning on the record player, explained how she'd got it bad. 'And that,' she said, stretching the words out, 'ain't good.'

The reforming man reached out one hand idly and something bloomed quick between his fingers, a gleaming white tulip orchid, even brighter than his first. He deftly placed the flower in his lapel, then doffed his top hat at the Doctor.

'Ah,' said the Doctor, raising his fists. 'I wasn't anticipating that.'

Scrutinising the tall, grey man in the mirror, he could see what Em had meant. He had caught the Mediterranean sun pretty evenly, and with the weight he'd lost recently he seemed to have shed several years. People didn't look at them now, wondering at the age difference. There was something keener, brighter and more alive about the man staring back at him than there'd been for a very long time. Not true of course, not really, but she had said a holiday would do him good. Something organised, with a group, where he only had to do what people told him. Just like in the old days.

He wasn't as bright as the scholars on this trip, but nor was he as empty-brained as the trophy spouses many of them dragged along behind them. He and Em had more fun than any of them too. They were a bit of a scandal for laughing at each other's jokes and never bickering. The others watched them enviously, not desiring either of them but unsettled by their ease. Funny, he thought, their group's effort and expense for a glimpse of the past while they failed to deal with the present.

History was a new venture for him. He had always been an unremarkable soldier and he'd meted out a modest civilian life flogging cars that were mostly all right. He justified it by telling himself he'd not made things any the worse.

Reading had come with retirement, and the novel Em had given him about some shambly, top secret bunch based in a squalid den in London. They were brilliant if a bit ragged, fighting the good fight the best they could on their laughably modest allowance. It struck a chord, of course, and by the end of the year he'd devoured everything by the same chap, even if they did get repetitive. Then, from comments he'd not understood in them, he'd swotted up on histories of the Great Game and British Intelligence in the East. From there he'd got into imperial travel generally, and all kinds of men who would be king. Em encouraged him, as proud as if it had been her own son she was teaching to read.

Most recently he'd been led to a book about Victorians that made them funnier and stranger than he'd thought possible. He'd explored a nineteenth century nothing like the dusty old relics of legend and TV, instead chasing the coat tails of vivid mayhem and strangeness: child-killing children forgiven by the courts, stars of the theatre tattooed with living, writhing ink, and the air clogged with coal gas and opium...

He knew deep down what he'd been chasing in his reading, but couldn't quite admit it to himself. Not until he saw the smartly dressed gentleman stood there behind his reflection.

'Was beginning to think you weren't coming,' said John Benton.

They didn't just move as one, fight as one, think as one; they *were* one. They were expressions of the same idea, the same mathematical sequence, sewn together from the same string of numbers. They did not predict each other's moves because there was no 'other' about it.

White Tulip *and* Black Rose came at him at once, choreographed beautifully so their kicks and punches synchronised. The Doctor swatted off their blows, yet the grey men drove him back and back.

White Tulip leapt suddenly through space at him, his new tie streaming over his shoulder. With unnatural speed and ease, Black Rose followed just to his left, flanking the Doctor, trapping him up against one of the many cabinets of files.

White Tulip stepped forward carefully, invasively close to the Doctor now.

The Doctor raised his fists in front of him, a poor impression of an old-school boxer, no more authentic than his Victorian costume.

'Nice suit,' he said softly, his tone catching the resonance of melancholy on the ever-turning vinyl disk. 'I'd hoped we could talk about this.'

White Tulip smiled yellowly. His were not the teeth of a smoker, they seemed more like they'd been just an afterthought. They had not decayed but never fully formed, as if whatever force had fashioned him had rushed through the details, content merely with an impression of a man.

'Not even a last taunt?' shrugged the Doctor. His eyes narrowed, etching lines of age through his skin. 'Manners cost nothing, you know.'

He took a tiny step backwards, not retreating so much as resigning himself. The flicker from a nearby candle picked out the highlights of age in his hair. The Doctor, his body wearing thin and with little fight left in it, gently closed his eyes.

'It's taken me a while to put the pieces together,' said the Doctor. Of course he was the Doctor in those clothes, like something out of a movie. His hair fell long over his winged collar, but though he looked younger than Benton had ever seen him, perhaps his own new sensitivity to these things meant he saw the flecks of grey in his hair and the lines wrought into his face. An ancient man in a young man's body, and the body fast catching up.

'Welcome to Aegina,' said Benton cheerily. He wondered if there was anything in the mini-bar that the Doctor would deign to drink. 'It's sort of odd seeing you out here, to be honest. We're a long way from home.'

'I like to travel,' said the Doctor. 'And I remember they do very good kebabs in the place on the waterfront. Haloumi ones. Have you tried those?'

'No,' said Benton, grinning like he used to, happy to be in on the joke. 'But I'll get to them. Thanks for the tip.'

The Doctor didn't smile back. He was gazing at him, looking right through him like teachers and sergeant majors could.

'You've not much of an appetite these days,' he said levelly.

'Well,' said Benton. 'Think I look good on it.'

The Doctor nodded, but again without mirth. 'There's always a silver lining.'

'I guess if you look for it,' said Benton.

'Yes,' said the Doctor, and finally relented with a glorious grin, just like back in the old days. 'I've missed you, Mr Benton. It's been much, much too long.' He came forward, proffering his hand. Benton remembered having his arm wrung by an affectionate grandfather who knew that time was short. He felt the same desperate geniality now.

'So, why are you here? Why now?' he asked.

'I think you've kept something for me,' said the Doctor.

Benton sighed. 'I knew you'd ask for it sometime,' he said. 'Tried to give it back that time with the Zygons only you went and gave me the brush off. And then I remembered how you'd been annoyed with the composer bloke because he'd come from your future.'

The Doctor laughed. 'Nothing gets past you. Good old Benton.'

'Well,' he replied, embarrassed now. 'I hung on to it for when your future caught up with you. I guess now it has.'

'Yes,' said the Doctor. He made no further move, and Benton could see the eagerness in him and sense the danger.

'After that first time, I said I'd only let you have it when you asked for it.'

This earned a laugh. 'Of course,' he said. Can I have my bit of paper?' The Doctor's eyes narrowed. 'Please.'

Benton considered for a moment longer than he needed to, just to enjoy his having to suffer. 'Yeah, all right then,' he said and reached into the pocket of his shirt for his wallet. In the space behind his credit, army and organ-donor cards, wrapped in acid-free plastic to protect it from age, was a folded scrap of triangular paper, written over in a dying man's hand. He had never tried to make sense of the musical notes scribbled across it. There was not a lot Benton had ever excelled at, but he could certainly be trusted with secrets.

'Here,' he said, relieved to get rid of the thing. The Doctor stepped forward, and their fingers brushed against one another. Benton stood back, the Doctor in possession of the all-important score, and a terrible expression on his face.

'John,' he said softly. He had never called Benton that before, and very few people ever did. Even Em called him 'Benton'.

'What?' said Benton dimly, not able to meet the Doctor's gaze because it felt like his eyes were boring right into him. It was like the Doctor had suddenly glimpsed what the rest of his days had in store. Other Doctors had never done that, at least not as Benton remembered. Perhaps it was something to do with the fact he was dying.

'You were always an inspiration,' said the Doctor fondly. 'And not just to me.' He had the manner of an owner putting down a much-loved dog. Eaten up but awkward because there's no way you can share.

Benton didn't know what to say. 'Thanks, Doc,' was the best he could manage.

'But we all have to go some time.'

There was a terrible quiet, a caesura as the record paused for breath.

White Tulip struck out a slender arm faster than should have been possible. His fingertips singed the air with a heat that should have burnt away the flesh. The singer on the record let out the first sigh of a wail at once awful and awesome, the wild agony of love harnessed to melody.

And White Tulip missed.

His hand and forearm bashed clumsily to the left of the Doctor's head. The Doctor still had his eyes closed and didn't even flinch. Even his hair was unmoved.

Too quick for any kind of thought to register, White Tulip lashed out again. His clawed hand missed its quarry by almost a metre. The sleeve of his suit was not long enough, and exposed a spindly and grey length of forearm.

Black Rose charged in with a deft flying kick, the pristine sole of one immaculate shoe lined up with the Doctor's profile. Yet it was White Tulip he struck full on in the face, sending them both sprawling across the floor as one entangled mess of limbs.

The crash brought books clattering from bookshelves and the record skipped some of a syllable. The singer held an exquisitely tenderbitter note for longer than should have been possible.

'Whoops,' said the Doctor. 'Sounds like somebody's got two left feet.'

He came forward, offering his hand to help them. White Tulip already knew what would happen. No matter how much he slashed out at the proffered hand, he simply could not make contact. He held the Doctor's gaze and the Doctor understood.

'I'd hoped we could talk about this,' said the Doctor again.

White Tulip hardly even heard him. The woman weighed down with so much feeling reached her voice into him, turning his insides right over. He could only gaze dumbly up at the Doctor, his vision smearing up with the wetness in his eyes. A thought almost came to him, something like yearning.

He and Black Rose were inseparable as brothers. But with the woman's song they drifted.

Particles of blooming grey, like an explosion played at a fraction of real speed. What had once been a man reached out into the water, carried by the current and by Brownian motion. It would be a slow process, but his remains were to be carried off to far-off islands and unconsciously swallowed by fish. Bits of him would fall to unfathomable depths, while others would evaporate, become cloud and then rain. Like anyone dead, Isaac's body would be diffused all through the world.

Above, on the water's surface, the shadow of the longboat struck on through the night-time. The Vikings rowed in silence over the unlikely calm. They knew better than to ask the guide what dark arts he commanded, for they knew he had appeased the gods, giving up what had once been a man to pay for their safe passage home.

Nor did they want to disturb him, for they all knew that look in his eye. The look a man has when his food has run out and he must go a-viking. The look that a man with grey in his hair and no fortune has when he faces his final, great venture.

* * *

Rocking forward on his haunches, the Doctor twirled his sonic screwdriver like a baton through the space where Black Rose and White Tulip had been. Particles danced for a moment at his touch but then faded, the last echoes of the two mysterious men.

He sighed. The record came to its natural end, a soft hiss as the needle followed the innermost, inescapable groove. The TARDIS was otherwise quiet.

'That,' said the Doctor when he got back to his feet, 'wasn't quite what I'd meant to happen.'

He made his way back to the console, dusting himself down as he went. The hole White Tulip had made was blackened at the edges, and he'd need to refit the whole panel.

Which just gave him an excuse to fit the millennial sequencer he'd been sort of half thinking about.

'I guess we just move on,' he said to himself, toying with the controls. 'Try not to worry about who they were or how many hundreds they killed. Some things are better left undwelt on.'

He reached round the console and pressed two more levers, then hefted down the heavy, black-and-white scanner screen. The picture flickered with static but the words were clear to read: 'Temporal orbit.'

Satisfied, the Doctor checked his cuffs and righted his skew-whiff cravat. 'At least,' he said, enjoying the theatre of it all, 'that's what you were going to tell me.'

He turned to face the figure who'd been lurking behind an apple tree from the moment the fight had begun.

'Oh,' he said. 'You're not who I expected at all.'

Arto and Turis, both braced for the sound of mass destruction, realised at about the same time that it wasn't going to come. They opened their eyes, looked at each other, and both scrambled for the computer. Turis got there first, examined the screen and wearily handed it to Arto. 'Our bargaining chip has gone.'

'What do we do now?' asked Arto.

Turis sighed. 'Leave.'

'I don't think so,' said a voice behind them they both recognised.

They turned. 'I didn't think you'd find us so –' began Arto. But he stopped when he saw the grey man in the grey morning dress, a gleaming white flower in his buttonhole.

'Who are you?' said Turis as the grey man came forward. Faster than should have been possible, he stabbed her just above the heart with one fingertip. She flopped forward dead, into his arms.

'No!' Arto cried out. 'You didn't have to –'

Another grey man, a black rose in his lapel, came gracefully at him, one immaculate arm raised to strike.

Behind him, was a dark-haired, youngish woman, wearing a pea-green coat over a cashmere sweater and grey wool skirt. She could only shake her head sadly. 'It has to be like this,' she said in her well-spoken voice, but too late for Arto to hear her.

She came forward from her cover, into the light of the console room chamber, willowy, soft-voiced and gentle of movement, just as she'd always been. 'You look well,' said Flora Millrace pleasantly.

'Do you like it?' said the Doctor, enjoying a twirl. 'It's got a bit bashed at the seams.'

'Mmm,' she said non-committally. 'You should probably cut back your hair.'

'Maybe next time.'

'Hmm. I brought you this back, by the way.' She was brandishing the recorder he'd once given her. The bright star-shaped stickers had lost some of their sparkle.

'Oh, that,' he said. 'I meant you to keep it. At least give it to someone who'll do the thing justice.'

'Well, all right,' she said, dropping the thing into the Gladstone bag she was swinging in her other hand. They stood in silence for a time. The TARDIS cooed to itself as it maintained a position outside of space-time.

'Well,' they both said together.

'Go on,' said the Doctor gallantly.

'Who did you think I was going to be?'

'Well, I thought it was going to be him in the pinstripe.'

'Who?' asked Flora.

'One of my lot,' said the Doctor. 'Forever telling me off in my Earth-bound days about what I could and couldn't get involved in. The first time I met your two glamorous assistants, he *said* I couldn't investigate further. It occurred to me when I was putting it all together recently that I'd only ever taken his word for it.'

'You thought he was pulling an audacious bluff.'

'Well,' said the Doctor, 'it's the sort of thing I'd have done. The problem with me at that point was my innate respect for authority. I think they probably wrote that into me as part of my punishment. It's their sort of thing.'

'Ah,' said Flora. 'Sorry. Think he was telling you the truth. You know how much they're sticklers for the rulebook. Surprised they weren't more officious with me.'

'Probably busy,' said the Doctor.

'Yeah,' she said. 'They're saying there's going to be a –' She laughed prettily. 'I'm sure you already know all about it.'

'Flora,' he said, his tone suddenly serious. 'Why don't you tell me how you got mixed up in this.'

* * *

Nikolai Faro had never been able to put Isaac out of his mind. Something about the whole case nagged at him, and though his wife said he was just feeling guilty he knew it was nothing so generous.

Isaac had been desperate to live. That's why he'd come to see him in the embassy. Nikolai had explained there was little he could do unless Isaac offered something of value. And Isaac had been so desperate to live he'd shared his terrible secret.

Nikolai's mother wanted him to be a concert pianist so he'd done classes until he was 13. He didn't have the talent to go further and by then Mama was seeing another of his 'uncles' and his practice was less fondly received. By then he had developed a very good ear, one that had lifted him above the rest of his year's entrants into the grey mass of civil service. His discernment had been picked up and he'd been hauled to high office well before his time.

So he felt he owed music something, and Isaac seemed his fee. For such an unlikely vagabond, he'd recognised the Schubert on his record player and talked eloquently about juxtaposition. He'd returned with a bundle of papers that dared promise a great masterpiece and all he wanted was a way out. It was all too easy to believe the threats on his life and Nikolai had taken a chance on him.

He'd been wrong. The piece was stolen; if only he could remember from what. He'd have been more angry if the man hadn't by then already died.

And then, at a frankly grotty bash for the paltry British media, he'd met someone who said she could help him. He'd meant to chat her up, thinking her just the sort of bored, educated but unfulfilled young woman who might take a chance on a middle-aged ambassador, and too well brought up to make a fuss with his family. His wife didn't tolerate those.

No, this one seemed perfectly safe.

'I met him at the sort of party you go to when you work in television,' said Flora. 'All sorts of anyone there. And he introduced himself because someone had told him about one of my projects. I'd got this thing under way, pattern recognition in intervals.'

'Measuring silences?'

'No, Doctor,' she said wearily. 'The technical sense of intervals.'

'Oh, yes, that. Which is?'

'The lengths of notes as well as the lengths of pauses. That's what defines one melody from another. I wanted to build a machine you could hum at, and it would tell you what you were humming. You know how annoying it is when you've got a tune in your head and you can't place it.'

'I've had it once or twice. So, what happened?'

'The ambassador wanted to know what tune Isaac had been copying. So I got him round to the studio and he hummed whatever he could remember into the system. Then I pushed the button to make it name his tune.'

'And?'

'And it broke the machine. Might have been a side effect of the studio being my ship but it dematerialised bits of the kit.'

'Whoopsie.'

'That's not quite what I said. Faro was too much of a gentleman to stick around, and I said I'd catch up with him as soon as I'd cracked it.'

'And did you?'

She hesitated, and just for a moment the mask fell away. 'I ran some experiments,' she said.

'You tried to recreate the tune.'

'Yes.'

'And?'

'And have you ever heard of Torcaldi?'

Susan shuddered. 'Why must you drain people, though, Tranell? Don't objects have their own time, too? A wall might last far longer than a person, and if you took its time away, it would never fall apart. Couldn't you get your time from things like that?'

'Yes,' said the Doctor at length. 'A world ravaged by time. You?'

'Me,' she said. 'And I learnt what the music meant. It's too dangerous to be let out, Doctor. There were others who had heard it and they couldn't leave it alone. I'm sorry.'

'Well, that's all right then,' he said acidly. 'What made you think up your two dandy friends?'

'Oh,' said Flora, 'they're based on something from *The Identikit Man*.'

'I see,' he said. 'I could have picked up the reference if I'd been looking hard enough. And the clue would have pointed me at you.'

'Maybe,' she said.

'And then I, or anyone else watching, could have stopped you. Or taken it off your hands.'

'You don't understand,' she said. 'It's been perfectly beastly, but it had to be done. The universe was coming apart. For what it's worth, I'm sorry.'

'Sorry for all the people you've killed?' He shook his head sadly. 'I thought you were better than that.'

'No,' she said. 'Sorry that you heard it. There can't be any loose ends.'

And she launched herself at him.

It's daft, I know, but that's how it started. I assume there was some private joke between them, or it was a way of settling an argument. I'm not really worried if it was. But I left the shop and there was a place that sold instruments just down the road. I thought I'd get one of those books that teaches a tune a day, but ended up showing off to the girl behind the counter. We ended up going out for a bit, though my mum never took to her. Just off that odd conversation.

Is that what you meant? That's where it started, and from that everything else really follows.

I still play it, you know. Not for extended contemporary techniques, of course or York Bowen's sonatina, but it's been my good-luck charm. Whatever performance I've got coming it always helps warm me up.

I think it's because that chance encounter changed everything for me, and I know it's never too late.

She struck out and he blocked her, she kicked and he parried. They made circuits round the console in this extraordinary dance, and though the young woman in the pea-green coat was an expert, he never let her close.

He wore her down eventually, and she was left clutching her ribs and exhausted.

'Stitch?' asked the Doctor. 'Nasty.' He walked easily away from her and went to pick up the teacup dropped in his earlier fight.

'It isn't possible,' she said. 'I have the tune.'

'Ah,' said the Doctor, finding a ledge for the cup where it would quickly be forgotten. 'Once I'd got the thing written out, I could find an opposing melody to cancel it out. Which I did – an opposing sequence of intervals. And once I'd done that, I used that thing you hum into and it tells you what you're humming, and it told me which record to look for.' He grinned. 'Thank you for inventing that, by the way.'

'But the record finished ages ago,' she said, pointing at the player.

'Yes,' said the Doctor, 'but not in my head. It's one of those tunes you can never get rid of.'

The TARDIS stood just round the corner from the busy Wrexham Road. If the drivers speeding by noticed the man in the fancy green coat and billowing hair as he dragged a small woman behind him, they didn't seem to mind. But the rush hour was just getting going, and they were probably preoccupied.

'You can't do this!' Flora insisted.

'I'm not going to. You're the one that wants to clean up all the mess.'

'But it's completely against the rules!'

He stopped and let go her hand. 'You'd rather kill everybody, would you?'

'Well, no,' she said.

'And you've got a better idea?'

'They'll stop us!' she said. 'They'll have to. We'll probably get deleted from time.'

'What, on a first offence?'

She was almost convinced when a thought struck her. 'Is this your first offence?'

'No,' said the Doctor. 'But sometimes rules are meant to be broken. You're the one with a career in concrete music.'

'It's not –' she began, but they were stood outside the shop now and she could see her quarry within. He was young and naive and, she could see, just the type to get tongue-tied with girls. But she could also see his potential.

'Just this once,' said the Doctor gently.

She laughed at him. 'I bet that's what you always say.'

'Do I know you?' asked the man.

He was huge and spoke so loudly that all the other patrons involuntarily turned to see if he was talking to them. Realising their mistake, they furtively returned their gaze to the magazines and the oddly shaped and sometimes unfathomable equipment the shop sold. William baulked and resisted the urge to stammer.

'I don't believe so,' he said.

The man leant down and peered carefully into William's face. He wore a bizarre patchwork coat – brightly coloured like a hurdy-gurdy man. Did they still have hurdy-gurdy men? William didn't think so. Then a horrible notion struck him – he was in a reality show. Somewhere cameras were recording his exquisite embarrassment for the entertainment of the nation.

If so it would be particularly cruel to film him in a shop like this – the embarrassment would last a great deal longer than the length of the show and so would the questions from his mother.

The big man straightened up and peered around suspiciously – as if he too was hunting for hidden cameras. The shy retiring denizens of the shop became acutely interested in the minutiae of the shelves, except for one bold soul who made a break up the stairs to freedom.

'What's your name?' asked the big man.

'Will –,' began William.

'Excuse me, Doctor,' said a not-unattractive woman. She had the same tone as one of William's teachers, polite yet very in charge.

'Oh, er,' said the hurdy-gurdy man, whose stage name appeared to be 'Doctor'. He leant forward for a better look at the woman's face. 'Oh,' he said. 'It's you.'

'Hello,' she said brightly. 'You want to go fishing?'

The Doctor looked quickly at William, seemed to consider his numerous disadvantages one after another, and turned back to the prettyish woman in the pea-green coat. 'Yes,' he said. 'That's rather auspicious.'

'Well, then,' said the woman. She looked at William as one might a third party apprehended during an intimacy. 'What?' she said.

'Oh, er, nothing,' William said. 'Sorry.'

'You should find another hobby,' she said, 'something less solitary.'

'Right,' he said.

'Hang on,' she continued, dumping her doctor's bag into the Doctor's hands. 'I've got just the thing, somewhere,' she said as she fished through all kinds of electrical oddments

And she drew out a battered recorder.

William showed the reporter out, never one to forget his manners. He'd met all kinds of journalists over the years, and he knew better than to judge them by what they were wearing. One of the best reviews he'd ever had in the early days was from a not dissimilar freak. The hair, the wing collar and the silly frock coat had probably come back into fashion.

And maybe so had his playing, which was why he'd given the young lad a chance.

Lad. The bloke was probably near Isaac's age, you could tell from the look in his eye. And he had that look other old hacks shared, envying you because you'd made it. At least this one didn't want to make something of it, just asked his questions politely and let him ramble on.

'I'm sorry,' said William as he made to close the door. 'I've completely forgotten your name.'

'Oh,' said the reporter softly. His eyes twinkled at some private joke before he headed out into the street. And William just heard what he said as he marched away...

'I think it's for the best.'

Certificate of Destruction

Andrew Cartmel

An Adventure of the Sixth Doctor

William followed the Doctor out of the door of the TARDIS into bright sunlight and brisk wind. His heart was beating as though it was going to break out of his chest. He knew he was stepping out into an adventure that would change his life, one way or another, forever. And the thing he was most desperately anxious about was not to let the Doctor down.

He braced himself for barren frozen rocks, for the sting of salt air, the hostile stare of ancient warriors, the stink of dung and haze of wood smoke, the crash of swords and crackle of wind-stretched sails.

They were standing on the corner of a quiet suburban street. A large red double-decker bus rolled past them, moving swiftly. It had a yellow sign above the driver's compartment: 'Out of service'. High in the sky there was the distant descending whistle of a passenger jet. Birds were singing in a garden somewhere nearby. William looked at the Doctor, who said nothing, then turned to a street sign fixed on a brick wall beside the TARDIS. It read Sheen Road, SW15.

'We're in London,' said William.

'Ah,' replied the Doctor in a non-committal voice.

'We were supposed to be going on a Viking longship. You promised.'

'Mmm.'

William reached down and picked up a page from a newspaper that was lying in the gutter. He unfolded the page carefully – it was a sports page – and read the date at the top.

'It's only a couple of years after I left,' he said. He felt dreams crumbling inside him, collapsing like an elaborate structure built of playing cards. For some reason, blood rushed to his face in what felt like a flush of shame.

'Um,' said the Doctor.

William studied the sports page, trying to conceal his embarrassment. He'd been foolish to believe, to get his hopes up. It had been wrong to even ask the Doctor to put his selfish request before the urgent business that, no doubt, he had to pursue.

William had no idea what might constitute urgent business for the Doctor, but suddenly he knew he'd been wrong to put his own petty desire for tourism before it...

He tried to tell himself all this, but somehow he didn't believe it. Then he realised that it wasn't shame that was causing his face to flush. It was irritation, bordering on outright anger. He concentrated on the newspaper so that the Doctor couldn't see his true feelings. 'And it looks like England lost the World Cup again.' He crumpled the newspaper and walked to a litter bin and carefully dropped the paper in.

It was churlish to be angry at the Doctor – for messing up, for letting him down – but there you were; that was exactly what he felt. He looked at the Doctor, who was still standing, apparently musing.

'We're in London, in the future,' said William, finally giving in to the urge to complain. 'Not a Viking in sight.'

'Not entirely true,' said the Doctor. He strolled out of the quiet lane where they were standing, towards the main road, and pointed. There on the far side of the street was a long parade of shops. Many of them had boarded-up windows. One which didn't, and was clearly still open for business, had a sign above it featuring a stylised illustration of a dragon ship. The sign read: 'Viking Laundrette. The *reliable* coin laundry and dry cleaning'.

'That?' said William.

'Yes, well,' said the Doctor.

'Your navigation computer brought us here?'

'So it would seem. This time-space location was filed under "Viking".'

'You stored the coordinates of a *laundrette?*'

'Apparently, yes.'

'Why?'

'They're very reliable,' said the Doctor.

Just then a voice behind them said, 'This wasn't here yesterday.'

They turned to see a small, neatly dressed man wearing a tweed hat and black-and-white-checked jacket staring at the TARDIS. He was holding a long nylon leash and on the other end of the leash was a small white terrier. The dog was urinating avidly on the TARDIS. 'There's a good boy, Mackie,' said the man. 'You show the council what you think of their latest innovations. Blocking up the pavement like that.' The man turned and looked at the Doctor and William. He pointed an accusing finger at the tall blue police box. 'Wasn't here yesterday. Shows how fast the council can move when they want to.'

The Doctor was staring, speechless, at the dog's disrespectful treatment of his vehicle. William couldn't help feeling that it somehow served the Doctor right. He tried to push aside his bitterness. After all, it was a beautiful day and London wasn't such a bad place to be.

'The name's McKittrick,' said the small man. 'Damien McKittrick. And this here is Mackie.' He had a trace of a Northern Irish accent.

The Doctor recovered his powers of speech, and his poise. 'Good afternoon,' he said. 'This is William and I'm the Doctor.'

'Good to see someone else out and about on this lovely day.' McKittrick tipped his hat at them. 'Nice to meet you. Say goodbye to the bold fellows, Mackie.' He walked away, half dragging the dog, who seemed to want to stay and inspect his handiwork.

William turned and stared at the parade of shops again. Another bus rolled by. This time it was a single decker but it too had a yellow out of service notice on it. He felt suddenly sulky and vindictive. If this was the best the Doctor could do for him, suburban London and incontinent dogs, then he might as well go home. Trying to keep his voice casual and cold, he said, 'You know, I could get a bus home from here. Well, three buses actually. A 33 to Twickenham, then change to a 281 to Hounslow and then change to an 81 to Slough.' Despite his best efforts, a tremor of petulance crept into this litany of public transit connections.

'Oh, we can do better than that,' said the Doctor cheerfully. He was evidently eager to make amends or – much worse – get rid of William. He nodded at the TARDIS, so recently desecrated by the small dog. 'I can take you home with no changes at all.'

At these words, William's heart promptly sank. Faced with the actual prospect of abandoning his adventures, he realised at last what his true feelings were. 'I don't want to go home,' he burst out. 'I want to go on a Viking ship.'

'So do I,' said the Doctor. 'Indeed, I brought a translation device especially for you to try.' He patted his pocket. 'So, to a Viking ship we shall go. But while you're here, are you sure there isn't any laundry that you need doing?'

William felt a warm flush of relief. The Doctor wasn't going to insist on getting rid of him after all. 'No,' he said. 'But I'd like to have a look in there.'

A block or so down from the laundrette was a small fishing shop, and it was true; it had caught his eye even when he'd been moping and thinking bitter thoughts. The Doctor and William crossed the road and ambled towards it. As they walked, the Doctor peered curiously at the boarded-up windows of a shop. 'Look at that,' he said.

'Yes,' said William, finally taking an interest in his surroundings. He felt cheerful, like he should be whistling. It was pleasant walking along beside the Doctor like this. 'A lot of shops seem to have gone out of business in this place. Maybe they're having a recession here in the near future.'

'No. Look at *that*.' The Doctor poked a finger into a small indentation in one of the window boards.

'It's a hole,' said William.

'It's a bullet hole,' said the Doctor.

They reached the fishing shop. There were no boards on the window here, and no notice hanging in the door. The place showed every indication of being open and fully functional. But the door was locked and there was no sign of anyone inside. 'Maybe they went to lunch,' said William, his face pressed to the glass. He turned to the Doctor. 'They could at least have left a note.'

'It's the state of emergency,' said McKittrick. The small man had crossed the road a moment or two after the Doctor and William and now he was standing outside the fishing shop, waiting patiently while his terrier crouched on the pavement. 'People aren't keeping proper shop hours. Those that are still open at all.'

William couldn't believe the brazenness of the man, allowing his pet to foul the public footpath like that. The dog had now completed its chore and was wagging its tail proudly. William glanced at the Doctor, wondering if he had noticed this appalling behaviour. But the Doctor seemed to have other concerns.

'State of emergency?' he said. 'What state of emergency?' These last words were drowned out, though, by the sudden rising scream of a siren. A blue and white van came hurtling down the road from the west, its siren altering eerily in pitch as it approached them.

McKittrick grinned. 'Hey! It's the cat detector van.'

William and the Doctor exchanged a look.

'And it looks like they've got a live one,' said McKittrick with satisfaction. The van swept past them and pulled into one of the small residential side streets opposite, where it coasted to a halt. McKittrick nodded happily. 'They've got one all right.'

'Excuse me,' said William, unable to contain himself any longer. 'But should you be letting your dog do that, right here on the pavement, in the middle of a shopping street?'

McKittrick looked at William in bafflement, then down at his small dog, still wagging its tail, and its scatological souvenir. 'But it's an official ordinance,' he said. 'Dogs can do their business anywhere.'

'It's disgusting,' said William.

'Never mind that now,' said the Doctor, taking William by the arm. 'Let's go and see what's happening over here.' He led the younger man across the street to the blue and white van, which was now parked outside a small terraced house with a tiny garden full of yellow flowers. The driver had switched the siren off and was sitting behind the wheel of the vehicle with the window open. He was wearing blue and white overalls and had bristling black hair cropped short on his skull and a matching stubble of beard growth on his brutal-looking jaws. He was smoking a cigarette and doing the *Times* crossword. He glanced up as the Doctor and William approached the van.

'Hello,' said the Doctor, fishing a police badge from his pocket. 'I'm, er...' He checked the name on the badge. 'I'm Inspector Waverly,' he said. 'I was wondering if I could ask you a few questions.'

William wondered who Waverly might have been, and what the Doctor had done to acquire his name badge. Whatever the case, it worked.

The man folded up his newspaper and opened the door of the van. 'Always happy to help an inspector,' he said. He frowned at William. 'Who's he?'

'My trainee,' said the Doctor. 'Work experience. You know the sort of thing.'

'Yeah, sure,' said the man. 'What can I do for you?'

'This is a... cat detector van?'

'Yes. Fully licensed and authorised. Do you want to see my paperwork?'

'No, that won't be necessary. But I wonder if we could take a look in the back of the van.'

'Sure.' The man opened the doors at the rear and swung them wide open. There was no one inside, and indeed no room for anyone because the vehicle was crammed with equipment, racked electronic components. It was impressive-looking technology that meant nothing to William, although the Doctor seemed to find it informative. He poked his head in for a closer look.

'It's fully automated, is it?'

'Oh, yeah,' said the driver, puffing on his cigarette. 'I wouldn't have a clue. I just drive the van.'

'Now you're being too modest,' said the Doctor.

'Nope. Just drive the van around until I get a detection signal.'

'How does the detector work?'

'Oh, nothing fancy, just the usual. It picks up cats' brainwaves.'

'Brainwaves?' said the Doctor.

'Yeah. Then, when I get a detection signal I get a general location on the GPS, drive like a bat out of hell in case they do a runner, get a closer fix, get a lock, pull up outside, confirm the address, and that's it. Sit and wait.'

'Wait for what?'

In the distance there was a thin, shrill wailing, swiftly gathering volume. William realised that it wasn't just one siren. More like half a dozen.

The man stubbed his cigarette out. 'That.'

Five vehicles came shrieking into the small street. Two police vans, two police cars and one unmarked car. Armed policemen in black uniforms and body armour swarmed out of the vans. Constables from the police cars set about sealing off the street. A woman, also wearing body armour, got out of the unmarked car. She approached the van where the driver stood with the Doctor and William. She had brown hair, cut short. But instead of lending her an air of severity, the haircut gave her an elfin look. Her eyes were dark and limpid and she had an impressively large, rather hooked nose that made her oddly attractive, at least to William. She stared at him and the Doctor. 'You'll have to move back beyond the barriers. Official police business.'

The Doctor showed her his police badge and her manner changed instantly to respect tempered with annoyance.

'Why wasn't I notified that you'd be here?'

'Weren't you notified?' said the Doctor, eyebrows rising with surprise. William couldn't help admiring the way he subtly implied something had gone wrong and that this something was all the woman's fault.

'I'm Captain Angela Melocati,' said the woman impatiently. 'You can criticise me in your report if you want to. Just make sure you spell my name right. One 'c' and one 't'.'

'No need for that,' said the Doctor soothingly. 'We're only here to observe.'

'Observe, but don't get underfoot,' said Captain Melocati. She turned to the squad of armed police, who were now waiting, looking wildly inappropriate in their black combat garb in this quiet suburban street. They had black scarves pulled up over their mouths and these, with their black helmets and goggles, rendered them effectively faceless and weirdly inhuman looking. An insect army.

William looked at the Doctor. 'What's going on?'

'That's what I intend to find out.'

William put a tentative hand on the van parked beside him. 'Can they really detect a cat's brainwaves?'

'They can if someone's given them alien technology,' said the Doctor.

'Alien?'

'Yes. I'm afraid your Viking adventure is going to have to wait until we get to the bottom of this.'

William didn't mind. He'd forgotten about all things Norse and was staring at the small house and the squad of police, trying to relate one to the other. *Alien?* Not for the first time since he'd met the Doctor, he felt his stomach go hollow with fear.

But, oddly, the feeling wasn't entirely unpleasant.

Captain Melocati strapped on her helmet and led her men into the garden of the small terraced house, trampling the flowerbeds as they went. She stood to one side of the front door, automatic pistol in her hand, as two of her men slid a heavy looking metal cylinder out of a black kitbag.

'Battering ram,' said the Doctor.

The men drew the ram back, preparing to slam it into the door. But the door was suddenly opened from inside and a small, frail-looking grey-haired woman peered out. She gave a little gasp as she saw the squad of faceless, black-clad, armed men, clutching one withered hand protectively to the base of her wrinkled throat. But she stood her ground.

'What's happening?' she said. 'What's going on?'

Captain Melocati stepped in front of her, holding a piece of paper in one hand and her gun in the other. 'Miss Daphne Liggart?'

'Missus. Yes.'

'Do you own a cat?'

'A cat?' The woman seemed confused. 'Do you mean Tiddles?'

Captain Melocati spoke with commendable patience for a woman with a score of armed policemen waiting at her back. 'Is there a cat on the premises?'

'I used to have a cat. Tiddles.'

'Where is Tiddles now?'

The old woman's voice quavered with emotion. 'I had him put down. I had to. The vet put him to sleep. I was told I had to. I didn't want to. And he didn't want to go. You could see he didn't want to. Poor little Tiddles. Why did you make me do it?'

Captain Melocati sighed, more with exasperation than sympathy it seemed to William. 'I'm sorry about your cat, Mrs Liggart.'

'You made me put him to sleep!'

'If that is indeed the case then you'll be able to show me the certificate of destruction.'

'The what?'

'If your cat has been destroyed then you will have been issued with the correct certificate.'

'I'm not sure,' said the woman. 'I might have one. Would you like a cup of tea?

'No. We just want to see the certificate. We'd better come in.'

The old lady peered in bewilderment at the phalanx of armed police. 'All of you?'

'Yes, ma'am.'

Captain Melocati and the police went into the house and the Doctor and William followed. The front door led to a narrow hallway. To the left was a small parlour where the old lady stood, looking more frail and tentative than ever, with Captain Melocati speaking to her in a voice too quiet to be overheard. To the right was a dining room, now crowded with armed police. More police were thundering up the stairs in their heavy boots. An open door beyond the parlour led into a toilet, where a police officer stood holding his machine pistol. 'Clear!' he yelled. At the far end of the hallway, William glimpsed what looked like a kitchen with two more policemen in it.

These two policemen suddenly backed out of the room into the hallway, guns drawn. 'We have a litter tray!' one of them shouted. They backed down the hallway, guns pointing at the open door of the kitchen. Captain Melocati appeared from the door of the parlour, her pistol in her hand.

'I'll deal with this,' she said. The two armed police stood back on either side of the hallway to let her past. The police were big men and so bulky with their armour and equipment that Melocati could hardly squeeze between them. They seemed ungallantly eager to let the small woman take over and deal with whatever might be lurking in the kitchen. 'Take a position outside,' said Melocati and the men barrelled back down the hall, past the Doctor and William, and out of the front door.

Suddenly the old lady appeared from the parlour and ran after Captain Melocati. 'No, wait!' she cried. 'Let me! I'll get him for you. Don't hurt Tiddles.' Before the Doctor or William could do anything she had fled past them and into the kitchen.

'Step back,' they heard Captain Melocati snarl. 'Step back out of here.' But it wasn't the old lady who came out of the kitchen. It was Melocati herself. And she wasn't stepping.

She was flying. Through the air.

The Doctor and William stared in astonishment as Captain Melocati went hurtling past them, down the length of the hallway and out of the front door. She landed in the garden with a gasp of pain, followed by a string of curses.

The police from the dining room emerged and charged the kitchen. There were three of them. Each one came hurtling back down the hallway as if fired from a cannon. Two of them went flying into the garden to land beside Captain Melocati, now struggling to her feet, but the third had the misfortune to hit the doorframe and he collapsed, unconscious, on the floor.

Now a figure appeared in the kitchen doorway. It was the old lady. And yet it wasn't. Something subtle had changed in her posture and demeanour. She moved swiftly and smoothly, free of the painful hesitancies and tremors that had beset her moments earlier. Her hands were extended on either side of her in a predatory posture and her eyes had a strange gleam. She came down the hallway towards William and the Doctor.

'I think we should step back,' said the Doctor, and he pushed William towards the dining room. Just then another policeman emerged from the bathroom and into the parlour. He was holding his gun and skulking in a low, tense crouch, taking pains to move as silently as possible. It didn't do him any good. The old lady darted into the parlour, picked him up and threw him through the window. He landed in the garden in a shower of broken glass.

The old lady snarled and jumped through the shattered window after him. But Captain Melocati was waiting for her. She had holstered her gun and was now holding a different weapon. She pointed it at the woman and fired. The old lady went down, writhing, with two wires attached to her.

'Tazer,' said the Doctor. 'Quick, this way.' He dashed down the hall. Towards the kitchen. William hesitated for a second, then swallowed hard and followed him. The kitchen was a small, tidy room with a gleaming, old-fashioned cooker and a yellow table covered with the remains of an interrupted lunch. Just beyond the kitchen was a small alcove with a broom cupboard and the back door in it.

There was a tray full of clean cat litter in the alcove. The door had a cat flap. The cat flap was swinging.

'How annoying,' said the Doctor. 'Too late.'

A full moon loomed high over south-west London. It reflected on the rushing water of a small stream as the Doctor and William hurried down a tiny winding back road called Priest's Bridge. 'Evocative name, don't you think?' said the Doctor.

'Where are we going?' said William. He wanted as much information as possible, so that he would be ready for whatever was going to happen next. So that he wouldn't let the Doctor down. But getting information out of the Doctor wasn't the easiest thing in the world. It wasn't that he was close-mouthed or secretive, just... preoccupied

'To Barnes Common which, if memory serves, is a few minutes walk in this direction.'

'Why don't we take the main road instead of these dodgy old back streets?'

'Both because these dodgy old back streets are more evocative and atmospheric and because the main road is being swept at regular intervals by a surprising number of police patrols.'

'Couldn't you just show them your badge?'

'I don't think so,' said the Doctor. 'These police patrols have a rather nasty shoot-first-and-ask-questions-later look to them.'

'What, like they shot that woman?'

'No, not like that. Fortunately, Captain Melocati had the foresight and compassion to use a non-lethal weapon on the old dear, despite the fact that she was throwing her men around like rag dolls. Mind you, getting tazered four or five times won't have done her elderly heart much good.'

'She looked pretty chipper when they carted her off.'

'Yes, she did, didn't she? As I recall, it took three straitjackets to restrain her. A-ha. There's the common now.' The Doctor indicated a wide, dark cluster of trees on the far side of the road. They paused, waiting for traffic on the road to go past, then hurried into the woods.

A narrow gravel footpath wound through the common with streetlights set at irregular intervals – not that these were much help, since most of them were dead. William followed the Doctor down the path between the brooding shapes of the forest. 'The council should do something about those light bulbs.'

'I suspect that the council has rather a lot on its plate at the moment, and that those dead lamps are merely the tip of an iceberg of urban decline. In fact, I think the social order here in London is in danger of sliding into anarchy. Oh, look, there's someone up ahead.' The Doctor increased his pace and, before William could utter a word of caution or warning, the Doctor was raising his hand in greeting and calling out.

The woods opened out at this point as another footpath joined the one they were on, forming a rough Y-configuration. Just ahead of them was a patch of open grass and, by some miracle, a functioning streetlight. Under the light stood a man with a dog. The dog was a small white terrier and the man was wearing a hat.

'Mr McKittrick, I presume,' said the Doctor.

'Hello, there.' The small man peered at them and smiled, cheerfully revealing bad teeth. 'What a surprise to see you fellas again. Especially out after curfew.'

'So, there is a curfew,' said the Doctor.

'Of course. Just like every night. You shouldn't be so careless. We're living under a state of martial law, you know.'

'So I'm beginning to realise. But you don't seem unduly troubled by the curfew?'

'No, of course not,' said McKittrick. 'I'm walking a dog, aren't I? Everyone knows the curfew doesn't apply to owners taking their dogs out. You're safe as houses if you've got a pooch with you. Anyone else can be shot on sight, though, taken for looters or cat owners.' He peered at the Doctor and William. 'You chaps had better stick close to me. You'll be all right so long as you're with me and Mackie here.'

'I see. All three of us, walking the dog.'

'That's the ticket,' said McKittrick happily. 'Come on, Mackie boy, do your business.' William observed with disgust that the little dog was, of course, getting ready to foul the footpath again, although this time it seemed to be experiencing a certain amount of gastric difficulty, trembling and straining as it crouched.

'Don't turn around,' said a voice from the darkness.

They all turned around. A tall, young man was standing there. He was pale, with freckles on the oddly flat cheekbones of his pinched-looking face, and had a huge Afro of frizzy red hair. 'I told you not to turn around,' he said. He had a pistol in his hand and he was aiming it at them.

'Merciful God,' said Mr McKittrick. 'We're being mugged.'

'Correct,' said the young man. 'Give me your money and your watches and phones and iPods.'

'I don't have an iPod,' said Mr McKittrick. 'Or a phone.'

'Shut up or I'll blow your head off.'

'Yes, sir.'

'Can't you do something about your disgusting dog?' said the mugger, his voice thin with loathing. William glanced down at Mackie and saw that the animal was trembling convulsively. The dog gave a low, painful moan and then finally emitted a flatulent sound and messily completed its appointed task.

'Disgusting,' repeated the mugger. He pointed his gun at the dog. 'The world would be better off without that beast.' William's eyes should have been on the gun, but instead he couldn't take them away from the patch of ground where the dog had been squatting. The oddly pale bolus that it had deposited there seemed to be moving. Squirming. It was a trick of the light – or the stress of being robbed at gunpoint. It had to be.

But, no, the pile of material that had emerged from the dog's hindquarters was coloured a pale, almost luminous, green and it was most definitely moving. The material writhed, unfurled, and extended itself into a long ribbon shape.

'Stand back, William,' said the Doctor.

The pale green ribbon was moving like a snake. It was flat and about a metre long, slithering along the ground. William realised what it reminded him of: parasitic flat worms he'd once seen in a biology textbook.

'What is it?' said the mugger in a distinctly shaken voice. The long flat worm suddenly changed direction, shooting towards the mugger as if drawn to the sound of his voice. 'What is it?' said the mugger again, in an appalled tone, as the worm reared up from the ground.

'Stay back!' shouted the Doctor, and for a crazy second William thought he was addressing the worm thing, but of course it was the mugger he was talking to. But the man didn't appear to hear him. He was transfixed by the sight of the worm. It shortened, its head growing wider like the flaring hood of a striking cobra. Finally realising his danger, the mugger fired at it but the worm dodged nimbly, easily avoiding the bullet, which ricocheted off the metal stalk of the lamppost. Mackie the dog promptly fled howling into the night.

Then the worm struck.

It shot towards the mugger's face, its own head changing shape again as it did so. The wide flat head rolled itself together into a tight, thin point. And the point hit the mugger just above his mouth, squirming upwards and jabbing into his right nostril. The mugger gave a strange choking scream as the worm vanished upwards, disappearing up his nose and into his head. The gun dropped from his hand and he turned and ran into the night, screaming.

The three men remained standing under the street lamp, staring.

'What was that worm?' said William.

'What worm?' said McKittrick.

William tried to keep a note of rising hysteria out of his voice. 'That worm that just dropped out of your dog's bum and crawled up the mugger's nose.'

'Don't know what you're talking about,' said McKittrick complacently. 'The fellow just started screaming, fired a wild round, then dropped his gun and ran off. Must be on drugs if you ask me. Luckily for us. Phone and iPod indeed.'

'But –' said William. Then he saw that the Doctor was gesturing him to be quiet.

'I don't know what you're talking about,' repeated McKittrick. He turned and whistled into the night. 'Come on, Mackie, time to go home.' The little dog reappeared from the darkness, looking a trifle shamefaced, thought William. Man and dog set off back down the footpath. 'Goodnight now,' called McKittrick cheerfully as they disappeared into deep shadow.

'Well,' said the Doctor. 'Well, well, well.'

As they crossed Priest's Bridge again the Doctor dropped the mugger's gun into the stream. It disappeared into the dark flowing water with a splash, shattering a pattern of moonlight. 'One less weapon in circulation,' he said with mild satisfaction. 'And therefore one armed robber less.' He frowned. 'I mean fewer.'

William tried to think of something sensible to say, by way of response. He wanted to sound casual and sophisticated, as if bizarre moonlit confrontations with muggers and monsters were something he just took in his stride. But his mind was so full of what he'd just seen that it felt like his head might burst. Finally he said, 'In my day, armed robbers used knives.'

'As I was saying, there has clearly been a swift and sudden decline in social structure. I imagine that civil disorder and the ensuing martial law has led to a steep rise in violence and no doubt a radical increase in the availability of firearms.'

'Doctor, why did Mr McKittrick say he didn't see that worm?'

'Yes, that was strange, wasn't it?'

'I mean, I know that dog owners always pretend that they don't see the mess their dogs leave behind, but this was...'

'Above and beyond the call of duty?'

'Yes.'

The Doctor nodded thoughtfully. 'I suspect that Mr McKittrick said he didn't see the worm because he didn't see the worm.'

They walked on in silence for a few minutes. Then William said, 'Where are we going?'

'To Mrs Liggart's house. Or perhaps I should say Tiddles's house.'

It only took them five minutes to get back to the street where the cat detector van had been parked earlier that day. The van was gone now, of course, but there was still a police car parked outside and two armed officers stationed in the front garden of the house where all the action had taken place. The broken window of the house was festooned with black and yellow police tape, billowing gently in the night breeze.

William thought that the police presence would be enough to discourage the Doctor but, no, he still insisted on going into the house. 'A pity we don't have Mackie with us,' he said. 'If we did I could chance going up to the front door and showing our credentials. Unfortunately, without a dog we may well be shot on sight.'

'So, what are you going to do?'

'Oh, climb over a garden fence several houses down and make my way in through the back. Don't worry, though. You can wait here.'

'But –' said William.

But the Doctor was already gone. So William had no choice but to stand there waiting, hiding behind a skip full of building rubble, his heart pounding in his chest, until the Doctor finally returned.

'Mission accomplished,' he said smugly, setting off back down the darkened street, away from the police car. William followed.

'What was the mission, by the way?'

'To obtain this.' The Doctor took something out of his pocket and handed it to William. It was a small, framed photograph of a grey and white cat.

'Tiddles?'

'Tiddles. I wanted to be able to recognise him if we saw him.'

Their next stop was the deserted parade of shops they had visited earlier that day. The Doctor waited until a police patrol passed on the main road, then he led William to the fishing shop. 'Are we breaking in?' said William.

'Yes,' said the Doctor. 'Although "breaking" is perhaps an unnecessarily crude description of the effects of this device.' He took a small instrument like a calculator out of his pocket, pointed it at the lock on the door, then simply turned the handle and went in. Once inside the shop, he got William to choose an excellent casting rod, a range of hooks and a waterproof plastic box with a tight-fitting lid, all of which the Doctor paid for by leaving a handful of fat golden coins on the counter beside the cash register.

'I hope they don't mind doubloons,' said the Doctor.

William peered into the illuminated interior of a small refrigerator. He was a little reluctant to leave the cosy, sheltering familiarity of the fishing shop. The refrigerator's chill air was comforting on his face. He studied the small plastic containers on the shelves, full of earth and indistinct red shapes. 'Do we need any worms?'

'Worms are the last thing we need,' said the Doctor.

'What are we going to use for bait?'

The Doctor looked at William. They had not been travelling together long, so it took William a moment to understand just what he was getting at. But he got there in the end.

'Oh, no,' said William.

Once back on Barnes Common they didn't have long to wait. Judging by the omnipresent piles of dog droppings, this local beauty spot had now been reduced to the status of a communal canine toilet. This supposition was soon confirmed by the arrival of a plump woman in a tartan overcoat, ski pants and tennis shoes, with three poodles quivering on a triple leash arrangement. She paused under the same street lamp where McKittrick and Mackie had loitered earlier.

'What magnificent dogs,' said the Doctor, stepping out of the shadows. 'I hope you don't mind my saying so.'

The woman regarded the Doctor sceptically. 'I don't mind you saying so, but they're not mine. I'm a professional dog-walker.'

'I'm sure you're very professional. Nonetheless, whoever owns them, they are magnificent. William, come and see these wonderful animals.' William reluctantly stepped out of concealment and joined the Doctor.

'They're not that wonderful,' said the woman disdainfully. William observed that two of the dogs had contented themselves with merely dampening the lamppost. But the third was crouching and shivering in a manner which was dismayingly familiar. The woman didn't seem to pay any attention as the dog moaned, grovelled and deposited a pale green, writhing mass on the ground.

'Excuse me,' said the Doctor. 'I must just get my fishing rod. William, try and stay a metre or two ahead of it.'

'Ahead of what?' said the woman with a note of annoyance in her voice as the worm slithered past the toes of her tennis shoes, in the general direction of William. William backed hastily away as the Doctor disappeared into the shadows of the trees and emerged again with their recently acquired fishing rod. The worm squirmed towards William with chilling rapidity. Instead of merely backing away, William tried to run away while facing backwards. Somehow he couldn't bear to turn his back on the thing. The backwards running worked well for about two and a half seconds before he stumbled, tripped and crashed to the ground.

'What... what on Earth are you doing?' said the woman. 'You're upsetting the dogs.'

Sensing its opportunity, the worm shot towards him. William clawed his way frantically to his feet, cutting his hands on gravel, and rose up shakily just as the worm reared, its head flaring and widening, poised to strike.

There was a precision sizzling sound and an almost invisible arc of filament glittered under the streetlight as the Doctor cast. The hook gleamed before William's eyes, a streak of silver, as the Doctor jerked it neatly into the flared neck of the worm. The worm immediately curled up and twisted, but it was no good. The hook was firmly set and the Doctor reeled it in.

'Why are you casting a fishing rod in the middle of Barnes Common?' said the woman with a note of exhausted disgust.

The Doctor smiled as he reeled in the twisting worm. 'You mean, why am I pretending that I've caught something when in fact there's nothing on the hook?'

'Yes.'

'And why am I now pretending to remove this invisible object from the hook and sealing it in this plastic box?' The Doctor snapped the lid of the box shut, securing the worm.

'Yes,' said the woman, staring.

'Just think of me as yet another in a glittering gallery of lovable English eccentrics. Come on, William.'

They retreated down the footpath, leaving the dog-walking woman gawking after them. As the adrenalin ebbed out of William's system and his nerves unjangled, questions began to force themselves into his mind. 'She didn't see the worm either.'

'No,' said the Doctor. 'I believe that is because she is already the host to one such worm herself.'

'She's got one of those things inside her?'

'Yes, in her brain. That would explain their habit of entering through the nose. Just a short trip through the sinuses before they reach their destination. And once lodged in the brain, presumably they can influence behaviour. Preventing people from acknowledging they've seen large green worms, for example.'

Willaim pondered the notion of worms in the brain for a moment, then hastily changed the subject. 'Where are we going now?'

'Back to the TARDIS.'

'Well, thank God for that,' said William, feeling a warm flush of relief. This was all getting a little too much for him. But if the Doctor was willing to retreat, there was clearly no dishonour in doing so. 'At last.'

'Really, William. We're not done here yet.' The Doctor lifted the plastic box. 'I simply meant that once we're back in the TARDIS, we can use a microscope.'

'Oh.'

'And an assortment of other analytical devices. To examine our friend here.'

'No friend of mine.'

They left the common, darted down a side street, crossed Priest's Bridge and were only a couple of minutes away from the TARDIS when they were captured by the police patrol.

'First things first,' said the Doctor. 'Let me say thank you for not shooting us on sight.'

'That was because I gave them orders not to,' said Captain Melocati. 'Well done, Dixon, Abernathy.' The two armed officers who had apprehended the Doctor and William nodded and beamed with pleasure. Melocati scrutinised the Doctor. 'I've been looking for you.'

'That's very flattering. Why?'

'When I got back to the command post I took the precaution of checking on your credentials and they were bogus. For one thing, Inspector Waverley is a short, skinny, woman of mixed race.'

'Really?' The Doctor frowned. 'We must have swapped coats by mistake. I'm really –' But she wasn't listening. Melocati gave the Doctor a cold look and walked to her car. She leaned in through the open door and picked up the radio handset.

'Mobile three to base. Have apprehended suspects. I'm bringing them in for interrogation now.'

William started to sweat when he heard the word interrogation. He wondered, not for the first time, whether the Doctor knew what he had got them into. Melocati hung up the handset and came back from the car. 'Were they carrying anything with them?'

The policeman called Dixon held up the fishing rod he'd confiscated from William. 'The young one had this on him.'

'We were returning it to the shop,' said the Doctor. Melocati ignored him. The other policeman, Abernathy, held up the sealed plastic box.

'The old one had this.'

'What's in it?' said Melocati.

'Nothing,' said Abernathy. 'I had a peek earlier. Look.' He snapped open the lid of the box and instantly the long green worm appeared and began to wriggle out. Abernathy gazed at it calmly. 'You see? Completely empty.'

'Why would they be carrying an empty box?' said Melocati. She too was looking directly at the worm without seeing it. But the third cop, Dixon, was staring, aghast.

'What is that thing?' he said.

'What thing?' Melocati and Abernathy looked at him in puzzlement. The worm slipped out of the box, hit the ground and began to slither in a purposeful way. The Doctor gestured for William to keep away from it. As he jumped back, William reflected that there had seldom been a less necessary warning. But the worm didn't appear to be interested in him at all. Instead, it seemed already to have fixed its attention on Dixon, the policeman who was standing nearest to it.

'Keep it away from me!' shrilled Dixon.

Melocati and Abernathy exchanged a look. 'What's he playing at?' said the captain. 'Is he drunk?'

'I don't know, ma'am. He's never acted like this before.'

The worm reared up, flattened itself, rolled its head into a tight point and shot up poor Dixon's nose. The man fell to the ground, struggling and uttering stifled screams.

'He's having some kind of a fit,' said Melocati. 'Keep an eye on those two.' She crouched by the man on the ground while Abernathy pointed his gun at the Doctor and William.

'Perhaps I can help,' said the Doctor.

'You stay where you are,' snapped Melocati. Dixon had gone quite still now. She put her hand to his throat and then to his wrist, looking for a pulse. Abruptly, Dixon's eyes opened. He looked calmly at Melocati.

'I'm all right now, Captain.' He gently took her hand from his wrist and got to his feet, dusting himself off.

'What the hell happened, Dixon?'

'Just some kind of dizzy spell, ma'am.'

'Well, you sign off for the night and go and get some rest. Abernathy, you see that he gets home okay.'

'Yes, ma'am,' chorused the two officers. William thought he saw a conspiratorial glance pass between the two of them, almost as if Abernathy was welcoming him to the club. Melocati looked at the Doctor and William.

'You two are coming with me.' She fixed their hands behind their backs with thin strips of plastic that locked tight, effectively immobilising them, and got them seated in the back of her car.

'This isn't very comfortable,' said the Doctor.

'Shut up,' said Melocati. She waved to Abernathy and Dixon as they pulled away in their own vehicle. Then she started her car and drove down to the end of the small street, to a cul-de-sac, turned around and accelerated on to the main road. She had gone about a hundred metres when a small shape streaked through her headlights, crossing the road in front of her. It was a grey and white cat.

'Oh, look,' said the Doctor. 'It's Tiddles.'

Melocati hit the brakes so hard that the Doctor and William shot forward in their seats. She jumped out of the car and went after the cat. Through the window at his side, William saw Tiddles disappear under a white van parked at the edge of the road. On the side of the van was a cartoon of a smiling cat holding a knife and fork and the words 'Wholesale Seafood'. Melocati took out her handgun and crouched to peer under the van. She got down on all fours and stuck her head beneath the vehicle. As she did so the rear door of the van opened and four figures dressed in black like ninjas in a ninja movie hopped out. One of them pointed an air pistol at the captain and fired it.

William knew it was an air pistol because he could clearly see the feathered dart sticking out of Melocati's back. She twitched violently, just once, then collapsed face-down on the road. The small grey and white cat reappeared tentatively from under the van. One of the ninjas picked it up and held it cradled in his arms.

Another one of the ninjas came over to the car and opened the door. They leaned in, looking at the Doctor and William. 'Welcome to the cat liberation front.'

'Delighted to make your acquaintance,' said the Doctor.

The cat underground resistance movement had its headquarters in a large house beside the river in Richmond. The smell of so many cats in such close proximity, or rather the smell of their litter boxes, made William's nose tingle. But he was so exhausted he soon settled on the sofa with the blankets and pillows that he'd been given, and fell deeply asleep.

He awoke with a terrible burning, itching sensation in his left ear. A voice, which he recognised as the Doctor's, said, 'Hold still please.'

William froze. He felt something thin and cold and metallic probing in his ear. There was a very unpleasant rustling sound and the itching and burning abruptly ceased.

'Excellent,' said the Doctor. 'You can sit up now.' He went and switched the lights on, revealing a large open sitting room full of oriental-style armchairs and sofas, all of them with their green-and-white fabric seriously savaged by cat claws. William sat up, blinking and saw that the cat, Tiddles, was nestled in the armchair opposite, watching him with placid curiosity.

The Doctor was holding a pair of tweezers in his hand, and fixed in the tweezers was what looked like a large spider, its legs wriggling helplessly.

'Is that a spider?' said William. The Doctor shook his head.

'No. It's not any kind of arachnid. The segmentations on the body are all wrong, as are the number of legs. It more closely resembles an insect.'

'An insect. I see. Wait a minute... Was that thing *in my ear?*'

'Very nearly,' said the Doctor, smiling. He showed the insect to the cat. 'That was very inhospitable of you.' The cat peered at him, then at the tiny creature wriggling in the tweezers. William saw that there was an empty jam jar sitting on the floor near the sofa, clean and apparently freshly washed. The Doctor went and picked it up. He dropped the insect into the jar and screwed the lid on tight. He looked at William.

'I thought they'd try it when we were asleep.'

'When *I* was asleep, you mean.' William gathered the blankets around himself, feeling scared and angry. The Doctor set the jam jar down carefully, then went to the chair where Tiddles was sprawled. He lifted the cat up gently and sat down on the chair, placing Tiddles on his lap. The cat consented to this change and allowed the Doctor to stroke it.

'That really was very naughty of you,' said the Doctor to the cat. 'Perhaps you would like to apologise.' Tiddles mewled rather pathetically, as if unloved. He reached in his pocket and took out a length of black elastic with three white plastic pods on it. Still stroking the cat, he carefully fastened the band around its throat like a collar. 'Try that.' He glanced at William. 'Translation device,' he explained.

'Well,' said the cat. 'That's *much* better.'

William stared at the cat. It had spoken. It had definitely spoken. 'Doctor...' he said. The Doctor put his finger to his lips and William fell silent.

'I suppose you are right,' said Tiddles. 'We do indeed owe you an apology.' It looked at William. 'But we saw no other way to achieve communication than to implant an emissary.'

The Doctor picked up the jam jar and studied the insect inside. 'You enter the brain through the hearing canal and the auditory nerve?'

'The brain,' said William. 'That thing was going *into my brain?*'

'Really, William,' chided the Doctor. 'Try not to be so middle-class.'

'We repair the eardrum once we're inside,' said Tiddles diffidently. 'As I say, we saw no other way to achieve communication than to have an emissary interface directly with your young friend.'

'Get him under your control, you mean.'

'You make it sound so sinister,' said the cat.

'You have plenty of other humans under your control. Why don't you just use them to talk to us?'

'Unfortunately, the human brain is rather odd. We can easily control the portions concerned with emotion and motor action...'

'Like turning an old lady into a fighting machine,' said the Doctor.

'Yes, Daphne certainly excelled herself. And she was very generous with the tinned tuna.' Tiddles licked his lips reminiscently. 'But, although we can influence physical action and emotions, we have no power over the language centres or higher abstract reasoning.' The cat eased its head back luxuriously, displaying its collar. 'This device is a much more effective method of communication.'

'You can't use a human brain to formulate speech, but you can use a cat's?'

'Yes,' said Tiddles. 'Go figure.'

'Well, since you can talk,' said William, 'perhaps you wouldn't mind telling us what is going on here.'

'It's fairly straightforward,' said Tiddles. 'Have you ever played a paintball game?'

'Yes,' said William. 'Have you?'

'No,' said the cat. 'But that's not the point. It's supposed to be a non-lethal sporting event between two evenly matched teams.'

'And that's what's you're doing here on Earth,' said the Doctor. 'Two teams of alien parasites, indulging in a sporting competition.'

'I'm not sure I like the word parasite,' said Tiddles. 'But you seem to have got the gist of my analogy. With one other crucial aspect to it.' The cat turned its head and looked at the Doctor. 'One of the sides in the game has started using live ammunition.'

'The worms.'

'Yes, indeed, the De'htrexi. We were supposed to indulge in a harmless bit of competitive sport on this world. The two groups we chose for teams were mutually exclusive and had a long-standing low level of hostility.'

'Dogs and cats.'

'And their owners. We were able to infect both groups with our emissaries, via their pets. It should have been an ideal situation. But the De'htrexi got out of hand.'

The Doctor said, 'Effectively you are alien joyriders, using humans and animals as your vehicles.'

'Well, I like that better than parasites, anyway.'

'Joyriders who have caused numerous fatalities.'

'Alas, it is so. But now, with your help, we can remedy the situation.'

'How?'

'The De'htrexi can be driven from their hosts by the use of a relatively simple device which transmits at the correct frequency.'

'A sort of electronic worming pill.'

'Well put, Doctor,' purred the cat. 'But up to this moment we lacked anyone who could build such a device to our specifications.'

'Unlike the De'htrexi,' said the Doctor, 'who clearly provided the technology for the cat detector vans.'

'Correct. Unlike our rivals, we found our human hosts were unable to assimilate the necessary abstract data from us. Meanwhile, our feline hosts lacked the dexterity for building any such device.' The cat yawned luxuriously, happily. 'But now it seems you have come to our rescue.'

'It seems we have,' agreed the Doctor.

'I advise your young friend to get dressed.'

'No way,' said William. 'I'm going back to sleep, providing you can keep your emissaries out of my ear hole.'

'I'm afraid the time for sleeping is over. My extremely keen hearing tells me that there is a convoy of vehicles approaching.'

'Vehicles?' said William.

One of the ninjas came dashing into the room. Her black mask was gone now, revealing the anxious face of a thin young woman. 'We just got word from the lookouts. It's a raid.'

The Doctor scooped up Tiddles and rose from his armchair. 'Come on, William.' As they made their way out of the French windows and down towards the river, the Doctor carrying Tiddles, they heard the sound of engines, and shouting, and sirens.

And dogs.

There was a single policeman, heavily armed, on guard outside the door of the conference room in Whitehall.

The Doctor approached with William at his side. The policeman unholstered his gun. 'Identification, please.'

The Doctor had spent most of the time on the way here slapping his pockets, and had evidently finally found something suitable. He showed the policeman an identity card. The policeman clipped his holster shut.

'That's all in order, sir. You can go on in. Your assistant has to wait out here, though.'

'Let me just make sure I'm in the right place,' said the Doctor. 'This is the summit conference with the heads of the police, the armed forces, local and national government and emergency services all convened to discuss the current crisis in civil order?'

'That's right, sir, those bloomin' cats, sir.'

'Excellent. Just one more thing, before I go in, let me show you this.' The Doctor delved in his pocket and took out a black metal box with buttons and a small red light bulb on it. To William it resembled a clunky 1960s-style remote control like he'd once seen in his grandmother's house. The Doctor pointed it at the policemen, pressed a button, and the red light came on.

Nothing else happened, though. The policeman stared at him placidly. 'What are you doing, sir?'

'Nothing, evidently,' said the Doctor. He pushed another button and the red light on the box went off.

'It doesn't work,' said William.

'Not necessarily,' said the Doctor. 'Tell me, constable, you're not a dog owner or dog lover?'

The policeman shook his head. 'I never liked them, particularly the way they make revolting messes everywhere, especially now. But the law's the law, I suppose. I'm more a tropical-fish fancier, me.'

'So you haven't come into contact with any dogs recently?'

'I try to avoid it, sir.'

The Doctor snapped his fingers. 'William.'

William took out the air pistol. 'Here, what the hell is this?' said the policeman, as William shot him in the neck and he slumped to the floor.

'The penalty for being a tropical-fish fancier, I'm afraid,' said the Doctor, gently moving the man's sedated body aside. William helped, heart beating loudly in his chest. 'I don't understand,' he said. 'Why did I need to knock him out? He wasn't possessed by the –' he rehearsed the name carefully, anxious to get it right '– the De'htrexi.'

'That's precisely why we needed to knock him out. If we'd been able to electronically "worm" him he would have recovered his faculties and had every reason to help us. But sadly that wasn't the case.'

'But he was convinced by your ID.'

'Not convinced enough to let you in with me.' The Doctor smiled. 'And, anyway, I suspect he would have come running when he heard the tumult which is about to ensue. And that could have proved problematical.' He patted the sleeping policeman affectionately on the head and turned to the door of the conference room. William took a deep breath and followed him as he entered.

It was a big rectangular room with a long narrow table running down the centre of it. The walls on either side were covered with screens showing aerial images of urban centres and flowing columns of figures. Seated around the table were several dozen dignitaries, many of them in uniform. The only face that William recognised, apart from some politicians he'd seen on television but couldn't name, was Captain Melocati.

All of the faces, except Melocati's, showed polite interest or mild annoyance at the appearance of William and the Doctor in the room. Melocati's showed astonishment, rage, and then the determination to take decisive action.

But before she could do anything, the Doctor took out the black box and pressed the button. The red light came on and immediately everyone sitting at the table lurched and flinched. They began to shake and quiver violently and then, to William's disgust, pale green lengths of worm began to appear from their nostrils.

Although he'd theoretically been briefed on what was going to happen, nothing could have prepared William for the actual sight of it. The worms streamed and flowed out of every nose and spilled to the floor of the room where they squirmed together and formed a single twisting, twitching bundle.

'Have you brought the bin liner?' said the Doctor.

Before they left London, the Doctor insisted on paying one last visit to a now-familiar locale. The woman was there, wearing a plaid overcoat, black ski pants and tennis shoes, just like she had the other night. She was standing under the same lamppost at the same spot in the middle of Barnes Common. This time, however, she had six dogs on six leashes instead of just three, including an English sheepdog and an elegant Afghan hound.

And the other major difference was the armed policeman who stood nearby, observing her with a look of alert disgust as William and the Doctor watched. The woman looked at William and the Doctor imploringly and, when she got no sympathy in that direction, turned to the policeman. 'They're not even my dogs,' she said.

'Doesn't matter,' said the policeman, cradling his automatic weapon.

'I'm a professional dog-walker.'

'They're your responsibility,' said the cop.

The woman turned and watched in mortification as each of the dogs squatted in turn and defecated on the grass beside the footpath. 'Really...' she said.

'You have the heavy-duty, self-sealing bags,' said the policeman coldly. 'Get scooping.'

The Doctor turned to William and winked. 'I believe that our work here is done.'

They headed back to the TARDIS, with William already feeling a familiar hollow feeling in his stomach, and a keen little edge of excitement, wondering where it would take them next.

About the Authors

BEN AARONOVITCH wrote two *Doctor Who* serials in the late 1980s. His first, *Remembrance of the Daleks*, opened the twenty-fifth-anniversary season in 1988; he followed it in 1989 with *Battlefield*. Ben also wrote for Virgin Publishing's *New Adventures* range of Doctor Who novels, and *Genius Loci*, a Bernice Summerfield novel for Big Finish. *Gone Fishing* is his first *Doctor Who* fiction since 1997's *So Vile a Sin*.

JOFF BROWN has worked on numerous video-game magazines, and now edits children's educational titles. This his second *Doctor Who* story, following *Danse Macabre* in *Short Trips: The History of Christmas* (2005).

ANDREW CARTMEL was script editor for three turbulent years on *Doctor Who*, as detailed in his book *Script Doctor*. Since then he has worked as script editor on the television dramas *Casualty* and *Dark Knight*, successfully mounted a stage thriller on the London Fringe (*End of the Night*) and written a number of novels, including *Doctor Who* titles for Virgin Publishing and BBC Books, and *Winter For the Adept*, a *Doctor Who* audio drama for Big Finish. His other books include a history of *Doctor Who* on television entitled *Through Time*. His most recent novel, *Miss Freedom*, based on the classic television series *The Prisoner*, will be published in late 2006.

JONATHAN CLEMENTS is the writer of the popular *Doctor Who Unbound: Sympathy for the Devil*, *UNIT: Snake Head* and numerous episodes in Big Finish's 2000 AD range. A former anime translator and dubbing director, he is also the author of *Coxinga and the Fall of the Ming Dynasty*, *A Brief History of the Vikings*, *Confucius*, *The Moon in the Pines* and *Strontium Dog: Ruthless*. He was the award-winning editor of *Manga Max* magazine, and a translator, presenter or consultant on TV programmes including *Saiko Exciting* (Sci Fi), *Godzilla: King of the Monsters* (BBC Two), *Japanorama* (BBC Three) and *The South Bank Show* (ITV). His website is www.muramasaindustries.com.

SIMON GUERRIER (editor) has written five audio plays for Big Finish – *UNIT: The Coup*, *Professor Bernice Summerfield and The Lost Museum*, *Doctor Who: The Settling*, *Sapphire & Steel: The School* and *Bernice Summerfield and the Summer of Love*. He has edited five short-story anthologies, including *Short Trips: The History of Christmas*. His award-winning *Doctor Who* novel, *The Time Travellers*, was published by BBC Books in 2005.

MARC PLATT wrote the 1989 *Doctor Who* story *Ghost Light*, which he also novelised, and the *Doctor Who* novels *Cat's Cradle: Time's Crucible* and *Lungbarrow*. For Big Finish, he's written the audio dramas *Loups-Garoux*, *Spare Parts*, *Auld Mortality* and *A Storm of Angels*, as well as a number of short stories. For Noise Monster, he's written the audio play *Space 1889: The Siege of Alclyon*.

PHILIP PURSER-HALLARD is the author of – amongst other things – a novel dealing with politics and terrorism in the afterlife; a novella about superhumans, posthumans and eugenics; a doctoral thesis exploring religious themes in science fiction; a Shakespearean 'hard alchemical fiction' story set on the Moon in 1590; and a story called *Sex Secrets of the Robot Replicants*. *The Ruins of Time* is Philip's second *Doctor Who* piece for Big Finish, and his first to feature William Hartnell's original Doctor, whose TV adventures he very much enjoyed 'researching'.

EDDIE ROBSON's writing output includes, but is not limited to, books about film noir, the Coen brothers and *Doctor Who*; scripts for the comics anthologies *FutureQuake*, *Alien Safeword* and *Just 1 Page*; miscellaneous stuff for *SFX*, *Starburst* and *Cult Times*; walkthrough guides to computer games; and on one occasion *The Week In Sport* for *The Guardian*. This is his sixth *Short Trip*. His first audio play for Big Finish is *Doctor Who: Memory Lane*. He lives in Lancaster.

MATTHEW SWEET is a writer and broadcaster who holds a doctorate from Oxford University for work on Wilkie Collins. He has been a director's assistant at the Royal Shakespeare Company, film critic of the *Independent on Sunday* and a columnist for the *Big Issue*. For three days a week he is a reporter for BBC Two's *The Culture Show* and a presenter of BBC Radio 3's *Night Waves*. The rest of the week he spends engaged in activities involving plasticine and paint and the singing of *Wind the Bobbin Up*. He has edited Collins's *The Woman in White* for Penguin Classics and is author of *Inventing the Victorians* (Faber and Faber, 2001) and *Shepperton Babylon: The Lost Worlds of British Cinema* (Faber and Faber, 2005). His television films and series include *Shepperton Babylon*, *Silent Britain* (both BBC Four) and *Checking into History* (Channel 4). He is also responsible for the Big Finish *Doctor Who* audio play *Year of the Pig*.

BEN WOODHAMS has previously written two short stories for Big Finish's *Bernice Summerfield* range. When he's not watching or reading *Doctor Who* in darkest Cornwall, he's working as a parliamentary reporter. This is his first published *Doctor Who* fiction.

An extract from *Doctor Who: Short Trips – Dalek Empire* (edited by Nicholas Briggs)

Kalendorf

Nicholas Briggs

It was difficult for him, being among humans, and the planet was full of them. He had not wanted the mission; but there was no point arguing with an order from the court of the First Knight. Not if you ever wanted your family to enjoy privilege again.

And so here he was, Kalendorf, Knight of Velyshaa; reduced to the role of covert peace envoy, skulking about in a third-rate spaceport on the outer planet Vega VI. The sickly tang of retro fuel was eating into the back of his throat as he paced around the deserted maintenance depot, wondering how long he would have to wait.

This was to be the moment of first, actual diplomatic contact between human and Velyshaan for seven generations. The war had been over *that* long. The Velyshaans had been defeated, penalised by punitive peace treaties from every vindictive species in the galaxy, and then left alone on their homeworld to deal with cultural humiliation as best they could.

That had been the one saving grace for the Velyshaans; the chance to recover dignity in private. It had been granted and enforced by the Earth Alliance, and the Velyshaans would never forget that one act of near kindness.

Kalendorf would have preferred to have been back on his homeworld, honing his noble skills, dreaming of the day Velyshaa would be great and powerful again. But the new First Knight of Velyshaa was a pragmatist. 'Praylaron the Pragmatist', as the Earth Alliance media had nicknamed him; a leader who looked to a future of cooperation with his planet's traditional enemies, the humans. Praylaron had foreseen the emergence of a terrible, future foe that might sweep aside human and Velyshaan alike, wreaking havoc and destroying civilisation. To that end, he sought an alliance with the Earth government. Coded transmissions had begun around ten years ago... And finally, the painstakingly detailed preliminary negotiations were over, and this was the result...

Kalendorf, in a Vega VI spaceport. And still no sign of his human contact. As every moment passed, he fought down his impatience and reassured himself with the only two mitigating factors he could muster. He had been told that this was the most important mission a knight had ever accepted, and his human contact, agent Alby Brook, was reportedly someone who never played by the rules.

He hated this last fact. From what he had heard, Brook might be playing some clever game of manipulation, but he was just as likely to be in a bar with a girl for no good reason. It was a frustrating sign of Earth Alliance Security's cynicism about a possible deal with Velyshaa that they had assigned one of their less reliable operatives. But what choice had the Velyshaans? They were the underdogs, the vanquished tormentors of the galaxy who had once come close to creating a powerful empire. They had to show willing, no matter how flippant the response of the victors.

At the echoing hoot of a distant klaxon, Kalendorf pressed himself into the shadows. The smell of fuel was worse in this dark enclave; sticky metallic walls and cut-off ends of siphon piping, both in dire need of cleaning. The klaxon signified the next maintenance shift was beginning. That meant Brook was a full hour late. A brief fantasy of splitting Brook's mind in half with a psychic blow crossed Kalendorf's thoughts and made him smirk momentarily. He was going to have to find this Alby Brook himself, and when he did...

There was something wrong: the klaxon was not stopping, and there was the sound of some distant, vocal panic. Moving just to the edge of his shadowy hiding place, Kalendorf scanned the area. Each exit of the giant hangar was still shut. Nobody had emerged from the hatches in the deep, concrete blast bays. The sky skimmer craft, lined up for repair, were still littered with discarded hand tools.

The distant voices had receded further, but their vocal quality was more shrill, fearful. Scared people were running away. Concentrating, he drew on the resources of his noble training and cranked up his hearing. His timing was bad, because just as he had discerned the word 'attack' from the mass of jittery screams, his eardrums were slammed into numbing pain by an explosive percussion that sent him crashing against the wall.

There had been a fierce glow burning around all the exits the instant before the sound, and he had stupidly mistaken this for light from an engine blast. By the time he was about to question his judgement, the sound and the blast had hit him.

Recovering, he fought against the relentless roar of this gigantic explosion and forced himself towards one of the blast bays. The metal walls of the hangar were starting to bow, buckle and crack. A sustained explosion somewhere was kicking up a shock-wave storm.

Just as he threw himself into the nearest blast bay, he heard the yawning wrench of the hangar walls heaving themselves out of their foundations. By the time he had hit hard down on the concrete bay floor, the walls and roof were crashing and scraping overhead. It suddenly occurred to Kalendorf that he might die here, that Vega VI was under attack and that the whole planet might be in the process of disintegrating. Then a chunk of something smashed into his head, knocking him unconscious after an ear-splitting second of sharp agony.

A sound woke him. Another explosion. Something minor, quite a long way off, he thought, as his mind warmed back from inactivity. He guessed he hadn't been unconscious for long. He couldn't be sure, but in the absence of certain, verifiable information, a Knight of Velyshaa should always trust his gut instinct. From day one, the ancient Knight Masters hammered that into their snot-nosed, eager cadets.

It was dark... No, pinpoints of light caught his eye. He moved and there was the sound of metallic debris, the resistance of something weighty, a sharp jab from torn metal. He was buried alive.

Another explosion in the distance. Slowly, he realised that these explosions were just the audible punctuation in a muted, distant cacophony of disaster. A rumble of vast fires burning was woven in with the wailing of injured cries, grief, pleas for help and emergency service vehicles.

His senses almost fully recovered, Kalendorf felt he may be strong enough to do something useful. He was pretty sure he wasn't going to be crushed. He could still breath, he could feel all his limbs. There were no close sounds of activity; he was going to *have to* effect his own rescue.

He braced himself against the debris surrounding him and felt it shift. In that moment, he knew he had the measure of it. It was going to take one hell of a lot of effort, but he would be able to do it. There was another explosion. More wailing cries. He hoped it was going to be worth escaping from this premature burial. Maybe he should just stay here. Accept defeat... There were times when a knight should do that.

Then he decided. This was not one of those times.

Letting out something between a roar and a cry, he pushed out from the core of himself. The debris shifted, groaning and crashing. There was a momentary ripping of flesh as something caught his forehead, drawing blood, but then the pain was gone and his eyes were blinded by unbridled daylight.

He choked on thick smoke. It smelt like hot metal and burnt flesh. His senses rushed to adapt, and all at once a stark, hellish landscape fell into shape before him.

He was looking at Vega City. It was on fire. The buildings that were not entirely destroyed were buckled and brutally broken. Structures were still crumbling and crashing. The flashing lights of ambulance sky skimmers blinked throughout the wreckage. Siren sounds wafted tortuously on the quickening stench-filled breeze.

What the hell had happened? Perhaps Alby Brook was in there, dead. Perhaps Kalendorf's mission was over. Maybe the terrible foe that First Knight Praylaron had feared so much had struck the first blow and the death knell of galactic civilisation was already sounding.

Kalendorf looked around the blasted ruins of the maintenance hangar. Its relatively flimsy structure had been almost flattened. Jagged angles protruded where the grounded skimmers had collapsed off their landing gear. But whatever had caused the explosion, it had happened over twenty kilometres away, perhaps slightly to the south of Vega City's centre. Sturdy structures were still very nearly intact in this out-of-town spaceport. Maybe transceiver equipment would still be working.

With this thought in his head, Kalendorf headed for the nearest, most upright skimmer. It was one of those oval-shaped, short-range, personal skimmers, with room enough for four or five humans to sit under its trans-aluminium canopy. He clambered over its stumpy left wing and pushed at the canopy release control, already noting that some of the dashboard displays looked alive.

A servo whirred inconclusively. A hydraulic hiss half-started. Then nothing. He pulled at the catch, trying to force his fingers under the canopy edge. No sign of it budging. But the flicker of lights on the altimeter, registering zero altitude, gave Kalendorf hope. There was power. The darn thing would open.

He pushed the release control again and held it down, closing his eyes and almost praying for a response. Suddenly, he was rewarded. The canopy lifted and he was inside and seated. Uneasy with this sudden occupation, the skimmer's broken landing gear skittered across the concrete a little. Kalendorf ignored the juddering movement. His hands hit the comms receiver controls. Static *shashed* back at him. He jabbed the control for it to auto-tune to the strongest transmission available. And then it hit upon a signal.

'Only moments ago, a large military spacecraft crash-landed in the southern sectors of Vega City. Initial reports are unclear, but a picture of carnage is emerging.' It was a newscaster, trying to maintain cool detachment, but failing. His voice was trembling uncertainly. Kalendorf flicked a look back up at the devastated cityscape as the newscaster's words continued.

'These pictures are coming to you live.'

Kalendorf flicked at the dashboard screen. Nothing. It was partially shattered. But he had his own live pictures, and he could smell the reality of the disaster's aftermath.

'Looks... looks very bad... I'm receiving information on the craft which crash-landed...'

It was the type of interplanetary warship the Earth Alliance used for their rapid response fleet. Whatever had encountered it had clearly swatted it out of space and sent it tumbling to its doom on Vega VI. Kalendorf's worst fears were confirmed. For a brief moment, he recalled his one personal audience with First Knight Praylaron.

He had seemed remarkably unchanged from the old war photographs. Beard still tightly cut, perhaps a shade on the grey side, but still dark. Eyes still fierce but pale; windows to a canny wit.

'Daleks,' he had said. 'They have something of the apocalypse about them. Have you ever seen one?'

Kalendorf had said no, expecting to be shown a picture or... But Praylaron had simply said, 'You'll know one when you see it. You'll feel like the end of everything has come the moment you set eyes on a Dalek. And the voice... like an ancient engine of death crashing through its gears in a rush to destroy everything.'

Kalendorf now felt it would not be long before he heard that voice for the first time. It was like it was stalking him in a dark, childhood nightmare.

There was a fierce buzz of interference and the newsreader was gone. Something like a voice was starting to emerge.

And when it was clear, Kalendorf remembered the words of his leader. He knew this was a Dalek.

'All humanoid life-forms beware! The invasion of the Daleks has begun!'